"YOU'VE GIVEN ME TONIGHT, SABRINA...."

Thorn's words echoed hollowly in her heart. She twisted, caught his hand to press it to her lips. "It's not enough if we can't marry!" she cried. "What kind of life will we have?"

"It will be sheer hell...but we'll try to forget each other," he breathed into her hair.

"You may try," she countered. "But there's something I want you to remember...." Her lips trailed enticingly down the column of his throat. "I'm yours, Thorn."

He groaned deeply, crushing her in his arms, his fingers biting into her flesh, his kiss inflaming her. She felt a tremor shake his powerful body and murmured, "I don't think you'll ever forget me completely...."

AND NOW...
SUPERROMANCES

Worldwide Library is proud to present a
sensational new series of modern love stories —
SUPERROMANCES

Written by masters of the genre, these longer,
sensuous and dramatic novels are truly in keeping
with today's changing life-styles. Full of intriguing
conflicts, the heartaches and delights of true love,
SUPERROMANCES are absorbing stories —
satisfying and sophisticated reading that lovers
of romance fiction have long been waiting for.

SUPERROMANCES
Contemporary love stories for the woman of today!

SARA ORWIG
MAGIC OBSESSION

A SUPERROMANCE FROM
WORLDWIDE

TORONTO · NEW YORK · LOS ANGELES · LONDON

To Dr. Gary Boring and Kenneth May
with many thanks.

Published March 1983

First printing January 1983

ISBN 0-373-70057-1

Copyright © 1983 by Sara Orwig. All rights reserved.
Philippine copyright 1983. Australian copyright 1983.
Except for use in any review, the reproduction or utilization of
this work in whole or in part in any form by any electronic,
mechanical or other means, now known or hereafter invented,
including xerography, photocopying and recording, or in any
information storage or retrieval system, is forbidden without
the permission of the publisher, Worldwide Library,
225 Duncan Mill Road, Don Mills, Ontario, Canada M3B 3K9.

All the characters in this book have no existence outside the
imagination of the author and have no relation whatsoever to
anyone bearing the same name or names. They are not even
distantly inspired by any individual known or unknown to the
author, and all the incidents are pure invention.

The Superromance trademark, consisting of the word
SUPERROMANCE, and the Worldwide trademark, consisting of
a globe and the word WORLDWIDE in which the letter "O" is
represented by a depiction of a globe, are trademarks of
Worldwide Library.

Printed in Canada

CHAPTER ONE

IN THE CIRCULAR AREA of the lower level of São Paulo's Congonhas Airport, Sabrina Devon searched the crowd. Smoothing a strand of golden hair away from her face, she spoke to the man beside her. "There's not a sign of anyone to meet us, Roddy!"

Dr. Roderick Hughes, Sabrina's tall blond coworker at the World Food and Agricultural Outlook Board of the US Department of Agriculture, shifted his weight and frowned. "It's been half an hour since we finished with customs. I'll go back to that gate and see if anybody is looking for us." Checking his watch, Roddy murmured, "I'll stay there another half hour. You watch here for someone, then meet me on the second level in front of the post office."

Sabrina nodded and turned her attention to the people milling around her. São Paulo, Brazil, she mused. More than ten million people in the city and no one to meet them. She sighed with mounting concern, because to complicate matters, neither she nor Roddy spoke Portuguese.

She thought of the anticipation she had felt fourteen hours earlier on Tuesday, when they had left Washington, D.C. on assignment to Brazil to study the crop methods—specifically sugarcane—of Thornton Catlin, one of the country's most successful plantation owners. After the flight from New York to Rio they had changed to a DC-9 for Congonhas Airport, where they had come in for a breath-stopping landing on a short runway. Now to be stranded at the airport, when they had been assured they would be met, was unnerving.

Smoothing the skirt of her blue cotton dress, Sabrina drifted toward the glass doors and mulled over the fact that it was difficult to be met by someone they didn't know. It occurred to her that Mr. Catlin or one of his employees might be waiting outside, so she opened a door to investigate. When she stepped outside, she encountered a warmly wafting March wind as the morning traffic whipped past. Only a few feet away at the curb travelers whistled taxis into place from lines farther down in front of the international wing of Congonhas.

Deciding no one was waiting, she was about to turn away when a horn blasted. She looked around to see a red-and-white taxi at the curb. Squarely in front of its bumper, blocking the vehicle's path, stood a large shaggy dog. At the sight of the dog's uncertainty sympathy rose in Sabrina. It looked as lost as she felt. While she watched, the dog turned its head frantically, as if searching for direction or an owner.

Other taxis departed around the irate driver. A passerby laughed and whistled. Wishing the dog would move, Sabrina watched while the animal observed the whistler, the taxi, then settled on its haunches. The driver beeped his horn discordantly, then swung his fist at the dog.

Wondering why someone didn't go to the animal's aid, Sabrina edged closer. A few people cast bemused glances in the direction of the confrontation, but most ignored it. The horn honked again. Then the driver stepped out. Curious about his intention, Sabrina waited, wishing he would try a little kindness to move the dog.

More than six feet tall, clad in an open-necked dingy shirt and baggy black trousers, the burly man spewed out an angry stream of Portuguese at the mongrel. Still the animal refused to move. Sabrina felt a rush of horror as the driver swung his foot and planted a solid kick on the creature. She gasped as the animal yelped and rolled onto its side. Everything within her cringed for the dog, but at the sight of its helpless roll to the pavement anger replaced fear.

The man thrust out his lantern jaw, and another kick hit the dog. It yipped but didn't budge, lying on its back, dirty paws in the air, gazing up with imploring brown eyes.

Sabrina couldn't bear any more and decided that the bully must stop his cruelty. Impulsively she dashed forward to step between man and dog. Even if they didn't speak it, Brazilians understood Spanish. *"Terrón! No!"* she cried. "Clod" was the first word that had come readily to mind.

Her heart began to pound wildly as she looked up at the driver, who loomed over her like a giant. He spat out unintelligible Portuguese, then waved his hand in a gesture for her to move. She wanted to run; instead she stood her ground.

While cars rushed past in the next lane, a crowd began to gather on the curb behind them. "Don't kick him again!" she warned.

The driver's lips firmed; he reached out, his huge hand closing around her slender wrist. Shocked that he would touch her, she pulled against his grip.

Out of the crowd behind them a man emerged and stepped to her side. Sabrina glanced briefly at the rugged features above the dark blue suit and tie.

The stranger spoke in a deep calm voice touched with a hint of laughter. Sabrina couldn't follow the flow of words, but the driver released her immediately. While the black-haired stranger talked, he slipped his arm around her waist. She didn't mind—was, in fact, grateful for his protection.

The driver glared balefully at them. Suddenly, without warning, his fist shot forward. The tall stranger was caught unawares. The blow landed squarely on his jaw and sent him sprawling. Horrified, Sabrina watched while some onlookers gasped. Instantly the stranger was on his feet.

His burly assailant swung again. This time the stranger side-stepped in a little movement. The driver growled and ran forward, and Sabrina uttered an inarticulate cry of dismay.

Again the stranger dodged easily. He thrust out his foot, and the driver tripped, then stumbled forward. As he fell over the curb, the crowd parted. Someone pushed, and the driver sprawled onto the concrete.

Whistles and cheers went up from the crowd. Sabrina's sigh of relief changed to a chuckle when the stranger bowed slightly toward his audience. As he straightened, she was startled by a shrill whistle from the opposite direction.

Instantly the floppy gray ears perked up. The dog leaped to its feet and galloped away, almost knocking Sabrina down. The stranger steadied her with a strong arm, then as quickly released her. Sabrina's gaze followed the dog as it bounded down the walk to where a boy on a bicycle waited. He began peddling away, the dog loping behind.

Laughter at the ridiculousness of the situation bubbled up in Sabrina's throat as she turned to the stranger. "A thorough ingrate!" he declared. "After all your efforts on his behalf!"

She smiled, then noticed a cut on his lower lip. "You're hurt!" she exclaimed. "Oh, I'm so sorry," she added, searching in her purse and withdrawing a handkerchief to dab at the cut.

"Thank you for coming to my rescue. It's terrible that you were hurt...." She held the handkerchief lightly against his lip and looked up. Any other words she might have uttered died in her throat at the expression in the cool gray eyes that met hers.

In that moment she went from concern for a stranger who had come to her aid to acute awareness of a man who was regarding her with a mixture of appreciation and mocking amusement. She jerked her hand away from his jaw as if she had patted a steaming kettle.

Apparently unperturbed, he took her arm. "Come have coffee," he invited, and steered her back toward the airport's main doors. Without a glance they passed the driver, who was sitting up by now, shaking his head fuzzily. Sabrina thought of Roddy then and looked at her watch. It would be another quarter of an hour before she had to meet him—time enough for a quick cup of coffee if she wanted. She glanced up at the man beside her and decided she did want. What harm would there be in spending fifteen minutes over a cup of coffee with a stranger? He looked at her, one dark eyebrow climbing in a quizzical arch. "Your name?" he asked.

Beneath his heavy-lidded gaze she experienced an absurd breathlessness. "Sabrina..." she murmured before they stepped through the door and conversation ceased. They headed for the stairs to the airport restaurant, and once there he guided her to a deserted corner of the busy room. When he sat down across from her, he appraised her in a lazy sensuous way that brought color flooding to her cheeks.

A waitress appeared, and he ordered. "*Cafèzinho*, please." Then he paused and looked at Sabrina. "Unless you'd prefer the American version?"

She shook her head. As soon as the waitress departed, Sabrina asked, "What's the difference in coffee?"

"*Cafèzinho*, or espresso, will be served in a demitasse, along with sugar, if you like. Traditionally Brazilians don't use cream. If you prefer cream and a regular-size cup, have it the American way."

"Brazilian is fine," she decided.

"Good. If you'll excuse me a moment, I'm here to

meet some men on a business matter. I'll have them paged. Then I'll be right back."

Before she could protest, he was gone, heading for the door in long easy strides. Light from the hall briefly outlined his broad shoulders and black hair.

Sabrina was suddenly struck by an urge to flee. All she was going to do was drink coffee with a stranger she would never see again, yet half her mind argued escape, while the other half held her rooted to the seat. She couldn't fathom any reason for her feelings—apart from disturbing looks she had received from those teasing gray eyes. Her opportunity disappeared as the stranger slid back into the seat opposite and smiled at her.

She couldn't resist asking, "When you came to my aid, what did you tell that taxi driver?"

Those eyes twinkled merrily. "That I have a very tenderhearted wife."

Sabrina laughed at the deception, noting the lines of amusement that bracketed his mouth. "You find that laughable?" he asked.

"It's absurd, but I'm thankful you did."

"I don't look as if I could be a husband?" he bandied back.

Matching his tone, she answered, "You spoke to him in Portuguese. I spoke in Spanish and English."

"Some things transcend the language barrier," he retorted, while his eyes conveyed clearly that he found her very attractive. At that moment the waitress placed tiny steaming cups of black Brazilian coffee before them.

He raised his cup and looked over the rim at her.

"Do you always rush to the aid of stubborn mongrels?"

"Do you always rush to the aid of someone in need?" she countered lightly.

His voice was warm and husky. His firm lips curved in a smile. "Always—when it's to the rescue of a beautiful woman!"

She smiled briefly. "I'm sorry you were hurt. He was a terrible man."

A fine web of crinkles showed at the corners of the stranger's eyes when he laughed. "Ah, such fire in those lovely blue eyes. The man was obviously a— what was the term you used—*terrón*?"

She blushed from his teasing. "It was the only word I could think of that adequately covered my feelings."

His deep baritone laughter rang out, and his eyes danced. "Perhaps I should teach you some adequate words!"

"No, I hope I never need any again. I don't speak Portuguese, and the Spanish came to mind. I don't usually call people names."

"What do you usually do, Sabrina?"

She wished she weren't so conscious of him. "I'm in Brazil on an assignment."

He relaxed and sipped his coffee. "This job sounds very important," he stated with a smile.

Sabrina couldn't guess whether he was being pleasant or was teasing. She didn't want to be laughed at. She knew many men found it difficult to accept the fact that she was an agronomist who specialized in the production of farm crops. Her work concerned improving methods of farming by studying soil, fertilizers and plant breeding, as well as farm management. Even without that knowledge this man didn't seem to take her seriously, so she merely answered, "I deal with natural resources, but it's complicated to go into. It's very important to me. If I get what I want, I'll be able to more or less do as I choose when I go home."

"Ah, you hope to obtain something valuable, indeed!" His eyes were full of curiosity. She was certain her evasive answer had aroused his interest, but she refused to elaborate.

With a fleeting smile he asked, "Now what can a beautiful woman obtain in São Paulo that will provide her with everything at home?"

She blushed. "Thank you," she stated, acknowledging his compliment and noticing his flare of amusement, as well as curiosity. She also suspected he was misinterpreting her statements, imbuing them with far more intrigue than a direct answer would have.

Just as she started to explain, he asked, "Where is home, Sabrina?"

"Tennessee," she replied.

He still hadn't revealed his name, but that shouldn't matter, because she would never see him again.

He leaned forward and took her hand, placing it on the table. At his touch an unaccountable warmth ran through her. Leaning closer still, he studied her fingers, then looked up. "No wedding ring?"

"No." She attempted to withdraw her hand, but his fingers closed firmly over hers.

"Such lovely slender fingers," he murmured.

Sabrina gazed at the strong hand dwarfing hers. Along the back a sprinkle of thin dark hairs disappeared under a slim gold watch and white shirt cuff. In spite of his cosmopolitan appearance, the skin pressed against hers felt hard and callused, and Sabrina wondered what he'd done to cause this. His fingers moved, lightly trailing over hers, while his lips widened in a smile.

Her cheeks were suffused with heat. Every tiny nerve in her hand was sensitive to his touch. She remarked on the cruelty of the taxi driver, the stubbornness of the dog. Yet she had a suspicion he was no more listening than she was thinking about what she was saying.

While she talked, she studied him. Curling above wide gray eyes were long thick lashes. His arrogant appearance was partially due to his straight thin nose, and a finely delineated mouth offset the harshness of his rugged features. But when he laughed, those features were transformed into irresistible merriment.

"You're alone in one of the largest cities in the world and you don't speak the language...." His voice faded, and Sabrina blushed at the unspoken speculation in his words. She jerked her hand away. He made it sound as if she were some sort of suspicious character.

She rose to her feet abruptly. "No, I'm not alone, and I have to meet him now."

He let out his breath. "Ah, a man. I should have known." With a lithe movement he stood and moved in front of her. She was pinned between the table, the stranger and the wall. Helplessly she looked up, wishing her heartbeat hadn't quickened. The man was a total stranger; she didn't even know his name. Yet he could set her pulse racing.

As if he could read her thoughts, he startled her with his own. "You stepped into my life. Now you'll step out of it. A brief encounter, beautiful Sabrina." Her name rolled off his tongue with a slow emphasis that conveyed intense sensuality.

His voice dropped, and his finger traced a line down her cheek. "One quarter of an hour that will be absolutely unforgettable."

She couldn't believe his words. In the background she heard the clink of silver and the low buzz of conversation from customers. Tiny spots of gold flecked the stranger's eyes. Light and clear, they were as compelling as magnets. In a deep voice he observed, "You run a great many risks rushing to the aid of helpless dogs."

Why was it so difficult to speak? "I didn't stop to think about it," she answered softly.

A smile tugged at the corners of his mouth. "Impetuous and passionate...."

"No, I'm not," she protested, conscious of how difficult it sometimes was for her to convey her thoughts.

He continued. "You're tenderhearted, more impetuous than you realize. I like the unpredictable." His hand tilted her chin upward. "It adds a spice to everyday living that makes the world half enjoyable."

Half enjoyable? The man looked as if he had a real zest for life—and enough arrogance to mold events to his total satisfaction.

His gray eyes darkened. No matter how much she longed to, Sabrina couldn't look away. His broad shoulders blocked her from view as he leaned forward and bent his head. Warm and fleeting, with feather lightness, his mouth brushed hers. The merest touch—yet a quiver shook her. Again came the sweet brief sensation of lips upon lips.

A cape of oblivion dropped over her. She felt devoured by gray eyes, as if she were drowning in their depths, losing all consciousness of the people surrounding her in the restaurant. His eyes changed. She felt as though she saw mirrored in them her own feelings—a tremulous surprise, a wonder, a sense of the impossible. She knew he would kiss her again. Beyond belief she wanted him to...watched as he leaned closer.

Lost in awareness of his firm mouth, she had only a vague knowledge of his arms wrapping themselves around her. His lips pressed harder, and Sabrina's rosy mouth opened at his heated caress. She swayed against him and returned his kiss.

Suddenly she realized the extent of her response. With clarity of reason she pushed against him. Instantly he shifted and looked solemnly down at her.

Burning with embarrassment over the manner in which she'd reacted, she gazed up. With a questioning look he cocked his head to one side while he murmured, "I think I'll always be fond of shaggy dogs."

Touching her cheek lightly with his finger, he added in a strange tone, "That mysterious something you've come to São Paulo to obtain...I wonder if you'll get it."

He had misinterpreted her statement, but she didn't want to tell him now that she'd been talking about agronomy. With breathless urgency she whispered, "Goodbye." Keeping her eyes on the door as she left, she felt too embarrassed to see if anyone was staring.

Dazed, she rushed toward the post office. Above the crowd she spotted Roddy's blond head and hurried to him with an apology on her lips for being late.

Before she could utter it, he spoke. "There you are! Come on, Sabrina. Thornton Catlin will meet us downstairs at the Varig Airlines desk."

"Did you talk to him?" she asked, her shoulder blades growing icy with reaction. Somewhere behind her was a stranger she'd just kissed. Her lips still tingled from the touch of his. She couldn't believe herself. How could she have allowed him to kiss her in the first place? How could she have responded to a total stranger? Never in her life had she done anything like that. But never before had she encountered a man like that.

Roddy glanced at her. "Are you all right, Sabrina? You look pale."

"I'm fine," she stated, not inclined to reveal what had happened during the past few minutes. She wondered if those mocking eyes were watching her leave with Roddy. Attempting to keep pace with his long-legged stride, she was unaware of the bustling people, all her thoughts on the man she had just left. Her cheeks still burned from the episode.

They had descended a flight of stairs, turned a corner and headed in the direction of the sign indicating Varig, when Sabrina's heart lurched.

CHAPTER TWO

AHEAD WERE unmistakable broad shoulders, a dark blue coat tapering to a slim waist and thick black hair curling against a tanned neck. His back was to them, but Sabrina immediately recognized her stranger.

Her throat went dry. She couldn't face him again, see his amused smile. If only he'd move along. But with every second that passed, the space between them narrowed, until they were just a few feet apart. His back remained turned, his arms folded across his chest.

Sabrina's heart thudded. "Hurry, Roddy," she whispered, more to herself than to him.

"I'll see if he's here," Roddy stated. The next moment she stared in disbelief as Roddy spoke in a slightly raised voice. "Mr. Catlin?"

The stranger turned. The smile that had begun vanished.

Sabrina's heart pounded in her ears as she gazed up at him. Not him! Even while she was hoping not, somewhere deep inside her a sudden strange elation was growing.

For an instant, a flicker of breath, his eyes narrowed and something flashed—a cold harsh look that made Sabrina want to cringe. Now he'd know the answers to his curious questions about her mission. She hadn't come to steal his secrets about cane production. She'd come at his invitation. So why did he look so angry? The look vanished with such swiftness that she decided she'd been wrong.

His wide mouth curved in an aggravating grin as he shook hands with Roddy and introduced himself, then turned to Sabrina. Taking her hand, he gazed down at her and commented, "Ah, we've met."

"You've met already! Sabrina, why didn't you tell me?"

Roddy's startled exclamation was almost ignored. Conscious of Thorn Catlin's warm hand holding hers, she couldn't take her eyes from his. "I didn't realize it, Roddy. Mr. Catlin—"

"Thorn," he interrupted softly.

She couldn't say it. "Mr. Catlin didn't make introductions."

A twitch of amusement hovered around Thorn Catlin's mouth, and she thought, *he didn't make introductions. He merely kissed me until I lost my wits.* Abruptly she yanked her hand free and turned her attention to Roddy, who was speaking in matter-of-fact tones but staring at Sabrina as if she'd just grown another nose.

Thorn Catlin was studying her carefully, as well. "So the S.J. Devon stands for Sabrina J. Devon. I expected to meet two men, but this is a pleasant surprise. Welcome to Brazil." He glanced at Roddy. "I'm sorry I'm late. I need to talk with both of you, but first let's get to your hotel so you can deposit your baggage. We'll have lunch there."

Roddy eyed Sabrina, and she felt certain he was wondering the same thing she was. According to the instructions they had received, they were to be guests of the Catlins. No mention had been made about staying at a hotel. Now they had no choice but to go along with Thorn Catlin.

Within minutes they were seated in a sleek white Excalibur. Driving with competent swiftness, Thorn headed toward the heart of the metropolitan area.

Sabrina had declined to ride in front and was well aware of Thorn Catlin's sardonic grin, indicating his awareness of her reluctance to sit beside him. He had placed their suitcases in the back seat, but not until they were on the road did Sabrina realize that, whether accidentally or on purpose, she was seated in a direct line with Thornton Catlin's gaze in the rear-view mirror.

"It seems strange to think of Americans transplanting themselves here," Roddy remarked.

Thorn shrugged one broad shoulder as he replied, "After the Civil War many Confederates fled to Brazil to preserve their way of life—as people of other countries and other conflicts have done. They established various colonies. One at Belém perished because of malaria, but several survived. From time to time they've been written up in newspapers and magazines."

He glanced in the mirror, and his eyes met Sabrina's before he continued. "Near São Paulo are the most successful colonies: Americana, which has grown quite large, and Villa Georgiana. My ancestors settled at Villa Georgiana, then later built Bellefontaine, our home."

It seemed strange to Sabrina to think of Thorn Catlin as American. He seemed more like a hot-blooded Latin American. She looked down at the eighteen lanes of traffic whipping beneath them on another roadway and asked, "Where are we?"

Thorn answered, "Below is the Anhangabaú, a central avenue. We're on Viaduto do Cha, which connects two major squares: Praça da Patriarca and Praça Ramos de Azevedo." He motioned with his hand. "The Old City, São Paulo's financial district, is east, while the Praça Ramos de Azevedo, the new municipal theater and a downtown shopping center, are west of here."

Again, he glanced at Sabrina. "If you're interested in art, two blocks east of the Praça da Patriarca is the Museu de Arte Sacra. It was a colonial convent and now claims to house the largest collection of religious art outside the Vatican."

With its horn blaring, a car cut sharply in front of them across several lanes. Thorn turned smoothly to avoid a collision and smiled at Sabrina, while Roddy muttered about aggressive drivers.

"Unfortunately the nature of many *paulistas*, or people of São Paulo, changes when they get behind the wheel," Thorn agreed. "There is a 'me first' philosophy that most embrace. Away from their automobiles people are polite and friendly." He turned a corner and added, "You're in a big city in a big country. Brazil has over three million square miles."

"I expected to come to an indolent slow-moving metropolis—not anything as busy as this," Sabrina observed.

Thorn laughed. "That's what makes São Paulo tick. The energy of its people shows in everything. Business is booming, and they say a building is completed every day."

Sabrina remembered details from a book she'd read on São Paulo. She was certain that as late as 1920 the population had reached only five hundred thousand. Now one of her guidebooks stated that Sao Paulo had more than ten million people living in more than six hundred square miles.

Roddy smiled at Thorn. "You sound as if you love the city."

Again their host lifted a broad shoulder and let it fall. "I do, but I like it better at Bellefontaine."

When Sabrina recalled the picture of Bellefontaine that Mr. Reece, her supervisor, had shown to her, she could guess why. The photo looked as if it could have been snapped in New Orleans or Atlanta or on any southern plantation that came complete with a magnificent colonial mansion.

Thorn spoke again. "São Paulo's the most exciting city in the world. It's the greatest industrial complex in South America, accounting for more than forty percent of Brazil's industrial output. If it continues its present rate of growth, in a few years it'll be the largest city in the world."

Assaulted by a cacophony of machinery, horns and motorcycles, by the strange blended odors of spices and baking bread, Sabrina gazed in awe at the shops and buildings. It looked as if a tornado had whipped the city into being. Up and down hills they zigzagged a meandering course between skyscrapers. Taking in the confusing jumble of names and avenues, Sabrina remarked in dismay, "Every block changes dramatically!"

Roddy looked over his shoulder at Sabrina. "I've been wondering, where did you two meet?"

"We met while I was waiting downstairs," she answered, and wished her cheeks weren't hot.

"A delightful and enlightening coincidence," Thorn drawled as he glanced in the mirror at her. Sabrina looked away quickly. They turned along Rua Barao de Itapetininga, past movie theaters and side streets lined with souvenir shops and bookstores. Shortly Thorn pointed out Edificio Italia, the tallest building in South America. Behind the forty-one-story edifice, across the street from their hotel, was a graceful curving office and apartment building designed by the famous Brazilian, Oscar Niemeyer.

Sabrina was dazzled by the bustle of people, the traffic and the winding maze of streets with names impossible to pronounce. Even more disturbing was the presence of Thornton Catlin. Why had she ever yielded to his kiss, to his teasing flirtation? She had an uneasy suspicion it might be difficult now to gain his respect.

They halted in front of the beautiful São Paulo Hilton. A triangular wedge beneath cylindrical upper stories, the hotel's facade gleamed in the bright sunshine. Inside, the coolness welcomed them, and

Sabrina hurried along with Roddy to register. She certainly didn't want to wait beside Thorn.

They signed in, deposited their luggage and met Thorn in the hotel dining area, seating themselves at a table beside an oval window that commanded a spectacular view of the city.

"It's unbelievable," Sabrina breathed as Roddy sat down beside her. Across the table, Thorn had his profile to her while he gazed out the window. "Sao Paulo is the heart of Brazil," he remarked. "This is a melting pot for many immigrants. We have the largest population of Japanese outside Japan. Liberdade is the city's Oriental district."

The waiter came, and Roddy glanced at Thorn. "Why don't you order for us? You know what these dishes are."

"Certainly," Thorn replied, looking at Sabrina for confirmation.

Stifling the urge to tell him she would have preferred to do her own ordering, she shrugged.

Taking her gesture for consent, Thorn suggested, "You must try *feijoada*. It's the national dish of Brazil."

She could understand why later as she ate the delicious mixture of black beans, chunks of beef, pork sausage, spices, tongue and peppers spread over white rice. It was served with *couve*, kale, and garnished with orange slices.

Bowls of manioc were placed on the table. Thorn sprinkled some over his *feijoada* and explained, "This is a Brazilian staple—like your potato. It's a tuberous root from the cassava. Ground up like flour, it's as common to the table as salt and pepper. When mixed with butter and onions, peppers or other ingredients, it's called *farofa*."

Sabrina sprinkled manioc, which resembled Parmesan cheese, over the *feijoada*, just as Thorn had. She tasted a bite on its own and found it bland unless mixed with the *feijoada*.

While they ate, Thorn related a brief history of Brazil, beginning with the Portuguese navigator, Pedro Alvares Cabral, who was the first European to reach Brazil in 1500. In 1809, escaping Napoleon's army, the king of Portugal fled to Brazil. Then the country became a kingdom under Dom Joao VI in 1815. After he returned to Portugal, his son, Pedro, proclaimed independence for Brazil on September 7, 1822 and was made emperor. Finally, in 1889 the country was declared a republic.

As Thorn talked, Sabrina studied him unobtrusively. Well aware that he was one of the wealthiest landowners in this part of the world, she wondered if he actively participated in the running of his plantation, Bellefontaine. Remembering the roughness of his hands and noting his deeply tanned skin, she suspected he worked often in the fields. She considered her assignment—to study and gather information on the Catlin methods of sugarcane production. At the thought of working in close daily contact with this man, she felt a strange excitement. She placed her fork on her plate and continued to gaze at him intently.

Cool gray eyes met hers. She hardly knew Thorn Catlin. Yet she felt there was now a coldness in those eyes that hadn't been there during their first encounter. Why was he discussing the history of Brazil at length instead of mentioning their assignment? From the moment they'd met at the airport he hadn't referred to their purpose in coming to this country.

As if reading her thoughts, he startled Sabrina by saying, "So you're an agronomist, Sabrina Devon. What does that kind of work entail?"

She suspected he knew. Yet she couldn't be rude, so she answered instead, "I study grasses, farm plants and weeds. I consider farm management ant field-crop production. I also collect soil samples, then study them in a soil-test lab to determine which type of cultivation best suits a particular area. Now that I'm with the World Food Board, I'm working on better methods of crop production so there will be enough food in the future. Since you've developed rust-resistant strains of sugarcane, this method should result in larger crops, and I'm certainly eager to learn about your methods."

A waiter interrupted them to bring dessert, *torta de castanhas-do-pará*, chocolate-frosted Brazil-nut cake with a creamy filling. Sipping his thick black coffee, Thorn leaned back and regarded them seriously. "I sent a letter to your office. I'm sorry I didn't get it mailed sooner, but that was an oversight. I telephoned, too, but you'd already left for Brazil."

A cold knot of apprehension began to coil inside Sabrina. She locked her fingers together and listened as Thorn went on. "Your government contacted my father, and he agreed to cooperate with your agency to provide information on raising sugarcane, but last month he suffered a heart attack."

After Sabrina and Roddy had murmured words of sympathy, Thorn continued, "My letter has now been directed to your supervisor. Our physician recommended my father wait a few more weeks before getting involved in anything. He's recovering rapidly, but he shouldn't overtax himself. I've asked for a postponement of your project."

With each word Sabrina suffered a deepening pang of disappointment. For two months she'd been getting ready, hoping and planning to work in Brazil, thinking ahead. She intended to apply for the position of county extension director at home. She wanted that job, the opportunity to be in charge of a county and work closely with the local farmers on any problems related to crop production. The work in Brazil would give her special experience that other applicants wouldn't have. Now, with each of Thorn's words, her chances for director seemed to be evaporating. Her whole family was counting on her return to Tennessee. As Thorn talked, she thought of her mother and the elder of her two brothers, Jeff.

For an instant she remembered clearly the last time she'd been home. Over cups of hot chocolate at the kitchen table, Jeff had discussed their mother's medical bills with her. Back trouble and a hip operation had put Mrs. Devon in the hospital several times during the past year.

She had a small gift shop, but it was getting more and more difficult for her to maintain. Besides Sabrina's worries about the bills, there was the problem of Andy, her fifteen-year-old brother. Sabrina couldn't guess where Andy got his wildness, but he needed a constant firm hand, and her mother wasn't able to cope with him any longer.

It weighed heavily on Sabrina that Jeff had had to postpone college last year in order to work and supervise Andy. She needed to get home to take over and let Jeff have his chance for an education. Apart from career considerations, the job as extension director would increase her salary and make it possible for her to be with her family.

Sabrina had always had a strong sense of responsibility. She had diligently completed her undergraduate courses in agronomy in three years, then earned her master's degree the next year. All her efforts had been concentrated on an education and a career, and now to have the Brazilian project canceled without warning was a bitter blow. Her thoughts returned to the present with a jolt as she glanced up and caught Thorn watching her intently.

She had to try to get around him. "Is your father the only person—"

"I could go over everything with you," Thorn interrupted, "but I don't want to take this project away from my father. He needs something to occupy his time, and he can't get out in the field anymore. It's regrettable, but I sent a check to Washington that should cover your expenses for the trip, as well as a donation for the Food Board's continuing research."

As if to close the matter to further discussion, he straightened and added, "I'll show you the sights of São Paulo today and tonight. Then tomorrow I've arranged for you to join a tour group. Friday morning a Varig flight leaves for Rio and the United States. I've cabled your office that you'll be returning."

On the surface his words sounded reasonable. Yet Sabrina was aware of his close scrutiny, of a controlled anger. She sensed there was something more to this affair than he was telling them, but disappointment crowded out everything else. Her throat felt tight. She squeezed her fingers together, striving for control.

Roddy looked at her and swore softly. His deep blue eyes flashed angrily as he began, "Mr. Catlin—"

"Thorn," he corrected at once.

"Thorn," Roddy replied, "this is damned discouraging. Don't misunderstand. We're both sorry about your father, but we've been looking forward to this assignment."

"I regret this, but it's unavoidable."

"We appreciate sight-seeing," Roddy persisted, "but it's really of little interest in comparison to the opportunity to study your farming methods. Our supervisor, Mr. Reece, briefed us about Bellefontaine. You've developed varieties of cane with higher contents of sugar, as well as rust-resistant strains. This is a major breakthrough in research and development. Isn't there some way we can work without disturbing your father?"

"I'm sorry, but my answer has to be no. As I've said, I'm postponing this project so my father can still be involved in it when he's able. At that time you may return and have our complete cooperation."

Roddy's face flushed, and Sabrina studied his features beneath the thick hair that was as golden as her own. Roddy was extremely handsome. Yet she had never felt anything more than a sisterly affection for him. They had gone through some college classes together. Then Roddy had helped her get the job with the department. She knew his work was his first and only love, that he was totally dedicated to it. Many times she had watched women at the office try in vain to stir a response in him, but a stock of wheat would have stood a better chance. There was more to his resistance, of course. He had admitted to Sabrina once that he was scared of marriage. Both his parents had remarried several times, and Roddy had grown up in boarding schools or being shuffled back and forth between families.

Thorn rose to his feet, interrupting her thoughts. "Now that we've settled that problem, let me show you Sao Paulo."

She stood up, too, and looked at Roddy again. She knew he felt the same way she did. The chance to return later wouldn't do her any good and might not materialize for Roddy. She didn't want to give up this assignment. She decided to try to think of some way to convince Thorn Catlin to allow them to stay.

At first it was difficult to concentrate on Thorn's conversation as he pointed out the sights to them, but the Butanta Snake Farm and Museum caught her interest. She learned the history of the institute—that in 1888, a scientist, Dr. Vital Brasil, had been awarded a farmhouse by the government as a research site.

His theory was that snake serum could save the life of a person bitten by a snake. He started with sixty-four snakes to treat the horses of São Paulo's cavalry.

They were in time to witness a demonstration of "milking" snakes and discovered that the institute kept serum available to send anywhere in the world. More than sixteen thousand snakes were housed in little red clay igloo-shaped houses shaded by jacaranda trees. In addition to snakes, there were thousands of scorpions, centipedes, lizards and spiders.

Next they drove to the São Paulo Art Museum, a modern building, complete with four concrete pylons, situated on Avenida Paulista.

As she strolled through the museum, admiring South America's largest permanent collection of Western art, Sabrina tried to think of convincing arguments to present to Thorn. His father's illness made the situation delicate but not impossible. While she viewed paintings mounted on plastic stands that gave the illusion of floating on air, she mulled over a likely means of approach.

Leaving the art museum, they strolled along the avenue, passing small open stands that carried copies of São Paulo's daily newspapers. When they returned to the car to drive around the city some more, she remembered her evasive answers to Thorn's questions about her goals in São Paulo. She wanted to explain her attitude to him, but there was no opportunity as he pointed out the *jardims*, gardens, and elegant mansions in southwest São Paulo. By the time they descended steep Rua Augusta, she'd dismissed her misgivings as unimportant. No doubt Thorn hadn't given a second thought to their earlier discussion.

Thorn parked along Alamedas Tietê so they could shop in the exclusive boutiques and galleries, where she purchased a small sterling pin for her mother and a straw hat for Jeff. Undecided about her third choice, she gazed uncertainly at a display until Thorn came up beside her.

"Are you looking for anything in particular?" he asked.

Sabrina smiled. "My little brother is interested only in his motorcycle." But she spotted a belt buckle then and decided it would do. After paying for her purchases, Sabrina was glad when Thorn suggested they step next door to a sidewalk cafe for a cool drink.

Once they reached a table, Thorn shed his coat, revealing that the broadness of his shoulders owed nothing to padding. An immaculate white shirt emphasized his deep tan, and while he continued to talk about his native city, she couldn't resist the chance to study both men. Roddy was within two inches of being as tall as Thorn. His shoulders were almost as wide, and his features were smoothly handsome, in contrast to the dark brooding ruggedness of Thorn's. Viewing the two men objectively, Roddy should have been the more appealing. Yet Sabrina found Thorn's looks more exciting. He also evinced a certain masculine appeal, a sexy charisma. She glanced at the faint trace of dark bristles along his firm jaw, the slightly full lower lip that was swollen on one side from the taxi driver's blow.

Suddenly her own lips felt dry, and she touched

them with the tip of her tongue. The sardonic gaze Thorn directed at her made her realize that he, too, had been watching her. Embarrassed, she quickly picked up her glass of water to cover her confusion.

Thorn's hand dropped lightly over her wrist. When she looked up in surprise, he smiled warningly. "Be careful, Miss Devon. To a newcomer the water may be dangerous."

"I think the water isn't all one must beware of!" Sabrina flashed back with a smile of her own.

He shrugged. "It was a harmless encounter, after all."

She suddenly felt foolish. That kiss had meant nothing to Thorn Catlin—and why should it? They were total strangers. He had taken advantage of the moment, and no doubt he found little female resistance at any time. Perhaps he was married. The thought brought a ridiculous twinge of disappointment, and she put it out of her mind.

Roddy was staring at them with obvious curiosity, and so Thorn explained his initial meeting with Sabrina. His gray eyes twinkled as he described the dog's plight, at which point Roddy interjected dryly, "No doubt Sabrina went to his rescue. Sabrina will befriend any stray. Once there was even an owl."

When Thorn looked questioningly at her, she shrugged and answered lightly, "I found an owl."

"You mean you took in a wounded owl," Roddy corrected her. "She finally found it a home in a zoo."

Thorn laughed. "So the incident this morning

wasn't out of character for you?" He said it lightly, but she sensed a seriousness behind the words.

"Why do you ask that?" she queried.

The waiter came then, and an answer was forgotten or ignored as Thorn ordered three *caipirinhas*, which he explained were made from *cachaça* or *pinga*. "It's cane alcohol, and common all over Brazil. There are some two thousand independent distilleries, and the drink is so typically Brazilian that you shouldn't return to the States without trying it. Taken alone, *pinga* can be less than appetizing, but with lime added it becomes *caipirinhas*—much more palatable.

"Why did you go into agronomy, Sabrina?" he asked, shifting in his chair to fix Sabrina with a deliberate total regard that made her feel utterly feminine and responsive to him.

"I grew up on a farm. Agronomy seemed like an interesting challenging field—and a natural choice for me. Already our earth's population is expanding at a rate of nearly two percent each year. We need to develop better crops to avoid world famine." Wondering if he would share these views, she added coolly, "I also felt there were good opportunities for women in agronomy."

She turned her attention to Roddy as Thorn said, "You're a plant pathologist. You study effects of disease on plants, then."

"Yes, and I'm interested in your results," Roddy said. "If you've developed a strain that's resistant to rust, it'll be a boon to world production of sugarcane. Our agency has tried for some time now to get

permission to work with you, and it's discouraging—
to say the least—to go back without getting what we
came for."

Thorn Catlin glanced at Sabrina. "I'm certain it's
a disappointment, but there's nothing more I can do
for the moment."

Sabrina suspected a hidden meaning in his statement, but she couldn't guess why he should be so
secretive. That feeling kept surfacing.... She recalled that first moment when he had turned to face
her at the Varig desk. Had the flash of coldness she
thought she'd glimpsed been real or imaginary? Were
his statements what they seemed on the surface?
When she looked at him, it was impossible to tell.
She gave up considering Thorn's actions and his
words as the waiter placed their drinks on the table.

Blended in frosted glasses filled with crushed ice
was a concoction of sugar, bits of lime and the *pinga*.
Sabrina took a sip. She choked and coughed, then regarded Thorn with amazement.

His eyes twinkled as he remarked, "It's a shock to
the unwary, but it wouldn't be Brazil without
pinga."

"It isn't fatal, is it?" she retorted, while Roddy,
too, recovered from his first sip of the deceptive
beverage.

Thorn laughed and shook his head. "Not at all,
but there are some brands that are about as appetizing as kerosene." Leaning back in his chair and
stretching his long legs, he added, "There is so much
to taste and see in Brazil. One could take a lifetime
and still not exhaust the possibilities."

After they had managed to finish half their drinks, they returned to the hotel. Thorn asked them to meet him for dinner later and left them once they had agreed. Roddy went over to the desk to see if there were any messages. Heading for the elevator, he extended a slip of paper to Sabrina.

"We're to call Mr. Reece. No doubt he's received Catlin's letter by now. It's been a hell of a day, hasn't it?"

She nodded. "I had been counting on this so much. I need this opportunity, Roddy. I don't want to give it up. I know the experience here would give me special qualifications for that job at home."

Roddy ran his hand distractedly through his hair. "For two years I've worked on controlling rust as well as other diseases in sugarcane. The Catlins have succeeded in doing it, and it looked as if they would share that information. To have the door slammed in our faces at this late date is quite a blow." He motioned toward his room. "Come in a moment and I'll place this call."

She crossed the threshold noiselessly on soft brown carpet and listened, first to sounds of traffic drifting up, muffled by walls and glass, then to Roddy while he related Thorn Catlin's conversation to Mr. Reece. After a few minutes he handed the phone to her. A brief conversation with her employer strengthened her determination to again attempt to reason with Thorn Catlin.

Finally she replaced the receiver and turned to Roddy. "He feels the same way we do. He told me to try our best to change Thorn Catlin's mind without interfering with his father's situation."

Rubbing the back of his neck, Roddy paced the floor. "I know, but it's going to be difficult."

Sabrina glanced at her watch. "There's a pool on the roof of the tenth floor. How about talking this over up there?"

"Okay," he agreed, smiling absentmindedly at her, "but I don't think it'll help much."

LATER, AT A POOLSIDE TABLE under a bright yellow umbrella, Sabrina read while Roddy swam. Her hair clung damply to her neck, rivulets of water still running across her shoulders from her swim. The chlorine odor was pervasive, but Sabrina's concentration on her book dimmed any possible distraction from the children splashing nearby.

Flinging a towel around his shoulders, Roddy sat down in a metal chair beside her and remarked, "Even on the tenth floor this city is noisy. I can still hear all that traffic." He glanced at the book in her hands. "What's that?"

A breeze riffled the pages as she held it up for Roddy to read the title. He squinted at her. "You're trying to learn Portuguese?"

She shrugged. "It bothers me not to know the language." She didn't add that it disturbed her to appear so unknowledgeable around Thorn. "From what Mr. Reece told us, we'd be at Bellefontaine and wouldn't need to know. But it hasn't turned out that way."

"I don't think you're going to use much tomorrow," Roddy said dryly. "It'll be our last day here."

She closed the book. "We've got to do something about that, Roddy."

"We'll just have to tackle Catlin over dinner tonight."

"I think I'll rest before I get ready to do *that*," Sabrina replied as she stood up. She spent the next few hours in her room thinking about arguments to present to their host. The prospect of an evening with Thorn caused her to dress with care. After slipping on a pale yellow chiffon sheath, she brushed her hair vigorously before fastening it behind her neck with a barrette. When she heard Roddy's knock, she called to him to come in.

"How pretty you look," he commented.

"And you look nice, too," she said with a smile, approving his dark brown suit and tie with his blond hair. For a moment they gazed into each other's eyes, and Sabrina remembered her few dates with Roddy.

Each time they'd ended up discussing their work. But while Roddy lived and breathed his research, there were times when Sabrina wanted to forget the office and everything about it. She never could when she went out with him, and their brief kisses had been uninspired.

Now Roddy planted his feet and placed his hands on his hips, the epitome of determination. "Sabrina, I'm going to try one more time to talk Catlin into allowing us to visit that plantation."

"We have to, Roddy. There should be a way to work this out."

"Oh, I doubt if the man will give an inch," Roddy

said, reverting briefly to pessimism. "This morning we never had a chance to object before it was decided we were on our way to sightsee. Those cold gray eyes are enough to freeze any man's blood. But I've worked on this project too long to give up easily." He turned and swung his hand in an arc. "Come on, Sabrina. We'll beard the lion in his den."

When they emerged from the elevator, Thorn was waiting. Dressed in a finely tailored charcoal pin-striped suit, he was leaning indolently against a lobby wall. Stubbing out his cigarette, he straightened and sauntered toward them.

Why did his smoldering perusal make her heart start pounding? Sabrina was aggravated by the reaction she seemed to have every time he focused on her. She hoped it was hidden by her smile and casual greeting.

Roddy launched into his appeal, and while the two men conversed, Sabrina wondered what it was in Thorn Catlin that caused her knees to turn to jelly whenever he looked at her. At that moment his head turned.

"Sabrina!" Roddy exclaimed impatiently, and she realized she had lost the train of the conversation. Both men were waiting expectantly.

A corner of Thorn's mouth curled in amusement at her obvious embarrassment. "What were you thinking about, Miss Devon?" he asked.

Damn him. She glanced at Roddy, wishing her cheeks weren't so warm. "I'm sorry. My thoughts were on something else."

Roddy gave her a strange look while he explained.

"I told Mr. Catlin—Thorn—that we've worked a great deal on cane production. Even if we can't stay, it would be helpful to visit one of his labs. Sabrina, you had some things you wanted to ask."

Before she could answer, Thorn interrupted smoothly, "Miss Devon has other things on her mind. Let's go to dinner and we can discuss it."

Without waiting for a reply, he took Sabrina's arm and headed for the door. When the Excalibur was brought to the curb, Thorn motioned for Roddy to slide into the back. Sabrina had no choice except to sit beside Thorn.

She glanced at him as he threaded the car through lanes of traffic. His strong brown fingers held the wheel firmly. Lean and muscular, he seemed to radiate vitality. He turned his head at that moment and gazed into her eyes.

She shifted quickly to study a rolling expanse of green lawn, well lighted by lamps and dotted with graceful willow and eucalyptus trees, with a large statue in view. "What's that?" she asked, hoping to distract him. He had the unnerving knack of guessing her thoughts.

"Ibirapuera Park with its Monumento des Bandeirantes," Thorn answered. "São Paulo was founded in 1554 by a Jesuit priest. That statue is dedicated to the *bandeirantes*, some of the first pioneers to settle here."

Both Roddy and Sabrina turned to get a better look at the statue—two horses and riders leading thirty-six mammoth figures. "Some of the locals have entitled it, 'Don't push!' " Thorn remarked lightly.

They finally pulled up to a long low restaurant set back in the hillside. Beneath a sign proclaiming *Churrascaria*, barbecue, flaming torches flanked the entrance. Thorn moved between Roddy and Sabrina to take her arm. He glanced down at her. "I selected this place so you could sample Brazilian cooking."

"Do you always make others' decisions for them?"

He merely smiled and replied enigmatically, "Only when I'm particularly interested in someone."

Conversation ended as they were led past flaming charcoal pits, where sizzling meat exuded a tempting aroma. Looking around, Sabrina decided it would be difficult to remain disappointed or depressed in such an atmosphere. Pots of ferns hung from a low-beamed ceiling, and they threaded their way past tables brightened by bouquets of red cannas and flickering candles to a garden overlooking a lagoon. Along the water's edge more flaming torches cast reflections across the shimmering blackness. In a niche of rocks near their table a small fountain cascaded, the splashing water mingling with the muted sounds of music emanating from a small dance floor inside.

Thorn held out a brown leather chair for Sabrina, then sat facing her, Roddy between them. She glanced across the top of the squat candle at their host. "You've already ordered for us, haven't you?"

Again there was a lopsided smile. "I hope you enjoy my selections."

As the waitress brought drinks, Thorn explained. "These are *batidas*, like *caipirinhas*, only juice is used instead of chopped fruit."

"Are these as potent?" Roddy asked cautiously.

Thorn laughed. "They can be," and he raised his glass in a toast. "To a shaggy gray dog."

Roddy's eyes narrowed, and Sabrina was aware he was looking intently at her, then at Thorn. They drank and Roddy remarked, "This is delicious."

Without thinking, Sabrina murmured, *"Gostoso,"* the Portuguese equivalent and one of the words she had just learned.

Instantly Thorn snapped up his head to study her. "You *do* know Portuguese!"

Before she could answer, Roddy said, "There won't be much chance to use it, since we go home in a day.... How much cane is produced around here, Thorn?"

"São Paulo State produces more than sixty-two percent of Brazil's sugar. Bellefontaine contributes a sizable portion of that."

While he talked, Sabrina was aware of his scrutiny, remembering that she'd told him earlier she didn't speak Portuguese. Now he'd think she hadn't been truthful, and she was determined to tell him otherwise the first possible chance.

Their waitress appeared and set platters on the table, and they were served *siri*, hot stuffed crab appetizers, followed by *canja a brasileira*, thick chicken soup made with rice and carrots. Bowls of manioc were also placed on the table. While they ate, Sabrina noticed Thorn's hands, blunt nailed and marked with tiny scratches. Recalling the feeling of his calluses when he'd held her hands, she recognized that there was a rugged earthiness to him physically that hinted at the toughness beneath the urbane sophistication.

Along with another round of *batidas* they were served *churrasco a gaucha*. First one waiter then another appeared at the table, each with a skewer of a particular type of meat, to slice chunks off onto warm plates.

Sabrina ate bites of beef, lamb, pork and chicken that had been barbecued. Afterward, enjoying fried bananas dipped in sugar, they discussed sugarcane and cotton. Any overtures they made to stay longer—any suggestions—were promptly and firmly denied by their host. Finally he rose and moved to Sabrina's side, taking her hand.

"Before we leave, may I have a dance?"

She nodded and rose, while Thorn excused himself to Roddy. Inside, the restaurant was warmer, filled with odors of food and smoke. A lively samba was playing, and Sabrina turned to face Thorn. They moved in perfect accord to the quickening beat, and both were breathless by the time the dance ended. But he didn't let go of her hand. "One more," he murmured. This time the music was slow, and he moved closer, adding softly, "It's been fascinating meeting you, Sabrina Devon."

At that moment, replete after a delicious dinner and two *batidas*, listening to soft music in a romantic setting while dancing with an exciting man, sugarcane was the last thing on Sabrina's mind. Looking up from beneath lowered lashes, she noticed that Thorn's mouth was still swollen from the driver's blow. "Does your lip hurt?" she asked.

While he shook his head, amusement filled his

eyes, and suddenly she realized how she must appear. She was gazing up at him like a star-struck teenager. Worse, her question about his mouth made it sound as if she wanted to kiss him.

At that thought she straightened abruptly and stumbled. Instantly his arm tightened around her waist.

Embarrassed, she looked up at him again. His face was inches away from hers, and the words she was about to utter faded from thought. He pulled her closer as he continued to look into her eyes.

She couldn't get her breath. She touched the tip of her tongue to her lips—then instantly wished she hadn't as he sucked in his breath to whisper, "You're bewitching!"

Her cheeks flamed, and she pushed against him, then spun away. "We'd better go," she murmured, heading for the door. Back at the table Roddy appeared startled when Sabrina snatched up her small bag and said, "Roddy, it's time to leave for the hotel."

All the way to the car Sabrina was oblivious to the two men's conversation. She was consumed by embarrassment. Thorn Catlin seemed to have the extraordinary ability of making her lose control of her reactions. She barely heard his words as he pointed out various sights on the return trip. But he seemed unaware of any discomfort, and gradually Sabrina began to overcome her awkwardness.

Two blocks from the hotel they slowed and halted for a traffic light. Sabrina glanced out the window, startled to see four candles burning on the curb beneath a lamppost. Incongruous amid the bright glow of neon signs and headlights, the tiny flames flickered and danced. "Why are there candles on the curb?" she asked.

"It's *macumba*," Thorn answered harshly.

Sabrina looked at him curiously, certain her question had aggravated him and wondering why. She couldn't resist asking, "What's *macumba*?"

"In Haiti it's voodoo. In Bahia they call it *candomblé*. Everybody who's lived on a plantation knows about it. Many Brazilians practice it. In some ways it's as Brazilian as Rio or *cachaça* or *feijoada*."

Then why does it anger you to be asked about it? she wondered. How was Thorn Catlin involved with *macumba*?

She glanced back at the curb and mused about the strange place she was visiting—one of the most modern cities in the world. Yet candles honoring gods were burned on street corners in an ancient mystical ritual.

In the hotel lobby Thorn shook hands with Roddy before he turned to Sabrina. "Even though you didn't get what you came for, it's been a delightful day and evening, Sabrina Devon."

As Sabrina thanked him and said goodbye, she felt a sharp edge of disappointment return. He had taken charge with a smooth arrogance that gave them no choice about canceling their plans. She didn't want to disturb the ailing Catlin, but Thorn could have at least discussed some of their farming methods. She glanced over her shoulder to watch him striding away in a casual yet commanding walk, as if he owned the world. His back was straight, his broad shoulders squared. As she watched, he turned and waved.

Wishing he hadn't caught her staring after him, she followed Roddy into the elevator. Waiting for the doors to close, she came to a sudden decision. "Roddy, I'm going to try one more time to ask him to help us."

When she held the doors open and stepped out, Roddy murmured, "Good luck. Let me know if he changes his mind. Otherwise I'll see you in the morning."

Afraid she would be too late to catch him, Sabrina rushed outside. He was at the curb, ready to get into his car.

"Thorn!" Sabrina called.

He straightened and she dashed up, then felt ridiculous for chasing him in such a manner. His smoldering appraisal made her wish she'd remained in the elevator with Roddy. Why had she ever thought she could change Thorn Catlin's mind?

"You cut it rather close. I expected you to stop me before I got through the doors." His cynical tone ended all hope of rational conversation. Her heart pounded in her ears, and she held the absurdly tiny evening bag in front of her waist like a shield.

She wanted to turn and run, but she took a deep breath and spoke. "Can't you reconsider working with us? I don't want to disturb your father, but if you'd just give us a little time. If you'd discuss your methods...." Under his heavy-lidded scrutiny words failed her.

He stepped nearer and tilted up her chin. His voice

was soft and husky. "I'll have to admit I'm tempted, but the answer is still no." His tone suddenly became harsh, and he removed his hand from her chin. "Better luck next time, Miss Devon!"

Filled with frustration, Sabrina stalked into the hotel. Not until she had reached her room did her heart stop pounding. The man was exasperating! She would never see Thorn Catlin again. Yet she had an uneasy feeling it would be a long time before she forgot him. It was impossible to think of sleep. First thing in the morning there would be another phone call to Mr. Reece. Contemplating how to explain their failure, she gazed out the window at the glittering lights of the city.

Vibrant, pulsing with life, Sao Paulo was an exciting city, she decided, filled with exotic things to see and taste. Bustling throngs of people conveyed a sense of energy. Then she laughed at herself. Was São Paulo really fascinating—or did she feel that way because the only view she had of it was through the eyes of Thorn Catlin?

SABRINA SLEPT for a few hours, then awakened early in the morning and dressed for sight-seeing. Before they left, she and Roddy talked again to their employer, who said he would contact Catlin, Junior in a last-ditch effort to change his mind.

São Paulo's museums didn't open until the afternoon, but they saw the Praça de República, a wonderful square filled with palms, then went on to a large outdoor market. They visited Ipiranga Park, with its converted palace and the preserved mud house where Dom Pedro I spent the night before proclaiming Brazil's independence. They saw as much as they could cram into one day, since tomorrow they'd be gone.

ON FRIDAY Sabrina got up early again and dressed in a pale blue cotton shirtdress, then ate a quick Brazilian breakfast of fruit and coffee. When she returned to her room to finish packing, she met Roddy coming down the hall.

With a broad grin on his face he announced, "Sabrina, I've just received a call from the desk. There's a car waiting to take us to Bellefontaine"!

CHAPTER THREE

ELATION SURGED through Sabrina. "We'll get to do the work we came for! Thank goodness!" she breathed. Yet deep inside a small voice told her that wasn't the only reason for her eagerness. Thoughts of seeing Thorn again, of possibly working with him, sent a quiver of excitement through her.

"Is Thorn downstairs?" she asked.

Roddy shook his head. "I don't know. The clerk merely said a car was waiting. Are you ready?"

She nodded. "I'll get my things." When they reached the lobby, Sabrina experienced a fleeting disappointment as a chauffeur introduced himself and informed them that Mr. Catlin had sent him to fetch them. And in the Rolls-Royce, headed out of Sao Paulo, she was struck by the first twinge of concern. She glanced at Roddy. "I can't understand this, Roddy. Thorn Catlin doesn't seem like the type of person to change his mind so completely."

Roddy shrugged, his white knit shirt stretched tightly across his shoulders. "I don't know, Sabrina. Maybe Mr. Reece had an influence. Just be glad of it."

She agreed with a smile, but as she gazed out the window at the rough red clay road, her uneasiness couldn't be shaken. The car eventually turned a bend, and on the hillside ahead she saw Bellefontaine.

Roddy's breath escaped in a sigh. "Wow!" he whispered. "Look at that house. It looks like a colonial castle."

Yes, she'd guessed correctly. It did remind Sabrina of a Southern mansion back home. Stately Doric columns rose from a sweeping veranda to a second-story gallery flanked by an east and west wing. A wide portico led off the west side, and fan transoms graced windows and doors. With a home like this, it was easy to understand Thorn's cool self-assurance.

The car passed two wide posts supporting a small iron sign that read: *Bellefontaine*. Below was another sign: *Entrada proibida*.

While Sabrina thumbed through a small Portuguese handbook, Roddy remarked dryly, "I can tell you. It means, 'No trespassing.'"

"You're right." Again she thought of her last minutes with Thorn in front of the hotel. Now why had he changed his mind and sent for them?

The chauffeur stopped the Rolls, held the door for them, then drove around the corner of the house. Feeling alone and slightly intimidated, Sabrina crossed the veranda with Roddy. A butler led them into a cool spacious room, three of its walls lined from floor to ceiling with shelves of books. Through a row of French doors light spilled into the room. Beyond the veranda two gardeners trimmed the hedges around a tiered fountain of splashing water.

Sabrina barely noticed the elegant furnishings surrounding them. She locked her fingers together tightly. Any moment she expected to hear a firm step and face the silvery gray eyes of Thorn Catlin. The mere prospect of greeting the man shouldn't be unnerving, but it was. To her surprise the door opened to reveal, not Thorn, but a young woman standing behind a man seated in a wheelchair.

The woman smiled and said, "I'm Laurel Catlin, and this is my father, Mr. Catlin. Welcome to Bellefontaine."

Even as she smiled and rose to her feet, Sabrina realized instantly that they hadn't been invited to Bellefontaine by Thorn. She was certain it was the elder Mr. Catlin who had sent for them.

While they introduced themselves, Sabrina studied Thorn's father. Even though his skin was ashen and his large-boned frame looked frail, it was obvious he had once been as handsome as his son. He had large gray eyes and thick white hair that gave him a distinguished look. There was an air of sadness about him until he smiled. Then, like Thorn, his whole face was transfused with warmth.

Sabrina glanced helplessly at Roddy; they couldn't turn around and leave. Yet she didn't want to do anything to jeopardize their host's health. Also, she suspected Thorn Catlin knew nothing of their presence in his home.

The wheelchair's motor made a whirring noise as Mr. Catlin moved farther into the room. He extended a hand that trembled slightly, and they each shook it. "We're happy to see you. I've been expecting you." He motioned to them. "Please be seated." As

Laurel Catlin crossed the room, Sabrina noticed she had the same gray eyes as Thorn and Mr. Catlin. Otherwise her coloring was different: curly brown hair, pale skin and a smattering of freckles. She was petite, almost Sabrina's size, and her yellow cotton skirt swirled against her legs as she sat down.

When they sat down on the brown leather sofa, Sabrina looked at Roddy and wondered if he felt the same way she did. She turned to Mr. Catlin and said, "We've met your son, Thorn."

"Ah, yes." He smiled. "I hope you enjoyed Sao Paulo."

With every passing second Sabrina grew more certain Thorn knew nothing about their being here, and she certainly didn't want to run into him. It would be a long time before she forgot the scathing tones of his goodbye at the hotel.

Her attention returned to Mr. Catlin as he said, "Laurel, see that our guests have a cup of coffee." He gazed at Sabrina. "I know my son scheduled a return flight for you. Those arrangements have been canceled. After coffee I'll have Laurel show you to your rooms."

In that moment Sabrina realized she was dealing with another arrogant self-assured Catlin male. Even though Mr. Catlin appeared physically fragile, it was evident he could be as unyielding as his son.

As much as she wanted the experience and knowledge to be gained from the Bellefontaine project, Sabrina didn't want to cause harm to Mr. Catlin. Since he really did look ill, she thought the best thing would be to return to their hotel and try again to reason with his son. She still hoped they could work out an arrangement, but she knew they should come to Bellefontaine at Thorn Catlin's invitation, not his father's.

Determined not to take advantage of this elderly man's hospitality, she said in a firm tone, "We don't want to impose. I think we should get back to our hotel."

Mr. Catlin waved his hand, dismissing her suggestion. "It's time for coffee." He glanced at the door as Laurel returned and a maid appeared with tiny cups of thick black coffee. It would be ungracious to refuse the refreshment, but Sabrina could barely concentrate on polite inconsequential conversation as they sipped the brew.

While Roddy discussed Sao Paulo's museums she glanced around the room. Large matching lamps had been placed on either side of the sofa. Beyond the grouping of chairs and sofa, near one end of the room, was an enormous oak desk. She noticed letters neatly stacked as if awaiting a signature and wondered if those were for Thorn, if he spent a lot of his time in this room. Her gaze traveled beyond the veranda. Watching the water in the fountain sparkle in the bright sunshine, Sabrina wished again that they were there at Thorn's invitation.

As if guessing her inner turmoil, Mr. Catlin commented encouragingly, "Miss Devon, don't look so worried. When Mr. Reece called this morning, I intercepted the call and told him you'd stay. I've no intention of overtaxing myself."

Stunned by his determination, Sabrina was beginning to wish she'd never met anyone named Catlin. Afraid to argue too much with the senior Catlin in his condition, she nevertheless had to state their case. "Mr. Catlin, as Roddy said, we may be able to come back, but we shouldn't stay now. You're putting us in a difficult position."

"I see my son's been very intimidating. I'll handle him. You've traveled thousands of miles. There's no need for you to go home without accomplishing something. You're both our guests." He shrugged his thin shoulders. "I've promised Mr. Reece. I won't overdo, and I'll talk to Thorn. You've no transportation to Sao Paulo anyway," he added with a smile.

Sabrina almost snapped, "We could walk!" but she held back the words. She'd rather walk all the way to the city than cause difficulty for Mr. Catlin—or face Thorn's wrath, she reflected wryly.

Roddy spoke up then. "Sir, we're trying our damndest not to be rude, but we don't feel we should stay unless your son approves."

"Nonsense!" He glanced at his daughter. "Laurel, take them on a short tour, then show them to their rooms so they can freshen up before we eat. While we're eating, you can give me your arguments," he added. "Now I'm weary, and it's nap time."

Sabrina gazed in consternation at him. How could she argue with an ailing elderly man who needed a nap? As Roddy shrugged, Laurel moved to the door. "If you'll come this way," she said.

As soon as they had moved down the hall into an ornate room with a high carved ceiling and French gilt furniture, Sabrina appealed to Laurel. "Laurel, will you please call a taxi for us? We can't impose on your father, and we should get back to São Paulo."

Laurel shook her head. "No, I'm sorry, I can't. Papa said I couldn't. He enjoys company, so please stay. Even if it's just for a day, it'll be good for him to visit with you." Wide gray eyes glanced back and forth between Roddy and Sabrina. "Please stay—at least until tomorrow."

Sabrina felt as if she were being pulled in opposite directions. She didn't want to be the cause of an argument between father and son. As much as she needed this job, she could understand and agree with Thorn's motives for not wanting to disturb his father. At the same time she could see the validity of Laurel's argument. She looked helplessly at Roddy.

"Please," Laurel urged. "One evening here won't hurt papa."

Roddy looked at Sabrina. "I don't know...." He frowned. "If we do, Laurel, will you get a cab out here in the morning with no more arguments?"

A bright smile revealed the dimples in Laurel's cheeks. "Thank goodness! Yes, I will. I'm so glad you'll stay, because papa needs to see someone new. His friends come, but they discuss the same old things over and over."

She turned for the hall and continued to show them through the rooms, which were odd mixtures of French, colonial and Portuguese styles. As they admired the ballroom, solarium, music room and formal dining room, Sabrina mulled over their decision to stay. She agreed with Roddy's answer—there seemed to be little else to do. Yet she didn't feel good about it. They would have to have Thorn's cooperation if they were ever to work on the project, and under the circumstances she didn't feel they would get it.

After they were shown the patio and a long rectangular swimming pool, Laurel led them to the second floor's east wing. She opened the door to a spacious blue-and-white bedroom chosen for Sabrina. "If you want anything, just let me know. A bell will ring when it's time to eat." She glanced at Roddy. "I'll show you to your room, Dr. Hughes."

As soon as Laurel and Roddy had gone, Sabrina walked around the room, taking in the four-poster bed of carved oak, with its white organdy bedspread. The bright colors in the handwoven rugs and chair cushions cheered her up a bit. Overhead a white fan revolved, stirring air freshened by the breeze blowing in through the open doors to the balcony.

Stepping into the blue-tiled bathroom, she washed and removed a brush from her purse to smooth the loose strands of her golden hair into a chignon. Then she glanced at her watch and walked down the hall to look for Roddy's room. Turning the corner, she ran right into Thorn Catlin.

Eyes blazing, he caught her shoulders roughly and looked angrily down at her. "You!"

Hostility, surprise and contempt were conveyed in that single word. Clad in a khaki shirt and trousers that held faint traces of the tang of tobacco and leather, Thorn seemed incapable of further speech.

Sabrina's heart pounded at the contrast this man

presented to the suave sophisticate of urban Sao Paulo. He had been transformed into a brawny rugged male who looked as if he had spent his life in the saddle. His fingers squeezed her shoulders, and he demanded, "What are you doing here?"

Sabrina felt as if she had turned to ice. She struggled to keep her voice steady. "Your father brought us to Bellefontaine."

He swore softly, and she gathered her nerve and jerked away. "We were told that Mr. Catlin had a car waiting for us. We thought you'd sent it."

His lips firmed, and he glanced around, then commented, "This is no place to talk." He took her arm. "Come into my room."

Sabrina allowed him to lead her along the hall. They entered a huge bedroom that did nothing to set Sabrina's jangled nerves at ease.

There was nothing impersonal about the room. From the large carved-oak bed to the display of guns, shields and knives along one wall, it revealed Thorn's tastes and hobbies totally. Shelves filled with books lined another wall. An enormous desk occupied one corner. Plants, bronze sculptures and watercolors added to the decor. On one side of the room a white hammock swung gently. He sat down in it, facing her. "Now go ahead...."

"There's not much to say, except that we thought you'd sent the car. When we assessed the situation, we asked for a taxi. But your father refused. It's difficult to argue with a sick man who says he needs a nap."

Thorn was watching her intently. "I know," he answered flatly.

"Laurel asked us to stay overnight," Sabrina continued. "She said it would be good for him to have guests. Then she promised she'd get a taxi for us in the morning. Your father says he's canceled our plane reservations."

Thorn planted his booted feet on the floor, rested his elbows on his knees and regarded her steadily. "Miss Devon, we're not far removed from the old feudal customs on these plantations. My father is strong willed and has ruled Bellefontaine with an iron fist. It's difficult for him to change. If you remain here, he'll insist on working with you. I'll have my secretary make reservations for you. I'll pay for rooms at the hotel and furnish your transportation back to São Paulo. Even overnight you're not to remain." His gray eyes were glacial. "You're not welcome under this roof."

Taken aback by his cavalier and blunt dismissal, she replied, "Your father insisted we stay to eat."

He stood up and looked down at her from his considerable height. "You'll find, Miss Devon, that it's not my father or sister with whom you have to deal—but me. You're to leave."

Indignation shook Sabrina as she shot back, "We had no intention of working here if it meant causing your father any harm. We had every intention of dealing with you." She remembered the moments of scrutiny in São Paulo, Thorn's veiled hints and double meanings. "Why don't you tell me the real reason you want us gone, Mr. Catlin!"

For an instant she thought she had been wrong. Nothing changed in his expression, but when he spoke the aggression was plain. "Get out, Miss Devon. In the airport, when you didn't know my identity, you gave yourself away. You're here for more than agronomy. As you said, if you get what you want here, you can do as you choose when you go home."

"That's right, but I *did* mean agronomy." She'd been right in the first place. In some way he'd misinterpreted her earlier statements. "I need this assignment," she began to explain, but his cynical smile only increased her aggravation.

Before she could say anything more, he reached out to tilt her face upward. "Such righteous indignation and innocent blue eyes," he remarked with scorn. "Agronomy, hell! Admit it," he demanded. "You're willing to go to any lengths in exchange for my cooperation. To get what you wanted, you were offering more than kisses that night at the hotel."

He ignored Sabrina's gasp. His eyes glittered wickedly, and his voice was filled with fury. "If I kissed that pretty mouth right now, how long would you resist? We'll see...." His arm slid around her waist and jerked her against his chest, while his hand locked in her hair and turned her face upward for his kiss.

Sabrina struggled, beating against his chest in a rage. Yet along with her fury flared passion. When her hands pushed against the rock-hard muscles beneath his khaki shirt, she knew she was fighting not only him, but also the current that coursed through her veins, a wild soaring abandon that threatened to engulf her.

Long and thoroughly, probing intimately, he kissed her, crushing her to him. Consuming fiery anger gave her the strength to resist, until finally he released her. Instantly she raised her hand and slapped him as hard as she could. Her palm connected with his cheek with a sharp crack, and she rushed past him toward the hall.

"Sabrina!"

She heard his call but didn't pause. She raced to her room, flung the door closed and leaned against it.

Her heartbeat thudded in her ears. Across the room she caught sight of her reflection in the mirror—pale face, eyes wide.

She couldn't understand his anger—didn't even want to try—and she couldn't forgive her own. Never in her life had she slapped anyone. Yet his accusation had been so insulting. She was certain now that those kisses at the airport had been disastrous. They had given him the wrong impression of her. How was he to know it wasn't typical behavior on her part? Now how could she hope to work with him? How could she even want to?

The dinner bell sounded, adding to her distress. Sabrina didn't want to join the Catlins for a meal. She certainly didn't want to face Thorn, but the insistent ringing made her realize the hopelessness of avoiding another encounter.

Shaking with frustration, anger and humiliation at Thorn's harsh treatment of her, she brushed back her hair and clasped it behind her neck. Grimly she headed for the door.

As soon as she descended the stairs, Laurel was there to meet her, exclaiming, "There you are! We're in the library. Everyone's here except Wade. Come on, Sabrina."

Moving beside Laurel, she was keenly conscious of the other woman's open curiosity. Suddenly Laurel asked, "Have you been with Thorn?"

"Yes." Her cheeks flamed at the admission, and she was thankful when they turned at the library door and walked in. Thorn's eyes narrowed as he rose to his feet. Mr. Catlin and Roddy were nearby. Beside Thorn on the sofa sat a slender dark-haired woman with pale flawless skin and black eyes that studied Sabrina coldly. In a manner fully as imperious as Thorn's, she waited while he introduced Sabrina and then added, "Miss Devon, this is my fiancée, Amanda Pickering."

Sabrina stared with stunned surprise at the woman and reflected that Amanda Pickering was exactly the type for Thorn. Strikingly beautiful, she should suit him well.

With every fiber of her being Sabrina wished she were somewhere else. If Laurel guessed so easily that she'd been with Thorn, most likely guessed he'd kissed her, how much more likely it was that Amanda Pickering would know.

Amanda studied Sabrina and remarked, "You're very young, Miss Devon, to have such a responsible job. It's unusual to be so wrapped up in a career. In my corner of the world women are still women."

Sabrina's gaze shifted to Thorn as she replied, "I enjoy my work immensely, and besides, sometimes necessity puts us in unexpected places."

"Doing unexpected things!" Amanda snapped, watching Thorn.

Embarrassed in spite of herself, Sabrina was relieved when a breezy greeting interrupted this exchange. She turned to face Wade Catlin.

Introductions were made, and her hand was shaken by a young man with brown hair, dark brown eyes and an engaging smile. Apart from his deeply tanned skin and straight thin nose, he bore little resemblance to Laurel, Thorn or Mr. Catlin.

"You're late." Thorn's flat statement brought a moment of silence to the group.

The brothers gazed at each other, and suddenly Sabrina deduced she was not the only one at cross-purposes with Thorn Catlin. Wade thrust his chin forward and jammed his hands into his pockets. "Sorry," he answered briefly.

Just then the double doors were opened to reveal a small informal octagonal dining room. Mr. Catlin led the way into the pale yellow room brightened by pots of red and yellow hibiscus.

Within minutes after they had been seated, it was clear to Sabrina that Amanda was interested in only two people in the room: Thorn and Roddy. Amanda sat between the two men near the other end of the table, and all her smiles were directed at one or the other.

While they were served *caldo verde*, broth, this one

with potato and shredded kale, Sabrina studied Amanda. Silky black hair curled softly over her shoulders, which were covered by the silk of a white dress embroidered with daisies. Pleating cascaded down the balloon sleeves, tapering at each pale wrist, only inches from her blood-red nails. Her voice was high with a childlike quality, and she startled Sabrina when she asked Roddy, "Is Miss Devon here to assist you, Dr. Hughes?"

Roddy glanced at Sabrina and laughed. "Hardly. It's more like I assist her."

Sabrina gave him a grateful glance before she remarked, "We work pretty well together."

"How romantic," Amanda remarked dryly.

The earlier discomfort Sabrina had felt from Amanda's cutting remarks returned. It would be unkind to Roddy to deny Amanda's implication, but silence would make it seem as if Amanda's assumptions were correct. Sabrina chose silence and longed for the meal to end.

"Papa Catlin," Amanda continued, "I had a letter from mother yesterday listing the things she's selected."

"Amanda's staying here because their home burned down," Laurel explained to Sabrina and Roddy. "They live next door to us. Her mother is in Paris buying furniture for their new house."

"What rotten luck, Amanda!" Roddy exclaimed. "Were you there when it burned?"

Amanda shook her head and flashed a smile. "No. We were vacationing in Monte Carlo. It spoiled what would have been a delightful trip. There are compensations, because I have a new wardrobe and soon we'll have a new house."

"How did the fire start?" Roddy inquired.

"The house was hexed...."

Instantly Thorn's eyes narrowed. "Amanda..." he said warningly.

She shrugged. "According to the report, faulty electric wiring caused all the trouble."

While Amanda continued talking to Roddy about her home, Sabrina studied Thorn, until he shifted and looked into her eyes. She couldn't guess whether the smoldering anger she saw there was directed at Amanda, his family, or at Roddy and herself.

As she turned away, she thought of his earlier angry words. Why did he think she was at Bellefontaine if it wasn't for agronomy? What else was there here to interest her? Remembering his kiss, she glanced at him again, her eyes straying to his firm lips. She clearly recalled the taste and feel of his mouth. Her lips parted. Her own breath was cool against them as she exhaled. She looked into his eyes and caught the glint of sardonic amusement gleaming from them.

Drawing a sharp breath, she shifted in her chair. Instantly she encountered Amanda's narrowed eyes and realized the other woman had been watching the interplay between her and Thorn. Sabrina's face burned as she looked at her plate, wishing even more fervently that the meal would end.

Mr. Catlin glanced at his youngest son. "Wade, this afternoon you can show our guests around."

Thorn spoke up then. "I have a car ready, papa,

and arrangements made again for their flight home."

For a minute Sabrina thought the matter was settled—until Mr. Catlin asked, "May I have the car keys, Thorn?"

Thorn hesitated briefly before anger flared in his eyes. He withdrew the keys from his pocket to hand them to Roddy. Before Roddy could pass them on to Wade, Mr. Catlin said, "Dr. Hughes, just keep those keys. After we eat, you can use the car to drive to the lab." He looked at his son. "Thorn, Bellefontaine is my home and these people are my guests—here at my invitation. Control over my activities still lies with me—not you and Dr. Andrade."

Thorn's gray eyes became opaque and icy. A muscle worked in his jaw, but his voice was low. "In an hour, Dr. Hughes, I'll meet you and Miss Devon at the sugarcane genetics and breeding lab. I'll drive you back to São Paulo after the tour."

Because Sabrina could think of many times she'd tried to help her mother and her efforts had been refused, she felt a sudden rush of sympathy for Thorn. She realized he was doing what he thought was best for his father. She glanced at Amanda and was startled by the intensity of the other woman's gaze. Lines bracketed Amanda's mouth as she pushed her chair away from the table and stood up.

"Papa Catlin, I'm so sorry, but you must excuse me. Suddenly I feel ill."

Immediately Thorn rose to his feet to accompany her upstairs. While he was gone, Laurel said to Roddy, "I'll go with you both to the labs. First you can drive past some of the cane fields and see them."

"We don't want to cause any difficulty," Roddy said. At that moment Thorn returned. When he sat down, he explained easily, "Amanda felt faint. She said she'd spend the rest of the afternoon in her room."

Mr. Catlin frowned. "Thorn, these people—"

"We can discuss this after we eat, papa," Thorn interrupted smoothly.

Mr. Catlin's gray eyes rested on his son, and Sabrina held her breath, fearful there would be an outburst. But the senior Catlin merely said, "Very well, we'll talk after we eat, as you suggested."

Sabrina glanced around the table. Even Laurel looked as tense and grim as Thorn and Wade. Although Sabrina barely knew the Catlins, it was clear that Bellefontaine was not a happy household.

Roddy spoke, and Sabrina felt as if he were voicing her feelings. "Mr. Catlin, I don't want to step into the middle of a family dispute."

"Nonsense!" Mr. Catlin said. "Don't let my son intimidate you, Dr. Hughes."

Roddy smiled. "I'm not intimidated."

"This is my house," Mr. Catlin said. "I want you to feel welcome here. I built this house, you know."

Sabrina looked at him in surprise and remarked, "I thought it was built by your ancestors who settled here."

While a maid removed the soup bowls and brought *moqueca de peixe*, a fish stew that included scampi and shrimp with coconut milk and *dendê*, or palm oil, Mr. Catlin answered, "No, Miss Devon. The original Bellefontaine was smaller. I had it leveled and rebuilt." A note of fierce pride was in his voice. "I've made this plantation what it is today. I built this house and purchased two-thirds of the land we now own."

"Papa," Laurel interjected, "be fair. Thorn's done a lot. He's constructed cane mills, increased production and started raising coffee."

Sabrina caught Thorn's quick wink at Laurel and saw Laurel's face flush with pleasure. Surmising she was facing an aging patriarch who did not want to relinquish his rule, Sabrina's opinion was confirmed as Mr. Catlin looked at Thorn and spoke harshly.

"I've built Bellefontaine, and I don't intend to be shoved aside like a worn-out plow!"

Thorn met his father's gaze, stating quietly, "No one will ever treat you in such a manner. You know my interests for Bellefontaine are the same as yours."

Mr. Catlin's eyes narrowed. "This is my house and I rule it." The challenge hung in the air. Thorn met his father's gaze, but he remained silent.

It was a relief when the meal ended. As they headed for the door, the uniformed nurse, Otília Alvares, appeared to remind Mr. Catlin it was time for his pills. He waved her away and motioned for Thorn to join him in the library, while the others moved into the hall.

At the door Sabrina stepped back inside the dining room and called to Thorn, who was just leaving for the library through an adjoining door. Aware that Mr. Catlin was within earshot, she spoke softly.

"We don't want to cause trouble between your father and you."

His voice was cold and unrelenting. "The difficulty isn't with my father, Miss Devon."

Stung by his implication, still she persisted. "Isn't there some way we can carry out our studies without interfering with your father's recovery? We don't want to intrude—"

"We're of one accord on that subject," he interrupted. "I'll meet you and Dr. Hughes at the lab in an hour. Now if you'll excuse me, I need to see Amanda."

He went striding off, leaving her frustrated. She followed slowly behind and encountered Wade waiting for her in the hall. "I see big brother is wielding his authority again," he remarked as he took her arm. "Come on, I'll show you around. Laurel's already gone with Dr. Hughes in the car to the lab. I thought you might like to see our gardens."

Angry that Laurel and Roddy had gone off without her—after all, the genetics and breeding lab had more relevance to her work than the gardens—she nevertheless agreed. It appeared they would be gone by tonight anyway. As Sabrina and Wade crossed the wide cool veranda, he took her arm to turn down a winding path. In the sunlight the water splashed and glistened in fountains surrounded by flowers. After a few minutes Sabrina glanced back at the mansion.

"When I look at Bellefontaine, it's difficult to remember I'm not in the Tennessee of bygone days," she remarked.

Wade raised his head and peered up at the clear

blue sky. The wind caught locks of his straight brown hair and tumbled them over his forehead. "We're cut off from the world here. We're not Brazilians, because we've kept to ourselves and clung to our old ways and traditions. Yet we're not Americans, because we've lived in Brazil for several generations now."

The bitterness in his voice surprised her, and she thought of her own home and their day-to-day money problems. "You have paradise. Yet everyone seems unhappy."

He glanced at her. "You're rather perceptive."

She shrugged. "Either that or it shows badly." She paused to admire a bright red arum, then moved on to a bed of pink and purple hyacinths. They reached a small lily pond, and she gasped with delight over the delicate crinum lilies with their thin white petals.

"These gardens are Thorn's," Wade said. "The farther from the house we get, the more changes you'll notice. Part of this garden is experimental. Thorn has recreated by artificial means conditions in various areas of Brazil. Our country has great development potential, since such a small percentage of the surface ground is cultivated now."

They turned to walk past the elongated red blossoms of a cockspur, and Wade continued. "Brazil is so immense. There's the undeveloped Amazon basin, which is three-quarters the size of the continental United States. West-central and south Brazil are known for their rugged hills and mountains, interspersed with grasslands and cattle. Here along the coastal belt we live on a plateau with an excellent climate for crop growth. This area has big coffee plantations, cotton, sugarcane, rice, cocoa and soybean, as well as valuable deposits of minerals and gems."

"I wish I had time to stay and see your coffee trees," Sabrina remarked. "I've never seen any."

"For generations we grew just cane and cotton," Wade explained. "Thorn has started fruit orchards and coffee growing, and papa doesn't like to acknowledge these developments, even though they bring more of a return than sugar. Thorn's always experimenting. That's how he's improved our cane crops so markedly."

"Your brother must be very methodical."

"He loves this work," Wade replied. "Papa won't give Thorn credit for what he's done, because he doesn't want to step down. I'm not certain I could be as patient as Thorn is in the face of such opposition."

Sabrina glanced at him. "You don't sound particularly enthused about any of this."

He placed his hands in his pockets as he walked on. "Thorn loves Bellefontaine more than anyone or anything on this earth." He spoke harshly. "This is his obsession, not mine. He wants to make it the biggest plantation in Brazil—and it will be when he marries Amanda. She's an only child and will inherit Fairoaks, which adjoins our land."

They had reached a tangle of vines, weeds and trees that looked incongruous next to the well-groomed garden. Separating the garden from this wild growth was a sturdy fence dotted with signs that read: *Perigo* and *Entrada proibida*. Sabrina remembered from the sign on the front gate that the latter proclaimed, "No Trespassing." She asked Wade about the other.

"It says, 'Danger,'" he answered.

Curiosity made her inquire, "Why is it dangerous?"

He shrugged. "There's a mine hidden under all that vegetation. It's closed and off limits to workers. That's where papa had his accident and was paralyzed."

"How awful!" she exclaimed. "Does the mine mark the end of your property?"

Wade laughed. "Except for the front drive, you'd have to ride all day in any direction to reach our boundaries. No, that's undeveloped land."

Sabrina looked at the shadowed darkness beneath the thick trees and vines. Suddenly she felt as if icy fingers were brushing the back of her neck. There was an ominous foreboding in the blackness.

"Our great-great-grandfather started the mine," Wade related. "Brazil has diamonds, emeralds, gold and silver in abundance. Anyway, they began to mine, specifically for gold, and he was killed in an accident."

"How awful," Sabrina murmured.

"That wasn't all," he continued. "Later one of his sons was killed, so for years it's been closed. Word gets around. Many thought there was gold and came to see if they could find any."

Wade bent down to pick up a stone, which he chucked into the tangle on the other side of the fence.

"Finally papa built fences around the site. While he was watching their construction one morning, walking around the mine area, he fell through an open pit. No one knew how long it had been there or why. It was covered with brush. Anyway, the fall crushed a vertebra, bruising his spinal cord. That happened two years ago; six months afterward he had his first heart attack. Now no one goes over to that damn mine except Thorn."

She gazed into the shadows again and shivered. Why would Thorn go there if it was closed down? Behind the lush vegetation she sensed something frightening, then decided her feelings were ridiculous. Yet it was a concealed forbidden place, and curiosity nagged at her. Finally she asked, "Why does Thorn go there?"

He shrugged. "Who knows why Thorn does what he does. That place is a jinx for our family, that's all I know."

Wade's words recalled the conversation at lunch. "Why did Amanda say their home was hexed?" Sabrina asked him now.

Wade glanced down at her earnestly. "Do you know anything about *macumba*?"

She remembered the candles burning on the curb in São Paulo. "Yes. Thorn said it's voodoo."

"It is also very, very Brazilian. Amanda was raised by a nurse who practiced it. Amanda might practice *quimbanda*, for all I know."

"What's that?"

"It follows the same *macumba* principles, except all is done for evil purposes."

As he talked, they continued to stroll along the edge of the garden. On one side were bright exotic blossoms; on the other, sinister dark wilderness. Sabrina felt lost in a strange world. There was an abandonment and a hint of savagery to life here. She thought of that first meeting with Thorn. Never in her life had she kissed a stranger and never before had she slapped a man.

Some strange force seemed to have taken possession of her since she first set foot in Brazil, and now Sabrina didn't want to hear anything more about *macumba* or hexes or magic. Even though the sun was bright, she felt a menace in the air. On top of all the uneasy undercurrents, Bellefontaine was torn by the feudal struggle between father and son, and that tension seemed to permeate the plantation. "Can we go to the lab now?" she asked uneasily. "Thorn expects to meet both Roddy and me there."

"We're headed there right now," he answered. "Unfortunately your coming has created another problem for us. Thorn wants you to go—papa wants you to stay. Ironically, this project was Thorn's idea in the first place. He thought it would give papa something of interest to do. It's the first time Thorn's agreed to share our methods. Others have been here to discuss an exchange, but he's never consented."

"Why?" she asked.

Wade shrugged. "I think it's Thorn's nature. He's aggressive, competitive and a loner. He wants Bellefontaine to outproduce everyone else." Wade sighed and continued. "Thorn's right about waiting on this project, though. Dr. Andrade told papa to rest and regain his strength, but no one's ever been able to tell papa what to do—not even Thorn. On the other hand," he added bitterly, "Thorn can be ruthless. He'll stop at nothing to get his way." He glanced at her and added, "Amanda wants you out of here, too. I saw the looks she gave you at the table. She's every bit as ruthless as Thorn."

Emerging from the garden, they had started across an expanse of lawn behind the house when Wade suddenly muttered, "What the devil?"

Sabrina looked up to see a dark-skinned boy running toward them. Dressed in a white cotton shirt and pants, he was waving frantically.

"Senhor Catlin! Please come!"

As he approached the boy, Wade asked, "What is it, Vicente?"

Gasping for breath, Vicente halted abruptly in front of them. "Senhorita Catlin and her guest are hurt!"

CHAPTER FOUR

"ARE THEY HURT badly?" Sabrina asked quickly.

The boy waved his hands helplessly. "Please come. Senhorita Catlin sent me to find you."

"Fine, Vicente," Wade interjected. "Go up to the house and get Otília. Where is Senhorita Catlin?"

"They're at the labs. They've wrecked a car."

Wade drew in a sharp breath and took Sabrina's arm. "Come on."

She hurried beside him as he cut across the grounds in long strides. He was tense and quiet while they passed stables, a corral, then a row of long low buildings. They rounded a corner, and Wade pointed. "There they are."

A greenhouse was ahead. In front of it a black Ferrari had smashed into a tall sycamore. Beneath the tree's dappled shade Laurel stood holding a handkerchief to her head. Sabrina's heart thudded against her ribs at the sight of Roddy stretched out on the grass.

Trembling and pale, her face streaked with tears, her forehead cut, Laurel ran to Wade. When he put his arms around her, Roddy gazed up at them. "The brakes failed," he muttered painfully.

The air reeked of gasoline as Sabrina knelt in the

grass to take Roddy's hand. He groaned when she examined his skinned cheek and jaw, the dirt smudges on his forehead and hands. His trousers were twisted and ripped around his knees.

She heard a motor then and turned to see Thorn rounding the corner in his car to stop nearby. One look at his angry countenance chilled Sabrina to the marrow.

As he approached, Roddy looked up at him. "Sorry about your car."

Thorn waved his hand. "It's you and Laurel I'm worried about. I've sent for a stretcher from our infirmary and told Antonio to get the plane ready. Vicente told me about the accident."

"The brakes failed, Thorn!" Wade said.

Thorn's head whipped around, and his eyes narrowed. Suddenly Sabrina felt an undercurrent of tension she couldn't understand. Remembering Wade's words only minutes earlier "—Thorn can be ruthless. He'll stop at nothing to get his way—" she stiffened. He had warned them to leave Bellefontaine. He hadn't expected Laurel to be in the car with Roddy. Could he have contributed to Roddy's accident?

She shook her head. Her imaginings were impossible, and she wouldn't give them credence. Yet something strange was going on....

She squeezed Roddy's hand and felt her heart twist at the pinched look on his face. Behind her Laurel sobbed softly against Wade's shoulder. All the while Sabrina was aware of Thorn walking around the wrecked car, studying it in frowning silent scrutiny.

A Jeep turned the corner a few minutes later, and

two young men climbed out with a stretcher. From that moment on, through the quick ride in the Lear jet with Thorn at the controls until they reached the hospital, Sabrina moved in a numb haze.

Leaving Sabrina and Wade in the hospital waiting room, Thorn disappeared with Dr. Moreira, Laurel and Roddy. It seemed that a man with his influence was welcome anywhere. Sabrina waited quietly, sitting in a deep leather chair, conscious of Wade pacing back and forth, the heels of his shoes making repetitive clicks on the tile floor. Finally Laurel returned with a narrow bandage on her left temple. As she sat down beside Sabrina, she said, "I'm fine. Thorn's with Dr. Hughes."

Sitting quietly, Sabrina guessed the others felt as little inclination to chat as she did. Time seemed to pass with interminable slowness until Thorn reappeared. They moved to meet him. Yet it was impossible to guess anything from his impassive features.

Sabrina's spirits sank lower after he announced that Roddy had broken both legs. Reaching into a pocket of his khaki shirt, Thorn withdrew a pack of cigarettes and offered one to Sabrina. When she declined, he lit one and exhaled before he related that Roddy had simple nondisplaced fractures in both legs and would have to remain in bed for a time.

Laurel looked stricken. "How awful!"

Thorn looked down at Sabrina and drawled, "In spite of all your arguments, your visit's finally terminated—although under unfortunate circumstances, I will admit."

His cold cynical words stung. She raised her chin,

but before she could reply, Laurel spoke, "Not at all, Thorn. There's no reason Dr. Hughes can't recuperate at Bellefontaine. After all, he was hurt there. We should allow him to recover in comfort."

"Oh, no, Laurel," Sabrina began, but Wade broke in.

"Don't be ridiculous! He can't travel, so you can't go home anyway. He'll be more comfortable at Bellefontaine than here at the hospital, and we have all the help you'll need. It won't be a problem."

Laurel grasped Sabrina's hand. "Say yes—please. Don't make him stay here."

"Very well," Sabrina sighed. She glanced at Thorn—and instantly regretted her capitulation. His features grew harsh, and anger smoldered in his eyes. But he was not inhumane, and Wade's and Laurel's pleas left him little choice.

"I'll make arrangements to move him to Bellefontaine," he said abruptly, and turned and left.

NOT UNTIL THE PLANE set down at Bellefontaine and they had stepped out did Sabrina talk with Thorn again. As they started on the short walk up to the house, two men behind them carrying Roddy on a stretcher, Thorn spoke in a low voice that only she could hear. "You're getting the opportunity to return for a prolonged stay—just as you desired."

She looked up and couldn't resist saying, "Are you disappointed Roddy merely has two broken legs and not something worse?"

As soon as she asked, she regretted it. When he

spoke, each word was clipped. "And just what do you mean?"

A gust of wind blew against her, and she pushed a tendril of hair away from her eyes. "The b-brakes failed on that car..." she murmured unsteadily.

Thorn sucked in his breath sharply, and his face flushed. "You think I caused an accident that settles both of you here indefinitely?"

"Y-you couldn't know that would be the result. You've been trying to get rid of us from the s-start."

"It's more likely that Dr. Hughes injured himself deliberately so you could stay!" he snapped.

"Roddy wouldn't do that! It's unthinkable!"

While the others went on, he halted to face her. Laurel glanced briefly over her shoulder at them, then turned to keep pace with the stretcher-bearers. Thorn looked at Sabrina with narrowed eyes. "It seems we've got carried away by anger. But you have a knack for bringing that out in me! I think we're both saying things we don't mean."

He turned and went on ahead, his long-legged stride widening the gap between them, his hand-tooled leather boots catching dull glints of sunlight. He soon passed the others, and Laurel glanced back at Sabrina and waited for her to catch up.

"Laurel, I'm sorry about this," Sabrina said. "We shouldn't be returning to Bellefontaine now. It'll just be harder on your father."

"Oh, no! Papa will feel better if you're here. It'll be good for him to have someone else to worry about."

As they crossed the large expanse of graveled

driveway leading up to the house, a rider left the stables. A wide-brimmed white hat shaded his eyes, and a pistol was strapped to his side, its leather holster dark against the white cotton of the man's shirt and pants.

"Who's that?" Sabrina asked.

Laurel followed her gaze and answered indifferently, "One of our guards. They patrol the property."

Sabrina wondered why an armed guard patroled the plantation. What was the danger? She thought of the fenced-off abandoned gold mine with its grim warning signs, but surely fields of sugarcane shouldn't need protection. Then it occurred to her that there might be more than one reason Thorn didn't want visitors at Bellefontaine. Perhaps there was something he didn't want her or Roddy to see, something of value. Again a cape of gloom settled around her. Roddy's accident, Thorn's anger, armed guards and danger signs—there were too many things going on here that she didn't understand or like.

Overriding any speculation about the plantation and the guards was the memory of Thorn's last critical statement: "You have a knack for bringing that out in me...." The words wouldn't fade, and they stung. She thought to herself, *you have a knack, Thorn Catlin, for disturbing me!*

She went straight to Roddy's room and asked for a dinner tray to be sent up for them both. Later, after phoning Mr. Reece to inform him of the accident, calling Roddy's father and mother, then calling her mother to tell her the stay in Brazil would last longer than the two weeks they had originally planned, she went to bed early. Sabrina had taken all of the Catlins' presence she could cope with for one day. Life at Bellefontaine was growing increasingly complicated, and she wondered if they would ever get the chance to study Thorn's crop-growing methods.

THE NEXT MORNING Thorn appeared as Sabrina was finishing breakfast. He leaned casually in the doorway and gazed at her. "Good morning."

After she had returned the greeting, he startled her by saying, "I've asked Amanda to take you shopping in Sao Paulo. I thought that would entertain you."

Appalled at the prospect of spending Saturday in town—especially with Amanda—Sabrina protested, "I didn't come to Brazil to be 'entertained.' I'll be happy right here."

Raising an eyebrow, he drawled sardonically, "I'm certain of that, Miss Devon, but the arrangements have been made. Don't disappoint Amanda. She's changed her plans for you."

"She shouldn't have done that," Sabrina answered stiffly. "I'd really rather—"

"Ah, there you are." Amanda's high-pitched voice interrupted their conversation. Dressed in a breathtaking blue silk suit, she stopped beside Thorn and slipped her arm around his waist.

After he had kissed her lightly, she glanced at Sabrina. "Are you ready?" Without waiting for an answer, she eyed Sabrina's dark slacks and white blouse. "I'll wait while you change to a dress. It'll give me a moment with Thorn."

Sabrina rushed past them. She didn't want to go to

Sao Paulo with Amanda, but she couldn't argue with both of them. Why did it hurt to watch him kiss Amanda? She wouldn't consider the reasons but dressed hurriedly in her blue cotton dress.

When she returned, Thorn was gone. Closing a magazine, Amanda stood up. Her tone of voice suggested she was resigned to a bitter task. "This way. My car's in front."

Once they were in the red Ferrari, Amanda drove at top speed. It took a real effort for Sabrina to resist commenting on it, but she bit her lip and watched the scenery flash by, until Amanda asked, "Why are you here, Miss Devon?"

"To study the Catlins' methods of growing sugarcane."

"What else did you come for?"

"That's all," Sabrina murmured, wondering why Amanda frowned.

"You know, if you really want to, it would be possible to get Roddy on a plane to the United States."

Irritation flashed through Sabrina. "A fourteen-hour plane ride might be a bit uncomfortable for him right now," she stated dryly.

Amanda shrugged. "It could be better than remaining at Bellefontaine."

Wondering what she meant, Sabrina glanced at her curiously. Was Amanda issuing a warning? Why would Amanda care if an agronomist and a plant pathologist were guests at Bellefontaine?

Sabrina's curiosity vanished as they reached the highway. Without pausing to look, Amanda merged onto the multilaned pavement. Sabrina gasped at the sight of a large dilapidated truck bearing down on them from behind. The driver leaned on the horn, slammed on his brakes and began to skid toward them.

Certain they would collide, Sabrina closed her eyes. She clutched the door as the car slid across the road, lurched and bounced off the shoulder, then straightened. At the roar of the motor, Sabrina opened her eyes. They were speeding along the road once again, and relief flooded through her. Glancing over her shoulder, she saw the truck had turned sideways on the road; the driver was shaking a fist at Amanda.

Sabrina looked at Amanda and bit back an impulsive condemnation of the woman's abysmal driving. "Are you late for an appointment?" she couldn't resist asking.

Amanda smiled, revealing her white even teeth. "Are you frightened, Miss Devon?"

"Yes," Sabrina admitted. "Not to mention furious."

Amanda laughed easily. "Sorry, but that's the way I am. I can't bear to be conventional and boring." With a maddening lightness she added, "If I wreck this car my father will buy me another."

Sabrina silently fumed and resolved to rent a car in Sao Paulo. She didn't want to depend on the Catlins, and she certainly didn't want to return to Bellefontaine with Amanda!

When they reached Sao Paulo, Sabrina clamped her jaws together until they ached rather than comment upon or show any reaction to Amanda's city driving. By the time they parked, Sabrina had counted five close scrapes.

Climbing out of the car, Amanda laughed almost delightedly. "You really don't approve of my driving, do you?"

Sabrina tried to force lightness into her tone, sensing this spoiled woman thrived on opposition. "We each have our own way."

Amanda laughed again as they strolled along a crowded sidewalk to turn into an elegant shop. Beneath a large crystal chandelier, a deep blue carpet stretched before them, luxuriously thick. A slender woman emerged from behind a draped doorway and greeted Amanda in Portuguese.

During the introductions, rather than make a mistake or have Amanda laugh at her accent, Sabrina said good-day in English. They were led into a small room with white Louis XIV furniture, where they were given demitasses of coffee. As they sipped, a model appeared, wearing a dress of flowing bronze silk.

"If you see something you'd like to buy," Amanda said, "say so. Since you're with me, they'll take your check. That one costs—" she paused to speak to the model in Portuguese "—in American dollars, seven-fifty."

"It's beautiful," Sabrina murmured. Seven hundred and fifty dollars! That seemed like an enormous amount for one dress.

Anger returned, both at Amanda and at Thorn. Why had they sent her to town to waste the day?

Thorn should have guessed she wouldn't be interested in shopping with Amanda, and she was certain Amanda was equally as uninterested in taking her. Why had Amanda brought her to such an exclusive shop, too? She should know Sabrina couldn't afford any of these clothes. But Sabrina realized Amanda might not care. She was doing what she wanted anyway, merely bringing Sabrina along because Thorn had requested it.

Amanda purchased three dresses totaling almost two thousand dollars and Sabrina continued to sip thick black coffee. Amanda signed a credit ticket and allowed Sabrina to help her carry the boxes. As they placed them in the Ferrari, Sabrina was thankful they took up so much room, because it gave her an even better excuse to get a rental car for the return trip.

But at that point Amanda insisted they have some tea, and Sabrina sought to avoid friction by agreeing. They wound through the crowded streets in another alarming ride. Tall buildings and busy crowded walks gave way to smaller structures, old and rundown factory buildings and crumbling tenements. Scattered between the derelict buildings were small nondescript shops. Sabrina had begun to wonder about their destination when Amanda finally stopped the car on the outskirts of town. Cracked plastered walls showed behind a high wrought-iron fence that was covered in vines and orange trumpet flowers.

Stepping through the creaking gate, they entered an empty darkened restaurant. A sweet exotic odor Sabrina couldn't recognize hung in the air. They sat down at a wooden table, and a woman appeared through an arched doorway to greet Amanda.

The two women engaged in a rapid exchange in Portuguese with continual glances at Sabrina, convincing her she was the topic of discussion.

Finally the woman disappeared through the arch, and Amanda remarked, "I've ordered tea and rolls for us."

From the moment they'd left Bellefontaine, Sabrina hadn't enjoyed her day with Amanda, and the feeling hadn't changed with the visit to this restaurant. In fact, the sense of foreboding she felt around Amanda had grown stronger.

Sabrina glanced around. There was no one else in the room, and Sabrina wondered why Amanda had come to such a place. She seemed to know the proprietress well, so she must come often. Yet it was totally unlike the elegant shop they'd just left. Initials were cut in the rough wooden table. Nicks and grooves scarred its top. The entire restaurant was rundown, but Amanda seemed content with the atmosphere.

"This is different," Sabrina remarked.

Amanda smiled, and her black eyes glittered. "Brazil has many facets. Some can be delightful—and some can be dangerous."

Although there was no reason for it, Sabrina felt as if the statement had been directed at her. Suddenly she had the same cold feeling she'd experienced in the garden with Wade. She wished she had never come to this place with Amanda. But she shrugged away the notion as ridiculous.

A man stepped through the arched doorway at that moment. He wore tight black pants and a vest. His bare chest and arms rippled with muscles as he bent over a table and began polishing the top, though not before he had brazenly appraised Sabrina.

She turned away, but she had seen his look. Her gaze met Amanda's, and Sabrina was startled by the intentness in those dark eyes. Instantly the expression was gone, hidden by long black lashes as Amanda looked down until the woman reappeared with two steaming cups of tea, which she placed before them.

Amanda listened to the ensuing stream of Portuguese, then glanced at Sabrina. "In a moment she'll bring the rolls." As the woman moved away, she added, "She's able to see the future. If you like, she'll predict your fortune."

Glancing around, Sabrina caught the man watching her again. The waitress cast a quick look in Sabrina's direction before she disappeared through the door to the kitchen. Amanda was studying her intently once more. Sabrina looked at the cup of tea, watching a thin trail of steam rise from the brown liquid.

She wanted out of the small room, away from three pairs of cold hostile eyes. She felt in danger, and all the logic in the world could not dispel that conviction. Were Amanda's actions deliberate? Had she driven so wildly to disturb Sabrina, or was that her usual style? There was no way for Sabrina to know for sure. Yet she felt consumed by an unreasoning panic. It was growing by the second, mushrooming inside her. Her palms were damp; her mouth felt dry.

Amanda drank her tea in silence and watched Sabrina, then suddenly demanded, "Thorn has kissed you, hasn't he?"

The question caught Sabrina by surprise. At a loss for an answer, she merely looked at Amanda. But by then it was too late—the answer was obvious by her silence. "It didn't mean anything, Amanda," she murmured helplessly.

Amanda's dark eyes flashed. "I'm certain it meant nothing, Miss Devon."

Sabrina wondered if a kiss was the reason for Amanda's hostility. She raised her cup to her lips, and just then a premonition of disaster shook her. She didn't want to touch the tea. Whether it was her wild imagination or a true portent of evil, Sabrina sensed the beverage was laced with something harmful. It was absurd to react in such a manner, but she found it impossible to shake off her uneasiness. With the tip of her tongue she tasted the fiery liquid, finding it bitter and hot. Keeping her lips against the rim of the cup so that none of the tea would go into her mouth, she tilted the cup, then lowered it to the saucer. "The tea tastes unusual," she commented.

"It is," Amanda replied casually. "It has herbs in it."

Peril seemed to ooze from the aged dark wood, the hostile glances, the strange-tasting tea. It hung in the air as much as the cloying sweetness of other curious odors. Sabrina couldn't stand another second in the room. Feeling faint, she stood up. "I don't feel well,

Amanda. I have to leave." The words tumbled out. "I'll rent a car and get back to Bellefontaine myself." She whirled around and dashed outside. Pushing open the gate, she ran along the walk and collided with a man.

His breath was fetid with rum. He laughed and grasped her shoulders. Really frightened now, Sabrina jerked free and ran blindly along the walk, then around a corner. In a few minutes she was lost in an area of tenements, factories and slums.

Gasping for breath, she halted. Why had she acted in such a ridiculous manner? In the bright sunshine of a warm afternoon, her actions seemed ludicrous. Yet all she had to do was to recall sitting in the cool darkness of that room with those three staring at her, and the same feeling shook her.

She had to get out of here! Taking stock of her surroundings, Sabrina was relieved to spot skyscrapers above the roofs of shacks and old buildings. She turned and headed in the direction of several cathedral spires and two tall office buildings.

Not until she was in a busy thriving part of the city did the stiffness leave her shoulders. She found a sidewalk cafe and sat down weakly to order coffee, totally unnerved by her experience and feeling foolish. Nothing Amanda had done could be declared outright dangerous or threatening—except her driving habits, of course. Yet Sabrina had felt the threat beyond all doubt. She would never be able to explain her actions to Roddy or Thorn. Thorn! How humiliated she'd be when Amanda related the day to him.

She ran her hand across her eyes. What an assignment this was turning into! She hoped it proved worth all the difficulties they'd encountered, wondering if Thorn would eventually change his mind and cooperate with them.

It took another hour to locate the rental car agency and get a yellow Volkswagen. Sabrina settled into the driver's seat with a sigh and leaned back to close her eyes. The car seemed like the first familiar ordinary thing she had encountered all day. Starting the motor, she drove to a cafeteria, where she ate before returning to Bellefontaine.

IT WAS EARLY evening by the time Sabrina pulled up at the long six-car garage. Her sense of dread increased with each step she took toward the house. How she hated to face Thorn! It would be too much to hope that Amanda hadn't related in detail the events of the day.

Entering the house, she turned for the stairs. Light spilled from an open door, and as she passed, she glimpsed Amanda and Thorn inside. Her spirits sank at Amanda's scolding words.

"Miss Devon! For heaven's sake! Where have you been? You gave me a time!"

Sabrina entered the room. Facing this formidable couple, she felt her cheeks flush with embarrassment. Thorn's gray eyes were as icy as she had expected. Amanda had changed into green linen and looked immaculate and cool, while Sabrina felt dusty and disheveled.

"Why did you run out of the restaurant?" Amanda asked. "Where on earth did you go? I hunted all over for you. Thorn was about to contact the authorities."

It had been a long disquieting day. Now to face an accusing Amanda was almost too much. Sabrina wanted to burst into tears. She was tired, frustrated and angry, but she answered quietly, "I told you, Amanda, that I intended to rent a car."

"I didn't hear you!" Amanda snapped. "I didn't know what happened to you."

Sabrina glanced at Thorn's harsh countenance and knew she'd never be able to explain this to him. "Well, it's certainly been a day!" Amanda exclaimed impatiently. "I told Thorn you were frightened of my driving, afraid of Sao Paulo, and nothing suited you where we went to shop. I'm sorry, because I tried to please you."

Sabrina burned with fury. It unnerved her that Thorn said nothing. She gazed speechlessly at Amanda, and Wade stepped to her side. "We know how much you tried, Amanda." His voice was bland and polite, but Amanda looked up sharply, and her eyes narrowed. Wade turned to Sabrina then. "Come on, Sabrina. I've been waiting all day to show you something." He propelled her through the open French doors, across the veranda and down the walk into welcome darkness.

She looked at him gratefully. "Thanks, Wade. I couldn't have taken much more of that."

"At least you don't have to for long. When you go home, you'll get away from her. No such luck in my case."

Sabrina felt some of her tension evaporate, and she

sighed. "Do you really have anything to show me?"

"No."

"Thank you again. How's Roddy?"

"He's fine—buried under a mound of books on plant diseases. Laurel's played chess with him all afternoon." As they strolled in silence, the moonlight seemed to brighten, and her eyes adjusted to the darkness. "There's a bench," Wade remarked. "Let's sit down."

She sank down gratefully, while he leaned against the trunk of a tree and looked at her. "What really happened today—if you want to talk about it."

She picked up a sycamore leaf that had fallen onto the bench. Spreading the wide leaf on her knee, she began to explain. "Amanda frightened me with her driving when we went to town. I don't know if it was done deliberately to bother me or not."

"No, that's the way she always drives. Thorn seems amused by it." He grinned. "You're not accustomed to the *paulista* style of driving."

She smiled ruefully. "Thank goodness I'm not! Thorn explained about it when we first arrived. Anyway, we went to an exclusive dress shop when we got into São Paulo. She said I wasn't interested, but there wasn't anything shown under five hundred dollars. That's beyond my working-woman's salary."

Wade swore lightly, then squinted at her. "There's something else, isn't there?"

After a moment's debate, she decided to tell him and began to describe the restaurant scene. Put into words, her fears sounded ridiculous. "Wade, the restaurant was in a terrible part of São Paulo. When the woman brought the tea, she watched me...the man watched me.... I can't tell you what it was like. It sounds absurd now, but it was frightening!"

"That bitch!" His countenance darkened, and he sat down beside her and took her hands. "Sabrina, don't apologize or feel ridiculous. It might have been all right, but it might not have been."

Sabrina looked down at his hands over hers. She felt as if she needed Wade's insight and support. She continued. "Wade, Amanda asked me if Thorn had kissed me. It was as if she were jealous. But there's no reason for her to be."

"She'd be jealous with reason or not!" he snapped. "You're a beautiful woman staying under the same roof as Thorn. And my brother isn't immune to females," he stated dryly. "She may feel threatened."

"That's absurd!"

"Sabrina, I think you did the best thing under the circumstances. You shouldn't have gone with her in the first place. Laurel or I could have told you that. You remember I told you about *macumba*?"

Sabrina nodded, and Wade continued. "*Macumbeiros* think that spirits affect our lives in both good and evil ways. Amanda is thoroughly wound up in this. Thorn doesn't believe in it, even hates it, so she keeps quiet around him."

Sabrina wondered why Thorn hated *macumba* to such an extent, but before she could question Wade, he stated, "I told you, Amanda might practice *quimbanda*, as well—" he turned to look at Sabrina "—or worse. I wouldn't put anything past her. She's spoiled, superstitious and determined to marry Thorn at all costs. I think you did the right thing in getting out of that place," Wade concluded, patting her hand. "You know, you might have disappeared in Sao Paulo, and no one could have done anything about it."

His words sent ice shivering through her veins. "Surely not!" she whispered.

He squinted at her speculatively. "Your sixth sense might not have been far off. Sao Paulo's a big city. You're a long way from home and family, Roddy's incapacitated and Amanda's wealthy enough to do whatever she wants." With a shrug he suggested, "The tea could have been drugged, and you might have spent an unpleasant week with those people, with Amanda pretending all innocence. I'm sure she'd have a good alibi. Who knows, Sabrina? Just stay out of her way."

His words were devastating, but for the first time since she had raced out of the restaurant Sabrina felt pleased about her actions.

"Wade, this all seems so impossible."

Stretching his legs, he folded his hands across his chest. "Not as impossible as you might think. *Macumba* is a more common practice here than you realize. I've been told over ten million Brazilians are *macumbeiros*, but I think that's a conservative estimate. During carnival in Rio, followers of *iemanjá*, also an Afro-Brazilian cult, gather on the beach making offerings to the Queen of the Sea. Lace tablecloths, fruit and perfumes are spread along the water's edge. Worshipers dance until midnight, when a wave is supposed to rush in to take the offerings to the goddess. If no wave comes, it means their offerings were rejected.

"Amanda lives in a different world than you do, Sabrina—one of strong beliefs and occult practices. Her mother has always traveled and left Amanda to be raised by nurses thoroughly indoctrinated in *macumba*." He patted her hand. "*Macumba* isn't bad in itself, though. It's *quimbanda* and the subsequent worship of *exu*, or evil, that can be dangerous."

Standing up, Wade offered his hand to pull her to her feet. "Come on. Let's walk some more and forget all about this depressing topic."

Sabrina moved beside him and asked, "When are Amanda and Thorn getting married?" The words had a hollow ring.

"I don't know. They haven't set a date." His tone became bitter. "Thorn will do as he damn well pleases—that I know."

She glanced at him, expecting further comment, but he remained silent. The only sounds were the crunching of gravel underfoot, the splashing of water in the fountains and the buzzing of insects. "It's beautiful out here at night," she commented.

His voice was suddenly sharp. "It's a beautiful prison!"

"You don't want to live at Bellefontaine, do you?" she guessed.

He shook his head, studying her with his dark brown eyes. "No, and that's blasphemy. This place was built under very harsh conditions by our ancestors.

"Our great-great-great grandfather, Thornton Beaumont Catlin, came to Brazil with other Confederates at the end of the Civil War. He was only eighteen years old, but he'd fought nobly with General Lee. His rifle hangs in our game room. He had three sons and two daughters over here. Tom, the middle one, died. Both girls married and settled here, but Beau returned to Georgia. The other son, the youngest, was my great-great-grandfather, Wade Delancy Catlin." He grinned. "You can see where we inherited our names.

"Papa told you how he's built this up," Wade continued, waving his hand expansively. "Adjoining plantations to the west and southwest belong to our cousins. My family, like many others around here, was raised to preserve our old ways. Life is changing—but not quickly enough for me." He kicked angrily at a pebble.

"You probably can't comprehend it, Sabrina, but we're still living under a feudal system. Day-to-day activities are ruled by men, and on each plantation, usually by one man. Papa doesn't want to hand the reins of power over to Thorn—that's Thorn's problem. I want out, and Thorn won't hear of it. For papa's sake, for the sake of generations past, for the sake of tradition, he's holding this family together. But it's my life, and I don't want to spend it this way!"

"How do you want to spend it, Wade?"

"Arrangements already have been made and I

have no choice," he answered flatly. "In two months I enter law school. I might as well be fifteen years old. I can't even fly our plane."

"If you do go to law school, at least you won't be living here," she pointed out.

"I'll still be tied to Bellefontaine—make no mistake about that." He smiled at her. "Enough of my problems. What are yours?"

The abrupt change of subject startled her. Then she laughed. "Most of mine center around wanting to get back home to Tennessee."

"Can't you just go?" He sounded surprised.

"It's not that simple," she replied. "I have to earn a living. I hope to get a position in an office in my hometown. As a matter of fact, I'd hoped my experience here would give me some special qualifications to help me get that job when I return. Thorn is getting much higher yields per acre than we do in the US. If I could study the strains, take samples home, I might be able to help our farmers increase their yields." After a moment she added, "I need to get home to help raise my younger brother, too. Andy's too much for mom to handle, especially since she's been ill."

Wade looked around at the vast property stretched out before them in the gloom. "You ought to send him here for a while. Thorn would work the devil out of him." Turning to face her, he placed his hands on her shoulders. "So there's more involved here than a government project."

"Officially that's all, but Roddy and I both had special reasons for wanting to come. I want experience to qualify me for this job. Roddy has worked on cane diseases in particular and is eager to gain more knowledge."

"I'll see what I can do to help."

"Thanks, but I don't want to cause—"

"So," a deep voice came from the shadows, "where you don't succeed with one brother, you'll try with another." Thorn emerged from the darkness and faced them. He addressed Wade. "When you're in São Paulo tomorrow, will you check with the caterer to make certain everything is ready for our barbecue?"

"Barbecue!" Wade exclaimed. "I'd forgotten all about it." He dropped his arms from Sabrina's shoulders.

Thorn turned to gaze contemptuously at her. His voice was harsh. "Wade has a weakness for a pretty face, Miss Devon, but he won't be able to provide anything you came to get, no matter how much you turn your charms on him."

"Thorn, that's an insult!" Wade growled.

Sabrina drew in a sharp breath but answered steadily, "It's all right, Wade. I'm becoming accustomed to your brother's rudeness."

"Thorn, you need to apologize."

Lazily Thorn's eyes shifted from Sabrina to Wade. He faced them in a relaxed stance, one hand in the pocket of his slacks. His voice was mocking. "Apologize, Wade, because I indicated that you have a penchant for succumbing to the wiles of an attractive woman?"

"You know that isn't what I meant!" he snapped.

"You implied she's using her looks to get something from me."

"For that I should apologize?" Thorn asked derisively.

Frustration shook Sabrina. She was tired; the day had been one emotional strain after another. Now she was the cause of an argument between brothers. She didn't think she could cope with one more difficulty.

"Wade—" she began, but he interrupted.

"Thorn, you could work with them."

"What do you think it would do to papa, Wade? I have to fight him too much as it is without arguing about what two visitors are up to around the place," Thorn replied angrily.

Wade took a deep breath. His fists clenched at his sides. "Apologize to Sabrina, Thorn."

"I see nothing to apologize for," he said evenly.

In rising desperation Sabrina implored, "Please forget it, Wade."

But the two men were now facing each other, tension crackling in the night air. Suddenly Wade swung at Thorn, who ducked with ease, straightened and moved to one side. "Wade, you'd better let well enough alone," he warned.

"Apologize, damn you!" Wade snarled, and to Sabrina's horror swung again. Thorn turned on his heel to walk away. Wade stepped forward, closing the gap between them. Oblivious to Sabrina's pleas, Wade grasped Thorn by the shoulder and spun him around. His right arm shot forward.

Thorn's left came up quickly, blocking the blow.

Then he swung with his right. There was the crack of bone against bone before Wade was sent sprawling, smashing a bed of red sultana as he fell.

At once he sprang to his feet, but Sabrina lunged between them and threw her arms around Wade. His eyes were glazed with anger as he grasped her shoulders to shove her aside. She held on tightly to his arms.

"Wade, please don't fight with him!" she begged.

His breathing was ragged as he glared silently over her head. She spoke rapidly. "Please, he doesn't need to apologize to me. It would be meaningless anyway."

Wade sighed heavily. "All right, Sabrina." He stepped away and turned toward the house. Making a supreme effort to hold back the tears, Sabrina found she was shaking violently.

Thorn regarded her in chilling silence, then spoke derisively. "I hope you're satisfied!" He walked away, his shoulders stiff with anger. His long legs widened the distance between them as Sabrina stared after him.

Once he was out of sight she ran to the house, and gradually the quiet in her room settled her jangled nerves. The bright rugs and oak furniture were comforting and normal, cheering her as much as getting away from the turbulent Catlins had done.

The blue-tiled bathroom filled with steam as she ran a bath, climbed in and tried to relax, concentrating on washing away all the day's calamities. She wriggled her toes and slipped down into the tub until only her face was out of water. Involuntarily she remembered Thorn's kisses, and a quiver raced through her. No one had ever kissed her the way he did. No one had ever been as angry with her, either, as he had been tonight.

Trying to forget Thorn, she slipped completely under the hot water to get her hair wet. Finally she bathed, then washed and dried her hair. It shone with golden silkiness as she dusted herself with lilac-scented bath powder before slipping into a practical high-necked long white nightgown.

When she emerged from the bathroom, the cool air struck her, and she glanced at the balcony. The doors stood open. Puzzled, Sabrina gazed at the delicate white curtains fluttering in the breeze, at the impenetrable darkness beyond. She was sure she hadn't left the doors open....

Her shoulders stiffened. Panic swept through her, bringing with it the certainty that someone had been in her room. She glanced quickly around and moved to lock the balcony doors. Although everything looked the same, untouched, she couldn't be sure because she hadn't studied the room before she went to bathe.

This time she looked slowly around the room, taking in every detail. The ticking of a clock sounded loudly in the silence. Sabrina shook her hair back from her face and clamped her jaws together, determined to remain calm. She put away her clothes and, as soon as she'd finished, turned out all the lights except the small one on her bedside table. Its soft glow through the white shade left the corners of the room in shadow.

Her eyes returned to the balcony doors, and she wondered if she was being foolish—letting the day's events cause her to jump at every shadow, to imagine things. But it was impossible to shake off that cold touch of fear.

Reminding herself that she was in a house full of people, that nothing could happen, Sabrina turned down the organdy spread and the top sheet.

Something dark lay in the center of the bed. Sabrina stepped closer, leaned forward cautiously, then screamed.

CHAPTER FIVE

SHE STARED aghast at the black hairy spider that crouched on the crisp white sheet. Within moments her door burst open.

Thorn brushed past her to glare contemptuously down at the ugly creature. Deliberately he reached down and picked it up, unlocked the balcony doors and moved through them to fling it over the rail. He turned to face her, and suddenly Sabrina preferred the spider to the anger in his eyes.

His glance went past her, and he strode purposefully back to the door, looking up and down the hall before he closed it and confronted her.

Even though her nightgown was made of heavy opaque cotton, she snatched up the organdy spread and wrapped it around her torso. Blushing furiously, she raised her head and met the diamond hardness of his eyes.

"Thank God papa couldn't hear you! His room's in the other wing." His scorn was evident as he added, "You must have seen a tarantula before. Or was that a clever little ruse to get Wade to come to your rescue?"

Sabrina's blush deepened with anger and embarrassment. "I'm sorry if I disturbed anyone," she faltered. "But it wasn't a ruse."

In two quick strides he narrowed the distance between them. Her heartbeat quickened as she looked into his blazing eyes. Glinting in the soft light from the nightstand, dark locks of hair tumbled over his forehead.

His voice was icy with derision. "Here you are, in a nightgown, the lights low, the covers turned back, screaming over a harmless spider. Do you really expect me to believe it's all mere coincidence?"

"It is!" she gasped indignantly. "The lights are low and the bed is ready because I intended to go to sleep. If I planned to seduce Wade, don't you think I'd choose something more enticing than a granny gown!" She flung away the organdy spread. It dropped to the floor with a soft rustle.

His eyes shifted, inspecting her in a way that made her feel a blush was creeping up from her toes. Instantly she regretted tossing aside the spread. Even though her nightgown covered her from chin to ankles, his burning assessment made her feel unclothed. Her face flamed as she reached again for her cover-up.

"I think I've made my point," she stated coldly.

All the harshness had evaporated from his voice. It was soft, almost tender. "*Pelo contrario!* On the contrary! On you it's not a 'granny gown.'" He stepped forward. Like a dancer following his lead, she took a step back. Pulling the spread up to her chin, Sabrina watched him warily and wished her heart would stop hammering so hard.

Raising her chin, he peered into her eyes. His fingers slipped to her neck, below her ear, not moving, warm and still against her flesh. He murmured to her, drawing out his words in a lingering husky manner.

"You smell like fresh lilacs...nice...." His eyes were full of curiosity. "You are a minx! You're most convincing. Who sent you here?" he demanded abruptly.

A knock on the door interrupted them, and Wade swung open the door at her call. "I thought I heard a scream—" He stopped dead when he saw Thorn.

Sabrina blushed even more furiously, and she moved away from Thorn. "There was a spider in my bed, and your brother has taken care of it." She looked directly at Thorn. "Thank you both, and good night."

Thorn's eyes flashed, and the harshness returned to his features. Glancing at his brother, he said, "If you'll excuse us, Wade, there are some things I'd like to discuss with Sabrina."

"Wade—" Sabrina spoke sharply "—you might as well wait for your brother." She turned to Thorn. "It's been a long tiring day. I'd prefer to talk tomorrow."

He raised an eyebrow and inclined his head, answering dryly, "Of course. I hope you're not disturbed again."

The moment the door shut behind the brothers, Sabrina sank down in a chair. She was left trembling and shaken from the encounter. What had Thorn meant by his question, "Who sent you here?" He knew she worked for an agency in Washington. Why would she pretend about that?

Even more worrisome was how had the spider got

into her bed? She thought of the moving curtains and the strange fear that had gripped her. Had the spider crawled in—or had someone deliberately placed it in her bed? In the warmth of the night Sabrina shivered.

Pondering these unwelcome questions, she sat quietly for a long time. First the brakes had failed in the Ferrari. Then she'd had that disturbing premonition about the tea. Now she'd discovered a tarantula in her bed. Each incident in itself wasn't so strange, but all three together.... Was it just coincidence, or were they meant to drive her and Roddy away from Bellefontaine?

Most disturbing of all—why was she so aware of Thorn? At any moment, without effort, she could conjure up an image of his thick dark lashes, his intense gray eyes, his mouth.... She recalled the intimate husky note in his voice as he'd said, "You smell like fresh lilacs...nice...." How could the man be so arrogant, so aggravating—and so seductive!

Not wanting to pursue that thought any further, Sabrina climbed into bed. But long into the night she recalled with clarity his gray eyes as he searched her face....

Finally she dozed, only to awaken to sounds of voices from somewhere on the grounds. She lay in bed and gazed out through the glass balcony doors. Light filtered up from the floodlights below. She heard a shout and hoofbeats, then after a time, quiet. She let darkness envelop her, and she slept again.

NEAR DAWN Sabrina awakened and went to sit out on the second-floor gallery, gazing over the misted grounds. The early-morning hush was broken occasionally by the melodic cries of birds, and somewhere in the distance church bells could be heard, faintly chiming.

Male voices drifted clearly to her from along the corridor. Then Thorn and Mr. Catlin came into sight, Thorn strolling alongside his father's wheelchair. His dark suit fitted to perfection, and Sabrina guessed he was dressed for church. He barely acknowledged her presence and continued arguing mildly but firmly with his father as they passed. Sabrina shook her head in exasperation. If only she could view Thorn with calm indifference, instead of suffering this quickening pulse every time she caught a glimpse of him.

Sabrina accepted Laurel's invitation to accompany her to a later service at the family church three miles from Bellefontaine, thereby avoiding running into Thorn and Mr. Catlin, but when they returned to the house, she met the elder Catlin in the hall.

He greeted her warmly, then said, "Let me have a little of your time, Sabrina. Would you come to the library for a few minutes?"

"We'll ride in forty-five minutes," Laurel said, and turned for the stairs, while Sabrina accompanied Mr. Catlin to the library. He moved to the desk and reached into a drawer to withdraw two notebooks. "Sabrina, these are journals I've kept. I've promised Dr. Andrade and Thorn—after much argument, I might add—that I wouldn't work on this project. But there's no harm in giving these to you to read and study. I think you might find them helpful."

Sabrina picked up the notebooks, opened one and scanned the neatly printed letters that indicated it was a journal on weed control. "Roddy will be interested in this, too," she remarked.

"Good. Now I'll keep my promise and say no more on the subject. I can do so little these days. Even this has to go." Reaching out, he patted a book that lay on the desk.

Sabrina glanced down and saw it was a Brazilian novel by Jorge Amado. "You're not allowed to read?" she murmured in surprise, then hastily apologized. "I'm sorry. It's none of my business."

He laughed. "Don't apologize. My eyes won't allow it. Otilia reads to me."

Sabrina realized Otilia's time was now partly taken up with Roddy, and because of that she suspected Mr. Catlin wasn't getting as much reading time in. "I've got a few minutes until Laurel is ready. I'll read to you if you like," she offered.

"That's kind, but I wouldn't dream of it."

"I don't mind," she replied, and opened the book to begin.

Mr. Catlin made no further objections but turned his wheelchair slightly to face her and settled back contentedly to listen.

When it was time to meet Laurel, she stood up. "If you'd like, I'd be glad to continue this later."

He studied her intently. "Only if you enjoy it."

"I do," she replied with a smile. "I'll see you this afternoon."

Sabrina stopped to visit Roddy for a moment, then changed and joined Laurel at the stable. As she swung into the saddle, Sabrina mounted a sorrel mare, Citánia.

They rode past gardens splashed with color—beds of purple lentens flanked by pink tulip trees and fuchsias. Darting bees made a steady hum near the flower beds, while the fragrance of hundreds of blossoms mingled with the whole, adding a tantalizing sweetness to the air.

After a quiet ride they dismounted beside a small stream, where Laurel pulled off her boots to wade. While clear water splashed against her ankles, she regarded Sabrina soberly. "I'm glad you came."

"Thanks. You may be the only person who is."

Laurel frowned. "That's absurd! We're all glad—" her eyes clouded "—except Thorn." She blushed and added hastily, "I didn't mean that like it sounded. It isn't personal, Sabrina. Since papa hasn't been well and mama's death, Thorn's like a wolf hovering over his pack. He's taken responsibility for Bellefontaine as well as our other plantations.

"Papa changed after his accident," she continued. "He used to be just like Thorn, only worse." She paused, then blurted out, "Sabrina, let me go home with you! Please.... Dr. Hughes said you live alone in an apartment. Let me go with you and share the apartment. You can help me get some kind of job. It might be the only chance I'll ever have to get away from Bellefontaine."

Aghast, Sabrina muttered, "Laurel, I don't think your family would consent."

"Of course Thorn won't consent!" she replied impatiently. "I'll run away."

Sabrina hid a smile. "If Thorn doesn't want you to leave, Laurel, he'll come to Washington to get you. Besides, you don't have the least idea what it's like to live in a small apartment in a big city."

Laurel waded out of the stream, shook her feet dry and began to yank on her boots. "I can't stay here! Thorn's a tyrant, and our ways are old-fashioned. *Paulistas* aren't as liberal as your country's people, but here at Bellefontaine—impossible!"

Feeling years older than Laurel, Sabrina gently asked, "What's impossible? You have everything you could possibly want."

"No!" Laurel exploded. "Soon Thorn will marry Amanda, and everything will change. Thorn is sending Wade to law school." Her eyes flashed angrily, and she jumped to her feet to stride up and down in agitation. "I'm the one who wants more education, but I'm not allowed to attend college now. Instead Thorn will send Wade, who cares not a fig for law. Wade doesn't want to be buried in dusty old law books. He wants to act!"

Lost in amazement, Sabrina asked, "Why doesn't Wade study acting, then? Surely Thorn isn't that domineering."

Laurel spun around. "You don't understand! You've never known anything like my family. When they came to Brazil, they brought Southern traditions with them. Papa was the absolute head of our household. Now Thorn is. In my family there has never been a marriage outside our own community, and the men have all stayed and worked to make Bellefontaine the plantation it is."

She took a deep breath then and answered Sabrina's question. "In college Wade studied dramatics, then joined a troupe of actors who did shows in Rio."

Sabrina thought of Wade's resonant melodic voice and could easily imagine him on stage.

Laurel continued. "Thorn would have put a stop to Wade's acting sooner, I suppose, but those were the years when papa had the accident, then several heart attacks. Everything seemed to happen at once. When Thorn took over, he changed, too."

Her scowl disappeared. Wistfulness filled her eyes, and Sabrina realized that in spite of their differences Laurel loved her older brother.

"Thorn used to be so much fun," the younger woman said with a sigh. "I couldn't wait for him to come home. He'd ride with me and take me to Sao Paulo for plane rides and to the beach—" She brought herself up sharply. "Then he found out about Wade and Estralita."

"Who is Estralita?"

Laurel sat down beside Sabrina. "She's a television actress. If you were a Brazilian, you'd know Estralita. She's beautiful and very, very Spanish. She's from Peru, and Thorn doesn't approve of her. He's done everything he can to break up Wade and Estralita. That's why he brought Wade back home from Rio, where they met." Laurel's gray eyes darkened. "Now Wade will go to law school and I'll have to marry Tom Rankin."

There seemed to be no end to Laurel's revelations. "I didn't know you were engaged," Sabrina said, baffled.

"I'm not, but the pressure is on from Thorn and Amanda, because she's pushing him to get me married and off their hands."

Sabrina laughed at Laurel's morose tone. "Surely not!" she exclaimed, suspecting a gross exaggeration.

"Yes, she is. She wants Thorn to herself. After they're married she'll get papa out of the main house."

"After they're married...." The words sent a chill through Sabrina. She didn't care to dwell on them—or her reaction, asking instead, "Could your imagination be running away with you, Laurel?"

"No, it could not. I overheard her talking to her mother. She'll wait until they're married, but she intends for Thorn to build a smaller house for papa."

"I don't think he'd do such a thing," Sabrina said to herself.

Laurel rose to her feet. "I'm not staying here, and that's that! Tonight we're having a barbecue. Everyone's coming, including Tom, and I don't want to be here." Her voice dropped. "Sabrina, let me take your rental car. Thorn doesn't know that I can drive, so it'll take him that much longer to find me. Please? I can get to São Paulo, turn it in there and be gone before I'm missed."

Sabrina stood up, too, gathered the horse's reins in one hand and mounted. "No, Laurel, I couldn't do that."

"Look—" Laurel grasped her hand "—I don't want Thorn to find me. You don't know how he can be when he's angry."

Sabrina gazed into her wide gray eyes and almost admitted she fully understood how he could be. Instead she replied, "Laurel, don't do something hasty that you'll regret later. Have you told Thorn about your feelings for Tom Rankin?"

"He knows how I feel."

"Try again," Sabrina suggested. "Discuss it with him and let him know exactly what you think."

"No! I know my brother. He'll do what he thinks is best for the family."

"Have you told your father about this?"

Laurel's eyes widened. "Oh, never! I can't burden him with more worries." She squeezed the hand she was gripping so fiercely. "Please give me your car keys."

Sabrina thought of all the Catlin cars and their long six-car garage; she bit back a smile. "No. My keys are in my room, but I wouldn't hand them over to you, Laurel, even if I had them. You haven't given this enough thought or really tried to talk it over with Thorn, I'm willing to bet."

"Would you talk to him for me?" Laurel's eyes were troubled. "If you won't let me use the rental car, then will you at least discuss this with Thorn? He'd know you're impartial and would listen to you. You're older than I am. Thorn thinks I'm a child." She paused and considered Sabrina. "He probably thinks you are, too, because he's so old."

Sabrina couldn't contain her laughter at Laurel's

statement. "Laurel, your brother isn't old!"

"Yes, he is. He's thirty-one."

Trying to control her amusement, Sabrina asked, "How old are you, Laurel?"

"I'm twenty-two. Wade is twenty-three."

Sabrina was surprised. Only four years separated her and Laurel. Yet she felt a great deal older. Perhaps Laurel's sheltered life had something to do with it, she decided.

"Please talk to Thorn," Laurel pleaded. "Sabrina, if you will, I'll do everything to see to it that you and Roddy—Dr. Hughes—gain something from your visit."

Her amusement vanished, and Sabrina studied Laurel keenly. "I don't want to cause difficulties for your father, and I don't think it'll do any good for me to talk to Thorn."

"Even if he doesn't listen, please try, Sabrina. I don't have a mother. There are only men in my family now, and Wade has his own problems."

"Okay, but I know little will come of it—except possibly to aggravate your brother," she added darkly.

Laurel squeezed Sabrina's arm. "Thanks. That's marvelous!"

Sabrina smiled wryly, wondering how long Laurel's enthusiasm would last. "Let's get back," she urged, waiting for Laurel to mount.

As they rode toward the house, Sabrina glanced at the other woman and could understand why Thorn would think his young sister such a child. She considered the entire Catlin family and remarked, "Your parents had two families really—raising Thorn, then having you and Wade later."

"Not really," Laurel replied. "We always call Thorn our brother because we've grown up that way, but actually he's a half brother. No one mentions it," she cautioned, "because Thorn's mother ran away. Papa married again, and we were born. Thorn loved mama and always treated her as if she were his natural mother."

Tilting her head to one side, she speculated, "I haven't thought about it in a long time, but in a way it was as if both papa and Thorn wanted to obliterate any memory of Thorn's mother."

"Did anyone ever learn what became of her?"

"Oh, yes. I think papa always knew," Laurel replied. "All we were told was that she died. Papa and Thorn are very close—although they weren't for a time and they always argue about what's best for Bellefontaine. I think Thorn was too wild for papa, and papa was hard on him. He was never as harsh with either Wade or me. Thorn ran away, too, once, but he came back."

Sabrina looked at her in surprise. "Maybe you should take a lesson from that, Laurel," she said.

Laurel frowned, apparently ignoring Sabrina's words. "Thorn's not as stern as papa used to be. I guess I'd rather deal with Thorn at that."

The heat of the afternoon sun was growing more intense, and Sabrina longed for Bellefontaine and a cool drink. Emerging from a lane of trees, they rode side by side across an open field, and another thought suddenly occurred to her. "What was the commotion last night or early this morning, by the way? I woke up once and saw lights outside."

"We had a prowler," Laurel stated calmly.

Startled, Sabrina glanced at her. "Was he caught?"

"No harm was done," Laurel murmured.

Sabrina thought uneasily about sleeping while someone prowled through the mansion. "Where did he break in?"

Laurel glanced at her and laughed. "Oh, not in the house! You'd have known that for sure, because there are alarm systems all over."

"Where was the prowler, then? What was he after?"

"Gold. We have an old mine."

"Wade told me," Sabrina remarked.

"Yes," Laurel said. "We always seem to attract people with gold fever. Last year a representative from a US food-processing company came to talk to Thorn about buying coffee from us. It turned out to be a front for his real purpose—hunting for gold. That's why papa deals only with your government or its representatives, but it's amazing he'll do even that. For years he refused to allow outsiders to visit. I think Thorn agreed to have you come originally for papa's sake." Laurel studied Sabrina and added inconsequentially, "Are you in love with Dr. Hughes?"

Sabrina laughed. "No! We work together, that's all."

"Yes.... You don't act as if you're in love with him." Then, abruptly changing the subject, she asked, "Are you coming to the barbecue tonight?"

"Your father invited me, but what shall I wear?"

Laurel cocked her head to one side. "It's casual. Just wear a skirt and blouse or slacks. We have barbecues often. They used to be fun, but now Tom Rankin is always underfoot."

A short time later they reached the stables, where they dismounted. Coming into the house, they glimpsed Thorn, and Laurel called out, "Thorn, wait!"

With a look of impatience he turned and faced them. His khaki clothes were dusty. His dark curls clung damply to his forehead. "Not now, Laurel," Sabrina cautioned under her breath. "He looks busy. Wait until a convenient—"

"It will never be convenient for Thorn!" Laurel snapped. "Thorn, just a minute," she said, and hurried toward him.

Reluctantly Sabrina followed. With a feeling of dread she listened to Laurel say, "Sabrina wants to talk to you." At the coolness in his glance Sabrina inwardly quailed. Laurel could have put the request less bluntly.

"Very well. Come into the library." He moved to hold the door for her, and she stepped inside and crossed the room. There was no sound except for the click of Thorn's boots on the polished floor. Having put as much distance between them as possible, she turned to look at him, and suddenly the coolness of the library vanished. The room became cloying and hot, the silence oppressive.

Thorn closed the door, his jaw set in a determined

line, his features severe. She'd been crazy to agree to intercede on behalf of Laurel! Sabrina wanted to retract that hasty promise. After all, she knew nothing of the situation except for what Laurel had told her.

His bold regard was difficult to meet, and for an instant Sabrina was tempted to tell him she had changed her mind, to escape. But she'd made a promise.

Taking a deep breath, she began, "I think I've made a mistake, but I agreed to talk to you for Laurel." She could barely get out each word. His insolence was almost tangible, his stiff demeanor conveying a contemptuous impatience.

It was unnerving to face him, the tension between them growing with each silent second. She raised her chin and spoke firmly. "You don't intend to make this any easier for me, do you?" When he didn't respond, she continued grimly, "Laurel says she's being forced to marry a man she doesn't love."

"Whether she is or not," Thorn replied coldly, "I can't see how it's any of your concern, Miss Devon."

He strolled closer, making Sabrina want to back away, but she stood her ground. The room seemed to close in on her, to be filled with him.

"You don't hesitate to rush into others' problems any more than you hesitated to run to the aid of that dog. I suggest, Miss Devon—" his voice was dangerously low "—that you stay out of my family's personal lives. Don't meddle in something that's not your affair. Do you understand?"

But Sabrina refused to be intimidated by his remarks, hitting back with, "Can't you understand why a young woman wouldn't want to marry a man she doesn't love? She shouldn't be forced to."

"Forced! You're behaving as foolishly as Laurel."

"She doesn't want to marry Tom Rankin. She wants to continue her education."

His eyes darkened. "Are you aware that only a year ago Laurel wanted to be a physician? And the year before, an artist? Laurel is suffering growing pains. She knows nothing of independence. This isn't Washington, D.C., and she isn't you, with your self-sufficient ways. She's been brought up in an old-fashioned manner. If I sent her to school, how long do you think she'd stay? Take a guess," he demanded.

Sabrina shook her head.

"Less than three months is the usual," he replied, and Sabrina's heart sank.

All his anger seemed to drain away then. He ran his hand across his brow, gazing outside into the distance. He was silent a moment. When he finally spoke, it was as if he'd forgotten her presence. His voice was low and somehow remote. "All I've asked Laurel and Wade for is a few months. Papa isn't expected to live much longer. I intend to see to it that his last days are happy peaceful ones, not filled with strife or arguments to upset him. But to the young a few months can be an eternity," he added softly.

For a moment Sabrina saw clearly the burdens resting on this man's shoulders. Even though he was arrogant and autocratic, she could appreciate the difficulty of trying to deal with such family problems while running a ranching empire. Somewhere outside a bird screeched mournfully. Thorn shifted and looked down at her.

"Laurel is uncertain about what she wants. She's filled with a young woman's fantasies and dreams of love."

Until he uttered that last remark, Sabrina had been taken in by his reasonable statements. She replied, "It's quite understandable that she might be undecided about her future, but surely it isn't mere fantasy for her to want to marry for love."

He shrugged. "That's a romantic notion promoted by your North American movies and television but not shared by the world."

"You're engaged—surely you love Amanda!" Embarrassment filled her at the lack of forethought behind her words, but as she looked into the depths of his eyes, the realization dawned that for him love wasn't the issue.

Her disquiet deepened as she waited for his answer. She couldn't take her gaze from his. While they looked at each other, it was as if a current passed between them, but his silvery gray eyes gave away none of his most private thoughts.

"It'll be a suitable marriage," he answered quietly.

"How can you marry if you're not in love?" she asked.

He crossed the room to her, catching her chin between his thumb and forefinger. In one of his mercurial changes of mood, hostility melted away, to be replaced by that magnetic charm she had come to associate with the interlude in Sao Paulo.

He smoothed her collar unnecessarily, his voice low and amused as he murmured, "You're like Laurel—young and full of sentimental ideas."

His touch was electrifying, making her quiver. She tried to speak calmly, but her voice came out in a breathless whisper. "It's not a romantic notion—or a sentimental idea—to care for someone heart and soul."

She was unable to turn away from his steady regard. Her heart, instead of her mind, spoke now. "It's not a whim to love someone more than your own life, to love even when it's unreasonable, when it hurts to do so and not merely because it's a satisfactory alliance for the family. That's the way it should be. I can't imagine going through with such a cold unfeeling arrangement as yours!"

Something flickered in his eyes, and suddenly Sabrina couldn't bear his solemn scrutiny after she had revealed her innermost feelings. Brushing past him, she fled into the hall.

Laurel, seated in an alcove, jumped up to waylay her. "What did he say?" she asked.

"I told you it would be useless!" Sabrina answered, rushing down the hall. She felt compelled to escape the house—and Thorn's probing disturbing presence. She hurried across the gravel drive until she reached the stables, finding Citánia still tethered where she had dismounted. Swinging into the saddle, Sabrina urged the mare forward into a canter. When they reached a grove of trees, she halted and looked back at the house.

A tall figure stood on the veranda. It was Thorn.

She was too faraway to see his features clearly. Yet she could picture in her mind's eye that unfathomable gaze. She tugged on the reins and carried on.

How foolish she had been to agree to Laurel's plea. Regret was compounded by the gnawing realization that Thorn's arguments were more reasonable than Laurel's in most ways. Leaving the path, Sabrina turned, and for almost an hour rode a meandering course over Bellefontaine's fields until she reached the cane.

An archaic windmill, no longer used, stood in mute testimony to the old methods of grinding sugarcane. Then she realized she was in an experimental field. Glass-enclosed towers to control sugarcane breeding were scattered throughout to protect the crop from windblown pollen. Row upon row had their feathery tops, or "arrows," covered in paper, also to protect them from pollen.

A gusty wind sighed through the tall stalks, causing strands of Sabrina's hair to escape from her barrette and curl across her cheeks. She dismounted and walked along a row of cane. It was Sunday and no one was working, but she hoped that tomorrow morning Thorn would allow her to take samples and measurements, discuss the varieties and growing conditions of the plants—although how she was going to talk him into it, she didn't know!

Finally she mounted to ride again and soon spotted the tangled growth and sturdy fence that indicated the forbidden mine site. Suddenly she felt alone and vulnerable. Why did Thorn keep everyone away from the mine? His actions were as enigmatic as his thoughts. And what must he think of her now? After her outburst, the prospect of facing him again filled her with embarrassment. She turned Citánia toward the stables, hoping she could get to her room without encountering Thorn.

Dismounting, she headed for the house. But just as she started up the veranda steps, the Excalibur roared out of the garage. Thorn was behind the wheel, and as he passed, he cast a black look in her direction.

Spewing gravel in a wide arc, he spun the car around to face her and braked. Leaving the motor running, he emerged, unmistakably furious.

Stunned, Sabrina waited, because with each long step it was clear he had a score to settle—with her!

CHAPTER SIX

IN SECONDS HE REACHED HER. "Laurel is gone, and your Volkswagen isn't here," he said, rapping out the words.

"Oh, no!" A sinking feeling hit her as she immediately recalled Laurel's request to take the car.

"Oh, yes—thanks to your meddling in our affairs. I didn't know she could even drive. Where did she go?"

"I didn't tell her she could take the car," Sabrina protested, and knew how feeble that sounded. "Perhaps she'll be back soon."

He shook his head. "She took a suitcase of clothes." His eyes narrowed. "Tell me where she is."

Sabrina shook her head. "I don't know. I'd tell you if I did."

Disbelief showed clearly in his eyes. He glanced past her and lowered his voice. "We're having a large party here tonight. I intend to find her and get her back to Bellefontaine without any disturbance. No one knows she's gone except one servant, you and me. It'll remain that way."

"I understand," she replied, and wished he would get in his car and go.

Relentlessly he demanded, "Where is she, Miss Devon?"

"I don't know. I didn't have anything to do with her taking the Volkswagen."

"After all you've said, I find that difficult to accept."

"I haven't been here," she protested. "I've been riding."

"What a convenient alibi," he muttered cynically. "Did she happen to ask you for your car keys today?"

Sabrina looked startled, and he frowned. "Yes," she replied, "but I told her she couldn't have them."

His eyes mirrored his scornful doubt, and his voice grated, "I warned you about remaining here. I'm warning you now for the last time to stay out of our lives. Stop interfering, or you'll regret it!" He returned to his car in long angry strides. With a roar it zoomed out of sight.

Helplessly Sabrina watched him go. Then she turned and entered the house, mulling over Laurel's escapade. She hadn't convinced Thorn that she hadn't aided and abetted his sister, and she didn't want to consider his fury if he came back without Laurel.

She walked aimlessly through the cool silent house, taking in the elegant furnishings and thinking about the tormented lives of its occupants. How would she ever be able to work with Thorn if he didn't find his sister quickly? Halting outside Roddy's room, she knocked lightly before she opened the door.

Her spirits lifted slightly at his warm greeting.

"How are you feeling?" she asked, and moved to sit down in a tall rocking chair facing his bed.

"Fine." He closed the book he had been reading on soil insecticides and studied her for a moment, remarking, "You don't look as if you feel well, Sabrina."

"I've been riding," she murmured, aware that it was an inadequate explanation. She gazed at the array of books spread around the patient and the chess set to one side of his bed. Roddy's blond hair was awry; a pale stubble of whiskers showed on his chin.

Smoothing the covers across his lap, Roddy glanced at the open door before lowering his voice to whisper, "Did you know Laurel's going to run away from home?"

Surprised, Sabrina asked, "How did you know?"

"She told me, and I'm still trying to talk her out of it."

Sabrina's amazement deepened. "Laurel confided in you?"

His face reddened. "She told me when we were playing chess, and I can't help but sympathize with her in a way," he stated. "Sabrina, Thorn really is a beast to her."

"Oh, Roddy, I don't think so," Sabrina protested.

"She's told me about him. The man has his good moments, I'll admit. He couldn't have been better at the hospital or when the accident occurred, but he's a tyrant to Laurel."

"I think some of her remarks about Thorn may be a little exaggerated, Roddy."

He frowned and scratched his head. "I don't agree, because she seems so levelheaded." He smiled. "A good chess player, too."

Sabrina laughed. "She must be very good. I can't recall your praising anyone except your friend Rudy, and he's won trophies." Abruptly Sabrina sobered. "Did she tell you where she was planning to go?"

He frowned. "No, because she didn't know. I'm worried about her, Sabrina." He looked at her intently.

"You have good reason, I'm afraid. She's taken my rented Volkswagen."

"She's gone already? Damn! And she's not an experienced driver!" There was a moment of silence. His frown deepened as he smoothed the blue blanket. "She was driving that Ferrari when we wrecked."

"Laurel did that!"

Instantly he motioned for silence. "Lower your voice. I told Thorn I was driving. They won't let me pay for anything so that's no problem, but she's terrified he'll find out, because she isn't supposed to drive. I didn't know that until too late. She's not a good driver, Sabrina."

"Oh, no!" She leaned forward in the rocker. "Roddy, you ought to tell Thorn about the Ferrari."

"That's not the important thing now. She shouldn't be driving to Sao Paulo, or wherever she's gone. Can you imagine an inexperienced driver in that city? She shouldn't be on her own that way! She's led too sheltered a life to cut all ties, even though, as I say, I can understand her wanting to get away from her brother's domination."

"Roddy, he's really not as domineering as she says," Sabrina remonstrated gently. "I've talked with him about her, and he has good reasons for his decisions—most of them. Anyway, he's gone out to look for her."

Roddy sighed with relief, then observed her keenly. "You're very defensive where he's concerned, Sabrina."

She blushed and stood up to study a vase of bright red hibiscus. "Can I get you anything, Roddy?"

"No, thank you. I just hope Laurel's all right."

Sabrina gazed out the window at the garden. Bright yellow butterflies circled in lazy arcs, moving from flower to flower. "I hope Thorn finds her quickly," she murmured.

Roddy leaned back against the pillows and sighed again. "I hope he's not too hard on her, but it's best if he finds her. She probably has very little money on her. She'll be lost in Sao Paulo. I don't know how Thorn will locate her."

"He'll probably start with the car-rental agency. There's nothing we can do but wait." She headed for the door. "Bye for now—and try not to worry too much about Laurel. I want to see Mr. Catlin before I get ready for this evening's barbecue." She knew she would have to put up a good front to avoid worrying Laurel's father. He mustn't guess that his daughter had disappeared.

She went downstairs to spend another half hour reading to the elderly man before she excused herself to go to her room for a bath and a nap. But when she stretched out, disturbing thoughts plagued her.

Thorn didn't love Amanda Pickering, he was merely marrying her to consolidate his estate. From all accounts he seemed obsessed with making the family plantation a success. But that was none of her affair, and reluctant to probe too deeply into her reactions to Thorn and his possible motives, Sabrina shoved the thoughts aside. Finally she dozed off, awakening in time to select something to wear to the barbecue.

Opening the closet to study the few dresses she had brought, she opted instead for olive-toned slacks and a cool cotton T-shirt. Laurel had said casual, after all. After she had secured her hair with a gold barrette, she stared at her reflection in the mirror.

She had always tanned easily, and hours in the sun since her arrival in Brazil had given her skin a golden glow. The woman in the mirror looked serene, cool and undisturbed. Wryly she wished she felt the way she looked.

Downstairs, shyness and anticipation swept over her as she gazed at the several hundred guests scattered across the lawn. The combined aroma of spicy herbs, fruit and hot breads filled the air, mingling with that of the burning coals and the meat barbecuing in an open pit at the eastern edge of the lawn. Exotic Bellefontaine, the fun of meeting new people, seeing a way of life far removed from her own.... The whole experience touched her with an eagerness that was dampened only by her concern for Laurel and her worry over Thorn. She smoothed her long golden hair, continuing to take in the scene.

Underneath the palms a band played steel drums that twanged and reverberated in melodic tones.

West of the swimming pool were long tables laden with gleaming crystal and silver dishes. As her gaze drifted over the yard, the tables of food and the lively guests, she was well aware she hadn't seen Thorn. It would be impossible to overlook him! A voice interrupted her thoughts.

"Ah, Sabrina, come and join us," Mr. Catlin invited. He was seated several feet away on the veranda in the shade. Sitting beside him was Roddy, dressed in a white robe, with a light blanket covering his cast-encased legs. Both were leaning over a small table holding a chessboard. Onlookers had pulled their chairs closer, and Sabrina sauntered over to watch the game.

After introductions to the other guests had been made, she remarked to Roddy, "I didn't know you'd be here."

"I didn't know it, either," he answered with a rueful grin. "I don't feel dressed for the occasion, but Laurel insisted."

"Laurel?" Sabrina asked, an unspoken question in her voice.

Giving her a long direct look, Roddy nodded. "She's here somewhere."

A few minutes later Sabrina moved away from the chess players and drifted down the steps. Catching sight of Laurel's curly head among the crowd, she crossed the lawn toward the tables.

Sabrina spoke, and Laurel turned. Her face was white, her makeup seeming to stand out glaringly against her skin. Her eyes were tinged with red, and Sabrina guessed she had been crying. The white bandage was gone from her temple. She had combed her hair forward, almost hiding the thin cut.

Laurel gazed back at Sabrina in silence, her disconsolate expression at odds with the gaiety of her red polka-dotted dress. She spoke in a flat tone. "You told him I'd gone, didn't you?"

"No," Sabrina replied. "Thorn already knew about it. He was going to look for you when I learned what you'd done."

Laurel searched her face. Then a frown creased her brow. "Thorn's a monster, Sabrina! I can't leave Bellefontaine for one minute unless I'm chaperoned! I can only find privacy around the pool and here in the garden. I can't even ride alone!" The tears in her eyes threatened to spill over. She wiped them away and gave Sabrina a sheepish look. Biting her lip, she spoke hesitantly.

"Thorn demanded to know if you'd given me permission to take your car." She grasped Sabrina's hand. "You don't know how stern he can be. I just couldn't tell him I took it without your permission."

Aghast at the younger woman's admission, Sabrina cried, "Laurel, you couldn't have!"

"He won't get angry with you. You're a guest," Laurel replied quickly.

"You must tell him the truth," Sabrina urged. "I've already told him I didn't give you permission to take it. Laurel, please."

Laurel looked down at the pale green daiquiri in her hand. "I can't," she whispered. "Let him calm down. Then I promise I will."

But the damage was done, and unless Laurel had a

change of heart quickly, there would be no undoing it. "All right, Laurel," Sabrina replied dejectedly.

"Come on, Sabrina, we should eat." Laurel handed her a plate. "I'll tell you about any dishes that are unfamiliar."

Sabrina turned to gaze at the opulent table. Large showy orchids with delicate purple petals graced the length of it, while at each end sterling silver compotes were brimming with pineapples, bananas, grapes and oranges. Nearby a crab-and-cucumber mousse was displayed on a silver tray, thin wedges of cucumber decorating it. Hot sauce made with *malaqueta*, peppers marinated in *dendê* oil as well as pepper-and-lime-juice sauce, filled bowls standing beside steaming clay pots of thick black beans.

Helping herself to some beans, Laurel glanced at Sabrina. "You're not eating anything. You have to try something. They'll bring the barbecued meat soon. Ours is done how Thorn likes it—cooked in the hide. He learned it from the gauchos when he lived on our southern cattle ranch."

Sabrina glanced across the lawn at the beef turning over the hot coals. So Thorn had worked with gauchos, which might explain his hard sinewy muscles and that general air of toughness about him.

"Here's what I like," Laurel said, and served herself some chilled shrimp. As she reached for more, she added, "I told you if you'd talk to Thorn for me, I'd try to help you with your work. Wade's promised to show you one of the research stations. Now I've kept my word."

Sabrina straightened. "That's fine, Laurel, but I'd

still like you to inform your older brother about the car."

"What's this about a car?" a voice behind them asked. Wade sauntered up and reached for the small peppers, but his gaze remained fixed on Laurel.

She sighed and looked down at her plate, her brown lashes shadowy against her freckled cheeks. "I let Sabrina take the blame for something I did."

He swore softly. "Laurel, that's a damned awful thing to do!"

She looked up. "You know how Thorn can be. Wade, will you tell him the truth for me?"

"Indeed not, sister, dear. You march right over and find him now and correct the mistake. You owe Sabrina an apology. It's time you learned to face up to the things you do."

She looked at Sabrina. "I'm sorry."

"That's all right," Sabrina murmured, hoping Laurel would speak to Thorn.

"It's not all right," Wade retorted. "Laurel, Thorn won't eat you alive. You always melt if he frowns."

"I'll find him," she promised, and moved away.

Wade regarded Sabrina admiringly. "How beautiful you look."

"Thank you, Wade," she said with a rather forced smile.

He cocked his head to one side, then reached out to take one of the orchids from the table and place it behind her ear. "Now you're wearing Brazil's national flower."

"Wade, you shouldn't take a laelia off the table."

"Why not? They belong to me. How'd you know their name?"

"I love orchids and I've studied them."

He stepped closer, and she caught a whiff of rum on his breath as he fumbled in his pocket. "I brought you a present."

She watched as he produced a tiny bit of tissue paper and unwrapped it carefully, revealing a sterling-silver necklace. A silver fist with the thumb protruding between two fingers hung from the thin chain. She looked up. "What is it, Wade?"

"A *figa*, an amulet to ward off evil spirits. Nearly all Brazilians wear them. It won't bring you good luck, though, if you buy it. Someone has to give it to you."

"Thank you, Wade," she said sincerely, and took it in her hands to study it more closely.

He accepted a drink from a passing waiter, then continued, "Don't lose it, Sabrina. If you do, all the bad luck it has warded off will descend on you."

She smiled. "I think I should have had one sooner."

"Here, let me put it on for you." Placing his drink on the table, he got her to lift her hair from the nape of her neck as he fastened the clasp. In a quick movement he slipped the *figa* under the scooped neck of her T-shirt, leaving only the silver chain exposed.

"Not everyone here approves of a *figa*," he said somberly. Instantly she knew it was Thorn who disapproved. But why did he have such strong feelings?

Her thoughts were interrupted when Wade stated,

"Thorn has a research station set up just a few miles from Manaus. He's studying the possibility of increasing crop production by improving the soil in the rain forest. He thinks the humidity and high temperatures there can make up for the lack of minerals in the soil and that our tropical climate aids decomposition of dead vegetation so that nutrients are quickly recycled. Anyway, we have a station there to test these theories. I thought the lab might be of interest to you, since it'll be different from anything you've seen before. Your going there won't interfere with papa or Thorn."

"I'd love that," Sabrina replied enthusiastically. "But isn't Manaus a great distance away?"

He shrugged. "I've already talked with Joao, our pilot, about it. It takes four hours, so if we leave early we'll have a few hours at the station before we have to fly back."

"I thought you said Thorn doesn't allow you to have the plane."

His gaze shifted, and he looked down at his hands a moment before he answered. "I can get it to take you to that lab." He raised his head. "Can you leave early in the morning?"

"How early would you like?" she asked. "Four, five—"

"Good God, no!" Wade interjected. "That isn't what I meant by early." He made a face of mock horror. "About seven is time enough."

She nodded and asked, "I'd hoped Thorn would agree to let me study the cane tomorrow. I'll ask him for Tuesday instead."

"You can settle that with Thorn when you get back," he mumbled. His face flushed, and he glanced away, suddenly causing her to feel uncomfortable. He was disturbed about something, but she couldn't guess what. Looking at her plate, Wade quickly changed the subject.

"See here, you have to eat." He took her plate and began to heap food on it in spite of her protests, until there was no room left for more. He returned it to her with a smile. "Now I'll get mine."

At that moment someone called to him, and he excused himself. Sabrina returned to the veranda, placing her laden plate within reach of Mr. Catlin and Roddy so that both could partake of the delicacies.

She knew instinctively the moment Thorn appeared. As if compelled by an unseen force, she turned and saw him step onto the veranda from the house. His thin aquiline nose and firm jaw were in profile to her as his gray eyes surveyed the crowd, including her. Observing his cool impassive countenance, she thought again how little anyone could guess of his thoughts or feelings. Why did she feel a sudden tightening in her throat as he strolled toward her?

Cream-colored slacks and a white embroidered shirt threw his dark tan and black hair into sharp relief. He really was too handsome, in spite of the anger and accusation Sabrina saw in his eyes. But he merely nodded to her and murmured, "Good evening," then turned to his father to ask, "Are you comfortable, papa?"

Mr. Catlin smiled at his son. "Yes, Thorn. It's a

beautiful evening, I have a good opponent and Sabrina just brought us all we can eat."

"Fine," Thorn remarked, and left the veranda as their attention returned to the chess game. Sabrina watched him stride away and casually descend the steps to the lawn.

"Thorn!" She hurried after him.

He swung around, his dark brows arched. As she approached, she wondered how he could be so aloof one moment and so warm and sensual the next. Dimly she heard a group of people chatting nearby, a woman's laughter. As she looked up at Thorn, she felt a cool breeze brush against her cheek. "I'm glad you found Laurel."

Slipping his hand into a pocket of his slacks, he looked relaxed and impassive. But his voice was filled with derision. "I can guess at the sincerity in your remark."

His reply stung. Laurel still hadn't confessed about the car. She wanted to cry out the facts. Yet she felt she should give Laurel the opportunity to do so. Sabrina bit her lip uncertainly; then the moment was gone. Amanda's high lilting voice intruded.

"Darling, I thought perhaps you'd forgotten me!" The heavy scent of her perfume wafted over them as she sauntered up to put her arm possessively through Thorn's, raising her lips to his.

He leaned down to kiss her lightly. Brief, almost impersonal though the kiss was, it was strangely disturbing to Sabrina. How easily she could imagine his warm lips against her own.... While she waited for an opportunity to excuse herself, she couldn't help noticing the way Amanda's aqua-and-maroon cotton dress hugged her figure. The elasticized bodice emphasized her voluptuous curves and the pale shoulders emerging from the strapless top. Shifting, she pressed herself against Thorn as she glanced coolly at Sabrina.

"Are you enjoying your stay at Bellefontaine? Any more frightening experiences?"

Aware of Thorn watching her quietly, Sabrina merely answered, "It's interesting here. If you'll excuse me, I need to find Laurel," and turned quickly away.

She found Laurel and Wade standing at one of the tables. Thick slices of barbecued beef piled on immense platters were placed before them. They ate for a while. Then later, after introducing Sabrina to innumerable guests, Wade drifted away.

All evening, in spite of the growing darkness and the crush of people, Sabrina couldn't lose her continual awareness of Thorn. If he danced a samba with Amanda, she knew, and more than once she glimpsed him laughing down into Amanda's eyes as she swayed in his arms.

Night descended; the lanterns glowed softly. Laughter rang out and music filled the air to compete with the crowd's chattering. In spite of herself Sabrina enjoyed the evening, dancing as first one, then another attractive man asked her.

She had just finished a bossa nova with Wade when Thorn called loudly for everyone's attention. He stood on the veranda, his arm around his fiancée. The aroma of still burning charcoal and the remnants of cooking meat mixed with the scent of sweet waxen blossoms.

Mr. Catlin sat slightly behind Thorn, Otília at his side. Great glass-and-copper lanterns cast deep shadows below Mr. Catlin's eyes and along his sunken cheeks and caught the blue black glints in Thorn's hair.

There were murmurs. Then a polite hush of anticipation settled on the crowd. In his deep strong voice Thorn began, "Papa must retire and bid you all good-night, but before he does, I have an announcement."

Sabrina locked her fingers together, bracing herself against an unreasonable feeling of gloom.

"My fiancée, Amanda," he continued, "has agreed to set the date for our wedding. The ceremony will be one month from today." Shouts of congratulation rose from the guests, and Thorn and Amanda turned to speak to Mr. Catlin.

Losing all sense of her surroundings, Sabrina watched Thorn smile into Amanda's upturned face. He leaned forward and kissed her briefly, then smiled again. Pain knotted inside Sabrina.

Wade sighed. "He's doing that for papa. Amanda couldn't have pinned Thorn down to a date this soon otherwise." He took her arm. "Come on, Sabrina, let's get some punch. We can give the happy couple our congratulations later."

She looked blankly at Wade. From the expression on his face she guessed he had been talking to her, but she hadn't heard a word, had even forgotten his presence.

"Sabrina, want some punch?"

She tried to collect her thoughts. "I guess."

His hand tightened on her arm, and he looked at her intently. "You're not in love with Thorn, are you?" There was incredulity in his voice.

"Of course not!" she snapped. "I'm sorry, Wade. My thoughts were drifting."

He continued to study her closely for a moment, then said, "Come on," and took her by the arm.

With relief Sabrina moved beside him through the guests crowded around the veranda steps. Her thoughts were in a turmoil. She couldn't ignore or understand her reaction to Thorn's announcement. She wasn't in love with him. Certainly she remembered some good moments—remembered his quick laughter in Sao Paulo when he'd rescued her and the dog had bounded away with sublime lack of gratitude. Remembered the moments in the restaurant, his kisses....

At the recollection her breath left her body, as if someone had punched her in the stomach. Sabrina ran her hand across her forehead. Maybe she was susceptible to Thorn's charm because she was influenced by the exotic background or because of her lack of experience with men. But even as she considered all these possibilities, she rejected them. She had dated enough and traveled enough that she knew this was something more. She became aware of Wade looking at her intently, extending a cup of punch to her.

"I'm sorry," she murmured. "What did you say?"

"I just said I wish I could help you and Dr. Hughes. But I don't know much about the crops or the research Thorn is doing." He glanced around vaguely. "This is home, but it isn't my whole life, as it is Thorn's. If necessary, he'd die for Bellefontaine. I wouldn't deliberately hurt papa, but I've got to live my own life!"

Half listening to his words, she continued to dwell on her reaction to Thorn. The fact that he was officially engaged shouldn't matter to her. Reminding herself that what was important was her study of Bellefontaine's sugarcane, she turned her attention to Wade.

"I'm sorry you haven't had a pleasant visit so far," he was saying. "If it's any consolation, I've enjoyed having you."

She smiled. "Thanks, Wade."

His fingers brushed her shoulder, and he pulled out the *figa* to look at it. "Maybe you need something stronger than this."

"This will be sufficient. I'll be gone soon."

He shrugged. "At least the big announcement should satisfy Amanda that you're no threat."

Sabrina gazed at him in amused surprise. "Me! That's ridiculous, Wade!"

"Sabrina, it isn't Thorn she wants—it's Bellefontaine," he stated grimly. "Because of that she won't allow anyone or anything to threaten her engagement to Thorn."

"Well, I certainly don't!" Sabrina exclaimed, wondering what had caused Wade to say such things.

"Thorn brought another girl friend home once,

long ago, you know. Amanda was only nineteen years old, but she drove that girl away in tears, frightened to death."

Sabrina thought of the restaurant in Sao Paulo, the spider in her bed, Amanda's dark glittering eyes. She placed the punch on a table and said, "Wade, I think I'll go in now—"

"Absolutely not!" He took her hand. "I won't have you sitting in your room when there's a party going on." He led her to the patio to dance, and after two numbers a guest took Wade's place. Sabrina noticed Laurel and Roddy with their heads bent over the chess set, then later, servants helping Roddy into the house.

After he'd gone Sabrina looked around for Laurel. There was no sign of her anywhere, and Sabrina wondered if she would ever confess the truth to Thorn.

The night was cool and pleasant as Sabrina strolled among the shadows. But there were sufficient lights on in the house that she could see to walk around the veranda without difficulty. Turning the corner of the west wing, she wandered aimlessly. The heavy sweet scents of freshly mowed lawn filled the air. Sitting down on a stone balustrade, she gazed at the bright flowers growing there.

"Ah, I had to search a long time to find you," Thorn remarked softly as he emerged from the darkness. Perching on the balustrade facing her, he leaned over, snapped a bright red hibiscus from its stem, then gently tugged the orchid from her hair to replace it with the blossom he had just picked.

His fingers were warm as they brushed against her cheek. Bristling, she leaned away from him a fraction of an inch. He raised one eyebrow. "You didn't want your beautiful orchid removed?"

Why must he tease her? "You've just announced your engagement," she said, and wanted to add, "To a woman you don't love!"

He laughed softly. "So it follows there's harm in placing a hibiscus in your hair?"

Blushing and feeling mildly foolish, she nevertheless replied evenly, "There can be with you."

She caught a flash of... something in the depths of his eyes. Tilting his head to one side, he examined her intently. "Why with me?"

"I think it's time for me to join the others," she said abruptly, rising to her feet.

He reached out and caught her wrist lightly. "I'll leave you alone. Sit down, Sabrina. Surely we can just talk." Without waiting for a reply, he added, "I owe you an apology. Laurel told me you didn't give her permission to use the car."

She turned to face him, aware of the lightest touch of his fingers. Certain the wise thing to do would just be to go, still she couldn't resist sitting down again.

"Apology accepted," she replied, glad that she'd waited to give Laurel a chance to confess. "And I understand some of your problems with Laurel, because I have two younger brothers myself." He hadn't released her wrist, and his fingertips moved lightly back and forth across the small bone, until finally she glanced down. "Must you?" she asked pointedly.

He, too, gazed down at his tanned hand holding her, as if surprised by his own actions. "With a beautiful woman it's a habit," he remarked in an odd tone.

"Compliments—from you?"

"Don't take it too much to heart," he responded shortly, and quickly added, "Tell me about those two younger brothers."

She shrugged. "Jeff is the elder of the two, and we agree on most things. It's Andy we both have to contend with." She remembered Thorn's blazing anger when he discovered his sister was missing and had to say, "I hope you weren't too harsh with Laurel."

"I should be. She's acting like a silly child. I know about the Ferrari, too. She admitted she was driving." He added dryly, "I'll see to it that my little sister gets lessons. I doubt that she caused the brake failure, though."

Startled, Sabrina looked up at him. "Wade and I think it odd. We keep our cars in good condition, and Laurel couldn't have just burned the brakes out while driving—unless she left the emergency brake on."

Sabrina thought of her own accusations against him, and her face flamed. "I owe you—"

He placed his finger against her lips and winked. "Shh.... It's forgotten."

His hand was gone instantly, but her mouth tingled from his touch. "Laurel just needs to grow up a little, as we all have," she said.

He laughed softly. "Ah, my old one. Are you any older than Laurel?" His hand moved to the back of her neck. His fingers softly twisted the silky strands of hair, causing it to brush lightly back and forth across her nape.

Each touch ignited a small flame, stirring tiny sparks into fiery awareness of his knee pressed so lightly against hers, his arm against her shoulder, his fingers barely brushing her neck.

Sabrina felt as if each inch of her were changing, slowly melting into a yearning warmth. Her fingers closed around his wrist. It was slender. She could feel the sharp bone. Yet she knew the terrible strength it possessed. Purposefully she removed his hand.

As his eyebrows arched with amusement, she faced him defiantly. "You're engaged. I couldn't bear it if my fiancé announced our engagement, then within the hour was seated somewhere alone with another woman—"

"With your fiancé it would be an impossibility," he answered on a decisive note that startled her. His tone had lost all its usual velvet sensuousness.

Before she could respond, he changed the subject. "I'm sorry you made the trip for nothing." He raised her hand. "No husband, but there must be a boyfriend. Are you in love with someone?"

His face was only inches away. His gray eyes were wide and inquiring. She thought of Wade's asking if she was in love with Thorn. It was impossible. Yet why was she always so aware of him, so disturbed by his presence?

They continued to look at each other, and Sabrina couldn't turn away. His hand rested lightly against her shoulder.

He could stir her so easily. Why was the slightest contact so volatile? That was no basis for love. Yet.... Leaning forward the few inches that separated them, he touched her lips with his, lingered, then took possession.

Warmth uncoiled, spread through her. "No," she whispered. She started to move away, but his arms closed around her and pulled her to him. Feeling the smooth curve of his taut muscles, Sabrina let her hands slide along his arms. As a protest rose inside her, he drew her closer still.

"Thorn!" Amanda's voice came from a distance.

Instantly they jumped apart. He eyed her narrowly, and under his scrutiny she felt the heat commence at her throat and rise to her face. She tried to keep her voice steady and casual. "Your Brazilian nights are filled with an intoxicating moonlight."

His voice changed, deepened, as he asked quietly, "*Are* you in love with somebody at home?"

Closer this time, Amanda called again. "Thorn!"

Uncoiling his long frame from the balustrade, he turned to stride toward the corner of the veranda. "Here I am."

"Darling!" She appeared and wrapped her arms around his neck, then tilted her face to kiss him. Her willowy body swayed against his, and Thorn's arms went around her.

Sabrina looked at the same arms that had just held her, now curved around Amanda's slender waist; the same warm firm lips now pressed against Amanda's, and an ache filled her.

Unable to watch them any longer, she rushed

across the veranda to the first open door she could find. Leaving behind the party, the noise and the people, she moved along the hallway until she reached the tall doors leading to the deserted ballroom. When she pressed a switch, a wall sconce blinked on.

The vast room was quiet, dimly lit by the sconce. Across the gleaming floor, in one corner, stood a piano. She moved toward it, her heels clicking on the polished wood floor. With a scrape she pulled out the bench, sat down and pressed a key. The lone note sounded forlorn, hollow in the empty room. Feeling the smooth ivory beneath her fingertips, she began to play.

Her fingers moved automatically. Music filled the ballroom, drowning out the faint sounds of the party beyond, but her thoughts prevented her from hearing her own music. With unseeing eyes, Sabrina stared into the gloomy darkened ballroom.

Cold logic told her she shouldn't, but Sabrina yearned for Thorn's kiss, for his touch, his quick laugh. He was downstairs, though, holding and kissing his bride to be.

What did she feel for Thorn? A dangerous physical attraction without question, but love was an unreasonable hopeless possibility. Yet the barest lingering brush of his fingers melted every ounce of her resolve. What foolishness it had been to allow him to kiss her. But she couldn't have made him stop. The memory of that kiss would remain as if seared on her soul. It would go with her when she returned home—and along with it, the vision of him holding Amanda in his arms. Her fingers landed on the keys in a discordant crash. She put her head in her arms for a moment, then straightened with determination.

She struck a note. The keys felt good beneath her fingers, and she flexed her hands, commencing the strong chords of "Malagueña." It wouldn't disturb anyone, because the rest of the family was in the opposite wing or outside at the party.

A shaft of light sliced the dimness as the ballroom door opened. Lifting her hands instantly, Sabrina looked up to see Amanda enter and close the door.

"I want to talk to you," she said without preamble. Sabrina waited quietly, sensing a storm to come.

"I was about to decide you'd gone to bed when I heard the music."

"Were you looking for me?" Sabrina asked in surprise.

A few yards from the piano Amanda halted. The same strong sweet scent of perfume surrounded her, overpowering the musty smell of the ballroom. Even though there was no reasonable basis for it, Sabrina sensed Amanda's antagonism every time they were together.

"Oh, yes, I've been searching for you," Amanda answered. "You see, on the veranda I happened to catch sight of you and Thorn before I called to him."

Sabrina looked steadily at Amanda. Even in the soft light the other woman's features were sharp. There was a petulant look to her mouth and two deep creases between her brows. Sabrina took a deep breath. "You know it meant nothing to Thorn."

"Men are fools," Amanda stated. "Since we were

children, Thorn and I have been expected to marry. You look shocked at that. Our customs are different than yours. Brazil is still very 'old world.' Thorn may be susceptible to the attentions of beautiful young women, but I haven't any intention of giving up Thorn or Bellefontaine. I'm destined to rule this plantation and the Catlin empire."

Her eyes narrowed, and she shifted impatiently. "To a working woman who trudges home to an empty apartment all this may look appealing, but you'll never succeed. I'm warning you now to stop trying to interfere. Thorn's father would disinherit him if he didn't marry me—of that I'm certain." She paused and looked coldly at Sabrina. "I'll promise you, to Thorn no woman is worth giving up Bellefontaine!"

Sabrina rose from the piano bench and spoke with dignity. "Dr. Hughes and I came to study sugarcane—that's all. As soon as our assignment is accomplished and he's recovered enough to travel, we'll leave."

"If I were you, I wouldn't wait for all those things. People grow sugarcane in other parts of the world. Go study it elsewhere. As you've already discovered, you're out of your depth in a foreign land...which can be filled with danger."

Sabrina felt her temper rise dangerously. Struggling to remain calm, she said, "Your threats are unnecessary, Amanda. Thorn doesn't have any interest in me."

"Who said anything about threats?" the woman countered sweetly with wide-eyed innocence. "But you're interested in him. You're madly in love with him, aren't you?"

"No! That's none of your—"

"He's my fiancé," Amanda interrupted, "and it's my concern. I know you're in love with him! But let me warn you again—Thorn will be mine! I won't hesitate to draw any line to get what I want. Thorn is older than I am and there have been women in his life, but they meant little to him. I'm twenty-eight, Miss Devon. I've waited a long time for this wedding. You're not going to interfere with it, no matter what you offer Thorn. Becoming his mistress will gain you nothing!"

Sabrina sucked in her breath, shaking with rage. "I think you'd better leave."

"And I think you're impertinent to order me out of a room that will be mine shortly—but I'll go. I've warned you. I suggest you take that warning to heart and leave Brazil!"

Twisting her fingers together, Sabrina watched as Amanda rushed out of the room. Beneath her anger lay a gloomy depression. How could Thorn find happiness married to such a person?

All hope for peace gone, she left the ballroom, colliding with Wade in the hall. He caught her by the arms. "Sabrina, I just passed Amanda and she said you were up here. If she's done anything to hurt you...."

"No, Wade, not at all. Please, I'm all right."

He studied her closely. "I don't believe you. When she's angry, she can be pure hell. I think you need a little more protection than a *figa* provides."

She laughed halfheartedly. "I'm fine, Wade."

But he ignored her. "Come with me," he urged, taking her hand. They descended the stairs and went outside. Instead of turning in the direction of the people and lights of the party, Wade steered her toward the shadows.

"Where are we going?" she asked.

"Just follow me. Thorn would have my hide if he knew about this," he muttered.

Sabrina looked at him, mystified, but said nothing. What were they going to do that would anger Thorn? Her curiosity increased as they skirted the house and started toward the cane fields, moving silently and listening to the sounds of music and people's voices fading behind them. Finally they left the lighted grounds and were swallowed up by the darkness.

"Can we talk now?" she asked.

"For a time," he answered, the slight slur in his voice making Sabrina glance at him sharply. The trace of rum on his breath was more noticeable than earlier in the evening.

"Wade, are you sober?"

"Sabrina, trust me," he replied. She nodded, but his answer stirred waves of caution in her. What was he up to? Why were they tiptoeing away from Bellefontaine late at night with such care that Thorn didn't discover them? She glanced at Wade again. Where were they going?

CHAPTER SEVEN

WHEN THEY REACHED the cane, Sabrina began to wish she hadn't come. Tall stalks rustled as they walked through, a whispering scrape of leaves against leaves that disturbed her. Above the diminishing sounds of the party a steady croaking of frogs could be heard. Eventually they left the cultivated fields for uncleared land, covered in trees and undergrowth.

For a time Wade held her hand, then relinquished it to move quickly ahead. Stumbling along in the darkness behind him, Sabrina was amazed at the distance they were covering. Each moment her tension grew, until finally she caught his sleeve.

"Wade, what on earth are we doing here?"

Her eyes had adjusted to see him easily in the gloom. His teeth flashed in a smile, and Sabrina's patience began to wear thin.

"I've worried you," he stated, "and I had no intention of doing that. I merely wanted to surprise you. Listen, Sabrina."

They stood quietly. Above the sounds of frogs and insects she detected another noise...a deep steady drumbeat. "What's that?" she asked.

"*Macumba*. You'll be interested in this."

Sabrina's curiosity was aroused in spite of her trepidation. "Do they let anybody watch?"

He shook his head. "Not out here, but they'll allow you to because you're with me. Come on and keep quiet. They hold these rituals to pacify evil spirits and please good ones," he continued. "In town the rituals are held in houses called *terreiros* and are led by mediums. Tonight the *mae-de-santo*, or high priestess, will be presiding."

Wade pushed branches out of their way. After what seemed hours later, ahead through the darkness Sabrina caught glimpses of a flickering orange fire. Again she thought of Wade's statement that Thorn would be angered if he knew where they were going. Was there good reason for her not to be with Wade or for both of them not to witness this ritual?

Wade glanced at her. "If the *mae-de-santo* speaks to you, answer, 'Good evening.' How's your Portuguese?"

"Not good, but I can say that much."

He nodded and added in a whisper, "Stay with me, Sabrina."

They hurried on. With each step the drums became louder, until the effect was overpowering. "Those are the *ogas*, the musicians summoning the gods," he murmured.

At last they reached a ring of people standing around a fire. To one side of the crowd a man stood holding a spear. "He's *indio mal*, symbol of evil," Wade informed her as he tossed a handful of dried beans at the man's feet and murmured a greeting in Portuguese.

Sabrina watched him uncertainly, then moved with Wade to stand beside the others around the fire. All joined hands and chanted—all except Sabrina.

At one spot in the circle was an altar decorated with flowers, plates of food and candles. A dark-skinned woman sat in a chair beside it. Dressed in white lace with a red turban circling her head, she kept her eyes closed as she chanted. Wavering flames threw dancing shadows across the broad flat planes of her face. On the ground before her was a ring of cowrie shells. While she chanted, she grasped another handful of shells from the altar and tossed them to the ground.

Three drums thumped in steady tempo. Flushed from the searing heat of the fire, Sabrina listened to the rhythmical unrelenting drums and studied the gathering of people. Some were elegantly dressed in expensive clothing; some in plain, even tattered garments. Several nationalities were represented, and Sabrina glanced at Wade, wondering what brought him here.

Perspiration dotted his brow, and his long-lashed eyes were almost closed while he continued to chant with the others. Sabrina found herself both awed and horrified by the magic of the drums, the crackling flames and the sweet narcotic scents that mingled with the acrid odor of burning wood. But she couldn't bring herself to join in.

Suddenly the *mae-de-santo*'s chanting rose to a harsh cry. Sweeping in an arc, her hand scooped up the cowrie shells from the ground. Then one long finger pointed directly at Sabrina. With a final loud flourish each drum was silenced.

After such an intense din the quiet was unnerving. The crackling of burning wood was the only sound, and Sabrina experienced a stirring of fear. *Why is she pointing at me,* she wondered. She felt Wade's fingers close around hers and pull gently. Reluctance filled her, and she resisted slightly. But he whispered, "Come on. Trust me."

Because she did instinctively, she stepped forward with him, halting in front of the *mae-de-santo*, who greeted them. Sabrina nodded and whispered, *"Boas-noites, minha senhora."*

Rising to her feet, the high priestess took Sabrina's hand. The woman's skin felt hot and dry. Her large black eyes studied Sabrina intently. Suddenly she tossed the handful of shells at Sabrina's feet, then knelt to peer at them for long moments. Finally she rose and looked deeply into Sabrina's eyes. Exhaling in a soft hiss, she declared clearly in English, "You are in great danger!"

Sabrina shivered at the somber warning. She had received warnings from Thorn and Amanda, warnings made in anger and jealousy, but this one seemed to carry an icy threat of validity.

Reaching into the folds of her robe, the *mae-de-santo* produced a necklace of tiny white shells, which she twisted in the air while she uttered an unintelligible incantation. Leaning forward, she dropped the necklace over Sabrina's head.

"Muito bem obrigada." Sabrina murmured a thank-you and felt Wade grasp her hand. People

shifted to make room for them again in the circle. Drumbeats commenced a moment before a dancer leaped forward.

Dressed in white lace, the young woman began to whirl in a circle around the fire. The flames gave a coppery sheen to her skin, while her black hair streamed out behind her.

Watching her, Sabrina touched the smooth shells that lay against her skin. "Why did she give me this, Wade?"

"To ward off evil spirits."

"How did she know to speak to me in English?"

"She always seems to know everything that goes on in our part of the world. She's probably known about you since the first moment you arrived at Bellefontaine."

Sabrina leaned close to whisper, "But does she always warn people like that?"

Turning his head, he gazed at her solemnly, and she guessed his answer before he replied, "No. I've only seen her do that occasionally." He frowned. "Sabrina, we'll go to Manaus in the morning. Promise me that as soon as possible after that you'll return to Washington."

Startled at his earnestness, Sabrina turned toward the fire. More frightening than the priestess's warning was Wade's solemn acceptance of it. Sensing her disquiet, Wade dropped his arm around her shoulders, and together they watched the dancer. Perspiration gleamed on her arms and forehead. As she spun around, her white lace skirt swirled high, revealing long brown legs.

Drumbeats seemed to be thumping out their own warning...danger, danger. Sabrina began to believe the *mae-de-santo*. She was living in a world she did not comprehend. Brazil was wild, savage and exotic. It attracted and repelled her at the same time.

Sabrina's gaze followed the dancer, but her thoughts went beyond the warning. She was determined to complete her assignment, because now, at long last, with Roddy incapacitated and settled at Bellefontaine, surely Thorn would allow her to work. Would there be any danger in remaining at Bellefontaine, or were the warnings insubstantial?

Someone removed the banana leaves from the top of a clay jar, passing it to allow each person to take a sip from it. Before it reached her, Sabrina stiffened. Deafening drumbeats and the chanting drowned out any other sounds. Yet Sabrina felt compelled to turn and look behind her.

She looked into stormy gray eyes. Only yards away stood Thorn, holding the reins to a black stallion. Stepping forward, he swept her onto the horse and mounted, turning the animal away from the ring of people.

It was done so quickly that she gazed at him in helpless surprise. "Wade and I...."

He spoke through clenched teeth as the stallion galloped away. "Wade had no business taking you to such a thing! He knows that." Brushing against her throat, his warm fingers locked around the shell necklace, and he yanked sharply.

Sabrina gasped as the white shells broke and tumbled over her knees to fall to the ground. She twisted

"Thorn," she murmured, struggling to voice a protest.

His cheek was warm against her temple as he whispered, "You're very beautiful, Sabrina."

"You must stop."

"Why should I? It's delightful, and you like for me to kiss you...here...and here. You do like it, don't you?" he murmured distractedly.

"Thorn, please..." she begged. But at the continued onslaught of lips against flesh, her words faded. She turned her head slightly to trail her lips down the strong column of his throat.

The cool night, the lush Brazilian countryside, the dying drumbeats behind them—all combined to color reality with a tinge of fantasy. Thorn's soft caresses were sorcery, turning each moment into magic. She felt as if she had lost all power to prevent his wandering hands from exploring—to fight her own response. She returned his kisses with a fierce ardor.

This was all wrong—yet soon they would part and she would never touch him again. She closed her eyes, and the vision of Amanda stepping into his arms flashed into her mind. Her eyes flew open. She straightened and pulled slightly away from him. "This isn't right. You're engaged, Thorn."

"That can't prevent us from enjoying this moment—I won't let it. I've waited too long...."

She felt as if he had closed his strong hands around her heart and was squeezing inexorably. This meant nothing to him. It was momentary amusement. "No!" burst from her forcefully. "You're engaged."

"No. I was listening to the drums and forgot everything else. Why were you out riding?" she asked curiously.

"I often ride over part of the grounds at this hour. It's a beautifully cool night—" his voice was almost seductive "—and I didn't feel like sleeping or lying awake in an empty bed."

The provocative words hung in the air. Sabrina wanted to say something, to speak up in matter-of-fact tones about an impersonal subject, but she couldn't collect her thoughts. Relaxing his grip on her waist, Thorn moved his hand up, following the length of her arm, tracing a line along her forearm with his index finger.

Her heart pounded as fiercely as the drums in the distance. She took a deep breath. Yet she couldn't bring herself to move his hand away. Drifting, his fingers settled against her collarbone in a lingering caress.

Sabrina felt on fire. If she had been attuned to him before, that awareness suddenly intensified a thousandfold. Reaching up, Sabrina caught his hand to remove it but instead found herself crushing his strong brown fingers in a convulsive grip. His lips touched her shoulder through the T-shirt, tracing its curve. With a deft movement he unclasped her barrette, and as her hair tumbled across her shoulders, Thorn caught it up and kissed her nape.

Laying her head back against him, Sabrina closed her eyes blissfully. She knew she was being a fool, that they must stop, but her intentions dissipated like smoke in a high wind.

in the saddle to look up at him. "Why did you do that? What harm is there in any of this? Wade said *macumba* is part of Brazil, part of your culture. You've said so yourself."

"That's right," Thorn answered, "but I don't believe in it. Nor do I like it. In spite of Brazil's progress, superstition is one of the things that holds us back. Wade has obviously given you a *figa*, as well. I should rip that off you, too! I don't care to see my family involved in practicing *macumba*."

Sabrina drew a sharp breath. "I'm not a member of your family. Why should you care if I watch?"

There was a note of cynical amusement in his voice. "Do you know anything of their rites?"

"No," she answered.

"Maybe I should have left you there. If you'd been in Sao Paulo at a *macumba* ceremony, it might have been interesting for you. But out here the ritual is primitive, sensual and earthy. Perhaps that was what you were seeking," he added in a sardonic drawl.

"I didn't know what to expect," she replied defensively. "I've found many things in your country that I don't understand."

"But you haven't found what you came for," he stated cynically, then fell silent.

"No," Sabrina admitted. He remained quiet, and she wondered if he was waiting for her to say more. He held her tightly against him, his arm clamped around her waist. She glanced up at his chin, so close, almost touching her temple.

Acutely aware of this man, she locked her fingers in the coarse hair of the horse's mane. She could feel

Thorn's body warmth, his steady heartbeat. Occasionally his chin brushed her forehead. Her knee was hooked around the pommel.

Soon her foot began to grow numb, and she shifted to ride astride, her legs pressing against his in the confining saddle. The hard length of his body was molded against hers, and it struck her then that she might find it difficult to forget Thorn Catlin. When she returned home, how long would it be before the remembrance of his kiss, his touch, diminished? When would she not be haunted by the image of gray eyes shuttered by thick black lashes? Shaking her head slightly as if to rid herself of such thoughts, Sabrina dislodged the hibiscus behind her ear.

She caught it quickly, but Thorn reached around to take it from her fingers, carefully tucking it in the neck of her thin T-shirt. At the brush of his fingers she caught her breath, then relaxed when he moved his hand away.

Closing her eyes, she listened to the fading drums. The stallion's pace had long since slowed to a clip-clop. The night air had cooled. A breeze blew softly against her bare arms.... Suddenly she was aware that she had let her head drop against Thorn's shoulder. Her eyes flew open as she straightened.

"Are you sleepy?" Thorn murmured.

His voice was husky, all traces of anger gone. His breath came out warmly against the curve of her neck and shoulder...a whisper of movement, but like a caress to her nerves, which were raw with awareness of him.

He sounded angry, almost wounded, as he retorted, "Yet you were willing to kiss a complete stranger!"

"Perhaps there was less danger in that!"

He sighed softly. "Of all times for you to develop a degree of caution!" Taking a deep breath then, he seemed to be trying to regain his self-control.

They rode in silence until they came into view of the house. Suddenly Thorn groaned, "It's no use, Sabrina. I can't resist you." He shifted her hair. Then she felt his lips, nipping and caressing.

The battle commenced again. A longing to yield to him stirred her. Yet cold logic made her want to withdraw. A flurry of kisses, his lips tracing small patterns on her shoulders, were like tiny rivulets of water rushing together, building to a torrent neither could resist.

Under the portico he reined in and dropped nimbly to the ground, then reached up for her, his hands circling her waist as he held her aloft. Slowly he lowered her against his body, and she slid the length of him until her feet touched the ground. With a will of their own, her hands roamed over his broad shoulders, coming to rest against the pulse beating madly in his throat.

She gazed into the depths of his gray eyes. Heavy-lidded, filled with an intentness she found unsettling, they clearly revealed his answering passion.

"Let me go, Thorn," she whispered in desperation.

His arms tightened, and he leaned forward. His

lips touched hers, and Sabrina pushed against his chest. "Thorn..." she began, but his mouth silenced her protest.

"Shh," he whispered before his lips came down on hers a second time. Like that first kiss in Sao Paulo, this one drove all rational thought away. It was impossible to break free. She had not imagined the magic of that first kiss, because she was experiencing the same tantalizing feelings now. Her arms locked around his neck, and Sabrina stood on tiptoe and responded eagerly.

Curving over her, Thorn smothered her in his embrace. His hand pressed into the small of her back, molding her softness to him. A wild surge of joy and longing swept through her. Why could he evoke this response in her? He raised his head, and for one brief moment she was certain he looked as shaken as she felt.

"Sabrina," he whispered huskily, desperately, then leaned forward to kiss her again.

And in that instant, when he'd looked into her eyes, Sabrina knew the *mae-de-santo*'s warning had been accurate. She was in danger—in danger of falling in love with Thorn Catlin. But even while she reasoned against it, she clung to him and arched her body into his.

His kisses burned, growing more torrid. One hand moved to caress her back between her shoulders. "Thorn, we should stop," she whispered.

His voice was low as he murmured, "Sabrina, I don't want to stop yet, and neither do you...." He kissed her throat. "Tell me you don't like this—" his lips trailed across her ear "—or this. Say it," he demanded. "Say you don't want me."

She trembled with each kiss, each caress, but insisted, "You'll marry Amanda, Thorn, and she loves you."

Gazing down at her, he shook his head. "She loves Bellefontaine, not me. That I understand. But I'm beginning to wonder if I understand myself," he added softly.

It was impossible to remain in his arms and conduct a coherent conversation. Then why did it seem so natural, so right, to be here? This rugged arrogant *engaged* man was a stranger. Yet in his embrace she felt complete, whole.

He leaned forward to kiss her again, and through his thin shirt, the fabric of her skimpy T-shirt, she felt his heart pound. As if he'd guessed her thoughts, he shifted, his breath warm against her ear, his voice intimate as he murmured, "Our hearts beat together.... You feel it as I do. You were meant to be mine."

His words started a trembling deep inside, and she had to be closer to that heart. Her eager fingers unfastened the buttons of his shirt, tugging it out of the waistband of his pants, caressing his broad chest with splayed hands. Thorn gasped, whispering huskily, "Sabrina, I've never known a woman until now who made me feel incomplete without her...."

Agony, exquisite burning, swept through her. She pushed against his chest. "That's impossible," she protested. "You know it's impossible."

He kissed her eyelids, the corner of her mouth. "Don't draw away."

Her determination to leave was crumbling. His expression was as overpowering as his kisses. If only he didn't look so...disconcerted, yet so serious, it would be easier. Breathing deeply, she tried to answer in a normal tone. "I can't stay another second."

"Yes, you can," he persuaded, his mouth trailing hotly across her shoulder.

Desperately she answered, "No, Thorn...."

"Why not? You feel this. Your heart is racing. You tremble to my touch."

Whatever she felt, whatever he felt, nothing but heartbreak could come of it. An instinct for self-preservation made her search desperately for an answer to distract him. "Because I'm in love with someone else!" she blurted out.

Instantly she regretted the words.

All traces of tenderness disappeared from his face, to be replaced by a guarded look. He pulled her close, but this time when he spoke, there was a cynical note in his voice.

"Do you know anything about love—about fidelity? You've given me your kisses freely. I've seen you with Wade's arm around you. You seem to live for the moment. Why not enjoy this one, then?" With a cry of despair she twisted out of his arms. Dashing up the steps to the house, she fled to her room.

As soon as she'd closed the door, she heard hoofbeats. Unable to stop herself, she rushed to the gallery, stepping out into the cool darkness. Riding away astride his black horse was Thorn. "Oh, Thorn..." she whispered despairingly.

Leaning against a warm wooden column, Sabrina placed her head in her hands. It couldn't be love, she reasoned, because they had nothing in common, no shared interests. They hardly knew each other. He was engaged, ready to marry soon. Sabrina Devon couldn't mean anything to Thorn Catlin.

Still, she couldn't forget that troubled solemn look on his face after they'd kissed. If she'd kept quiet, what might he have said? Now it was too late.

Returning inside, she undressed slowly, feeling confusion, misgivings and longing, while common sense argued she'd done the right thing. She had to forget Thorn.

She wouldn't admit to being in love with him, because it wasn't reasonable. What she felt had to be mere physical attraction. She touched the *figa*, still hanging around her neck.

Regarding it solemnly, she murmured, "It doesn't work, Wade."

By the time she'd climbed into bed, the *mae-de-santo*'s warning seemed dim and unreal, overpowered by the all too clear remembrance of her passionate encounter with Thorn.

Filling her thoughts was also the recollection of the husky note in his voice as he demanded, "Tell me you don't like this...." She groaned aloud and tossed around in bed, flinging the sheets from her body, which burned with longing for a man she couldn't have.

She slipped from between the sheets and moved to

sit out on the gallery again, gazing across the dark mysterious land of Bellefontaine. Somewhere out there was Thorn, riding his black stallion, alone.... Was he thinking of her, she wondered. A nightingale's melodic cry floated on the night air as the cool breezes blew across the balcony.

Finally she got up and returned to bed, forcing her thoughts to Andy and Jeff, to home and normalcy. Thinking about the problems that awaited her there, Sabrina fell into a troubled sleep.

SABRINA OPENED HER EYES to a room dusky with the gray light of dawn. In the distance she heard a rooster crow. She stirred, gazing around the bedroom, remembering the night, Thorn's kisses, the wild *macumba* dance, the warning.... In the security of her lovely bedroom at Bellefontaine she shivered, then pushed aside her fears. Another memory crowded in: she was supposed to meet Wade!

Dressing hastily in denim pants and a pale blue shirt, she tied her hair behind her head with a blue scarf, yanked on hand-tooled Western boots and snatched up her purse, camera, notebook and a battered khaki hat.

When she stopped by Roddy's room, he was seated on a chaise with a breakfast tray across his lap. "You're up early," he greeted her, taking in her appearance. "You look ready for fieldwork, Sabrina."

"Wade is taking me to the research station near Manaus."

"Well, dammit! How I'd like to go! Of all the times for me to be incapacitated. Amazonia is fascinating to me. I've been reading up on it, since I've had so little to do lately. I thought that was Thorn's field. I didn't know the younger brother was interested in research."

Sabrina sat down facing him. "Wade's not really. He just promised to do this for me. I'm sorry you can't come along. I'll take good notes and lots of pictures," she assured him, reaching out to pat his hand.

Roddy sighed with resignation. "That's just typical of everything about this assignment."

"Roddy, as soon as I see Thorn, I'll ask him if I can start our study tomorrow. It's high time! We've been sitting around doing nothing for long enough. I can take measurements and notes on conditions in the field, then give them to you to study and write up. How will that be?"

"Fine with me, if you think he'll agree to let you."

"I don't see how he can object, now that we're here for a prolonged stay." She straightened her shoulders. "If he doesn't agree, maybe Laurel or Wade will show me around."

Roddy grinned and leaned back against the pillows. "That's the spirit! Have a good day at Manaus. I wish I could go."

"I'll come straight here when I get back and tell you all about it," she promised, and left to drink a quick cup of coffee, then meet Wade at the hangar.

A plane was waiting, and Sabrina noticed another inside the hangar. There was also a helicopter on the landing pad nearby, and she wondered if Thorn was the only one of the Catlins who could pilot a plane. After introductions to Joao Fabrizio, the hired pilot, all three boarded the plane.

Monday's sun was high overhead when the rain forest's thick green canopy came into view. Edging closer to the window to look down, Sabrina was filled with excitement. Below, the foliage shifted from yellows to light and dark greens to blooming purple jacarandas. As the plane came in lower, a flock of brightly colored parrots scattered.

Manaus stretched along an Amazon tributary, the Rio Negro. When they began to lose altitude approaching the town, Wade pointed out the raft houses—small floating homes of river tradesmen. Glistening tin roofs were interspersed with houses topped by yellow green thatching, crammed together at odd angles.

"This is a colonial city that was built by rich rubber barons during the industrial boom before the turn of the century. Some of the original plantations would have made Bellefontaine pale in comparison."

"I find that a little difficult to believe, Wade," Sabrina remarked dryly.

"The merchants sent their laundry to Europe, which should give you an indication of the type of life they led. Manaus's custom house and lighthouse were built in England, then dismantled block by block, moved here and reconstructed. But in a relatively short time the boom was over. Rubber-tree seeds were smuggled out, spreading the industry to other parts of the world."

Since she showed such interest in the history of the

area, Wade decided to take her for a short ride around town. He hired a taxi to show her the Teatro Amazonas, an opera house facing into a dazzling plaza of black-and-white mosaics. They drove past the market, where natives in dugout canoes delivered tropical fish, fruit and vegetables from surrounding plantations. Explaining that during the rainy season the river would rise between forty to sixty feet, Wade pointed out the floating docks designed to accommodate the high water levels.

When they passed some women street vendors, Wade leaned forward to instruct the driver to stop while he stepped out to make a purchase. Returning, he handed a yellow gourd to Sabrina.

"What's this?" she asked as she noticed it was filled with liquid.

"Sip it."

She raised the gourd to drink the hot delicious soup. "It's *tacacá*," Wade explained, "a local concoction I thought you would enjoy. Let's stop and eat early so you can sample the food here. It's quite different from that of São Paulo."

When she agreed, he directed the driver to the Estrada de Flores restaurant. As soon as they were seated, Wade ordered. She ate *pato no tucupi*, duck in yellow soup that Wade described as a favorite Manaus dish. Sabrina enjoyed its spicy exotic flavor. Cutting into the duck's delicate pink meat, Wade urged her to try a bite. When she exclaimed about how delicious it was, Wade's eyes twinkled as he informed her she'd just eaten octopus.

Laughing, Sabrina cautiously ate more of the delicacy. Refusing dessert, she suggested they be on their way, since she only had a few hours to study the soil samples at the research station. Wade complied, and they drove to the dock to take the Catlin launch to the station.

Once on board, Sabrina gazed around with interest as they chugged steadily through the dark water. Flocks of parrots squawked and flapped amid the treetops along the banks, while monkeys chattered noisily. She felt marvelously free, as if she were leaving all her worries behind. While he steered, Wade spoke above the motor's drone. "I wish we'd had time to travel to where the Rio Negro and the Amazon merge. It's called the Wedding of the Waters. Each river flows side by side, one black and one brown, before they mingle all those miles downstream.

"Also, if we had gone in the opposite direction toward Belém and the river's mouth, we would have reached Santarém. Like Villa Georgiana and Americana, it was settled by the Confederates and still has many American descendants. It's enjoying a gold boom at present."

Within a short time the sunlight, beating down on them with increasing warmth, became a cloying sticky heat as they entered a tributary enveloped by green leaves, closing off any view of the sky. As they passed protruding tangled roots serving as a perch for scarlet ibis and white spoonbills, Sabrina gasped with delight. Their brilliant red-and-white plumage was dazzling against the dark green foliage.

"Look at all the vines, Wade," Sabrina marveled,

pointing at the thick vegetation along the bank. "They're lianas, aren't they?"

"Yes," he replied. "They can conceivably grow to seven hundred feet in length. They're not parasites, though, because they get nourishment from the soil. As you can see, once touched by sunlight they bear flowers and leaves—but you probably know something about this, in your line of work."

Although Sabrina did have a knowledge of botany, this part of Brazil was a whole new experience for her—a wonderworld of chattering monkeys, brightly colored parakeets, large multicolored butterflies, and everywhere the lush growth of plants.

Looking incongruous in the wild, a floating dock came into view. Wade cut the launch's motor, then drifted up to bump gently against the dock. Stepping out, he secured the boat and reached down to help Sabrina.

A narrow path overrun by vines led away from the landing. Wade moved ahead to walk up the sloping bank. "No one works here right now," he said. "Thorn's searching for a scientist, for the right person, but he hasn't the one he wants. I can't imagine why anybody would want to live in this godforsaken spot."

"But it's beautiful here, Wade."

He grinned over his shoulder at her. "Sabrina, I suspect you're happy wherever you are, whether it's Brazil, Tennessee or Washington."

She laughed ruefully. "You may be right." Stepping over vines as big as Wade's arm, she followed behind him until they reached a small building. Made of flattened bamboo and a thatched roof of acuri palm leaves, it was built on posts high above the ground. The roof cast long shadows over the wide porch.

When Wade opened the door, the odor of chemicals, stale tobacco and dank traces of mildew assailed her, but within minutes they improved conditions by opening several windows. Wade turned on two ceiling fans, which stirred up the steamy air and gradually brought some welcome freshness.

Sabrina looked at Wade with interest. "How do you get electricity?"

"There's a generator."

Sabrina strolled around the room and noted the cabinets filled with meticulously labeled notebooks, the small boxes of plants in long metal trays, the numbered and tagged cuts of timber. Hanging baskets of blooming plants lined the porch, but those inside were withered from lack of fresh air and water. She filled a watering can, optimistic about trying to revive them.

As she did so, she heard a pop behind her. Wade yanked free an electric cord, picked up a small radio and tucked it under his arm. Seeing her questioning glance, he casually explained, "I'm taking the radio into Manaus to get it repaired," and went out to place it on the bottom step of the porch.

Sabrina gazed curiously at the trailing frayed cord. Now it *would* have to be repaired, because he'd yanked the plug off—but why? She guessed the radio was their one contact with civilization, and now he'd severed it.

Frowning, she set down the watering can as he came back into the cabin, pausing in the doorway to gaze at her.

Seeing the look on his face, she felt a cold knot of fear. "Why did you do that, Wade?"

He reached out to take her hand in his. "This is goodbye, Sabrina. I'm leaving you here."

CHAPTER EIGHT

SHE LOOKED AT HIM and frowned. "What are you talking about?"

"I'm going back to Manaus, then to Rio, to pick up Estralita. We're eloping," he answered quietly.

"When Thorn returns to Bellefontaine at noon, he'll get the message I left to come and collect you. You'll only be stranded here a short time. Thorn will arrive on the wing."

Unable to accept what he was saying, she exclaimed, "You can't do such a thing! That's impossible!"

He shook his head. "No. I've made the arrangements carefully. By tonight Estralita and I will be on our honeymoon, where Thorn can't locate us. I'm sorry to include you in my plans, but you gave me an excuse to take the plane and get a head start on Thorn."

"Surely you're not leaving me isolated in this jungle! At least let me ride back to Manaus with you."

"No. From there you can get a commercial flight to São Paulo. If you're stuck here, Thorn has to come—which gives me time. He can't send a servant for you. Until he gets here, he won't know that I'm not with you. That's all the time I need."

"Who knows about this at Bellefontaine?"

He replied patiently. "I left word with Francisco, our chauffeur, to tell Thorn at noon today that we're stranded here because of trouble with the boat's motor. Until a few minutes ago it would have been possible to get messages relayed to Bellefontaine via Manaus by radio. Thorn will accept the news without question. None of the servants can get here without his guidance, so he'll come. I must have that time."

"You're as bad as Laurel—running away!" she snapped.

"I may have prompted her to do so. I told Laurel my plans."

"Won't she inform Thorn?"

He shook his head. "There's no danger. Today she's in Sao Paulo with an aunt for a clothes fitting."

Sabrina was rigid with shock. For an instant anger surged through her that Wade would use her so callously. But she also couldn't help feeling a bit sorry for him. "Wade, have you talked with your father about Estralita? Did you ask if you could bring her to Bellefontaine to meet everyone?"

"No, that would be useless. I won't run the risk, because it might bring on an attack. Then how would I feel? Papa is adamant. He won't give up his old traditions. I know he won't yield an inch. He'll never accept a woman from outside our closed community."

"But that's foolish. What if he has an attack when he learns you've run off and married a girl he's never met?"

"I know my brother. Thorn will break the news to papa gently."

"Please reconsider, Wade," Sabrina pleaded.

His jaw jutted out stubbornly, and Sabrina felt a flash of impatience as he replied, "No."

"Wade, give your father this much opportunity. Everyone, including you, says he has changed. He may have mellowed sufficiently to welcome Estralita. If she's your future wife, think how much better your married life will begin with the family's blessing."

Jamming his hands into his pockets, he paced the narrow aisle between two long rows of cabinets. "No! Dammit, Sabrina, I know papa and Thorn. You don't." He faced her. "It's their happiness against mine."

"Not necessarily."

"Within a month Amanda will be mistress of Bellefontaine. She'll never welcome Estralita, and Thorn will be furious that I've gone against his wishes. He'll see to it that I never have another chance to assert my independence."

Sabrina sighed. "You're a grown man. How much can he do to stop you from marrying whoever you want?"

His dark eyes flashed, and he spoke bitterly. "Thorn has enough power and wealth that he can make my life pure hell if I don't do as he wants."

She grasped his hand urgently. "Wade, this could cause a severe rift in a family that has held itself together—in spite of your differences—through generations, through a war, through migrating thousands of miles to establish a new home. If there is any way to avoid it, don't divide your family now. Call your father to discuss this. Anyway, you're not thinking clearly, Wade. If Thorn can do so much to destroy your happiness now, he'll be able to do as much after you get married."

He glared at her. "No. It'll be done and over with. He'll have to accept it then."

"Is this the way Estralita wants it?" she asked quietly. When his jaw firmed, Sabrina guessed she had struck a sensitive chord.

"Perhaps not, but she has no choice, either." He moved toward the door.

"Wade, you can't leave me here!"

"It won't be dangerous. The natives are friendly, although I don't think you'll see any. Just don't leave the lab. That would be the only danger. If you go six yards in any direction, you could be hopelessly lost. Thorn acts as if he were born here. He treks upriver quite often, but I wouldn't set a toe out of this clearing except to go as far as the landing. Lock the door and stay inside."

"I can't believe you're doing this!" she gasped.

Suddenly Wade's anger vanished, and his eyes clouded. He patted her shoulder. "I'm sorry. In case he doubts your word, I've written to Thorn, explaining you had nothing to do with this. The letter should reach him in a day or two."

"A day or two!" she exclaimed. "Can you imagine his anger when I explain what you've done?" Full realization dawned on Sabrina. "He'll blame me for everything, Wade. He'll think I helped you plan this."

Wade shrugged. "What difference does it make, Sabrina?"

She gripped his hand in hers. "It makes a difference to me!"

He looked down at her fingers, wrapped tightly around his. Gazing at her with narrowed eyes, he spoke gently. "Sabrina, don't care too much about Thorn. Go back to Washington and forget him. Thorn is arrogant and cold. I don't know why his charm has this devastating effect on women, but his feelings never go deep. Sometimes I think Thorn doesn't trust anybody except himself. I suspect he was deeply hurt when his mother left. He's my half brother, you know."

"I know. Laurel told me."

He tilted her chin. "It's good you're leaving before you get hurt. Thorn's never been in love in his life. Oh, there have been plenty of women, but he's never really cared for any of them. He'll never give up Bellefontaine, Sabrina. He couldn't marry anyone else even if he wanted to. Papa and Mr. Pickering promised each other years ago that their children would marry. Thorn doesn't love Amanda. He's high-handed and aloof—and that's why he doesn't understand my love for Estralita. All he loves is that plantation."

"It's not that bad, Wade," she answered with forced lightness. "I just don't want him to feel I've caused this."

"Sabrina, I swear I've never done anything I've hated more, but you can't come with me. For the past few months Thorn's kept me under his thumb. This was the only way—to take the plane and get away. But I'm sorry it involved you."

Desperately she persisted. "You're making a mistake. Please don't do this."

"I'm sorry. You'll be perfectly all right. I know Thorn will be here by sundown."

She drew in a quick breath. "You don't know! He could miss the message, or he could have gone somewhere today and not returned. I can't stay here alone tonight!" But she saw the resolve in his dark eyes.

"There isn't any way you can get into that boat if I don't want you to, and there's nothing to be gained by trying. I promise I'll call Bellefontaine this afternoon. If Thorn hasn't left to come and collect you, I'll send someone right away."

Wade backed away a few steps. "There's a supply of tins in the cabinet, a cot, books and experimental equipment. Also, you won't need it, but there's a weapon in one of the cabinet drawers." He put his hand on her shoulder. "Goodbye. I'll always remember you, and I hope you find as much happiness as I expect to find with Estralita." Leaning forward, he kissed her on the forehead.

It was useless to argue any further. Clenching her fists, Sabrina followed Wade to the door. He crossed the clearing, turned, waved, then disappeared toward the river. Sabrina closed the door and slipped the bolt into place. Isolated, thoroughly frightened, she began to search for the weapon.

In a lower cabinet she located a Colt automatic. Picking it up, Sabrina glanced across the room at a small mirror on the wall. Her face was pale, her eyes large, blue and frightened.

Suddenly she laughed. "You silly goose!" she said

aloud. If she had to spend hours in a jungle lab, she would make the most of them instead of quaking at every strange noise. Placing the automatic on a counter, she got out a microscope to study some of the dirt samples.

During the afternoon, when the sun was shining in the clearing and all was quiet and peaceful, Sabrina enjoyed herself. But as daylight faded, the noises began—birds, monkeys, insects, then high wild screeches and screams that jarred her raw nerves.

Dusk began to settle. Sabrina shrugged away her rising fears and stretched out on the cot with a book. She wouldn't entertain the thought that Thorn or someone from Bellefontaine wouldn't come.

Finally she heard a faint high drone in the distance. As it grew louder, she got up and stepped onto the porch. Her surroundings were still visible in the dying light. The motor's roar dwindled to silence. Someone was coming.

Her heart began to hammer. What if it was a complete stranger? If it was Thorn, would he be preferable to a complete stranger?

Within seconds Thorn's tall figure emerged, striding purposefully up the path from the river. She couldn't guess his feelings, but the moment she saw his eyes, darkened to the color of slate, she didn't have to guess.

He was dressed for the jungle, in khaki trousers, shirt and a wide-brimmed bush hat. Dark boots gleamed dully underneath his trouser cuffs. Sheathed and strapped around his narrow hips was a knife. Even in the ordinary clothing he looked ruggedly handsome. While she dreaded facing him, Sabrina felt her heart pound with that quick surge of excitement he always evoked.

Approaching the cabin in silence, he halted at the foot of the steps and looked up at her. "Wade isn't here, is he?"

She regarded him with surprise. "How did you guess?"

When he mounted the steps, his fury showed in the stiff set of his shoulders, the lines around his mouth. "Still meddling in my family's lives, aren't you?" he demanded roughly. "Did you and Wade plan this together, or was it your suggestion?"

In a ridiculous state of panic, Sabrina locked her fingers together and answered, "Until we got here, I didn't know anything about it."

"He's run off with Estralita, hasn't he?" he asked. When she nodded, he continued, "I've had men looking for him all afternoon." Glancing over her head, he added, "We'd better start back. Let me check things over before we go."

He brushed past her, and Sabrina followed. Seeing him pause to look at the slides and books she had been studying, Sabrina hurried toward them. "I'll put things away. I didn't know when you would come." She knelt to replace the microscope inside a cabinet, then stood up to collect the books.

Thorn picked up the automatic and raised his eyebrows. "Wade told me where I would find it," she explained quickly.

"If I hadn't returned to Bellefontaine from town

this morning, do you realize you could have spent several days here?" he remarked dryly.

She straightened and faced him squarely. "You still think I helped Wade plan this, don't you?"

He shrugged. "It doesn't matter now. Are you ready?"

"Quite," she replied, and stepped outside. But her cool manner began to wane as she approached the swirling waters and realized that within moments they would be on the river, in darkness. When she glanced at Thorn's angry scowl, Sabrina bit back her words of concern. She had no intention of allowing him to see how worried she was.

Reaching the boat, she steadied it as she stepped inside. "Want me to help push off?"

"No," he answered as he shoved the launch away from the dock and leaped agilely in. They were caught by the current and began to drift from the bank. As the boat glided silently through the water, Sabrina looked at the darkening jungle and recalled clearly the *mae-de-santo*'s words: "You are in great danger!" She shivered and clutched the side of the boat.

The motor kicked to life, and Thorn reached into his pocket to hand her a vial. "Here, this is insect repellent. You only need a few drops. It's not the rainy season, so mosquitoes shouldn't eat us up, but there are other insects to combat."

She silently dabbed on repellent and glanced at him. "Is this safe—to be on the river after dark?"

"I try to avoid doing so if at all possible," was his calm reply. Reaching into an upper pocket, he withdrew a pack of cigarettes. "You don't smoke, do you?"

When she shook her head, he selected a cigarette, lit it, then put the lighter back in his pocket. His answer had been disturbing—disturbing to have this strong powerful man admit they were in danger.

Her uneasiness was like an aching tooth she couldn't ignore. She gazed at the black water rushing alongside the boat and asked, "Is there any danger of getting lost?"

He nodded. "That...and other things. Smugglers for one—"

"Smugglers!" She glanced nervously around. "What would anyone smuggle out here? There's nothing except wild animals."

His voice was more chilling than the prospect of losing herself in that forbidding jungle. "Oh, no, Miss Devon. There's gold."

Sabrina grew quiet at his tone. The night seemed to take on an ominous quality. She felt as if eyes were peering out from the darkness all along the bank. What sort of frightening creatures swam below in the opaque water? "What's dangerous in the river itself?" she asked, not sure she wanted to know the answer.

"Could it be that a little of your self-reliant fearlessness is beginning to wane, Miss Devon? Perhaps you might be regretting this latest escapade."

Sabrina caught the mocking derision in his tone and, wishing she'd never asked, compressed her lips. All fear fled, replaced by anger.

"To answer your question," he continued blithely,

"there are considerable dangers. There are the *bagres*, catfish that can weigh up to three or four hundred pounds. Not deliberately vicious, one might happen to make a meal of your arm or leg."

In a can in the bottom of the boat Thorn stubbed out his cigarette before he continued. "There are piranhas, stingrays, various poisonous snakes, caimans—you'd call them alligators—"

"You needn't go on."

"Oh, but I haven't even begun. There are ten thousand tributaries in the Amazon. In many places the river doubles back on itself, so we could become hopelessly lost in a maze. You can't trust currents because some tributaries cause water to flow in the opposite direction from what you would expect. There are whirlpools—"

"Then why are we out here!" she snapped.

Angrily he replied, "Because I don't have an endless amount of time to trek around and rescue you from disaster!"

She sighed and lapsed into silence. She heard a soft hiss from far off in the equally silent night and turned to see an oil lantern on shore, which cast a circle of blue white light across the river.

Finally they reached Manaus. Sabrina jumped to the dock before Thorn could help her. After stopping to get sandwiches and a thermos of coffee to take with them, they went to the airstrip, where a Catlin plane waited.

The sky was heavy, overcast. Thorn helped Sabrina inside, then sat down behind the controls. Settling into the seat, she willed her mind to become a blank.

She refused to worry about Thorn's anger or wonder if Wade would ever bring his bride home to Bellefontaine. The Catlins had disrupted her life in more ways than she wanted to consider.

The plane circled over Manaus. The lights were bright below. Then darkness enveloped them as they gained altitude.

Depression sank over Sabrina, and she resolved to apply for any position with the county extension office at home—anything to escape Brazil and the volatile Catlins! Thoughts of her relatively nice, ordinary family were a comfort, until she glanced again at Thorn.

She could still see the hostility mirrored in his face. His jaw was clamped shut, and his eyes had a shuttered look. 'I couldn't have stopped Wade,'' she stated quietly. His gray eyes rested on her without wavering. He made no comment, merely turned away.

Sabrina clenched her fists in her lap and gazed out the window. Wisps of gray cloud trailed past. Leaning her head back against the seat, she closed her eyes wearily.

When Thorn asked if she wanted any coffee, she accepted and sat up to get the sandwiches. They ate and drank in silence. Then she put away the thermos and lay back, closing her eyes again to doze fitfully.

Sabrina had no notion of how much time had passed before she was jolted upright by a sudden dip. Jagged lightning flashed overhead. They hit an air pocket and dropped. Then Thorn steadied the plane.

Apparently unconcerned, he peered ahead. The

plane rocked violently. Big drops of rain began to splash against the windshield. Determined not to distract him with questions, Sabrina tensed and bit her lip. Thorn reached for the microphone. Flashing lightning struck with a deafening crack.

Dazzling in its fiery brilliance, it tore across the plane. Inside the cabin there was a crackling popping noise, followed by the heavy drumming of rain. Suddenly the flash was gone, and they were plunged into darkness.

A lick of orange flame erupted at the wing root and danced outward. Sabrina gasped at the sight and clutched the arms of her seat. "They both flamed out!" Thorn muttered, working frantically with the controls.

"What happened?" Sabrina asked.

"We've been struck by lightning. Everything is failing," he stated grimly.

Even as he answered, the bright orange flames spread over the fuselage. The tense silence that enveloped them was broken only by peppering rain. Gray acrid smoke began to fill the interior, stinging Sabrina's eyes and filling her throat and lungs until it was difficult to breathe.

"Buckle up. Get your knees up and your head down," Thorn commanded quietly. "We're going to crash."

CHAPTER NINE

AS QUICKLY AS IT HAD STARTED, the rain ceased. With a high-pitched whine the plane hurtled toward earth.

"I'm throwing a blanket over you," Thorn said quickly. "Stay down until we've completely stopped. We may bounce, then hit again."

The last thing she saw before the heavy blanket obliterated everything was the dim smoky outline of Thorn's profile against the orange glow of fire outside the window. She heard him mutter softly, "Here we go...."

There was the excruciating sound of tearing metal, as if the plane were scraping across concrete, then a bang. Sabrina was thrown violently forward. The belt tightened against her. Then there was only exploding pain and darkness.

Later, opening her eyes to gaze blankly into the night, she tried to collect her thoughts but couldn't. A wave of dizziness washed over her, threatening unconsciousness again. She closed her eyes, struggling to remember what had just happened. Fright and terror enveloped her.

"Thorn!" The cry was a mere croak. Pinned beneath a crushing weight, she struggled to sit up. With great effort she heaved, then heard the crash of metal on metal.

Suddenly Thorn was beside her. His strong arms raised her and pulled her close.

"Thank God we're safe," she murmured as she hugged him wildly. A violent trembling seized her. Immediately his arms tightened, and he began to push debris aside in an effort to escape the wreck. Sheltering Sabrina in his arms, Thorn finally tumbled out onto the hard ground. Straightening quickly, he carried her several yards away from the inferno before collapsing breathlessly.

Her head against his chest, Sabrina listened to his steady heartbeat. While she clung to him, she faced the truth that she wouldn't acknowledge earlier. No matter how unwise or impossible, she could no longer deny her feelings.

She was in love with Thorn Catlin.

In that first moment of consciousness, not knowing whether he had survived, she had been overwhelmed by a fear that erased all doubts. She loved him desperately.

Shifting to press her lips lightly against his shirt, Sabrina felt his warm flesh through the material. It was the barest touch. She didn't think he could feel it, but, as if in response, his hand moved to smooth her hair back from her face.

Resolve filled her. Because she couldn't bear his pity, she wouldn't let him know about her love. Something wet ran down his cheek. Sabrina reached up to wipe it away and noticed a smear of blood on her hand. "You're cut!" she exclaimed.

"Not badly," he answered. Glass tinkled as he shifted. "We'd better take stock. Let me see if I can find a light."

Her eyes were beginning to adjust to the darkness, enabling her to see scattered bits of the wreckage. A small flame flared with the click of his cigarette lighter, its light shedding a circle of visibility.

Sabrina's trembling increased at the sight of the gash across his forehead. Thorn pressed a folded handkerchief against his bloody temple, and she shook uncontrollably as she watched red gush over his hand down his blood-spattered shirt.

"It's not as bad as it looks," he concluded calmly. "Head wounds, even when superficial, bleed profusely."

"Is it terribly painful?"

He grinned suddenly, and she in turn relaxed. "I was about to ask you the same. You're cut yourself."

Looking down at her arms and hands in amazement, she discovered what he had said was true. "Except for shaking all over, I don't feel anything."

"We're both still in shock," he replied. "Soon enough you'll feel everything. Let's make certain there are no severed arteries." Gently he lifted her, but the moment she attempted to stand, white-hot pain shot through her ankle. Thorn caught her quickly as she swayed.

"Sit down again," he commanded.

"I'm beginning to feel several things at once now," she groaned, and glanced at the flickering flames surrounding the plane. They seemed to be diminishing. "Thorn, is there any danger of an explosion from the plane?"

He nodded grimly. "There is. That's why I dragged you from the plane so quickly." He glanced at the wreckage. "If anything was going to happen, though, it would have by now." Tugging gently, he removed her boot. His hands were warm against her flesh as he probed carefully with a light touch. Her ankle was red and swelling rapidly. Turning her foot in his hand, Thorn looked up.

"I don't think you've broken anything. Stay off your foot and let me see if I can find any bandages. I had emergency equipment. If it wasn't destroyed, there should be a first-aid kit." He wiped blood off his cheek. "Just stay here."

Before she had a chance to warn him to be careful, he had risen and returned to poke cautiously around the now smoldering wreckage. He didn't find the first-aid kit, but after ripping a strip of velour from a cushion, he returned to wrap it around Sabrina's shoulders. Kneeling beside her, he pulled it close under her chin. "There, that should make you feel a bit warmer."

She gazed at him solemnly. "Thorn, I think you should have a bandage on your forehead. It's still bleeding."

He shook out his handkerchief, and she reached up to pull the scarf from her hair. "Come closer," she instructed. Folding the white linen handkerchief neatly, she placed it against the cut, then bound her scarf around his temple.

As soon as she had finished, he rose again and

crossed to the smashed plane. After a moment of kicking through the debris, he swore softly. When Sabrina asked what was wrong, he replied, "The damn thermos is crushed. What little food we had is gone." He turned around. "I can't see enough with this lighter, and I don't want to build a fire. The best thing will be to wait until daylight."

He sat down beside her. "Think you can sleep?"

She shook her head. "No, not at all."

"I doubt if I can, either, but we might as well try. Let's move farther away from the plane, just to be on the safe side." Thorn supported her as she hobbled awkwardly for several more yards.

Although Sabrina's trembling had stopped, she was beginning to ache all over. Replacing the first wave of shock was a dawning awareness of the dark jungle and their predicament, and along with it came second thoughts about her feelings for Thorn. Rationally she argued she couldn't be in love with him. She decided that what she'd felt had been an emotional reaction to their close brush with death. She glanced sideways at him as he sat, his back against a tree trunk, knees propped up, eyes closed.

"How can you remain so calm?" she asked. "You act as if you're comfortably ensconced at Bellefontaine instead of lost in a rain forest."

He squinted at her and shrugged. "There's nothing else to do." With languid ease Thorn stretched out, placed his hands behind his head and closed his eyes.

His withdrawal made her feel so alone. Something screeched nearby. In the distance she heard a deep growl. But more disturbing than these noises were the small rustlings close at hand. Desperately she whispered, "Thorn."

He opened his eyes immediately, and feeling foolish but relieved to find him awake, she admitted, "I didn't really want anything. I don't know how you can lie down and close your eyes." She looked around. "Anything could crawl over you, off the ground or out of the jungle...." Her words trailed off, and she shivered.

He raised himself up on one elbow and turned to study her. "Frightened, Sabrina?"

"Yes, I'm frightened. If you weren't so damned arrogant, you would be, too!" The words were out in a rush before she realized what she'd said. She bit her lip. "I'm sorry, Thorn."

"Don't apologize," he chuckled. With a lithe movement he rose and walked over to kick through the debris. Sabrina heard a ripping sound and watched him pull something away, returning to place a strip of plastic on the ground. Sinking down on top of it, he motioned to her. "Come lie down here. I won't let anything carry you off."

Disconcerted, Sabrina looked at him. She had no inclination to stretch out beside him. "Thanks, no," she replied, and felt the warmth come into her cheeks.

His voice was filled with amusement. "Are you afraid of jungle beasties... or something else?"

His words hung in the air, and he laughed softly when she didn't reply. "Come on, Sabrina. There's nothing to fear."

"I won't be able to sleep anyway, and I don't know how you can," she repeated.

"Pretty easily," he drawled laconically.

His calm answer did nothing to soothe her frayed nerves. "We've just crashed in the Amazon. We're fortunate to have survived. It's impossible to calm down after that," she wailed.

"Come here, Sabrina," he commanded.

Just looking at him, she felt her heart race. If only he didn't have such a disturbing aura about him, she thought. But she shifted over to sit cross-legged on the plastic.

"Lie down and turn over," he ordered.

Turning her face away from him, she lay on her stomach. He began to massage her shoulders.

"If you sit up with me, you'll never get any sleep," she murmured. A bird's wild cry sounded, making Sabrina jump.

"Relax," he said softly.

Peering restlessly through the darkness, she sat up abruptly to face him. "I know you must ache and hurt as much as I do. We're surrounded by wild things—boa constrictors, jaguars, alligators...." The words tumbled out, and Sabrina began to lose control of her emotions.

Wrapping his arms around her, Thorn pulled her close. To her mortification, a sob racked her. Then she was lost in tears.

Thorn held her tightly, soothed her. She wasn't aware of the exact moment when he lifted her into his lap and cradled her against his chest. As she grew calm, she listened to the deep steady rhythm of his heart. "I'm sorry," she murmured, embarrassed by her outburst.

Tilting her face up, Thorn gazed down at her. In the dark it was impossible to read the expression in his eyes. "Don't apologize," he said. "You've been remarkably brave and cool. Laurel or Amanda would be having screaming hysterics. You've been through a hellish experience, and it takes time for the shock to wear off."

"You don't seem to be suffering from it!" she snapped.

He shrugged good-naturedly. "Maybe I show it in a different way." His voice was tender as he continued. "This seems like wild remote country—which it is—but it's home to the natives. Somebody lives here, likes it and is comfortable, so it is possible to survive. Look at it another way. Drop one of these natives into Washington, D.C., and he'd be terrified—which would seem absurd to you."

"I hadn't thought of it that way."

"There are dangers here," he added calmly, "just as there are dangers in Washington. Knowing what you have to cope with and being careful are what's important."

"Can you cope with this?"

Looking over her head into the thick brush beyond them, he said, "I've trekked through this area before. It's dangerous, but not impossibly so if we're careful. The real danger does not stem from the big animals but from the flies, mosquitoes and ants. Since prehistoric times they've survived, and they'll outlast the peccaries, jaguars, caimans, constrictors, endangered species and all other hardy animals. It's unusual to spot a jaguar, by the way. If we do, it won't harm us unless we disturb it. It's the flies that are relentless. By this time tomorrow night you'll understand what I'm saying."

She shivered. "I don't want to hear any more about it now."

His arms tightened around her. "Go to sleep," he whispered.

He seemed so calm, so in command, that Sabrina began to lose some of her fear. In the haven of his arms she felt safe and protected. Nestling her head against his shoulder, she listened to the strange night cries. An animal roared in the distance. Wrapping her arm around Thorn's neck, she finally fell asleep.

DISORIENTED, SABRINA OPENED her eyes. Her first awareness was of pain. Every muscle ached and throbbed, while drops of cool dew fell onto her from the leaves above. Sitting up, she groaned softly, hearing a strange cacophony of cries emanating from the bush. Memory of the night's adventure returned at the sight of the lush green leaves surrounding her. Yards away she saw the charred remains of the plane. Both wings and one side were sheared away, scattered in bits and pieces over the ground. Recalling the terror of the night, she stared at the wreck, even more amazed and grateful that they'd survived.

When the plane had gone down, it had toppled a stand of trees beneath it. Now they poked out from under the wreckage in an array of green leaves dotted with pink, yellow and purple orchids and red and golden vine blossoms. The sweet scent of jasmine permeated the air, and she shivered at the sight of the crushed blooms. The realization suddenly hit her that she was alone.

"Thorn!" She stood up to look for him. Instantly pain ripped through her ankle, causing her to sit down quickly.

"Here, Sabrina!" His voice came strongly from a distance. A few minutes later he stepped out of the bush. "What's wrong?"

She gasped at the sight of him in daylight.

One corner of his mouth lifted lopsidedly. "I look that bad, hmm?" he asked.

"Do I look....?"

He laughed and finished for her. "As bad as I do." He shook his head and crossed to drop his arm around her shoulders, his gaze traveling over her features. "No, you don't look bad at all—a little purple perhaps—" he touched her cheek "—and a bit yellow here—" his hand moved to her throat "—and this is a nice brown bruise...."

She gave a yelp. "Do I really look that awful?" When he grinned, she realized he had been teasing her. "I wish I had a mirror," she moaned.

"Here we are in the largest rain forest in the world—more than one billion acres. We're lost, have no food—and you're lamenting the lack of a mirror!"

She ran her fingers through the long strands of her blond hair, attempting to smooth out the snarls. "You make me sound quite vain."

Thorn chuckled as he reached into his hip pocket. "Here, I have a comb."

All her aggravation at his teasing disappeared when she studied him more closely. The blue scarf tied around his forehead and hanging down over one ear gave him a renegade appearance.

"Let me look at your foot," he said. While he knelt to carefully remove her boot, she gazed past him again at the wreckage.

"I don't know how we came out alive."

Thorn glanced over his shoulder. "We came in over those trees. With their shallow roots, they went down with us when we hit. Perhaps that cushioned the crash." He looked at her and spoke matter-of-factly. "There won't be any modern conveniences here. Just don't get too far out of sight when you need privacy." Probing her ankle gently, he finally concluded, "You're better. The swelling has gone down considerably." He helped her on with her boot and stood up. "While I salvage what I can, you sit here and conserve your strength."

She nodded, watching him move away to sort through the debris. He pushed bits of glass and pieces of metal aside, then retrieved something. Dusting it off, he walked over to her to hand her her battered hat, which she placed on her head as he returned to the wreckage.

Selecting assorted items, swearing when he found something smashed beyond use, Thorn worked methodically. Watching him, Sabrina realized it was Tuesday morning. Only a week ago she had been in Washington doing last-minute errands before leaving for the airport for the flight to Sao Paulo. Now that seemed years away, and she wondered vaguely if she'd ever be the same after knowing Thorn.

As he began to move in wide circles away from the crash site, she again noted the heavy sweet scent of the smashed flowers, the odors of decaying vegetation on the ground. Above them in the treetops, birds chattered noisily, too high above to be disturbed by Thorn's movements.

Suddenly he whooped and snatched up an object, hurrying toward her.

"What is it?" she asked. "Did you find food?"

"No. The first-aid kit."

"How can you be overjoyed by that?"

He opened the battered tin box. "The most important thing is to remain healthy. There's disinfectant and gauze here. Let's get these wounds clean," he added, tilting her chin and dabbing at her cuts and scratches with a torn piece of cloth and disinfectant. Next he took her hand and stretched out her arm.

In spite of his gentleness the disinfectant stung, and Sabrina tried to keep her thoughts off what he was doing. Looking around her, she asked, "Don't you think they'll send a search party for us this morning?"

He glanced at her. "They might not yet."

"How long do you think we may have to wait?" she asked.

Once again she noticed a brief hooded look cross his face. "They can't ignore the fact that we've gone down somewhere," she insisted.

He spoke grimly. "No, they won't ignore that."

He raised his head, and she detected stubborn determination in the set of his jaw. "No, they'll notify everybody we've disappeared." His eyes met hers steadily. "But the chances of them spotting the crash site are almost nil, Sabrina."

"How can you say that! You gave them your flight plan."

"Just remember we were caught in a turbulent tropical storm. During the last few minutes of our flight there was only a slim chance we were on course. Look, we've gone down in a rain forest. From above, all it is, is a sea of green."

"From above they'll be able to spot the wreck."

The thrust of his jaw gave her a cold stab of apprehension that intensified when he shook his head. "If they're directly overhead within the next day or two, maybe they can spot the plane," he replied. "In three days, Sabrina, you'll never know that anything ripped through those trees. If they pass directly above, fine—but we can't wait for that chance."

She gazed at him with increasing anxiety. "What are we going to do?"

"We'll return to civilization," he asserted in a voice filled with determination. "When he gets word of the crash, I don't know what it'll do to papa. We've got to get back as quickly as possible."

She'd been so numbed by the wreck that all her thoughts had been on it and their injuries. Now she began to develop new worries. "I hope they don't notify mother immediately," she murmured.

Wrapping a strip of clean white gauze around her hand, he replied grimly, "You know they'll have to.

If we can reach a village, I'll leave you there while I go on for help. I can't leave you here alone to wait."

"Heaven forbid!" she exclaimed, terrified at the thought. "I don't care to remain behind in a village, either."

His gray eyes rested on her. "I can travel much faster alone or with natives."

The implication that she was a hindrance was clear, and anger filled her. "I'll keep up, I promise. I won't slow you down."

He secured the gauze. "Don't make promises you can't keep. You have no conception of what it's like to travel through this area."

"How'll we know where we're going?"

"We've got to try. I hope we can reach a village soon."

"Are all the natives friendly?" she asked.

"No," he answered, "but most of them are." Rocking back on his heels, he assessed her. "Where else are your cuts?"

"That's all of them," she answered.

Untying the scarf from around his head, Thorn leaned forward for her to dress his wound. When she had finished there was a neat white bandage in place of the handkerchief and scarf. Next he stripped off his shirt and turned his back toward her.

Only inches above his belt was an ugly gash. Sabrina worked quickly, trying to be as gentle as he had been as she swabbed, yet acutely conscious of his smooth taut skin.

"Thorn, are you hungry?"

He chuckled and pulled his tattered shirt back on

when she'd finished. "As the proverbial wolf. We'll find something to eat."

In an effort not to be a nuisance, she bit her lip and held back her questions. He patted her shoulder. "Sit down. I want to see what else I can salvage before we go. I want anything we can use."

While she listened to the croaking of tree frogs mixing with the steady hum of insects high above, she settled against a jatoba tree to watch him sift through the debris again. A flock of small jungle partridges ran past nearby, startling her before they disappeared beneath a leafy bush. Her attention returned to Thorn when she saw him throw aside some rubble to scoop up what looked like a piece of metal.

When she spotted an automatic in his hand, Sabrina remarked, "I didn't know you brought that from the research station."

"I didn't. This Bernardelli was in the plane. The clip isn't full, but it'll do." He tucked the gun almost cheerfully into the waistband of his denims. After a time he jauntily raised his battered hat aloft to wave at her, then place it at an angle on the back of his head. His mood seemed to be improving, and Sabrina, too, took heart.

While he continued to work, he stuffed small scraps of paper into the band of his hat. "I think we're ready to go," he finally decided.

With an effort she scrambled to her feet, trying to ignore the pain. Immediately he stepped forward and said, "I can carry you."

"No!" she replied forcefully. "I'll tell you if it hurts badly."

"Very well, but no heroics. We're in good health. I want to keep it that way."

She nodded. "How can you hope to know which direction to take?"

"I don't. We'll hunt for a stream. Streams lead to rivers. Tributaries lead to the Amazon and civilization. Rivers are the roads of the Amazon." He glanced back at the wreck. "There wasn't a whole lot to salvage. I had a machete in there, but I couldn't find it."

He moved forward and slipped his arm around her. "Lean on me while you walk. Let's go."

She gritted her teeth against the pain when she placed her weight on the injured ankle and began to walk. During the first hours of dawn and early morning, the forest was filled with noises—raucous cries, screeching and chattering.

Thorn waved his hand. "I might as well give you a nature lesson while we're here. The ground is the 'basement' of the forest. Above us the crowns of trees are interlocked, forming the canopy, or so-called main level. Birds, insects and animals roam the corridors formed by the limbs. Between the canopy and the ground are trees growing at mid-level. Their crowns haven't yet interlocked."

He pushed aside broad leaves and continued. "The final level is above the canopy, marked by emergents, trees that shoot straight up through the canopy to grow about one hundred and fifty feet tall."

Sabrina looked overhead. "It's impossible to distinguish anything that high above us. The plants are so thick I can't pinpoint most of the birds we hear."

Thorn stepped over a fallen tree and commented, "As the day wears on, the air will grow stifling. But up in the canopy there's a breeze."

In spite of the pain from her ankle, Sabrina was fascinated by the multitude of plants. Gasping with delight, she pointed out first one variety of orchid then another to Thorn, until they came upon the tiny yellow orchids that carpeted the jungle floor, their sweet odor enticing brightly colored hummingbirds.

"Thorn, look at these! If only Roddy could be here." Reaching out quickly, she grasped his arm to get him to stop. As soon as he did, she sat down. "Wait a minute. Let's watch the birds."

Looking amused, he sat on a nearby log. Softly he said, "Brazilians call them *beija-flôres*—flower kissers."

Watching the hummingbirds' darting movements, she focused on a blue green one that hovered only a foot away. As it thrust its red bill forward, she whispered, "Look, Thorn, there's a spider inside the hypochilium...."

He laughed. "Inside the what?"

Barely hearing his question, she concentrated on the tiny hummingbird and whispered, "Inside the lip of the blossom— There! He ate the spider," she said with satisfaction.

"Don't talk about eating," he commented dryly.

She picked up one of the satiny yellow blossoms. "I think these are *Houlletia brocklehurstiana*."

Squinting at her, he grinned as he asked, "Now how the hell do you know that?"

"I could be wrong, but I've studied orchids. I think they're fascinating. So does Roddy."

"Well, it's a damn shame he isn't with us," Thorn said sharply, and rose to his feet. "Let's get going."

She looked up and wondered what had aggravated him. With an effort she rose to follow him and was soon battling lianas that scratched painfully. Everything was covered with moisture from the heavy morning dew. Her clothing was damp, and perspiration beaded her brow.

Pausing, Thorn raised his arm to point to his right. "Look, there's a sloth."

It took her several minutes to discover the animal that looked like part of the vegetation surrounding it.

"Its fur is covered with algae, and it looks as green as any plant," Thorn said.

"If it weren't for the claws, I wouldn't believe that's an animal," Sabrina replied. "It looks like part of the tree."

"His claws are wicked. He can be a nasty animal if bothered."

As the sun rose, the jungle cacophony died to a silence broken only by the hum of an occasional fly. The air became cloying and hot. Sabrina's foot throbbed. It was a struggle to keep up with Thorn's pace, but determined not to be a hindrance to him, she followed grimly.

Finally he paused and turned to face her. "Ready for a rest?"

She nodded with gratitude and sank to the ground. Thorn withdrew his knife, caught a liana and cut a section. Farther along the vine he made another slice, then handed it to her. "This should hold almost a pint of water. Care for a drink?"

"Thank heavens!" she murmured, accepting the vine. He cut another section for himself.

After a moment he asked if she was ready to continue. Sabrina rose, but when Thorn reached to put his arm around her, she shook her head. "I can manage."

He studied her a moment, then moved on. As the hours passed, Sabrina's hunger became all-consuming. The last good meal she had eaten had been in Manaus with Wade. She wished now she hadn't left half her sandwich when they'd eaten during the return flight.

She trudged along doggedly in Thorn's footsteps until she noticed a vine curling along the trunk of a *seringueira* tree. "Thorn, here are some red berries," she said. "Cut into one and I'll see if it's bitter. If it's not, the berries should be safe to eat."

He glanced at the tree. "I passed right by without noticing it." He cut open a berry, tasted it and murmured, "They're delicious. Thank goodness you saw them."

They sat down to eat for a few minutes, then continued the trek until Thorn halted again. "Sit down and rest," he advised. "We need something more substantial to eat." Looking overhead with narrowed eyes, he withdrew the automatic.

Sabrina sat down gratefully, leaned against a tree

and closed her eyes. Even the noise of the shot, the flapping of wings and the rustling of animals among the trees didn't disturb her. After a moment she opened her eyes to discover Thorn holding a parrot. He gathered dry twigs, removed some of the papers from his hatband and placed them on the twigs, igniting them with his cigarette lighter.

"Want any help?" she asked.

"You just rest." He moved a few yards away to dress the bird, and soon it was roasting, filling the air with a tantalizing mouth-watering aroma.

When they finally bit into their meal, Sabrina felt her strength returning with each bite. She smiled at Thorn delightedly. "This is the most delicious meal I've ever eaten!"

He returned a smile. "When we're back in civilization, I'll remind you of that!"

"Thorn, if there is a search for us, it hasn't been carried out around here. We haven't heard any planes pass overhead."

She caught his quick appraising glance. "So you noticed, too," he answered quietly, and reached over to squeeze her hand. "We'll get out of here, Sabrina."

She wiped perspiration from her forehead, longing to remove her boot. "There's so much to see here. In spite of our predicament, I find it strangely beautiful."

They both gazed around. Rays of sun slanted through the sparse openings high above them. The jungle was hushed and still. A shadowed gloom surrounded them. Bright, delicate, bluish pink orchids could be seen, and Sabrina pointed out tiny red arum blooms.

"When I'm in this forest, I'm always awed by the balance of nature and its ability to withstand any encroachment by man," Thorn said. He shifted to sit beside her. "It's as if there's no time here."

"I know. There wasn't any ice age—no glacial change," she said. "The equator protected it from that. Did you know the Amazon basin provides the world with forty percent of its oxygen and twenty-five percent of its fresh water?"

He turned to look at her. "Yes, I did."

She saw the questioning look in his eyes. "I read about Brazil before we came. Bellefontaine is about the same size as our state of Vermont, you know."

"You did your homework," he said softly.

At that moment a flock of toucans settled noisily in the canopy, sending leaves showering down on them, and Sabrina gazed up to see small kiskadee flycatchers flitting in the lower branches, which were covered with mosses and small plants, forming lush green paths for the animals.

Stretching out his long legs, Thorn commented, "I'm trying to develop a fertilizer for the rain forest. That's the purpose of that research station."

"I suppose the rain carries the nutrients away before they can be absorbed into the soil," Sabrina replied.

"That's right. We've come up with a nitrogen-producing plant that may be feasible. Do you know what biotite is?"

"It's a form of complex mineral, a mica."

"Right. It's found in eastern Brazil, and we've had some success in using biotite in fertilization experiments. Most of Amazonia's agricultural revenues come from rice and pepper. At this time the timber industry is small, although there's a large experiment going on with pulpwood. But when and if man moves into this area on a full scale, I hope it's in a knowledgeable manner."

"If not," she replied, "there could be worldwide changes in climate."

Thorn nodded, regarding their surroundings solemnly. "This is a fantastic area and still largely unexplored."

"I don't know much about the river itself," Sabrina admitted.

"From glacier-fed lakes in the Peruvian Andes, the Amazon begins and flows almost four thousand miles before emptying into the Atlantic with a torrent that drives back saltwater for more than a hundred miles. You might not believe it, but the Amazon's mouth is two hundred miles wide."

A morpho butterfly drifted past them, fluttering in great sweeping loops, its iridescent metallic-looking, blue wings shimmering. With a sudden loud crash, a distant tree toppled to the ground, pulling vines and flowers in its wake and leaving shallow roots and buttresses exposed. Disturbed by the fall, a cloud of yellow-and-green Phoebis butterflies flew skyward.

"You could feel the vibrations from that," Sabrina said, shivering. As she looked around, she became aware of life everywhere. When she met a pair of bright dark eyes, she uttered an exclamation of surprise.

In the high branches directly above them were three small, golden monkeys with black muzzles. Thorn smiled and explained, "They're squirrel monkeys called Chico-chico. We find them around our research station. They're friendlier than many other species."

Quickly shifting his arm around her shoulders, Thorn pointed with his other hand. "Look at that tree—at the trunk." He raised a length of vine and moved it toward the trunk. What looked like a piece of bark suddenly stirred, then fluttered to life. A moth flew away. Thorn looked down at her to gauge her reaction.

"See, that's their protection." He pointed again. "Look over there at the vine."

"Thorn, there are a hundred vines."

He pulled her closer and she followed the line of his gaze, but saw only a blue gray vine curling across a fallen tree. "Look to your right, along the vine," he said close to her ear.

"It's a snake!" Sabrina gasped. "It looks exactly like the vines except for the dark line of its mouth and eyes."

"Mimicry," Thorn replied. "It's evolutionary adaptation that enables these species to survive. I'll show you more examples if we come across any. There are all types of mimicry."

"Is the snake dangerous?" she asked.

"Not that particular one. It eats lizards and birds.

"Most animals in the Amazon have adapted to living in trees," he continued, gazing overhead. "There are some, of course, that don't, but most nutrients are in the trees. Monkeys and cats depend on them. Many other animals, agoutis and pacas, for instance, feed on things that have fallen from them."

But Sabrina was becoming far more aware of his closeness than of the inhabitants of the forest around them. "You're very familiar with all this, aren't you?" she asked.

He was only inches away. His familiar gray eyes had tiny flecks of gold near dark pupils. When her gaze shifted to his lips, hers parted involuntarily. She turned her head in rising panic, commenting on the first thing she saw.

"Look at those yellow blossoms so high above us."

Thorn sounded amused as he replied, "They're epiphytes, with aerial roots like the arum to catch and absorb nutrients from the air and the rain. The Indians call them 'daughters of the air.'"

Sabrina could feel Thorn's eyes on her, felt compelled to face him. But when she started to move away, his arm tightened around her shoulders. Looking into his eyes, she saw them darken with desire. Of all the things in the Amazon, she realized the most dangerous to her well-being was the man sitting beside her. Why was it that one smoldering look from him could send a burst of warmth melting through her?

Even as she thought this, his lips captured hers. A hungry longing rocked her, startling in its intensity.

Desperately she pushed against him and stood up. "Please don't," she whispered.

He didn't answer, but she was conscious of his intense gaze. She moved away, only to glance back and see a look of speculation in his eyes. He stood up without a word.

The crunch of their footsteps was accompanied by tiny constant rustlings as leaves dropped to earth or lizards scampered away. Lianas draped the trees like the furry green legs of giant insects. Sabrina spotted a bright red stemless heisteria flower growing on the bark of a tree near the forest floor. She called out to Thorn.

"The silvery fruit in its center is pollinated by ants and slugs," he pointed out. He directed her attention then to the fruit that hung like Christmas-tree balls from a nearby plant. "See that *visqueiro*? It's pollinated by bats. When they come for nectar, their wings brush the flowers. I'll show you another plant that's even more interesting if we come across it. It's called a cannonball tree."

As they trudged on, Sabrina caught sight of vines with graceful white-and-green leaves. "Look, Thorn, isn't that beautiful?" She pointed to the peperomia. "Even the mushrooms are lovely," she murmured when she noticed the tiny orange hoods that resembled small dolls' umbrellas. Close-by on a tree hung a delicate hairy fungus reminiscent of spiky golden eggs, bright against the rough brown bark.

Feeling soft sponginess underfoot, Sabrina discovered a bed of termites. Hurrying on, she was attracted by some beautiful white blossoms. She reached for one, and Thorn grasped her hand quickly. "That's a wild potato. The flowers are poisonous."

She laughed. "I didn't intend to eat them." Suddenly a piercing scream echoed through the forest, making her jump.

Thorn laughed at her reaction. "Relax, Sabrina. I'll show you the culprit." Dropping his arm casually around her shoulders, he looked around, searching for the source, finally pointing upward. "There's the scoundrel—a pia."

"That tiny bird!" she exclaimed as she spotted the small gray brown creature.

He smiled. "It's quite a common sight. Amazonians call the bird *daí-a-pior*, or 'worse to come.'"

"I hope not," Sabrina stated.

Thorn moved on and she followed, but after a time her interest in her surroundings began to wane. She no longer studied orchids or little animals or brightly plumed birds. Soaked with perspiration and suffering a constant throbbing pain in her ankle, she was miserable. Hunger returned as she plodded steadily along, biting her lip at the searing ache in her foot.

Thorn changed direction and his steps quickened, making it more difficult for Sabrina to keep up. The trees became a blur—until the moment when she looked ahead and Thorn was gone.

Suddenly alone, she felt panic overwhelm her. She called out to him, but the low cry seemed to come from far off as she sank into darkness....

SABRINA STIRRED. Consciousness returned, and she found herself looking up into Thorn's fierce countenance. No words were necessary to express his anger.

"Sabrina, I told you not to get separated from me!"

"I didn't mean to. I called to you." She struggled to get up, but he pressed her down against the leaves and raised her head to place her hat beneath it. He squinted at her in silence, then asked, "What happened? Is it heat or hunger or exhaustion—or all three?"

Before she could answer, a droning hiss pervaded the air. Thorn glanced up. "Here comes an afternoon rain. That should help." Big drops began to spatter down. For the first few minutes the thick upper canopy sheltered them, until the refreshing sprinkle began to drip through.

Effortlessly Thorn lifted her and moved close to the trunk of a tree for shelter. Wringing out his handkerchief, he wiped her brow. She lay back wearily and closed her eyes. A low moan escaped her lips. Instantly she realized what she'd done. Her eyes flew open in alarm.

Thorn was observing her intently. "What hurts?" he asked in clipped tones.

'My ankle," she admitted.

He removed her boot and swore softly, his eyes glacial. "I told you to let me know if your foot became painful."

"I didn't want to be a hindrance," she whispered.

With an obvious effort, he spoke calmly. "Look,

the most important thing, if we hope to survive, is to stay in the best physical condition we can. Now dammit, tell me when something aches."

"There's nothing you can do about it anyway," she answered tiredly.

"There damn well is," he retorted. "I can carry you and let it heal. Sabrina—" he paused and waited until she looked up at him "—promise you won't keep any aches or injuries from me anymore."

"All right," she agreed, and picked up the handkerchief to wipe her face again. "The water feels so cool."

The rain grew heavier and soaked them, a welcome relief from the oppressive heat. Thorn sat down beside her until the shower passed, then rose and removed the Bernardelli.

After checking the clip, he looked down. "There are seven shots left. I think I should save two or three for an emergency." He smiled disarmingly. "Now, m'lady," he murmured, "which would you prefer—roast snake, toasted frog or fried grasshoppers? The last will not entail use of the automatic."

Unbelievably, anything sounded tempting. Sabrina told him so and saw his white teeth flash. "Hunger does cause one to admit strange things." His eyes narrowed. "I'll be back shortly. Can I trust you to lie still?"

Trying to hide her apprehension, she asserted bravely, "Yes, Thorn. How can you find your way back?"

He patted the knife. "If necessary, I'll mark a trail." He grinned with an aggravating assurance.

"You can't lose me." Leaning forward, he kissed her lightly on the forehead, then walked away.

Gradually, with the weight off her foot, the pain receded to a dull ache. Sabrina shifted to sit up, watching small wrens hopping from branch to branch overhead. Intense quiet had settled in, broken only by the occasional twittering of birds. Within seconds all sounds of Thorn's steps had disappeared. In a short time she opened her eyes suddenly and realized she had dozed.

A crackling noise startled her. Sabrina straightened and glanced in the direction of the noise. She was certain it was not caused by Thorn. She sat up straighter. Her hands clenched into fists as she strained to catch sight of whatever was causing the disturbance.

A movement caught her eye, and she held her breath at the sight of three small brown animals, short, fat and sturdy, much like guinea pigs, running past her about twenty yards away before they were lost from sight.

In the distance a shot cracked, followed immediately by another. Anxiety gripped her, and she peered through the trees, longing for Thorn's return.

Silence enveloped her—only this time it was eerie. She felt a loneliness that seemed unending, as if she were the only human on a savage and alien planet.

When she sighted Thorn's broad shoulders at long last, Sabrina bit back a cry of relief. As he approached he raised his hand to reveal two macaws. "The menu is 'Macaw Supreme,'" he announced with a flourish.

Attempting to stand up, she murmured, "I was about ready to start on sticks and leaves as an appetizer."

"Sit down," he commanded. "I'll take care of this." She obeyed reluctantly and watched him move around, repeating the earlier procedure to build a fire. While he worked, she told him about the animals she'd spotted.

Thorn looked at her sharply and swore when she'd finished. "I should have stayed right here. We'd have had a better dinner and might even have found water."

"Why? Do you know what they were?"

"Capybaras, probably. They're excellent to eat."

"Are they pigs?"

He shook his head. "No. Actually capybaras are rodents. More important at the moment, they live around water. They're webfooted, which you probably couldn't see. The Indians use capybara teeth for chisels. In which direction did they go?"

Sabrina pointed. He stirred the fire contemplatively, then decided, "When we move, we'll head that way."

To accompany their meal, Thorn had procured a beverage of liana water. After they had devoured the succulent meal she gazed at him with admiration. "Thorn, that was better than roasted parrot."

"I'll accept that compliment gratefully and not question the reasons," he said, grinning and getting up to destroy the fire. After a time he crossed and helped her pull her boot on over the still swollen ankle. Then he lifted her easily.

Startled, she squirmed in his arms. "What are you doing?"

"We still have some light left. We're going to make the most of the time and continue the search for water."

"Put me down, please. You can't make any progress this way."

"I'll quit when you become too much of a burden," he replied cheerfully.

"I feel ridiculous. Let me walk."

"Be quiet, Sabrina. Let's listen for any sound of water."

Uncertain whether he really hoped to hear anything, or if he'd merely used the argument to keep her quiet, she fell silent, conscious of his closeness, of the odors clinging to his clothing, of him. Seemingly unimpeded by her weight, he strode rapidly on.

Finally Sabrina couldn't stand being carried a moment longer. She wriggled and pushed against him. "Thorn, I insist. Let me walk for a few minutes at least."

He set her down. "Only for a short time. Then I don't want to hear any more about it, Sabrina."

Within seconds she noticed that the jungle vegetation had changed. The lianas were now looped and tangled; the undergrowth had thickened. She could also see the excitement in Thorn's eyes. "We must be getting closer to water," he remarked. As if to confirm his words, the ground became softer, and Sabrina sank into rotting leaves.

Thorn swore, using his knife to hack at the lianas

converging on them. "If only we had that damned machete!"

Soon the soreness in her ankle wasn't Sabrina's only concern. With each step her feet sank deeper into earth, making slurping noises when she pulled free. Dead leaves were scattered thinly on top of bright green plants. The plants began to ripple beneath Thorn's feet as he forged ahead.

"Thorn, we're in water!"

He glanced over his shoulder at her. "I know, but it's stagnant. I don't know if it's a pocket or if a stream feeds into it."

She stared with loathing at the tiny leaves of water lettuce, their bright green dotted here and there with dark brown fallen leaves.

Dragon plants with long spiked leaves tore at her clothing. Large-leaved philodendrons barred her path. Thinking of all the possibilities of life under the camouflage of green, Sabrina shoved aside the wide leaves with distaste. Even the bright red blooms of the passionflowers had lost any appeal for her.

"Thorn, I hate walking through this. Can we go another way?"

"Just a little farther, Sabrina," he answered, and continued wading ahead. Above the steady squishing of their feet, a bird cried with a high forlorn wail that made Sabrina's skin crawl. She was terrified. Yet she didn't want Thorn to know it.

But when she noticed that each step brought them deeper into mire, her fright increased, because she was certain it would cover the tops of her boots in a few more minutes. Thorn seemed oblivious to any discomfort, as if he were strolling across the gardens at Bellefontaine.

"Thorn," she gasped, "it's getting dark! Night is coming. Suppose this goes on for miles. We can't lie down or sit down, and we can't climb any trees. If it gets any deeper, what'll we do?"

Reaching back, he grasped her hand in a comforting gesture. "How's the foot?"

"All right," she replied with a quaver in her voice.

"Look, we've been moving parallel to dry ground—see." He pointed to his left, and she turned to peer into the jungle.

"I don't see."

"Come along," he said gently. "We'll be all right. If we don't find a stream soon, we'll go back to dry ground."

Still holding her hand, he moved forward. Gritting her teeth against rising hysteria, Sabrina had no choice but to follow. Gnats and flies buzzed around their heads. The whine of mosquitoes increased, and she was bitten repeatedly, in spite of the heavy doses of insect repellent she had sprayed on.

They sloshed through murky gloom until it was difficult to see. Keeping her mind a blank, Sabrina concentrated on each step. Then, just as the water deepened dangerously, it began to grow shallow, until they were on dry ground. Thorn released her hand and moved ahead.

The distance between them widened, worrying her until she was about to call out to him. Before she could, she noticed a gurgling sound and waited a moment, listening.

"Thorn! I think I hear water!"

He joined her to listen, then grasped her hand and moved toward the noise. Within seconds they discovered a shallow narrow stream. With a whoop of joy Thorn spun and caught her up in his arms.

He grinned at her admiringly. "You don't need my help at all."

"Oh, yes, I do," she replied quickly as he lowered her gently to the ground.

"How's your ankle?"

Conscious of his arms still around her, she tried to remain calm. "It hurts," she answered truthfully.

"We'll stop. I'll build a fire. The smoke might keep down mosquitoes."

Within an hour her hunger and thirst had returned, but Sabrina refused to mention it. When night fell they couldn't see beyond the small fire, and when she thought of drinking water in the dark from the stream, her thirst fled—though she knew Thorn had done so.

He was now heaping up two large piles of leaves for their beds, his only a few feet away from hers. She settled down on the makeshift mattress, but no more than five minutes passed before an insect ran over her arm.

Brushing it away, Sabrina murmured, "I'll never get accustomed to sleeping on these leaves. I feel as if something is crawling all around me. There's a continual rustling."

He laughed softly. "Don't let your imagination start. The possibilities are endless and guaranteed to keep you awake throughout the night."

With another crackling of leaves, something scurried close at hand. Sabrina gasped and sat up. Thorn stretched out his arm and patted her shoulder, his voice filled with merriment. "Relax."

She swung around and glared at him. "How can you ignore all the crawling things?"

"I can't do a thing about them, so I might just as well get my rest," he drawled. His hand tightened on her shoulder. "Come here, Sabrina."

Aggravated, she yanked away. "I think that would be even more dangerous than staying here!" she snapped, then realized what she'd admitted.

With a strange note of curiosity in his voice he asked softly, "Why is it more dangerous?"

Grimly determined not to give herself away, she lay down again. "I'm quite all right," she replied, evading the question.

Every scrape, every snap set her nerves on edge. She glanced at Thorn, wondering if he was asleep or merely lying quietly with his eyes closed. A bird cried shrilly. The peace was definitely disturbed as howls and stirrings made a continuous din.

Then a wild scream split the air. Sabrina jumped and clutched Thorn's arm. "What is that?" she whispered.

His arm came around her, and he pulled her close. "A howler monkey. The little devils howl like banshees, which is how they earned their name." He tightened his hold on her. "Relax and enjoy the beauty all around us. Look up there."

Fireflies blinked in the darkness. A bird sailed through the upper branches of a broad-leafed tree with a flutter of white wings.

"Listen to the wild sounds." His voice was low. "You'll never hear anything like this anywhere else."

Slowly Sabrina's fears began to subside. She became aware of the length of his lean body pressed closely along hers. Her head was nestled in his shoulder, his arm around her. His fingers trailed along her arm, sending shivers through her. When he spoke again, it was softly. His breath was a whisper stirring her hair.

"At the moment I'm finding it increasingly difficult to remember that we're in desperate circumstances. The fire is chasing away the insects, the night is beautiful and I have a lovely woman in my arms."

She turned and began to protest. "Thorn...."

He placed his finger lightly against her lips. "Shh, Sabrina. Have you ever camped out?"

She relaxed against him. "Sure, but not in the Amazon."

"Did you enjoy it?"

He shifted slightly, and she snuggled closer. "Yes." They grew quiet and watched the bright dance of flames from the fire. Sparks shot upward, twinkling orange in the blackness.

She had no idea how long they were silent before Thorn patted her arm and remarked, "You're pretty easy to be around, very companionable to be lost with in the jungle."

"Thank you," she replied with a smile. "I can return the compliment. Right now I don't feel lost at all."

"What do you feel?" Thorn murmured, his breath warm against her temple.

"Perfect contentment," she answered honestly. "You have as many facets as a diamond, Thorn," she added, studying him intently.

He grinned. "How's that?"

Her gaze returned to the fire. "One minute you're fiery, the next you're calm. You can be so many different things."

His hand lightly caressed her arm. "So I'm like a diamond," he mused. After a time he asked, "Want to know what you're like?"

"I don't know that I want to hear."

"Like a deep lake," he said, ignoring her hesitation.

"Now explain that remark." There was curiosity and a touch of amusement in her voice.

Brushing her hair away from her cheek, he explained, "Because, Sabrina, on the surface you're peaceful—or you can be stormy—but it's still impossible to fathom what's beneath the surface."

"I'm not really that complicated, Thorn," she answered lightly, shifting to watch the fire. After a moment she asked, "You love the rain forest, don't you?"

"Yes. I spend one third of my time at Manaus, at the research station—at least I did until I took over full responsibility for Bellefontaine."

"Did you want to take over the plantation?"

He sounded surprised at the question. "I never gave it a thought. From birth I've been raised to accept the fact that one day I'd assume control. In a lot of ways we're not so different from many Brazilian plantation families," he continued thoughtfully.

"The father has authority over the entire family. It doesn't matter if the children are grown, either. Brazilians are descended from the Portuguese, who brought a way of life instilled in them by their Moorish conquerors. Even in the last century in Brazil men had harems. Women couldn't leave the house except for Mass or a festival. The head of the household was king, and when he took a long journey, the women were locked away in a convent."

"It sounds feudal and dreadful," Sabrina stated, growing more conscious of him every second, for he had shifted behind her to wrap one arm around her waist. His fingers continued to move lightly along her arm, sending small thrills of pleasure shivering throughout her body. Against her shoulder blades she felt the vibrations in his chest when he spoke.

"That way of life is changing rapidly—both in Villa Georgiana and Brazil as a whole. We should draw on the best of both worlds, I think. It's time for new ways, for a sharing and working together."

Raising herself up, Sabrina twisted to face him. "If you feel that way, why would you object so strongly to Wade marrying Estralita?"

Her flaxen hair tumbled down over her shoulder, and Thorn scooped a sheaf of it away from her face. He asked, "Sabrina, back at Bellefontaine you told me you were in love with someone. Who is he?"

The serenity she had found in his arms was instantly destroyed. She turned her head away from his probing eyes, but Thorn grasped her chin and pulled her around.

"Thorn, we have enough problems here. I don't

want to complicate them with true confessions."

His voice was light. "I merely asked if there was someone."

Once again she attempted to scoot away. His arms tightened. "Come back here, Sabrina. I'll say no more."

Knowing she was running a risk in doing so, she yielded. Settling her head against his shoulder, she asked, "You never answered me. Why do you object to Estralita if you feel the old ways are going?"

Thorn laughed softly. "Ah, questions are all right for me to answer but not for you. I don't object to Estralita. If Wade had just waited. All I asked was for him to be patient."

He was silent a moment, then said, "I'm not certain that Estralita is the one for Wade, but that's not my concern. I wanted *him* to think about whether they were right for each other. She's a beautiful, sophisticated, worldly actress. Somehow it's difficult to imagine my little brother captivating such a woman."

"Perhaps you underestimate Wade."

"Perhaps," he answered easily. "When I met her, she seemed truly devoted to him."

In the distance a deep-throated growl sounded. The jarring noise made her jump, and immediately Thorn's arm tightened around her. "It's a big cat," he murmured, "and not anywhere nearby."

"You must think I'm quite a baby," she replied.

"Not a baby at all," he drawled.

"Thorn, it's been a day now," she commented quickly. "Do you think...?" Her voice trailed off.

His tone changed, and she detected worry. "I'm certain our families know about the crash. We can't do anything about that, Sabrina." After a few minutes he asked, "How's your ankle?"

"Much better." Weariness swept through her, and she closed her eyes contentedly. Sleep quickly overcame her.

During the night she awakened and lay disoriented, blinking in the darkness. Her arm was thrown around Thorn's neck. Pressed against him, she was stretched out on her side, cradled in his arms.

But she was aware of something else—a stirring and slithering across her legs!

CHAPTER TEN

PERSPIRATION BROKE OUT across her forehead. Remaining absolutely still, Sabrina whispered frantically, "Thorn!"

His voice came back in a husky whisper, low and calm. "I know—don't move."

Feeling heavy muscles clench and pulse as the snake's body slid across her legs and over Thorn's, Sabrina lay immobile. She wanted to scream and jump up to get away from the reptile, but she closed her eyes and forced herself to count Thorn's heartbeat. Every second was torture.

Within a moment she became aware that his pulse was as deep and steady as ever. She opened her eyes and stared into space. The snake was gone.

Turning her against him, Thorn held her securely. Reaction set in, and Sabrina began to shake with fright. "Thorn, I can't stand this! I feel like everything under me is crawling, and now that awful snake...."

"Shh, Sabrina. We weren't hurt, and we've been here for hours without any harm coming to us."

His calm reply stirred an unreasonable anger within her. Pulling away from him, she sat up. "Don't you ever get scared? How can you let a snake crawl across you and not even get ruffled!" she cried.

He sat up, too, and smoothed her hair away from her face, then answered solemnly. "I'm accustomed to some of this. I've spent hour upon hour in the Amazon. None of this is new to me."

Chagrined and ashamed of her outburst, Sabrina sighed. "I'm sorry, Thorn."

Tilting her face up a fraction, he leaned forward and smiled. "You're very brave, Sabrina." Kissing her lightly, he gazed down at her upturned face.

All fears of the past few moments vanished as she looked into his gray eyes and saw them change. She knew he felt the tension between them increase, and she knew what he was going to do about it.

Her eyes closed as he drew her close to kiss her again. His lips were warm, captivating. His arms tightened, while his kiss conveyed pent-up hunger and longing.

As vibrant as the passionflowers she'd seen in the jungle, a flame spread through her, engulfing her with rapture. Her skin tingled from his touch as his hands moved in deft light caresses. Arching against him, she felt his hand brush the small of her back to tug her blue shirt free from the waistband of her slacks.

The thought that she must resist was like a leaf caught in a maelstrom. It flitted across her mind, powerless, torn away. She couldn't push him away; she couldn't take her lips from his. Twisting closer, she placed her hands on either side of his face. The tiny bristles of his beard scratched lightly against her palms, and she felt the hard bones of his cheeks, his jaw.

Sweeping her hair away from her face, Thorn kissed the curve of her shoulder and throat. His breath was warm, disturbing against her skin, and his kisses traveled in a slow sensuous trail up her throat, behind her ear. "Sabrina, darling...."

She pushed away from him with difficulty. "Thorn, if we don't stop now, I won't be able to in a few minutes."

His voice was soft, husky, as he nibbled at her ear. "Why stop something we both want? You know you want this...."

All reason was dissolving with each touch. In a quick movement she pushed away and stood up, her heart pounding and her breath coming in deep gasps as she looked down at him.

Straightening to a sitting position, he dropped one arm over his raised knee and eyed her angrily. "Sit down, Sabrina," he said roughly. "I won't touch you."

"No. I don't trust you!" Hastily she tucked her shirt back into her slacks.

"You mean you don't trust yourself," he challenged softly. Slowly, leisurely, he uncoiled himself and rose to his feet to face her, only a few feet away.

Any composure she'd just regained vanished as she interpreted the expression in his eyes. Somewhere above them she heard the melodic cry of a bird, but her thoughts were on the man in front of her.

"What game are you playing, Sabrina? One minute you give yourself to me willingly, the next you won't let me touch you."

It was difficult to answer, impossible to confess her feelings, so she said, "When I kissed you that first time at Congonhas it was a mistake, and I've regretted it ever since. But you took me by surprise this time."

"So it seems," he drawled sardonically.

She felt her frustration growing beyond all bounds. "I'm not playing any game!" she insisted.

He watched her a moment without moving before he whispered, "Come here, Sabrina."

She backed away a step, murmuring, "No...."

"Come here," he coaxed her in a voice of velvet filled with sensual promise.

A rising wave of desperation engulfed her. She knew it was hopeless, knew what he could do to her. Deep within her a response was born, began to unfold. Even though she hadn't moved, everything within her strained toward him, toward that husky exciting voice, and as he started toward her, she couldn't move. Helplessly, as if her feet, like the lianas, had grown roots into the ground, she stood transfixed.

His deep voice sent a ripple of delight through her. "I want you in my arms." He reached for her.

"Oh, Thorn!" She knew it was hopeless. From his first words of invitation her resistance had melted. She placed her hands against his strong arms as his muscles tightened and he crushed her to his chest.

While his hands roved over her body, inflaming and arousing her, he murmured against her ear,

"Quit fighting me. Stop protesting. Your body tells me you want this as much as I do." Then he kissed her, drinking in the sultry sweetness of her lips.

Why can't I resist him, Sabrina thought. *I can't do this. I mustn't....* She was drowning in exquisite anguish. With his hard body pressing against her they sank to the ground, lying on fallen leaves. The sweet rotting smells of decaying vegetation mingled with the earth-stained scent of Thorn's khaki shirt.

Dimly aware of his fingers at the buttons of her blouse, she felt him push it open. Her exploring fingertips followed the curve of his spine, drifting over his back to brush the bandage under his shirt. Suffering an aching need that grew intolerable, she returned his fevered kisses and caresses.

But when he paused, she moved a few inches away from him, gasping for breath.

He rolled to his side then and, with deliberation, propped his head on his hand and studied her through narrowed eyes. She was intensely aware of his scrutiny, of her open blouse. She pulled the flaps sharply together.

"Why?" he asked in a ragged voice.

"You're engaged to be married soon."

"What difference does that make! You told me you're in love with someone else. Yet you've clearly shown a very enticing response!"

His words were like a knife in her heart. Gazing down at her hands, her hair partially hiding her face, she forced herself to speak. "That was my mistake. I can't give myself to you that way."

The leaves rustled beneath him as Thorn sat up

abruptly. "Then why the hell do you keep tempting me?"

Unsure of the answer herself, Sabrina cried, "How can you be so unfaithful to Amanda?"

"I haven't taken any vows yet," he replied stonily.

She stared at him, aghast. "You're cold-blooded, Thorn. If I were engaged, I wouldn't want my fiancé to make love to someone else."

He raised his eyebrows, and derision tinged his words. "No? Well, then, I suppose I'm just immoral. But are you any better, Sabrina—any more faithful? I'll admit losing control, but you're very adept at leading a man on." His voice was harsh. "I suppose you've had lots of practice...."

"That's a disgusting thing to say! What right do you have to judge me?"

"What else do you expect me to think? Your kisses are a burning invitation, and you know it!" Their gazes locked and held in unbearable tension.

A weary cynicism sounded in his next words. "All right, Sabrina. What do you want? There's another reason you came to Bellefontaine, isn't there? Is that what you're holding out for, tempting me and then refusing?"

Thunderstruck, she could only stare at him. "What are you talking about?"

His eyes narrowed angrily. "Your innocence is convincing—but not quite convincing enough!" he snapped. "I'm tired of your games!" He closed the distance between them on the leaves and pressed her urgently to him.

Sabrina gasped and tried to fling herself away, but

she was held fast. His mouth met hers, and he kissed her wildly with hot demanding kisses, probing, eliciting her response. His body arched over hers, and she gave that response to him, hungrily. Her head was back against his shoulder. One hand was tangled in her hair to hold her fast, while the other arm circled her tiny waist.

She couldn't follow his sudden changes of mood, and she had to get to the bottom of his accusations. Battling her own desires as well as his, she gasped, "Thorn, what do you mean?"

"You know exactly!"

"I don't!" she cried. At the fury she saw mirrored in his eyes her heart pounded. "What are you talking about—holding out for what?"

"Gold," he replied.

"What gold?" she asked in amazement.

"The gold at Bellefontaine," he answered evenly.

Speechless, she peered through the darkness at him. "That doesn't even make sense!"

He straightened, and she sat up to scoot away a fraction. He was watching her intently, speaking in a cutting voice. "Are you certain of that, Sabrina? Or have those delicious kisses been deliberately seductive in a stall for more time?"

"What could I gain with more time?" she demanded coldly. "I don't understand at all."

"When I saw you in São Paulo—that first encounter at Congonhas Airport—and asked why you were here, remember what you told me?"

Numbly she shook her head. How could she have said anything then that would matter so much?

"You were more candid then," his chilling voice went on. "There was no mention of world hunger, of agronomy or of studying better methods of farming. Indeed not!" he snapped. "You told me you wanted to get something here that would give you everything you desire when you return to the States."

Her indignation reverted to amazement. "You can't believe—"

"How could I not believe, unless I'm a fool or blinded by your charms!" he interrupted savagely, his eyes blazing.

"You think I'm after gold at Bellefontaine?" she repeated, still stunned but suddenly remembering his strange behavior during their early encounter, the suspicion she'd thought she detected in his eyes.

"Under the circumstances it's a little difficult to accept your constant denials," he replied sardonically.

The world had turned topsy-turvy. It took a second for her to grasp the full implications of his last statement, but in dawning understanding she gazed at him while a deep fiery anger shook her. "Yes, circumstances! And that's exactly what you've got against me—mere circumstantial evidence! An exchange! You think I've been offering myself in an exchange for gold...."

His arm shot out and seized her, and he hauled her to him to kiss her. For one brief moment she forgot his cruel accusations and responded to the demands of his mouth, his hands and body. She sensed not only rage in him, but frustration, and his kisses provoked her, set her aflame. She knew now that that first wild kiss at Congonhas, their tempestuous encounter when he'd swept her away from the *macumba* ritual, had misled him, made him think she was playing a dangerous game.

Suddenly he tore his lips from hers. "How much, Sabrina? What's your price?" he demanded.

Within her, rage, frustration and hurt battled for supremacy. Anger won out, and blindly she raised her hand, swinging her palm to slap his face. His hand closed around her wrist in a powerful grip. "You got away with that once. You never will again!" he snapped.

Deep down a nagging kernel of logic made her realize that her own actions might have contributed to his suspicions. She had told him she was in love with someone else. Yet here she was, "leading him on," as he saw it. Still, she trembled with rage at his cool assumption of the worst. He had no real basis for believing she was invovled in gold smuggling.

She fought to control her voice when she asked, "Is there really gold for the taking at Bellefontaine?"

"I think you know the answer to that without asking," he replied coldly. "Yes, there is. I've started operations at the mine, but I'm keeping it from papa. The gold is there. It's abundant and reasonably accessible. Some have tried to acquire it—with disastrous results. They'll spend a large part of their lives in our jails. Evidently you haven't made a serious attempt, or the same fate would have been yours," he added harshly.

Tilting his head to one side, he studied her with narrowed eyes. The cynicism she had detected before was now blatant. "What is your price, Sabrina?" His gaze traveled slowly and insolently over her. "I may be willing to meet it."

She wanted to scream at him, to claw his arrogant face. Worst of all, she felt hot tears of pain springing to her eyes, betraying her.

She had lost her heart to him. There was no denying it. Otherwise she wouldn't be so totally vulnerable, wouldn't feel as if his sharp angry words were destroying her.

In unthinking fury, a mere angry retaliation to his accusations, she raised her chin and threw out a ridiculous figure. "One million dollars!"

Even though it was dark, Sabrina was close enough to see the varied emotions chase across his face. For one swift second she felt a stab of satisfaction and revenge, until his startled expression changed to anger. His eyes frosted. Sliding his fingers into her hair, he slipped his arm around her waist to jerk her to him.

With a fury that matched her own he growled, "That astronomical figure should go into the history books! Let's see how much of that you're worth!"

Any denial or protest was drowned by his fiery kiss. She'd gone too far. His lips were insistent, his hands insidious, arousing her, kindling with molten strokes a burning ache for him, demolishing reason and anger. She grasped his iron wrists, delighting in their strength. Effortlessly his nimble fingers peeled away her shirt, pushing it down her slender arms to toss it aside.

She joined with him in removing their remaining

clothing, all resistance melting at the touch of skin to skin. He was kneeling in front of her, one hand sliding up to her hip.

"Thorn," she began, but her words died in a gasp. Her experience had been limited. She'd never coped with such sensuality, such an explosion of passion. She swayed and trembled. His warm calloused hands drifted languorously up the back of her legs, sending an electrifying current coursing through her. The anger in him seemed to be fighting a losing battle with desire. How could he, with such ease, diminish all reality, all awareness of anything except him?

Sabrina leaned forward, her fingertips massaging the bunched muscles of his broad shoulders. "Thorn...." It was impossible to talk when her thoughts were befuddled by a sweeping tide of desire. His hands held her waist, and he pulled her down into his arms, lowering her gently to the ground.

Lifting his mouth from her shoulder, he spoke in a voice hoarse with passion. "I can't fight you, Sabrina, so why fight me? You've tempted me, wanted this since that first seductive kiss, your first offer...."

He knew how to read her trembling responses. Lost in the turbulent pleasure he evoked, she squeezed her eyes shut, clinging to him, feeling his sinewy muscles ripple with each movement.

Thorn's body shifted to cover hers, and for a startling moment she stopped writhing, was still. Her eyes flew open and she met his burning gaze. And in the gray eyes fixed on her she detected a tormenting conflict of passion and resentment, while his hands roamed and explored with adeptness, calling forth an instant response. She moaned and shoved uselessly against his shoulders, while he heightened the yearning she suffered.

The thick sultry heat of their bodies rose in scorching waves, overcoming the coolness of the tropical night. She lost awareness of the soft bed of leaves beneath her, the exotic scents of flowers high above.

He kissed her hungrily, achingly, then placed his hands on either side of her to raise himself up. They were hip against hip, her slender body arched beneath him as she strained upward. Yet her head thrashed back and forth wildly in a denial of what was happening.

In spite of their differences, she loved Thorn utterly and completely. But she didn't want their lovemaking to be born of misunderstanding and conflict. She wanted her body to be cherished, their minds to be one.

With a strangled cry she struggled to resist him before they went beyond the point of no return. But Thorn seemed to be a man driven.

Desperation swept over her. She did the only thing she could think of to dampen his ardor. "Are you going to pay my price?" she whispered.

He stiffened, looked down at her. The fires of hell could hold no more rage than she saw in his eyes. "You little bitch!" he growled savagely. In a supple movement he rose and stood over her. With his lean coppery skin rippling over his muscles, there was no question of his readiness or of his struggle for self-control. His fists were clenched. Glacial eyes swept the length of her body.

Snatching up her blouse, she rose quickly. "Thorn, please, it can't be this way, in anger. I didn't mean what I said—"

"Sabrina, you can take your own advice. Go to hell!" He spun around, grabbing his clothes and disappearing into the darkness.

She let him go, not knowing whether he would abandon her to the jungle but afraid to stop him.

Everything in her wanted to cry out, to tell him she loved him, to beg him to listen. She wanted to give herself wholly and completely, wanted to explain that she had to stop him only because she didn't want to forever remember that their coming together had been prompted by anger.

Why had she ever said one million dollars? The figure was so ridiculously high she had never expected him to believe her. But now the damage was done.

Shaken by wild sobs, she flung herself down on the ground, no longer caring whether he heard or not.

When her tears were spent, she got up and got dressed. There was still no sign of Thorn, but she was too exhausted and drained to worry. In the depths of despair, Sabrina lay down and gazed into darkness. Animals and birds moved around her, but she lay in numb exhaustion, until finally she dozed.

SABRINA AWAKENED with the sunrise and sat up, disoriented. There was still no sign of Thorn. After attempting to unsnarl the tangles in her hair, she went to tend to her morning ablutions. She realized it was Wednesday. A week ago was the first day she had met Thorn. Like a wind that had whipped into a tornado, he had swept into her life and smashed all her peace. Even so, she would never regret having known him.

Shaking her head as if to rid herself of these somber thoughts, she drank cool clear water from the stream. Refreshed, Sabrina straightened and turned, to find Thorn behind her.

He eyed her in tight-lipped silence. Lines bracketed his mouth. His voice was as icy and bleak as his gray eyes. "I'll take you out of here, Sabrina. Then you're to pack and get out of Bellefontaine immediately."

"Thorn—"

He waved his hand. "Spare me the clever lies, Sabrina. I think we cleared the air between us sufficiently last night." He turned away to walk downstream.

But they had labored under misunderstandings long enough. With a determined effort she stood her ground. "Thorn Catlin, you come back here!"

Her heart pounded in her ears as he stopped and turned, mild surprise briefly reflected in his face, then as quickly disappearing. "We've misunderstood each other right from the beginning, Thorn."

"This is old ground—"

"Thorn, I know, in your dealings with businessmen, you listen and let them have their say without interruption. You'd never be as successful as you are if you didn't. Now will you accord me the same chance—just five minutes of your time?"

She couldn't guess anything of his thoughts from his enigmatic expression. There was a silence. Her fists clenched tightly at her sides, trying to hide her fear, Sabrina tried again.

"You've misunderstood so many things. I'll admit I should have told you straight out why I came to Brazil. But I haven't been after your gold at all. I'm hurt and angry over your accusations. Nor was there a price for my favors—far from it," she couldn't resist adding, and continued after a pause. "The only reason I said that last night was to get you to stop. That day in São Paulo I was simply referring to the fact that I wanted to go home. My family needs me, and I have a chance to further my career in Tennessee. Soon there will be an opening in my hometown for a county extension director to work with farmers in that area. I felt if I did a good job here, my credentials would be much better and I might have a stronger chance at securing the job. If you care to bother, you can verify this with Roddy."

She lapsed into silence then, and he narrowed the gap between them. "If that's the truth," he stated quietly, "I owe you an apology. Sabrina, if you weren't bargaining last night—" his gray eyes probed hers intently "—why did you put me off?"

"You have other commitments, Thorn. You're engaged."

"You weren't thinking of that at the time!"

She blushed and looked away. "It bordered on rape."

"I would hardly say that," he drawled laconically,

and she glanced up in embarrassment, then looked down at her hands.

"All right, that isn't the right word. I wanted us to stop because, on both our parts, every act was the result of anger and suspicion." Her cheeks burned as she remembered what they had shared. Yet she kept her eyes averted for fear that if she met his piercing gaze, he would see clearly the love she felt for him. After all the emotional upheaval, the one thing she didn't feel she could cope with was his pity, for she knew he didn't love her in return.

The silence stretched between them until she finally met his eyes. She hoped her features were as expressionless as his.

"I'm sorry about last night," he said quietly. "I guess there's been so much trouble at that damn mine site lately that I was beginning to lose my perspective. Outsiders in the past have tried to worm their way into my confidence, and I jumped to the conclusion that you were doing the same. It's not like me to behave so impetuously, and I apologize for suspecting you."

She shrugged and turned away, devastated by the longing to throw her arms around his neck, to pull him back down on the ground and ask him to finish what he had started last night.

"It doesn't matter." She forced out the words. "You were a stranger a week ago, so I didn't want to tell you my purpose in coming. Many men are derisive about women in agronomy, and I thought you'd feel strongly about it. I didn't want to be laughed at. Then, too, I didn't suppose you'd care at that point why I was in Brazil." Smoothing her hands against her slacks, she glanced up at him and adopted a brisk tone. "Anyway, it's over. Which way do we go today?"

Thorn assessed her thoughtfully, and her heart began to pound in her ears. He raised his arm to point. "We'll move with the stream and hope it empties into a tributary," he replied, turning to lead the way.

She followed, and for more than an hour they walked in silence, until finally she spoke up. "Thorn, I'm getting thirsty. Is this stream safe?"

He paused and dropped down beside the water. "It's as pure as you could hope for. Any impurities in these streams have long since been carried away."

She knelt and drank, then splashed her face liberally. After he had done the same, he explained, "Rivers that feed into the Amazon are three different colors. The ones that flow down from the north, like the Rio Negro, are black. Actually the so-called black rivers are more red. They run off the Guyana Shield and their color comes from the humus in the silt. Rivers that flow from the west are called white, but they look yellow brown. These are impure, carrying mud and silt down from the Andes. Streams like this one, where we are, also flow ultimately from a rock shield and are blue green because of their clear sandy beds. There is almost no material in suspension in the blue and black rivers, so they're as pure as you could ever want."

He sat back, one arm around his raised knees. Eyes twinkling, he added, "That doesn't mean it's safe.

There's still the *sucuri* in these waters, the giant anaconda, which can reach as much as forty feet in length. There are eels and caimans—"

"Thorn, please," she protested laughingly. "We've been through this before."

He stopped his good-natured teasing and asked instead, "How is your ankle?"

"Much better than yesterday. Thorn, I could eat the rocks in the stream, I'm so hungry." She pointed. "Even better, there are some frogs."

"Not that fellow," he replied.

A brightly colored yellow-and-green-striped frog hopped from rock to rock. "That's an arrow-poison frog," Thorn stated. "Some of the flashier ones have the deadliest toxin in the world, and tribes use the poison for their blowgun darts. There is one frog in the Amazon so poisonous that the tribesmen merely rub the tips of their darts over its skin to gather the poison. As for dinner, we need to conserve the remaining shots in the Bernardelli, so we may have to settle for fried grasshoppers."

Suddenly he straightened and pointed. "Look. I told you I'd show you an oddity if I spotted it. There's a cannonball tree. If that fruit falls, you'll understand the reason for its name. It sounds like an iron ball hitting the forest floor."

She followed his gaze. More than a hundred feet in the air, amid masses of tiny yellow flowers at the top of a trunk, hung brown balls of fruit that resembled elongated coconuts.

"I'll tell you what, Sabrina—stretch out and rest while I get something for us to eat."

She was happy enough to comply and sank down on the leaves, falling asleep within minutes.

Later she awakened to Thorn shaking her shoulder. The delicious aroma of wood smoke filled the air, and he handed her a green leaf filled with charred tidbits.

"Sabrina," he remarked, "if I were you, I'd just eat. Don't study your food or ask questions."

She smiled. "Thorn, I think I could even eat something that was still alive, I'm so hungry." Using the leaf as a plate, she sat up, crossed her legs and popped the morsels into her mouth, munching happily enough. Nearby, Thorn squatted on his haunches while he ate.

"How did you get these cooked?" she asked.

"After the fire died down, I roasted them in the ashes. This won't hold us long, but it's sustenance for now."

After drinking some more cold water, Sabrina felt refreshed and ready to continue. Thorn offered his hand to help her up, immediately releasing it and moving away once she was on her feet.

From mere inches the stream gradually widened to several feet, and the foliage along the banks became more and more dense as they walked. Midway through the afternoon, Thorn suddenly stopped and let out an exclamation of joy. Not quite tall enough to reach the upper canopy, a sturdy coconut palm stood in their path.

Spines like whiskers ran the length of the trunk except for smooth rings that indicated the growth of older fronds. Thorn scaled the tree carefully. In a short time he was down, had opened the fruit, and they were feasting on sweet milk and the pulp of ripe coconut. An afternoon shower came and passed, drenching them, then turning the air to steam. As the afternoon dwindled, Sabrina's ankle began to throb and she grew weary.

Training her eyes on Thorn's broad shoulders as he plunged ahead, hoping they would stop soon, she noticed him draw the Bernardelli.

"Thorn, what's wrong?" she asked.

"Nothing," he answered easily, and glanced reassuringly at her. "I just want to be ready in case dinner flies past."

At that moment something darted out from a clump of leaves, and in an instant Thorn shot it, then turned and smiled triumphantly at Sabrina.

"Now we have dinner. If you're squeamish, Sabrina, don't watch."

"I'm so constantly hungry, Thorn, that it won't matter what you cook." She dropped down to the ground with relief and noticed his eyes narrow.

Crossing to her, he knelt and placed the automatic on the ground. He picked up her foot and carefully removed her boot, inspecting her ankle before he commented, "Be truthful now. Does it hurt badly?"

She nodded. "But not anything like it did yesterday."

"Good. It looks better than it did."

"I might as well see about the cut on your head," she offered.

She got on her knees to remove the bandage, and Thorn sat on the ground. Trying not to touch him except where necessary, she was still conscious of him sitting so near—only a fraction of space between them. She touched his shoulder; her hip brushed his. Every contact was disturbing.

She concentrated fiercely on the tiny roll of gauze in her hand. "Thorn, when I change this bandage and apply a fresh one, it'll use up all the gauze we have."

"How does the cut look?"

"It's healing just fine."

"Then don't put a bandage on it. Leave it alone. Just use a little disinfectant."

When she started to argue, he insisted, "We ought to save that last piece for an emergency," and took the gauze from her, putting it in his pocket before he stood up. "Now look at the cut on my back, please."

He stripped off his shirt, and she examined his smooth muscled back. Instantly she felt a stir of longing. She knew the feel of that sinewy back beneath her hands. Tugging gently at the bandage, she said, "It's doing better than the cut on your forehead, Thorn."

"Then we'll leave that off, also." He turned and took the old dressings away to burn.

While Thorn gathered leaves and twigs for a fire, she removed the bandage from her hand, then went to help him. When he was ready for the final step, placing the papers from his hatband on the fire, he looked up at her solemnly, and Sabrina felt a chill of foreboding. "Sabrina, we're out of lighter fluid."

"You mean we won't have any more fires—no

more cooking meat?'' she asked as the significance of his words dawned on her.

Not answering immediately, he picked up the automatic, removed a cartridge, forced it open and mixed some of the powder with the paper and leaves. "We'll have this fire, but not many more, no."

"What are you doing? Will you rub two sticks together?"

He smiled. "Not this time," and removed the wide buckle on his belt. Looking at it, she instantly recalled how it had bitten into her bare flesh, the hard cold touch of it against her skin.

Thorn found a stone, rubbed it against the buckle until it was hot, then pushed it into the pile of paper and powder. A puff went up, and she applauded as a bright orange flame appeared.

He bowed with a grin, but her smile at his jaunty reaction soon faded. "Thorn, how many cartridges are left?"

"Three," he answered quietly. Fanning the fire, he knelt with one knee on the ground, one raised with his arm resting across it. "We'll take each day as it comes, Sabrina, and do the best we can."

She marveled at his resourcefulness as he cooked and dressed the meat. When she bit into it, she found it delicious and asked, "What are we eating tonight?"

"A paca—another jungle rodent but an excellent meal. Indians eat them."

She studied Thorn thoughtfully. Rarely had he complained of hunger. He had divided everything evenly. Yet considering his size, his appetite would be much larger than hers. "You're very competent, especially since you come from a household where you don't have to lift a finger for anything," Sabrina remarked.

Thorn merely smiled at her and remained silent.

After dark Sabrina stretched out on the broad leaves that Thorn had picked earlier. A few yards away, he sat casually against the trunk of a tree, one arm resting on his knee in a familiar pose.

In the intimacy of the darkness and quiet, memories of the previous night weighed heavily on her. She couldn't ignore thoughts of his lovemaking, the recollection of his touch, his kisses.

His voice was deep as he asked, "Sabrina, are you in love with Roddy?"

Amused, she replied, "No."

"Who are you in love with, then?"

Her heart thudded against her ribs. "Thorn, I don't care to discuss it," she replied, and rolled over with her back to him.

After a moment he remarked in a bemused tone, "I thought most women liked to extol the virtues of their beloved."

"I haven't heard you praising Amanda!" she snapped.

"My marriage to Amanda has been determined since childhood, as you know," he stated flatly.

Sitting up, she turned to face him. "Haven't you ever been in love?"

He smiled indulgently, and she recalled their talk at Bellefontaine. "Sabrina, what is love? It's a romantic notion. In your country the right toothpaste and the best shampoo will bring you the man of your dreams, isn't that so?"

"You're avoiding the issue. I know there have been women in your life. Hasn't there ever been one you were in love with?"

"And what does 'in love' mean?" he persisted.

The amusement in his evasive question stirred her indignation. How could he sit there, so insulated from the torment she suffered? He felt nothing. Yet she loved him with all her heart and soul—no doubt forever.

Her answer burst forth impetuously. "It means caring about the other person beyond all reason, wanting them whether that wanting is returned or not, thinking of their happiness first—and never being able to stop those feelings. It is little things and big things: sitting by a campfire, walking in the rain, just holding hands, as well as feeling as if your whole aim in life is to find this one person, then give them everything you possibly can. Haven't you ever felt that?" she cried.

He shook his head with a smile. His voice was light and patronizing, as if speaking to a child. "You're very young, Sabrina."

"You've never once felt that way?" she demanded angrily.

He shrugged indifferently and waved his hand in a gesture of dismissal. "Perhaps for a fleeting moment, when I was around fifteen years of age. I survived that experience. Since then, in any relationships I've had, I've been honest and frank, making it clear that someday I would be expected to marry Amanda.

Either that was accepted from the first, or in some cases I've known women who have felt the same way as many men. They prefer their own independence and take relationships rather lightly."

A cynical note crept into his voice. "With some, a few baubles or a diamond bracelet—that sort of thing—softens the sharp edges of parting."

She stared at him in pain and consternation and longing. Why did she have to feel this way for such an arrogant cynical man? Yet even as the thought ran through her mind, she remembered the tenderness he had shown, the moments of solace, his teasing and laughter.

"Well—" he shifted and spoke brightly "—you've told me how you feel about love. He's a very fortunate fellow, Sabrina, in spite of your naiveté." Then one dark eyebrow curved in question. "But I still don't understand. If you have all these marvelous strong feelings for this man—that he's the other part of you, that you're not complete without him—then why won't you discuss him at all?" The lightness suddenly left his voice, to be replaced by harshness. "And why do you fall so eagerly into another man's arms?"

Hiding the desolation that swamped her, she stated flatly, unemotionally, "He doesn't love me, and since he doesn't, I find it difficult to resist your expert lovemaking."

Instantly his voice changed. "Sabrina, I'm sorry."

He made a move as if to cross to where she was sitting, but she waved her hand quickly to ward him off. Struggling to sound indifferent, she replied,

"It's nothing. Thorn, I'm tired and my ankle is beginning to bother me again. I'd like to sleep." She took a deep breath, locking her hands tightly together. "You'd make it easier for me if you wouldn't—"

"Sabrina," he interrupted, his voice filled with a tenderness far more crushing than all his anger.

She spoke quickly against her own threatening weakness. "If we're to get anywhere tomorrow, I have to get some sleep." She stretched out with deliberation and turned her back to him. Lying perfectly still, she struggled to breathe normally instead of yielding to the sobs rising in her throat.

Tears dripped off her face to fall onto her hand, and she said a small prayer that they would reach help soon. She couldn't take many more days of being alone with Thorn without revealing everything. She didn't want his pity. Even his anger was better than that. Sighing heavily, she pictured him sleeping peacefully only yards away. Brief and restless, sleep finally came to her.

THURSDAY MORNING SHE AWAKENED to Thorn regarding her intently with gray eyes that were dark and solemn. Cool dew dripped off a tree and splashed on her arm as she stood up and turned away. Their constant togetherness made every second increasingly difficult.

She hadn't taken two steps when his hands settled lightly on her shoulders and he turned her to face him. Speaking tenderly, Thorn said, "Don't you realize that if I can stir you, possibly the love you feel for this man isn't as deep as you think?"

Sabrina quietly studied each feature of his face, the thin bridge of his nose with a slight crook, the bruise on his cheek turning yellow, his dark lashes, the long thin cut. Her eyes moved to his mouth.

"I need some privacy to wash, Thorn. I'll be back in a minute." She paused. "May I use the comb?" Silently he handed it to her, and she hurried upstream out of his sight.

When she returned, he was pulling on his boots. The comb fell from her hands, and Sabrina bent down to retrieve it. As she straightened, she found herself looking directly into a pair of dark serious eyes in a brown face, peering from between the broad leaves of a nearby jungle plant.

CHAPTER ELEVEN

STARTLED, SABRINA GASPED and took a step backward. But thinking quickly while the man stared blankly back at her, she realized that he might mean help for them. She murmured a greeting that caused no change of expression on his face.

Attempting to convey her meaning, she spoke louder. "I have a friend. We're lost," she added, when from behind her she heard Thorn's Portuguese greeting.

The men spoke to each other. Thorn used Portuguese first, then lapsed into something unintelligible to Sabrina. While he talked, he waved his hands to punctuate his sentences.

Finally the man nodded and motioned to him to follow, turning and leading the way through the trees. With a smile Thorn took her hand, leaned close and brushed her forehead lightly with a quick kiss. "You found water. Now you've found a native. You're a marvel, Sabrina! You didn't need me at all."

Wordlessly she gazed after him, thankful that he had turned away. He noticed far too much, and she didn't trust her own responses to him—especially when he praised her.

After a short trek they entered a clearing that contained small patches of banana, tobacco, cotton and maize crops. Five malocas, communal houses made of palm fronds, faced into the open space, and in an outer ring were four smaller huts. Scattered around the village were white mounds of flour that had been made from the staple, manioc root. When some of the villagers came forward to greet them, Sabrina got lost in the verbal exchange, but it was clear they were welcome.

In a short time they were fed a sumptuous meal of bush turkey sprinkled with *farinha*, extracted from manioc flour. Sabrina delighted in every bite, relishing the mixture of bananas, coconut and *beijus*, roasted manioc cakes they had for dessert, so delicious after the sparse fare they had shared during their trek.

In the afternoon Thorn disappeared with the men, and Sabrina was left with the women and children. She watched the women work at weaving hammocks from strands of palm-leaf fiber and cotton thread, their smooth brown skin unadorned except for anklets and hipbands. Later, using a calabash shell to pour water, Sabrina bathed and washed her hair in a stream only a few yards from the point where it emptied into a narrow river channel.

By nightfall the men had returned, and they all ate fish, cakes and soup—another meal that seemed like heavenly fare to Sabrina when compared to fried grasshoppers. Afterward Thorn took her hand and led her toward one of the small huts.

They strolled across the village in any easy silence,

and after a time Sabrina said, "This has been an interesting day, Thorn. It's difficult to imagine living this way all the time, though."

He smiled. "They may have a better life than we do—not so many complications." His voice became solemn. "They may face a bleak future, too. Developers are planning new roads through Amazonia, and anthropologists are predicting disaster for the Indians if these roads are built. These people don't have much resistance to the diseases of civilization. Even colds can destroy whole tribes."

"They've been so nice to us, Thorn. It's horrible to think of them not surviving." She glanced around. "In all this quiet primitive living, it's also difficult to think of the bustle of Washington or Sao Paulo."

"I know what you mean. They've given us a hut for tonight, Sabrina. In the morning they'll provide us with supplies, a dugout and a guide for a few miles." And as he talked Sabrina wondered if she would ever again stroll in the darkness, walk in the rain or sit around a campfire without thinking of Thorn.

"A penny for your thoughts," Thorn murmured with a quizzical smile.

She looked down. "I just wondered how long I'll remember all this."

He halted and took hold of her hands. "I don't think we'll ever fully forget. It would be impossible." His gaze traveled around the clearing, then returned to rest on her. "I'll never forget anyway. Sabrina, you've been a help, you've been fun—"

"A virtual paragon," she remarked lightly, and attempted to turn away, but his hands tightened on hers.

"Sabrina, whoever he is, quit wasting your time on him. He mustn't have an iota of sense." He looked at her intently. "Forget him."

"Of course, Thorn." She forced a smile. "I'll do that first thing when we return."

He didn't smile but continued to gaze at her intently. Releasing her hands after a moment, he draped his arm over her shoulder to continue walking.

They entered the circular hut, where inside, hammocks hung from sturdy poles. The hut was also equipped with machetes, arrows and large baskets. "They make these huts round so there won't be any corners where evil spirits can hide," Thorn explained.

But Sabrina's attention was caught by the two hammocks so close together. As if guessing her thoughts, he commented, "They think we're husband and wife, and here it's customary for the wife to sleep in the hammock beneath her husband's."

"That's fine, Thorn," she answered quickly, and sat down in her hammock to remove her boots. The semblance of intimate routine, of being in the same room, of going to bed, made her far more self-conscious in Thorn's presence than she had been in the jungle.

Gradually her eyes adjusted to dimness, and she turned to see Thorn tugging his shirt out of his belt. His profile was to her as he unbuttoned the shirt and peeled it away from his broad shoulders. She couldn't take her eyes away. She knew how his bare smooth shoulders felt to her fingers, the hard muscles in his arms. Her mouth felt dry and her body tensed, burning with longing.

He turned to drape his shirt on the foot of his hammock, glancing down at her as he did so, and she was certain he could hear her heart thud against her ribs. Her eyes raked over his chest, remembering clearly how it felt against her bare flesh.

In a low voice he said, "These hammocks ought to be marvelous after our nights on the ground." She couldn't answer but lay silently watching him. His hammock sagged with his weight as he sat down above her and removed his boots before stretching out and placing his hands behind his head.

When he spoke, his voice was deep and quiet. "Djonoti, the man who led us here, indicated we're two to three days away from the first sizable village."

She shifted carefully and tried to think of traveling again, of the river, the jungle—anything except the half-naked man who lay only inches away above her. Turning carefully, she murmured, "That's good news. But I don't agree with you about this hammock. I may fall out of it during the night."

Chuckling deep in his throat, he said, "No, you won't. They're delightful after you get the knack. I have one in my room at Bellefontaine, as you know."

"How long did it take for you to get the knack?"

"Truthfully, I don't ever remember thinking it difficult, but I started when I was a small child."

"At least I don't feel like something is crawling around under me."

"That's why a hammock is so satisfactory in the tropics," he replied.

Their voices held the hushed softness of intimacy, and Sabrina struggled to keep her mind on other things, to forget the privacy of the hut, his nearness. Finally she heard his steady deep breathing and guessed he was asleep. She shifted and closed her eyes.

SHE AWAKENED TO DARKNESS, feeling stiff and uncomfortable. Slipping out of the hammock, she straightened, stretching her arms overhead, and looked down at Thorn, only a foot away in his hammock.

His head was turned toward her. His eyes were closed, the dark lashes feathered against his cheekbones. His bruised flesh had begun to heal; the cut was a dark line across his temple. His thick black hair, in disarray over his forehead, hid part of the wound. In sleep the harsh lines were gone from his face, giving him a gentle little-boy look.

A wave of longing washed over Sabrina, and she reached out to touch his hand.

But knowing how easily he could be awakened, she withdrew it. Her gaze ran the length of his relaxed body, as if memorizing him. Below his bare chest the ragged denims were tight across his trim hips and muscled legs. How could she love him so much—feel such a deep need for him?

With a slow lingering observation her eyes moved upward, watching the steady rise and fall of his bronzed chest, agleam in the moonlight filtering into the hut. In spite of the thick hair curling against the nape of his neck and full sideburns, his jaw was clean-shaven.

When she encountered his intent gray eyes, Sabrina gasped. Her face burned with embarrassment, and she struggled to sound calm. "I couldn't sleep," she stated. The words came out in a breathless whisper. At the intensity of his look her heart pounded in her ears.

"Come here, Sabrina," he commanded.

She couldn't take her eyes from his. Even though she was torn with unbearable longing, she shook her head.

In one lithe movement he swung his feet to the ground, reached for her and pulled her into his arms. A soft cry rose in her throat, but it wasn't uttered. Instead she wrapped her arms around his neck and shifted closer against him. A burning passionate kiss carried her beyond reason.

Golden strands of her hair cascaded over their shoulders, pale against his dark skin. In the distance the jungle was coming alive with the sounds of insects, bird cries and growls, but Sabrina heard nothing except their own heartbeats.

Her fingers slipped up the strong column of his throat to wind in his hair; she breathed in lingering traces of wood smoke.

Thorn kissed her slowly, with deliberation, while one hand caressed her back, pressing her slender pliant body against his. His other hand unbuttoned her shirt to explore every contour. His wide cold belt buckle bit into her flesh, but she ignored it in the rush of warm pleasure his touch evoked.

Sabrina was torn between bliss and agony, between the tempestuous arousal of her body and the small voice of sanity that warned of disaster. Time and again she returned his unbridled kisses, caressing his copper skin that looked so tough, yet felt as smooth as satin. She had to fight the declarations of love that automatically sprang to her lips. How right it seemed to be in his arms! She felt as if she belonged there. How would she ever be able to forget his rapturous kisses?

The hunger she'd known in the jungle was nothing compared to this insatiable need for him. Her pent-up longings burst free, and with increasing fierceness Thorn aroused ardent responses in her, kindling an unquenchable fire. Every inch of her cried out for her to yield to him, to give herself totally, body as well as heart. At the same time reason reminded her how empty life would be afterward.

If she succumbed to a passionate moment, how could she live each day with only a memory—unable to love him, to cherish his hard masculine body or give herself to him again and again?

She fought a silent battle, trying to decide which would be the greater disaster—to stop now and never know his body fully, to deny what she wanted more than anything else; or to yield—and then be forever tormented. Once they'd made love, how could she live with the thought that it meant little to him or that each night he would hold Amanda in his arms? Amanda, who would bear his children, care for him, love him....

With a sob deep in her throat she made her choice.

Pushing him away, Sabrina whispered, "Don't, Thorn. I can't go on."

His eyes were dark, stormy, as he snapped, "God, Sabrina! What do you think I'm made of? More than once now you've tormented the hell out of me. Then suddenly you stop cold."

"I'm sorry, but it's impossible," she whispered in anguish, turning to snatch up her discarded blouse.

He caught her easily and drew her to him. Stripped to the waist, he pressed his chest against her as he tilted her face up to his. "Who is this man you love, Sabrina?"

The last thing she wanted was his pity. She squeezed her eyes shut painfully. "Thorn, please don't ask."

"Answer my question, Sabrina."

She turned her face away, but he caught her chin and tilted it up. "Look at me," he ordered.

"Please, you're hurting me."

"I don't think I am," he answered gently. "Sabrina, tell me the name of the man you love."

She opened her eyes, looked into his and knew he could easily see his answer.

"Oh, Lord," he whispered. With infinite tenderness he leaned down to kiss her. His mouth was warm, his lips gentle, breaking her heart into a thousand fragments. She tasted the salt of her tears and tore her lips from his.

His arms tightened to hold her as he pushed her head against his chest and murmured softly, "I'm not worth one second of this. It's the tropics, the long distance from home and familiar faces. When you're back in Tennessee, you'll forget me, as you should."

Clamping her jaws together, she held back the protest that rose within her. In a moment, after she had regained her composure, she looked up at him. "Thorn, I didn't mean to be a tease."

His gray eyes were piercing, studying her with a deliberation that made her knees grow weak. Suddenly he groaned and leaned down to scoop her swiftly into his arms.

"We've got to get out of this hut!" he growled. In quick strides he moved outside, while Sabrina snatched up her blouse and scrambled to get it on and buttoned.

"Thorn! I'm not dressed!"

He set her on her feet and laughed. "Sabrina, every other female in this village goes around stark naked except for two bracelets." Fumbling in his pocket, he produced paper and a small pouch of tobacco to roll a cigarette.

She stood quietly, watching him a moment, before she asked, "Now that we're out here, what'll we do?"

He squinted at her through a small cloud of exhaled smoke. "Something sane," Thorn replied. "Wait a minute, Sabrina." He dashed inside the hut, then returned with their boots. As soon as they were on, he took her hand.

Sabrina walked beside him, willing her mind a blank, grateful that they had left the intimate atmosphere of the hut. Although covered with a sheen of perspiration, she shivered.

Thorn put his arm companionably around her shoulders and smiled at her. "Let's go down to the river and watch the fish swim."

She laughed. "That sounds safe enough, Thorn."

Silently they crossed the open area of the village, then headed for the river. "When I was with the men today, there was a place where some were swimming," Thorn remarked. "I'll show you."

After they had reached the spot, for some time they gazed silently into the beauty of the dark water. Silvery moonlight shimmered across its surface.

Suddenly inspired, Thorn turned to grasp first one liana, then another, testing their relative strength. Finally he found one that satisfied him.

With a rush he ran forward, clutched the vine and jumped. Sabrina gasped as he swung across the river and landed on the opposite bank. Uttering a wild whoop, he repeated the performance, landing beside her.

Sabrina laughed delightedly, and he looked at her and said, "Your turn."

Recklessness, plus a willingness to do anything to take her mind off the past hour, made her accept. His hand tightened. "Hey! I was just kidding."

"I'm not," she answered lightly, and ran toward the river. As the bank fell away, she locked her hands tightly around the coarse vine. The liana bit into her flesh. She'd swung just wide enough to reach the far bank. When she landed on the return, Thorn's arms closed around her and he took the vine. He sailed away with another whoop.

Suddenly a rustling and popping sounded in the

branches overhead. The liana snapped, and Thorn dropped into the river. Instantly he surfaced and with a jerk of his head tossed the water out of his eyes.

Sabrina doubled over in a fit of laughter. She sat down on the bank to wait for him and felt all the tension bubbling out in her laughter. Before she knew what was happening, Thorn was at the water's edge. His hand closed over her ankle, and he yanked her down toward the water.

"So you think that's funny!" he said.

She shrieked and attempted to scramble free. With a laugh he released her, then pulled himself up and flopped down on the bank beside her.

"Are you cold?" she asked.

"No. I'd like another cigarette, but that's out now." Looking down at her, he smiled. "I like to see you laugh." He tugged a boot free and poured the water from it. "Tell me about your family," he added. "You know far too much about mine already."

For nearly an hour they sat and talked. Then Thorn stood up, pulled her to her feet and took her hand as they strolled back to the hut.

When they reached it, he turned her toward him and rested his hands lightly on her shoulders. "You go in and get some sleep. I'll come in later."

"I'd rather do it the other way around," she replied. "You sleep."

He smiled and spoke gently. "Sabrina, somewhere there is a man who will make you far happier than I ever could." He touched her chin lightly. "Your love is flattering, but are you sure it isn't just infatuation?

Within a month after you're home you'll have forgotten all about this."

"Thorn, you act as if I'm a child who has scraped its knee. Wipe away my tears, take me down to the river for some laughs to take my mind off the hurt, pat me on the head and tell me everything will be all right—and that's that."

"Now Sabrina," he replied patiently, "answer me truthfully. Have you ever been in love before?"

She shook her head and whispered, "No, not like this."

With maddening cheerfulness he replied, "One day it will be the real thing—I promise you."

All the companionship, the calm of the past hour, evaporated. Hurt, embarrassment and anger filled her. "You've never been in love, Thorn," she said quietly. "You've said that before. I believe you now. For all your expert lovemaking, all your experience, you don't know anything about love. I wonder if your whole life has been a cold calculated taking of what you want without ever feeling anything."

"What you're experiencing is the impetuousness of youth," he stated, condescendingly amused.

"And you're so old!" she snapped. "Love comes at any age, Thorn! It's not something rational or the wisest course or even desirable. Do you think I like this! The only reason I held back from you is that I can't bear the heartache of not being free to love you...."

His arm went around her shoulders. "Sabrina—"

Infuriated by his composure, by his patronizing tone, she stepped back and cried, "Don't you touch me! If I have your pity, Thorn Catlin, then you have mine! Until you love you're not really alive. Love is more important than anything else, than a job or a plantation or money—''

"Sabrina, dearest...." he murmured again, and stepped toward her.

"Get away from me!" Running blindly across the compound, desperate to get away from him, she didn't stop until she reached the river, where she knelt down to splash water on her face, drying her eyes with her shirt.

She glanced behind her, but all was quiet. The first streaks of dawn were graying the sky; the stars had faded long ago. Sabrina sank down on the bank to rest, because she couldn't bear to go back to the confining hut and face Thorn.

A long time passed before she heard footsteps approaching, and looked up to see Thorn and Djonoti. They greeted her perfunctorily, then gazed downriver while Djonoti gestured and talked. Finally they turned back toward the huts. With a jerk of his hand Thorn motioned to her. "Come on, Sabrina. We'll eat before they send us on our way."

Brushing leaves off her clothing, she got up reluctantly and fell into step behind them, observing Thorn's long stride, his broad shoulders as he walked. He was dressed again in his khaki shirt and ragged denims. Black swarms of flies buzzed around their ankles, hovering about five inches off the ground.

They breakfasted on pineapple, coconut milk, varieties of banana and manioc cakes, then were given supplies to carry to the river. Bananas, coconuts, a pineapple, a spear, a machete, two hammocks and a sling made of bark, called a tumpline, were placed in the dugout. A guide, Benpire, accompanied them. After an attempt to convey their gratitude to the villagers, they shoved the dugout into the river. Djonoti waved and patted the Bernardelli that Thorn had given him.

There was no more insect repellent. They had used the last of it in the village. In its place, both Sabrina and Thorn were covered in coconut oil, which Sabrina had watched the women prepare the day before. After the white coconut meat was boiled in water, the oil bubbled to the surface, to be scooped off and ladled into a gourd.

Earlier that morning Sabrina had plaited her hair, and it now hung down her back in one long braid. She had also insisted that one of the village women take the *figa* as a gift for her hospitality.

It was their fourth day in the jungle, and Sabrina was sure that their families had been notified of the crash by now. Although neither of them discussed it, she knew it weighed as heavily on Thorn as it did on her.

She was thankful for Benpire's company, which helped to diffuse the tension between her and Thorn, and dreaded the moment when he would tell them goodbye. That moment came all too swiftly, because he refused to go too far from his village. When they halted alongside a long bank of sand, they all stepped out of the dugout. Benpire spoke briefly to Thorn, nodded to Sabrina, then disappeared into the jungle.

Thorn stared after him for a few moments, then motioned toward the dugout. "Get in and I'll push off."

"Can I help?"

He shook his head. "Sabrina, these waters are crawling with stingrays, piranhas, electric eels and other undesirable creatures. Don't yield to one of your impulses and jump in."

"Did you think that last night?" she asked.

"It was probably safer there," he answered quietly, then pushed off and jumped into the boat. It rocked, steadied, and he sat down to paddle.

While Sabrina pulled her paddle through the clear blue green water, she studied the lush vegetation growing along each bank and marveled that they had been able to trek through it. Even as she watched, there was a flash of movement. The largest snake Sabrina had ever seen slithered into the river, then swam alongside the bank, sending undulating ripples across the water.

"Thorn...."

"We've finally seen our first anaconda, Sabrina." The snake's head disappeared from view, but during the morning they sighted many other varieties of water life: fish, turtles, lizards, snakes and a host of wildlife. At times the current became sluggish. Once they passed a sandbank where dark green caimans stared sullenly back at them with unwinking black eyes.

As the hours passed the air became hot and steaming. Sabrina felt certain they had made a circle in a loop in the river, but she said nothing. Her shirt clung damply to her back and the thought of a cooling river swim seemed more and more enticing. At midday they moored along a sandbank to stretch and eat some of the food given them by the villagers. Shortly afterward they set out again.

The current was gaining force; they rounded a bend and found themselves being sucked into a short run of rapids. Behind her Thorn rowed violently, shouting commands to her until they were through the whirling water.

Sabrina felt limp with relief as he called out, "Good girl, Sabrina! That was excellent."

The shadows were gradually lengthening across the water now, and Thorn informed her that he was watching for a likely sandbank to pull up to for the night.

Sobering, Sabrina stared ahead. She dreaded the intimacy of those idle nighttime hours with Thorn. During long days of trekking through the jungle, they had been too busy to become concerned over personal matters, but during the quiet lulls of camping, waiting for a new day, it had been very difficult to remain impersonal—as Sabrina had discovered to her cost.

Her anxiety deepened when she saw him point in the direction of a long bar of white sand. They slid against it, and Thorn jumped out to tug the dugout above the water's edge. When Sabrina stood up, he reached over to lift her out. The moment his hands came into contact with her waist, a current of electricity seemed to course through her, and Sabrina knew Thorn felt it, too. His eyes were thoughtful as she stepped abruptly away from him. While she gathered twigs for the fire, Thorn squatted along the riverbank and hoisted the spear Djonoti had given him.

Curiosity overcame Sabrina, and she knelt beside him to watch. In a short time dark shadows appeared under the surface of the water—three fish swimming past. Suddenly Thorn sank the spear and lifted it in a rush. A fish flapped on the end, splattering drops of water over them. Sabrina moved away to build the fire while he cleaned the fish.

He worked silently until he had the fish on a stick, roasting over a fire. "We'll have a banquet tonight," he said with satisfaction, leaning back against a log and unplugging a gourd of water given to them by the villagers. He offered it to her, then drank after she had finished. Closing his eyes, he stretched out. When she glanced at him a moment later, she saw that he was asleep. Memories of last night crowded in, and she turned hastily away.

The fish was delicious, baked to perfection some time later. Darkness came, and Sabrina's self-consciousness increased by the minute. Restless, she crossed to the water's edge to gaze at the river. A bright moon shone down, reflecting on the water's rippling surface.

"Sabrina," Thorn called softly, "come back here. It's not safe there. I won't bother you, I promise."

With a sigh she strolled back to the dying fire, stretching out across from him.

THE NEXT THING she knew, the first light of dawn was streaking the sky. Thick fog lay on the river, surrounding them with gray, making it seem as if nothing else in the world existed except the small bar of sand and themselves.

While Thorn slept on, Sabrina decided to do something about breakfast. She picked up the spear and took it to the river. After half a dozen tries she finally managed to spear a fish. She built a fire, retrieved the knife and cleaned her catch. Just as she was finishing, she looked up to find Thorn watching her.

"I'll be damned," he murmured with amusement. "Where did you learn to clean fish?"

"From dad. I was the tomboy of the family."

"You really don't need my help at all."

"You come in handy sometimes," she answered, smiling.

His hand closed over hers, and he took the fish. "I'll finish up. Go freshen yourself up if you like."

She left him by the fire, and when she returned, the appetizing aroma of smoke and fish filled the air. Thorn was squatting beside the river, shaving with the gleaming sharp-edged knife. Thick swirling fog had begun to roll off the water, causing a chill to run through her.

As he crossed to the fire, Thorn saw her shiver and frowned. "Are you cold?"

"No—" Sabrina shook her head "—I just feel as if something is wrong."

"Don't tell me you have premonitions," he teased her.

Solemnly she answered, "No, but it's gloomy today. I suppose my mood is affected."

"Well, come cook breakfast. Slaving over a hot spit should raise your spirits."

She crossed to the fire but paused there. "Thorn, why were you so angry when Wade took me to see the *macumba* rite?"

His eyes darkened, and he poked the fire viciously. "I already told you. I don't believe in it, Sabrina, and I don't like to have it practiced at Bellefontaine." He met her eyes squarely.

"That isn't the only reason, is it?" she asked.

He shook his head. "No."

"I'm sorry. I didn't mean to pry."

"No, I want to tell you.... My mother was a great believer in *macumba*. I have some bad memories of it." His eyes narrowed, and he stirred the ashes beneath the spit. "My father remarried, Sabrina, and I feel like Laurel and Wade's mother was my mother—prefer to believe it, in fact. My own mother ran away."

She had a sudden suspicion he'd admitted something that he'd never revealed to anyone else. "I'm sorry, Thorn," she said again, knowing the words were inadequate.

He looked down and shrugged. "It doesn't matter anymore," he replied, and she had a quick picture of him as a child, locking away his feelings from a stern father. "Thorn, was there...anybody you could turn to when your mother died?"

He looked up with a quick smile. Ruffling her hair in a casual gesture, he answered, "I wasn't trying for sympathy, Sabrina," and removed the fish from the fire.

His reply was as revealing as a direct answer would have been. She knew then that there hadn't been anyone. His back was to her, and as she looked at him, she felt a rush of sympathy overwhelm her. She thought about their days together; this would be their fifth. In some ways it seemed as if she had known Thorn forever, and yet it seemed there were things about him that she would never understand. Interrupting her thoughts, he indicated that breakfast was ready, and she joined him to eat the fish.

It wasn't long before they were on the river again. They had paddled for only a short time when an island of green appeared. Thorn swore softly, but Sabrina heard him. "What is it?" she asked.

"This damn river is treacherous. I don't know which way to go. We could take the wrong tributary from this point and lose days paddling along some backwater."

She looked ahead as the island of spiked grasses, trees with large buttresses and tangled roots loomed closer. The current flowed steadily swifter, until Thorn suddenly called out, "To the right!" and they moved into a different channel and veered to the west.

Throughout the morning they were forced to make these split-second choices, and Sabrina could tell by Thorn's air of intense concentration that he was very worried. He paddled in silence for more than an hour before he asked if she wanted to stop to eat.

"No, I'm fine," Sabrina answered truthfully.

"Then we'll keep on." He continued to converse, seeming more at ease, and she realized they had gone for an hour without having to make a decision about which branch of the river to follow. Humming, he soon broke into a full-throated baritone, singing lustily. His voice carried over the river, and a chattering group of spider monkeys screamed their protests from the bank. Sabrina collapsed in a fit of giggles.

Thorn grinned at her. "I'm glad my audience has no tomatoes or rotten eggs to throw. I'm certain I'd get a direct barrage."

After a few moments he began a tune that she was familiar with, and Sabrina sang along. As the sun climbed, they paddled, their voices carrying across the water and mingling with the jungle sounds.

All at once Thorn grew quiet. "Let's row toward the bank, Sabrina."

She did as he instructed, realizing the current had grown stronger. Glancing over her shoulder, she saw the muscles in Thorn's arms bulge as he fought the strong flow of water. Gradually they began to move from the center of the river.

"Row, Sabrina! Pull for all your worth!"

But she found it difficult to paddle at all. Cold fear gripped her. Above the chattering of the birds and the splash of their paddles she heard a roar.

Although they were moving faster each second, pulling with all their might, they were still yards from the bank. They reached a bend and were swept around it. Trees rushed past. The water's roar intensified, until they rounded another curve and the roar swelled to a cascading rumble. Tumbling and whipping over rocks in swirling angry swiftness, the river dropped away before them.

Sabrina felt her heart lurch. They had had difficulties earlier on but hadn't faced anything as frightening as the rush of water ahead. "Thorn! What should we do?"

Sabrina looked back at him, and he motioned toward the bank, but she knew it was useless. He was working furiously, paddling first on one side, then the other, pushing against rocks, fighting with all his strength to combat the rapids. They were caught up in a torrent of white water then. The little dugout shot forward and dropped, tipping at an angle before it fell.

Sabrina lost her paddle and gripped the side of the dugout, panic-stricken. She could do nothing to help Thorn now. He struggled as they reached another drop, and once again the dugout tilted crazily, then rushed over the rocks.

Spray splashed over them, drenching them. The roar was deafening. The dugout rocked violently, then righted itself as they catapulted over a steep drop toward a boulder, landing, miraculously, intact.

Scraping over smaller rocks to the left of the boulder, they spun out over another drop. Spuming white water continued to thrust them forward. The dugout tipped, tilted, and Sabrina lost her hold. She fell. Cold foaming water rushed to meet her. She just had time to scream before it smashed over her....

CHAPTER TWELVE

COUGHING AND CHOKING, she bobbed to the surface, her lungs exploding before she managed to gulp in some air. Then the current sucked her under again. She fought with all her strength against the rushing water, but found herself helplessly slammed into a rock and went under again.

Flailing with her arms and legs, she burst above the surface. Thrashing to keep her head up, Sabrina flung off the hampering boots. The current carried her along for a few more torturous seconds before she saw ahead, like a nightmare realized, the dugout bobbing and turning, upside down in the water.

"Thorn!" The cry was torn from her, lost in the cascading roar of the rapids. Her muscles ached. She couldn't fight much longer. Ahead, blessedly, stretched a sandbar. Sabrina struggled to reach it and finally pulled herself to dry land.

She rolled, gasping and in pain, to lie stretched out on her stomach on the sand while she tried to draw sufficient air into her deprived lungs. "Thorn!" She called out again, his name a mere croak. Her shoulder throbbed, and she battled unconsciousness, then gave up as blackness enveloped her.

When Sabrina opened her eyes, she panicked, struggling to sit up. The world swam. There wasn't any sign of Thorn, and her voice didn't seem to work anymore. The sight of the vast river rippling and swirling in front of her filled her with fear.

Then she heard her name, and Thorn appeared through the brush, running across the sand to her. She threw her arms around his neck without hesitation.

"Sabrina, love," he murmured, and crushed her against him. Swinging her up into his arms, he held her tightly, and she clung to him as another wave of dizziness rocked her. "I was afraid something had happened to you, Thorn," she gasped. His shirt was gone, and she was pressed against his bare chest. Her blue shirt was torn, one sleeve almost ripped away.

He kissed the top of her head, her temples, her cheek, and overwhelmingly thankful that he was alive, Sabrina raised her mouth to his. Thorn kissed her tenderly.

"Thank heaven you're all right!" he exclaimed. "Are you hurt?"

She shook her head. "All over, but not seriously. I think I'll be all right in a minute."

"I need to see if I can find the dugout," he said, glancing around anxiously. "Sabrina, promise me you'll wait right here."

"I'll stay here," she agreed as he lowered her gently to the sand. Brushing her hair away from her face with a featherlike touch, he knelt to kiss her lightly on the forehead before he stood up, then hurried out of sight into the tangle of vines and trees.

After what seemed like an endless hour Thorn returned, moving along the shallows at the water's edge and dragging the dugout behind him. Tugging it up on land, he faced her grimly.

"We've lost everything—hammocks, food, the machete." Patting the knife strapped to his waist, he added, "This is all we have, but at least we're on the river and the coconuts are plentiful. I'll get something for us to eat."

He returned with a handful of berries, a pile of sticks and several coconuts. Using his knife, he cut into one so they could drink the milk and eat the sweet meat. Sabrina studied him surreptitiously, discovering his eyes on her every time she did so.

Finally she asked, "Are you worried about our chances of getting out of here now?"

"No. We'll get back. I don't have any doubts about that."

She swung her head around in agitation. "Do you ever have any doubts about anything in your life?"

Instantly she wished she could take back her words. Thorn's gray eyes had grown stormy and piercing, and with a quick movement he got up and went to wade into the river. Selecting a large flat rock, he carried it up onto the hot sand. While he worked, cutting a wide strip of bark from a tree to place it beneath the rock, she noticed his boots were missing. The denim pants were ripped in jagged lengths just above his knees.

Taciturn and solemn, he broke open more of the coconuts, scored the outside of the kernels and placed them on the rock in the hot sunshine.

"Thorn, what are you doing?"

He turned brooding gray eyes on her. "It won't take more than two hours before the sun causes the coconut oil to drip out onto the rock. From there it will run down onto the bark I put underneath. I'll hollow out a coconut shell to use for a container, drain the oil off the bark into it—and we'll have insect repellent. There are hundreds of ways to use coconuts."

She watched as he whittled away at the ends of the sticks he'd gathered until he had a makeshift spear and a bundle of stout sticks with sharp points. Sabrina thought she should be helping him, but he seemed so unapproachable, silent and morose, and she couldn't guess why. Surely her words hadn't angered him that much. Yet something continually nagged at her, something she couldn't call to mind.... She wriggled her toes, the action reminding her of those frantic moments in the river when she'd kicked off her boots.

Thorn rose, lashed the sticks together with vine ropes, then drove the sticks into the ground, constructing two simple frames, which he covered with stout palm fronds.

"Why go to all this bother?" she asked.

Deep as slate, and as opaque and unreadable, his eyes rested on her. "I've seen some caiman tracks and, what may be worse, flies and sand ticks buzzing around. Don't thrash around or you'll be buried in sand."

She nodded and lay down gingerly to gaze at the darkening sky. She was bone weary, still hungry and troubled at the change in Thorn. Was there some terrible danger ahead that was worrying him?

Exhausted, she closed her eyes—closed her mind, too, to all thoughts of Thorn, oblivious to the moment when he lifted her gently and placed her in her shelter for the night.

SHE AWOKE TO A BREAKFAST of baked fish. Before they ate, Thorn opened two coconuts, then told her he wanted to look for more to place in the dugout. She watched him stride away, covered in coconut oil, his muscles glistening and rippling in the sun, his bronzed body lithe, tough and perfectly fit.

Sabrina plaited her hair and secured the braid with a short length of vine. A sudden movement caught her eye, and she turned quickly. Hanging from a liana, a small brown monkey, a capuchin, stared at her. On impulse Sabrina snatched up a chunk of coconut and extended it.

The monkey dropped to the ground, dashed a few yards deeper into the jungle, then turned to stare back at Sabrina with bright black eyes.

Speaking in a coaxing voice, Sabrina moved cautiously forward. The monkey scampered farther away, then halted again to look at her.

Talking softly, she slowly narrowed the distance between them. Finally she reached the little animal and offered the coconut. The monkey grasped it eagerly, jumped a few feet away and sat down to eat, watching Sabrina all the while.

Sabrina edged forward until she reached the small capuchin and picked it up. It wrapped a furry arm trustingly around her neck and continued to munch.

"Sabrina!" Thorn's voice thundered her name, and she spun around.

"Here!" she called, hurrying through the brush.

"Sabrina, where are you?" he called again.

"Over here." She was near enough now to see him through the trees. He stood with his back to her, hands on his hips, his black curls glistening in the sunlight.

"Thorn!" she called again. He swung around, and she exclaimed, "Look at this darling monkey!"

"Dammit, Sabrina! Why can't you stay put! What are you doing with a monkey?"

Her patience snapped. While the monkey tightened its arms around her neck, she glared at Thorn. "Don't use that tone with me, Thorn Catlin! You're frightening him."

"And what do we do if you get a nasty capuchin bite? Did you think of that?" he asked sardonically.

She blinked in surprise, suddenly contrite. "I hadn't considered it."

His anger drained away then, and he spoke wearily. "Let him go, Sabrina. We should be on our way."

As the canoe slid into the current, Sabrina looked back and saw the capuchin scamper into the brush and disappear from view.

All day they traveled, with little said between them. Late in the afternoon, as the sun began to slant across the water, Thorn grew even more morose. Occasionally Sabrina would turn and catch him staring at her, but he'd look away silently. It was their sixth day together, and she knew that in those six days she'd changed. She had become more self-reliant, but at the same time she'd lost her heart. Finally she asked him when they would stop for the night.

"We haven't found a clearing or a sandbar. If we don't soon, we'll have to tie up along the bank. But the jungle is so thick along here, I don't relish the thought."

"Why? Is it dangerous because of the caimans?"

"No—because of the mosquitoes."

Within an hour Sabrina knew why he'd been concerned. She felt as if insects had bitten every exposed inch of skin. "Thorn, can't we push out to the middle of the river?"

He slapped at his cheek. "We don't dare take the chance. Even the damned coconut oil hasn't stopped these devils."

Sabrina put her head down on her knees and covered her face. The continuous high whine of mosquitoes was stretching her nerves to the breaking point. She groaned and heard Thorn swear.

"Here, Sabrina, I know one thing that will give us relief." When she heard his palm slap his skin, she looked up, then gasped. Thorn had scooped layers of mud from the riverbank to spread a thin coat over all exposed areas of his body. He motioned to her. "Come here."

She needed no more urging but shifted closer in the dugout so that he could spread the welcome cool mud over her arms and legs. Reaching out with the palm of his hand, he smeared mud on her cheek.

Sabrina gazed up at him as he rubbed it across her

forehead and over her nose in quick deft strokes. "I hope I don't have skin like sandpaper after this," she murmured.

Pausing, he looked down at her, his gray eyes startling against his dark mud-covered cheeks. "You couldn't possibly have skin like sandpaper," he drawled laconically.

Sabrina wondered at the compliment, but Thorn had already moved away to spread more mud on himself. When he attempted to reach the middle of his back, she offered to do it for him and scooped up a handful to spread over his firm smooth muscles. "There—all done."

He turned and appraised her with an intensity that surprised her. Then he shifted to the bow. The dugout rocked, then steadied. "Stretch out in the bottom to sleep if you want," he said.

Instead Sabrina sat down, drew her knees up, wrapped her arms around them and placed her head on her elbow. They spent a painful miserable night on the bank of the river, as Thorn had predicted, and by midmorning the next day Sabrina was thoroughly wretched. The mud had dried, caked and stretched her skin. She was thirsty and hot. Thorn had fashioned paddles from the stiff bark, and they were unwieldy articles.

Stretching into the river ahead, a bar of white sand glistened. To their right, on the other side of it, blue water tumbled and rippled over rocks into a wide shallow tributary.

Thorn called out to her to head for the sand. Once they reached it and stepped out of the dugout, they could hear the splash of a waterfall nearby. Within seconds they discovered it. Only a short distance up the tributary, cascading water tumbled over rocks and boulders, dropping into a shallow bed about eight feet below.

Sabrina stopped in her tracks, amazed by its beauty. Orchids of various sizes and colors bloomed everywhere—on rocks, on trees, on vines. Tall ferns with delicate fronds also grew in profusion, along with epiphytes and bromeliads.

"Thorn, isn't it beautiful?" she breathed. Without waiting for him, she clambered over roots and rocks to reach the falls.

Refreshingly cold water rushed over her bare feet, and spray blew against her. Then she stepped right under the falls, where the roaring gushing flow drowned out all other sounds. Water beat against her head and shoulders. Her clothes were plastered to her skin as the dark caked mud began to wash away. Sabrina squeezed her eyes shut to prevent the mud from running into them as the grime slid out of her hair. She noticed Thorn beside her doing the same. He grinned, then stepped behind the falls to climb on an outcrop of rock. Leaning down, he lifted her to sit beside him.

Wet, cool and refreshed, they sat together to gaze out from behind the curtain of falling water. The world on the other side was a shimmering green, gold and pink, while bright rainbows shot through the spray.

"This is the most beautiful place in the world!" Sabrina gasped.

"At the moment I agree with you," he drawled lazily, his good humor resurfacing after a day and night of ill temper.

"Brazil is magnificent in many ways," he continued. "But with millions of peasants, starving, illiterate and superstitious, powerful landowners should be doing all they can to change the situation. It can't stay the same if this country is to compete in the modern world."

"You surely don't care to dismantle Bellefontaine, do you?" she asked.

"No, not at all, but much of the wealth should be channeled off and used for housing and schools for those less fortunate. Everything is here. We just need intelligent development." He gazed around. "With the returns I expect from our gold mine I'll be able to do more. I'd like to build a research center in Manaus, too."

"If you feel this way, why won't you work with me for the Food Outlook Board?"

He turned his head and regarded her steadily, and suddenly Sabrina became self-conscious, aware of every inch of her body, as well as his. She slipped off the rock and stepped under the falls when it was clear he wasn't going to answer her.

Cold water splashed over her head and shoulders, running down her body but not quenching the fire that burned within her. Thorn clambered nimbly down and crossed to the bank, leaping from rock to rock. His hard tanned body glistened with water, and it took an effort of will for Sabrina to look away from his strong shoulders. She gazed with consternation at her mud-streaked clothing.

"Thorn, I'll never get rid of this mud unless I wash these clothes. Turn your back and let me take them off."

For a moment he observed her quietly, then moved away to sit down on a rock, his back to her. Under the falls she stripped off the few garments and washed them, glancing once at Thorn.

His back was still to her, his knees drawn up, his arms locked around them. She wrung out her clothing and spread it on the bank before stepping back under the water to bathe. Leaning over, she let her hair hang down while she ran her fingers through it to get out the grime. Straightening, she lifted her face to the cool spray, reveling in it as it splashed over her shoulders and streamed down her body. She held out her hands to let water fall over her palms. Her arms were deeply tanned, dark against her pale golden body.

Finally, with reluctance, she crossed the slippery rocks to the bank, reached for her clothing—and found Thorn staring at her.

He stood only a yard away. Slowly, his smoldering gaze traveled over her from head to toe, then met hers again.

Never had she seen such naked desire in a man's eyes. A tremor ran through her, and warmth filled her cheeks. Feeling devoured by those eyes, she whispered, "You promised."

"I didn't keep my promise," he stated flatly, and with a groan reached out to take her in his arms. Crushing her trembling naked flesh against him, he cradled her head in the crook of his elbow and kissed her hungrily. There was no slow awakening—only a burst of flame as desire flashed through her.

Sabrina murmured his name over and over against his lips. He kissed her lips, her throat, her flesh, cool and damp from the water.

"My love," he whispered. Then Sabrina remembered what had been nagging at the back of her mind since that catastrophic spill in the rapids. When she had regained consciousness, Thorn had addressed her in the same manner.

"Thorn...."

He looked down at her. His eyes were filled with desire as he spoke huskily. "You don't know what I've suffered." He crushed her to him and spoke against her hair. "Sabrina, when we went into the water in the rapids, I couldn't find you. I couldn't bear the thought that something might have happened to you."

Hardly daring to hope, she raised her face and looked at him wonderingly.

His eyes clouded as he looked down, then kissed her, his mouth savoring her lips... kissed her deeply and passionately, yet with poignant tenderness.

Finally he released her, and his voice was filled with pain. "I thought I had all the answers, that I had such complete control, but I've never felt this way about anyone. It won't make any difference, though," he said grimly. "I've asked Amanda to marry me, and I can't take that back."

Of all the hurts he had inflicted, none had ever equaled this one. She couldn't speak—couldn't look away from the gray depths of his eyes.

"You were right—I haven't known what love is. But, Sabrina, honor is everything in my part of the world. I couldn't insult my family, our name or Amanda."

Amanda. Beautiful, sophisticated and part of his world—also immensely wealthy, with an enormous plantation that adjoined Bellefontaine. Small wonder he would not give all that up. She suspected he longed for her to say she understood, but she couldn't. All she knew was that she loved Thorn wholly and completely, and now he had admitted his love for her.

Seeming to guess her thoughts, he pulled her close again. "Lord, what a blind fool I've been. I don't know when I began to feel this way—it might have been with that first kiss in Sao Paulo. All I'm certain about is that I felt like my world had ended back there when we went into the river."

Sabrina slipped her arms around him and raised her eager mouth to his. The kiss scalded, arousing a sweeping hunger within them. "I've been fighting my feelings for you for a long time now," Thorn growled, and she pulled away to look up at him. His face was shuttered and dark as he looked solemnly into her eyes.

"You're unhappy with me, though," she murmured.

"You've just complicated my life. It was all so simple and easy before." He ran his hands agitatedly through his hair, and she was torn with anguish.

"That's why you've been quiet, isn't it?"

"Sabrina, it upsets everything...."

She stiffened, pushing against him to get away. Snatching up her wet clothing, she boldly faced him to lash out with angry words...and encountered his burning gaze consuming her, moving in a slow scrutiny down the length of her nude body.

"Dammit to hell!" he muttered, and pulled her to him. The kiss was fiery, passionate and demanding; his lips were unbearable in their insistence. Her hips thrust to meet the hardness of his body, and she lifted the sweetness of her eager lips to his, to be ravaged by a hunger that shook them both.

"Thorn, I love you," she breathed. The longing of her heart and soul poured out.

"Oh, Lord, Sabrina," he groaned, and crushed her in his arms.

Dropping the clothes, she tightened her arms around his waist to glory in the feeling of his furred chest, the flat hard stomach against hers.

"Sabrina, I have to go back to Amanda. You'll have to return to your country. There's a man waiting for you, isn't there?"

"No."

He looked at her intently. "I can't believe that."

She shook her head. "No, Thorn. I've dated, but there's never been anyone I've loved except you."

His dark brows flew together. "No other love... no other man?"

When she shook her head again, he kissed her fiercely, passion driving away their words.

In a magic world of waterfalls, rainbows and orchids, all she knew was the hard brown body clad in tattered khakis. Her fingers fumbled at the waistband of his denims.

Suddenly he straightened. "No!" he grated. "Not

this way—not here, Sabrina. You're too precious."

She reached for him, curling her arm seductively around his neck. "Thorn, I love you!" she insisted.

He swore softly, then caught her wrists and held her hands away. His face was as dark as a thundercloud. "No, not here on a sandbank in the jungle. This tropical place warps the senses. We're in a dreamworld."

"Thorn, I know what I'm doing!"

His voice was a rasp. "Nothing is rational here. You may feel entirely different when we get home."

Looking up at him, Sabrina guessed he was actually expressing his own feelings. He didn't want to accept what he felt. He didn't want to be in love with her—he had admitted as much—and he hoped the feeling would go away when he returned to the familiarity of Bellefontaine.

She set her jaw, determined not to let the searing pain show. "You're right," she answered, and motioned with her hand. "Go on ahead. I'll get my clothes and catch up."

She couldn't bear to face him. As soon as he headed for the dugout, she struggled into her clothing. A violent trembling seized her. She looked at him striding away, the healthy vigorous body honed to a tough leanness by their days in the jungle.

Any joy from his declaration of love was destroyed by the grim knowledge that he didn't want to be in love with her—that as much as possible he was fighting it. Yet even as she reflected bitterly on his words, Sabrina knew that if he returned right now and took her in his arms to make love to her, she'd yield.

Wiping the tears resolutely from her cheeks and steeling herself to hide any hurt, she hurried to catch up with him. At the bend Sabrina looked back once more, trying to capture in memory a magical place that already seemed unreal.

"Come on, Sabrina," he murmured gently.

Certain that part of her remained behind forever, she turned. A measure of her joy in life was locked away beside those falls. Blinking rapidly, she hurried along.

Numbness set in as they returned to the river, and a strained silence lasted between them for the rest of the day. And that night sleep wouldn't come. Sabrina stared into the dark, hearing the words over and over: "It upsets everything."

THE NEXT TWO DAYS ran together in a blur. On Thursday, their tenth day since the crash, as they were drifting in the dugout with the current, they spotted a man and child fishing on the bank.

Thorn called to them in Portuguese. There was a brief exchange before he turned to her exultantly. "We've made it, Sabrina!"

CHAPTER THIRTEEN

"How CAN YOU be sure?" she demanded.

Another conversation ensued, the man on the bank gesturing, and Sabrina began to see the two of them through his eyes. Sabrina looked at herself, at her filthy stained clothing. The legs of her slacks were frayed and torn above the knees. Her blue shirt was ripped and faded. Against the sun-bleached paleness of her hair, her skin glowed a deep golden brown.

Clad only in ragged denims, Thorn appeared fierce and disreputable with his long black hair and burnished copper skin. At that moment he stood up and let out a whoop that echoed across the water, scattering birds and rocking the dugout wildly.

Sabrina shrieked and clutched the dugout. "Thorn! You'll have us in the river!"

Grinning broadly, his white teeth flashing, he sat down and began paddling.

She gazed at him, bemused. If he had been fit before the crash, he was even more so now. His powerful muscles rippled with each stroke. She looked away quickly.

Within a quarter of an hour a landing came into view, then huts, then more docks. They had reached a village on the Rio Tapajós tributary. Thorn shouted and waved at everyone they saw, who, to Sabrina's surprise, shouted and waved in return.

It was sundown by the time they pulled up to a dock and climbed out. She waited while Thorn conversed in Portuguese with a dark-skinned man who was unloading fishing gear from a boat.

Finally Thorn took her arm. "We're in a village—and apparently it's growing by leaps and bounds. Last year a Brazilian industrialist started up a pulpwood business here, and now the village is featured on one of the Amazon tour routes. So there should be enough modern conveniences to make us feel at home. Come on. The fisherman told me where to find the hotel." Within minutes Thorn had registered them in connecting rooms at the small but comfortable hotel. Next he placed calls home to both families.

Certain that his family would want to talk to Sabrina, Thorn insisted they call together from his room. They got Tennessee on the line first, to allow Sabrina to talk to her mother and brothers. When she wept at the relief in her mother's voice, Thorn's arm closed warmly around her shoulders. She glanced up at him as she spoke to Jeff. His familiar voice was a welcome sound, and after answering his questions, she listened anxiously as he told her about Andy's motorcycle accident. She talked to Andy and learned he had broken his arm and totaled the motorcycle before Jeff spoke to her once more. His voice made her long for home as he laughed and said, "Between you and Andy, mom's had a time."

Assuring him that she really was fine and that she

would write with further details, Sabrina finally handed the phone to Thorn. "Mom wants to speak to you."

She watched him while he made polite comments. Then he said, "She took care of me, too." The husky tone of his voice and the warmth in his eyes made the moment poignant, and pressing her face against his shoulder, she struggled to hold back the tears. Why did it have to be this way? Why had she fallen in love with a man engaged, bound by duty and honor, yet whose every look devoured her with love?

Thorn handed her the phone, and she struggled to keep her voice normal as she said a final goodbye. As soon as she hung up, he turned her into his arms and held her quietly against him. While she listened to his heartbeat, his hand stroked her hair. Not a word was spoken, but she grew calm and gained control over her emotions. "You'd better call your family now."

He kissed her forehead and kept his arm around her while he turned to pick up the phone. It was clear that Laurel answered. Her voice was loud in the first moments of excitement. Then Thorn's wide grin disappeared and his eyes clouded as he asked grimly, "When did it happen, Laurel?"

His sister's rush of words was unintelligible to Sabrina, but Thorn exhaled and murmured a relieved, "Thank God!" As Laurel continued to talk, he covered the mouthpiece and whispered, "Papa had a stroke."

"Oh, no!" Sabrina exclaimed.

Immediately he added, "Laurel says he's recovering, though." He listened again for a few minutes before he raised a dark eyebrow and muttered, "I'll be damned! Let me talk to him."

Surprised, Sabrina looked at Thorn and uttered softly, "Wade?" then blushed with embarrassment for intruding on his call. Deciding it would be best to give him some privacy, she turned away.

But he reached out and caught her arm as he said hello to his brother. Trying to catch the drift of the conversation, she got another surprise when Thorn asked, "You're not married?"

Her gaze met Thorn's, but it was impossible to read his thoughts. After giving Wade instructions on getting a plane for them and sending them some money, he spent a few more minutes talking to Laurel. There was a pause. Then Thorn spoke briefly, choosing his words with care as he talked to his father. Finally he spoke to Roddy and handed the phone to Sabrina.

At the sound of Roddy's voice, pleasure rushed through Sabrina. "Sabrina, we've been so worried," he said. "Everybody has prayed for both of you. Laurel said you would get back. Have you talked with your mother?"

"Yes," she laughed. "My mother and my brothers. Roddy, you'll never believe the things we saw."

"I can't wait to hear. Laurel wants to know if you encountered any boa constrictors."

She laughed again. "I'll discuss it with you later, Roddy. Here's Thorn."

When she handed him the phone, his eyes were intent, a deep slate gray. He spoke in a level voice. "Roddy, is Amanda there?"

Sabrina balled her hands into tight fists. Just hearing him say Amanda's name hurt. She turned again to go to her room, but he reached out and caught her arm to pull her against his chest, kissing her tenderly and holding her close.

Sabrina listened to the deep steady rhythm of his heart and was near enough to hear Roddy's voice, too. Thorn ended the conversation and hung up, then looked down at her. "I had to do that," he said solemnly. "I couldn't ignore Amanda. She's not there at the moment." He sighed. "I'm going to get us some other clothes. Then we'll bathe and see what kind of feast we can have."

Lifting the receiver, he called the management and spoke in Portuguese. Sabrina desperately wanted a bath, but she waited politely for him to finish.

Typical of the tropics, she thought, was the sparsely furnished room allotted to Thorn, with its dark gleaming floors and louvered shutters at the windows. Overhead a fan turned lazily, and on one side of the room was the inevitable hammock. For a brief moment Sabrina remembered the last time Thorn had slept in a hammock.

Determined to remain calm, she dismissed those memories and went through the connecting door to turn on one of the small lamps that decorated the bamboo tables in the room. She had requested a bed, but otherwise the room was identical to Thorn's. The white plastered walls and vases of brightly colored paper flowers lent the room an air of cozy cheerfulness. Sabrina felt as if she were in a palace—especially after the jungle.

When Thorn hung up, he glanced across at her. "We're getting some clothes. God knows what sort, although the man assured me it won't be a problem. He said there's a new store in town and he knows the owner. Do you want to come, or do you trust me?"

"I trust you," she replied with relief, moving back to the door that separated the two rooms. "All I want is a hot bath."

Thorn glanced down at himself ruefully. "Right now I might not be welcome in the best restaurants."

Sabrina giggled at the understatement. "They'd probably send us to the alley and throw out some scraps."

He grinned, then turned as the phone rang. When he answered, his eyes narrowed and the laughter faded from his voice. Sabrina felt certain it was Amanda, and she couldn't bear to listen to him talk to her. Hurrying through the connecting door, she closed it quietly, then began to get ready for her bath.

Soon she was relaxing in the tub. The hot soapy water felt like the most luxurious thing she'd ever experienced. Hearing a rap on the bathroom door, she looked up. From the other side Thorn said, "Your clothing is on the bed, love. I'm heading straight for a shower. Then I'll take you to eat."

Sabrina dried herself, wrapped the towel around her and emerged to look at the outfit Thorn had placed on the bed. She glanced at his closed door with silent gratitude. In addition to the necessities—a toothbrush, hairbrush, pins, stockings, handkerchief, sandals and dainty lace underwear—she found a white peasant blouse and a full skirt of heavy exquisite handmade lace.

After she had dressed, Sabrina surveyed herself in an oval mirror. How much she had changed! Even though she had the same wide blue eyes, the same full rosy lips, now, against her deeply tanned skin, the blue of her eyes seemed lighter and brighter, her hair more golden, pale and shimmering as it tumbled over her shoulders. Catching it up, Sabrina twisted it and fastened it in a chignon behind her head. Yes, subtly she had changed, and she felt certain it was not just the deeper tan or sun-bleached hair that were different.

"How beautiful you look," Thorn commented from the doorway.

She swung around to face him. Noiselessly he had opened the connecting door and was now lounging against the doorjamb, watching her. His ravenous measured gaze was as powerful as his caresses had been.

He was the most handsome man she'd ever seen, dressed in a white dinner jacket and dark slacks with a white shirt. The only indication that the clothes hadn't been tailored for him was the jacket's snug fit across his shoulders. Against the white shirt and jacket his skin was a startling contrast. Rugged features, the scar along his temple, the slight crook in his nose—all only served to heighten his masculinity.

Sabrina tightened her lips. If she didn't take care, he really would break her heart.

"You don't look as if you've been lost in the Amazon," he stated softly.

"I was thinking the same of you," she replied.

He straightened at that, his gray eyes challenging her as he approached.

"Thorn," she whispered, "please, let's go—right now...."

Without hesitation he advanced to take her in his arms and bend her against his body. His mouth came down on hers. Sabrina yielded, melting against him, returning his passionate kiss. Finally he loosened his hold, looking down at her with heavy-lidded eyes.

"Thank you for the clothes," she murmured. "I don't know how you found them."

"I told you. There's a new store here." He flexed his arms. "Although this jacket isn't the best fit, it will do, and your dress is handmade by local women." He smiled. "But the clothes were a small matter. The store owner also had a small unpacked crate gathering dust in the back...with this among its contents." Reaching into his pocket, Thorn withdrew a small bottle of cologne, placing it in her hands.

"Oh, Thorn, thank you!" she gasped with delight. After all the days spent in the wilds without even soap, the cologne was a marvelously luxurious gift to receive. Opening it, she inhaled deeply of the fragrances of muguet, lily and carnation.

His fingers brushed hers as he took the bottle from her, tilted it against his forefinger and dabbed a drop of cologne behind her ear. She looked up at him solemnly as he repeated his action, dabbing some behind her other ear.

Tilting the small round bottle again, he brushed

the scent lightly in the cleft between her breasts. Even though it had been the barest touch, Sabrina's heart began to pound. His eyes never left hers as he applied several drops to each wrist.

With deliberation he closed the bottle, then leaned down to kiss her. "You are irresistible," he murmured, taking her arm and heading for the door. They left the hotel and strolled along the wide dusty main street of town.

They found a restaurant at the river's edge, where they were seated at a table in a secluded corner overlooking the shimmering water.

Inside, dim lighting revealed broad dark beams, white-washed walls and a rust-red tile floor. Candles flickered, sending bright little circles of light across the gleaming dark wooden tables. The enticing aroma of roasting meat, chilies and onions filled the interior.

"It would be best to eat only a little," he teased, "since we're on a diet." After a moment he lowered the menu and gazed at her with dancing eyes.

Sabrina laughed. "All this food—it's overwhelming!"

"Would you care for a coconut—or perhaps a slightly raw fish?" he suggested, tongue-in-cheek.

The waiter came, and Sabrina handed Thorn her menu. "Please order for me. You've taken care of my diet all these days now."

To start, Thorn ordered a green salad with *palmitos*, hearts of palm, then *lombo de porco*, pork loin. After a moment of study he ordered a bottle of dry white wine and asked for coffee later.

When the waiter had gone, Sabrina murmured, "I feel I want to gorge myself, to indulge fully."

"Indeed, I'd like to indulge myself, too," he retorted huskily, and reached across to grasp her hand.

His meaning was instantly clear. All the laughter died in Sabrina's throat as she looked at him. The candlelight danced over his features, highlighting the bridge of his nose, the prominent cheekbones, the pale gray eyes that flamed with desire.

"Thorn...."

Reaching up, he placed a finger against her lips. "I can see the protest in your eyes. Sabrina, by this time tomorrow we'll be back at Bellefontaine, and everything will change." He gazed into her eyes, then at her cheeks, her mouth, her throat, down to the soft rounded curves above the scooped neckline of her lace blouse, before returning to meet her eyes.

"Just for now, let's forget the world—forget that we won't walk out of here together forever."

Without taking his eyes from hers, he lifted her hand to his mouth. Slowly, lingeringly, he drew his lips across each knuckle. "Please, Sabrina," he whispered.

"You make it so difficult," she stated solemnly. Each touch kindled desire, stirring her until she wanted to fling herself into his arms.

"Give me only these hours, Sabrina. I won't take your innocence, love—only a few hours of shutting out everything else," he murmured. "In our part of the world a woman's purity is highly valued. I won't violate that. You can trust me. Just give me this brief time."

"And my heart," she added. She licked her lips, then became aware of what she had done as his gaze focused on her mouth with a consuming intensity. It was difficult to breathe—even more of an effort to speak. "You must stop what you're doing now, Thorn, or I'll be in your lap in a few seconds. I've lost my appetite." The sounds and tempting aromas, the clinking dishes and silverware—everything in the cozy restaurant ceased to exist for her.

"I've lost mine for food," he returned, his voice a husky drawl. "I want to reach over and take each of those pins out of your golden hair. I'd like to feel its softness over my shoulders."

"Thorn, you don't know what you're doing to me," she whispered.

Boldly his eyes undressed her in a languorous smoldering appraisal that made Sabrina's cheeks flame.

"Thorn!"

The corners of his firm mouth lifted, and he replied dryly, "I'm just sitting here, Sabrina."

"No, you're not!" she replied breathlessly. "You're making love to me right now—and you know it!"

He held up both hands. "I'm not doing anything," he replied with mocking innocence, "except letting my eyes touch you where my hands would like to. Like there, Sabrina, and there...and there...."

Sabrina felt on fire from the low intimate drawl and the direct silvery gray gaze, each as real as a fiery touch to her quivering flesh.

Longing to melt into his arms, she caught her

breath and shifted in her chair. "I don't want to eat. I can't when you're doing that," she whispered.

"I haven't moved," he murmured. "I'm just sitting still thinking about what I want to do, where I'd like to kiss you...."

She drew a sharp breath. The room was stifling; her own heartbeat drummed in her ears.

The mocking note faded in his voice. Solemnly he appraised her; his gaze lowered. "I'd like my mouth to touch you there, Sabrina."

"Thorn," she whispered, her excitement growing, "you're seducing me, and I can't do anything except sit here and think about what you're saying."

He settled back in his chair, his gaze slowly moving, lingering a moment, drifting.... It was impossible to stay still in her chair. She shifted again. Every inch of her blazed with awareness beneath his sensual scrutiny.

A waiter walked past. On the other side of the restaurant, dimly, she heard a guitar. But she couldn't take her eyes from Thorn. Licking her dry lips, she crossed her legs.

The faintest smile lifted the corner of his mouth as he whispered, "You always respond...whether consciously or not. You're a sensual desirable woman."

"If I am, it's because you make me feel that way," she answered. "I can't do anything else except respond to you. That's what you haven't understood, Thorn. No one else can do this to me...."

At the quick blaze in his eyes her words faded. She saw the flare of his nostrils as he inhaled sharply, and she had to lean forward to hear his reply.

"You have the softest skin...."

"Thorn, I can't eat," she murmured. "Let's leave...."

"We have all evening."

With an effort she looked away from him—looked at the restaurant, the flowers—anything to avoid his eyes, which sent a current of longing coursing through her that she couldn't ignore. She knew he was watching her, watching her in the same hungry sensual way.

"Thorn, will you please say something sane, something on a safe impersonal topic?" She was still concentrating fiercely on the floral arrangement.

In a deep drawl he said, "You have the most beautiful hair, Sabrina. I'll always remember how you looked under that waterfall, with your golden hair streaming down your bare back...your long tanned legs...."

She turned then to gaze into his eyes. Each word made her want to reach for him, to pull him to her so she could wrap her arms around his powerful shoulders. Too well she remembered how he had appeared at the falls, the rippling muscles beneath the smooth copper skin.

Finally she could tell him, "Your kiss at Congonhas, Thorn—I've never kissed a stranger before. You see, from the first you've been able to command this instant physical reaction in me...."

"You think you were the only one of us to feel it, love?" he whispered.

She was stunned by his confession and hoped these

weren't mere words—that she could stir in him what he aroused in her.

He saw her thoughts in her eyes. "Oh, yes, Sabrina," he said huskily, "I'm older than you. I'm experienced with women. But there are moments with you.... I feel as if I haven't had a woman's kiss before. If I'm unique to you, God knows, you are to me. Those big blue eyes can turn my knees to water and make me want you beyond all belief...."

Her heart's hammerblows drowned out everything. *He does feel it, too,* she thought. Exultation flared within her, a molten joy that brought with it unbearable yearning.

She forgot the restaurant and the people and reached across the table to take his hands. His brown fingers closed over hers, and she felt the warm callused palms against hers. "I didn't know a man's body could be so marvelous, Thorn.... I love to feel your shoulders, your smooth skin...."

His eyes darkened as he turned her hand to kiss her palm, his lips, his tongue brushing the sensitive skin. Raising his head, Thorn smiled his familiar crooked smile and said on a long breath, "Now you're tormenting me, Sabrina. I've spent a lifetime learning to discipline myself, doing what I had to do, not what I wanted to do. But you're putting a—an almost irresistible temptation before me."

At that moment the waiter approached with a bottle of chilled white wine. Releasing her hands, Thorn smiled, a smile meant for Sabrina alone, a smile that burst through her like sunshine flooding into a dark room.

Thorn leaned back and spoke in mocking tones.

"Sanity returns with a grand cru Chablis, a vintage year—" he paused and glanced at the bottle "—1967." The waiter uncorked the wine, lifted a clear tulip-shaped goblet and poured the green-tinted wine. With a flourish he handed the glass to Thorn, who tasted it slowly, then nodded. Smiling brightly at Thorn's approval, the waiter served Sabrina, then Thorn and departed.

Thorn lifted his glass in a toast. "To the survivors." Sabrina raised her goblet and clinked it against his, aware of the most casual contact, the mere brush of his hand against hers. She gazed at him over the rim as she sipped her wine, then lowered the goblet to the table.

"I'm not so certain I have, Thorn," she stated solemnly.

"None of that—not for the next few hours," he replied with a deep-throated huskiness. "There isn't any tomorrow...only now."

Conscious of the dangers involved in disregarding tomorrow, Sabrina nodded, willing to take the risk. A guitar player appeared and approached their table. For the first time Sabrina glanced around at the tables and discovered there were only a few other people in the restaurant.

"Sabrina," Thorn said, "when we get back to Bellefontaine, I'll work with you. There are enough other projects in the works that papa can get involved in when he's better. Let me help you."

"Thank you," she accepted quietly, knowing he was doing this to assist her in getting the job in Tennessee. The thought of separation was too painful, and she looked away quickly.

Dressed in a full-sleeved white shirt, a wide cummerbund and tight-fitting black trousers, the guitar player strummed softly and sang a love song. Sabrina smiled at him in polite appreciation, aware of Thorn's gray eyes resting on her.

Finally it was impossible to resist. Her gaze swung around to meet his, and she saw the passion in his eyes. Warmth crept up her cheeks. She looked down at her hands in her lap to hide it.

The singer finished, and those in the restaurant applauded. With a smile he acknowledged their response. Thorn spoke to him in Portuguese for a moment, after which he began to strum the deep vibrant chords of a haunting melody.

Sabrina sipped the dry chilled wine and watched, mesmerized, as Thorn placed his arm on the table and held out his hand to her, his shirt cuff white against his tanned wrist. She placed her hand in his, feeling his warm fingers close over hers. In the flickering candlelight their eyes remained fixed on each other while the musician sang softly.

Thorn's dark hair was a deep blue black in the muted glow, long and curling on his neck. She knew how the silken strands felt to the touch and had to resist an impulse to touch them now. His heavy sideburns were gone. The strong jaw was clean-shaven, and his eyes had darkened to a flinty gray.

Why did he have to be this way—sensitive, provocative, sensual—and absolutely unreachable?

The musician moved on to another table, the waiter appeared with their dishes, and still Thorn held her hand while the chilled salad was placed before them. Shifting his long legs underneath the table, he released her hand and straightened. "Now, Sabrina, you may have what you've dreamed of lo these many nights."

Her eyes never left his face as she shook her head slowly. She thought of how much she wanted him, loved him, and knew he could see it in her eyes. Too clearly she recalled the nights she'd lain in his arms and wanted more than his kisses.

"No, Thorn," she whispered, "this isn't what I've dreamed about."

His fork halted in midair as his eyes bored into hers. Slowly, he lowered it to his plate, pushed back his chair and rose to his feet. Wondering what he was doing, she looked up at him inquiringly. One glance into his gray eyes gave her the answer. Her astonishment changed to disbelief as she watched him step away from his chair to reach for her.

Sabrina glanced wildly around the restaurant. No one was looking their way. Thorn's hand closed around her wrist, and he pulled her to her feet.

His intent was as clear as if he'd announced it.

"Thorn, you can't...."

He tugged her wrist. "Sabrina," he coaxed huskily.

"Thorn, sit down! Please...."

His voice was warm. "Sabrina, just one kiss...."

"Thorn, you can't! All these people—"

"I don't give a damn." He tightened his arms around her, then leaned down. His mouth silenced her as he bent over and kissed her.

Any protest was momentarily drowned, swept away with his kiss. Then she pushed against him. "Thorn, please sit down!" Her face was burning and Sabrina was too embarrassed to glance around the restaurant for anybody's reaction.

Laughter danced in his eyes as he slipped into his seat. "Sabrina, you don't know anybody in here and you'll never see them again. What difference does it make?"

She relaxed and smiled at him. "And if I threw convention to the winds in the same manner, Thorn, then what would happen?"

With a devilish grin he retorted, "I'll tell you, Sabrina. First, you would throw your arms around me—"

"Thorn!" she interrupted with a yelp. "Never mind! Don't ever accuse *me* again of yielding to impulses too easily, Thorn Catlin!"

He smiled. "I suspect you're exerting an influence on me. I'm changing."

Not enough, my darling, she thought, but merely laughed and said, "You're making a habit of kissing me in restaurants."

"I find you irresistible—as I've told you before."

Later, after listening to some more music and eating only half their meal, they left the restaurant to stroll back to the hotel.

The night was cool, the dark shadows of the jacaranda trees lining the wide dusty road. Reaching an arched bridge, they sauntered across, stopping in the center. Thorn placed his arm around her shoulders and stood close beside her, gazing down at the river. Fishy odors drifted up from below.

"Does it look the same from here?" he asked.

"No." Sabrina felt peaceful and content. She realized that contentment would soon be shattered, but at the moment Thorn was at her side, and it was a beautiful night.

She leaned her head against his shoulder, and he shifted to hold her tighter. He spoke softly into her hair. "It looks so serene and romantic—not treacherous and bug-infested."

Not knowing what she was answering, Sabrina murmured softly. All she could think of was his arms around her, his face above hers.

Turning then, Thorn leaned down to kiss her, crushing her in his arms. His warmth sheltered her, kept the cold air away from her arms and bare shoulders. She could smell the clean scent of soap that clung to him as she stepped into his embrace.

At that moment a truck rumbled along the road, its headlights catching them full in their beam. Two men were in the front, two more standing in the flat bed at the rear. As the lights played over Thorn and Sabrina, a cheer went up from the men.

Holding her lightly around the waist, Thorn grinned at them and waved, while Sabrina smiled, a hot flush of embarrassment creeping up her throat. When they roared past, cries of *"Belissima!"* and *"Linda!"* as well as whistles rose above the rumble of the truck.

Thorn smiled down at her. "They said the *senhorita* is very beautiful."

"I can imagine." She laughed, wondering what else they'd said.

He took her hand, and they continued their stroll to the hotel. Its outer walls were painted in a muted patina of pastels. Soft yellow faded into tints of rose or green in the rough plaster, its paleness broken up by the dark wrought iron that graced each balcony. The hotel had only four floors, and a climbing bougainvillea soared to the roof and spread red blooms and branches across the orange tiles, lending a delicate beauty to the plain structure.

When they crossed the threshold to enter the quiet deserted lobby, the coolness of the night was replaced by a warm stuffiness. A creaking elevator rose to the second floor, where they got off and walked down the hall to Sabrina's room. With each step her pulse quickened. Remembered words and images of Thorn flitted through her mind. In a remote hotel in an exotic corner of the world, she wanted to give herself to this man whom she loved fiercely. She watched as he unlocked the door to hold it open for her.

He followed her into the room, then turned the key in the lock. After switching on one of the small lamps that shed a dim glow, he looked around expectantly. "Ah, there's what I ordered before we left."

Beside the open doors to the balcony, a bucket of ice, containing a bottle of champagne, rested on a table. As he reached for it, she said, "Thorn, I haven't thanked you properly for the dress or the other things. They fit remarkably well."

His gray eyes flicked over her and he smiled. "I would say so, yes."

"I want to pay for them," she said a little breathlessly. "What did they cost?"

He popped the cork, poured champagne, then crossed to hand a glass to her. "I'm having all of it put on my hotel bill, Sabrina. I've made arrangements with the proprietor." He looked down at her with amusement. "You're the only female I've ever known who continually tries to pay for every gift."

She sipped the bubbly champagne. "It's not really your responsibility."

He drank, then smiled at her. "And what is my responsibility?"

Gazing up at him for a moment in silence, she spoke in a small voice. "Not one thing where I'm concerned, Thorn."

He had raised his glass to his mouth, but at her answer his eyes narrowed and he paused. Turning, he placed his glass on a table, then hers beside it, before he pulled her into his arms.

His gray eyes darkened as he tilted up her face. His lips touched hers, possessed her mouth, and desire shook them both. A chord of music floated upward. Somewhere outside a lilting song was being sung. Finally Sabrina noticed and pulled away to look up at him. "I think we're being serenaded," she said.

Thorn released her. Crossing to the balcony to look below, Sabrina discovered the guitar player from the restaurant. Without a pause in his singing, he bowed and smiled. Thorn strolled out to join her.

"You asked him to do this, didn't you?"

He nodded. The singer finished, they applauded and Thorn requested another song. As soon as the music began, Thorn turned her into his arms to dance, gliding back and forth in the small space on the balcony.

After a moment he folded her closer. The moonlight illuminated his firm wide mouth and strong features. Cool breezes blew over them, but she felt them only slightly, since she was shielded by his arms. "Under the waterfall seemed like paradise," she whispered. "Now this does."

His voice was deep and husky as he replied, "Paradise is where you are, love."

The music ended, and they applauded. Another song commenced, and Thorn handed Sabrina her glass of champagne.

She sat on the balcony railing and leaned back against the wall. Prickly and rough, the plaster had retained some of the heat of the day, and she welcomed its warmth. The wind blew a branch of bougainvillea against her arm, the barest brush of paperlike blossoms. She watched as Thorn refilled her glass then his, before he moved to stand nearby in the shadows. His gaze, intent and hungry, rested on her.

Her heart thudded against her ribs. She closed her eyes and listened to the music, until his hand brushed her forehead and she looked up to see him snap a bougainvillea blossom to tuck it in her hair. His fingers trailed a line down the side of her face, along her cheek to her chin. Tilting her face upward, he leaned down and kissed her.

Every touch sent a thrill through her, a longing that gained in urgency. She wanted to love him wildly, to entice him, to feel the strength of his arms, of his hard body. Yet she sat perfectly still, kissing him sweetly.

Straightening, he removed his coat to drape it over a chair. The dark tie followed. Then he loosened the top button of his shirt and slipped off his shoes. It would have been impossible to take her eyes from his as he approached and leaned down to close his fingers around her ankles, one by one, and slip off her sandals. Then he took her in his arms to dance again.

They drifted from the balcony into the room, where he wrapped his arms around her while they merely swayed languorously to the music. She was aware of his height, the breadth of his shoulders, as his lips followed the graceful curve of her throat.

Their feet moved soundlessly over the floor. In his deep baritone he murmured, "Now, love, I can do all the things I wanted to when we were in the restaurant." Removing a pin from her hair, he let it fall to the floor as he whispered, "I want to take down your hair, to hold you in my arms, take away all those clothes, to kiss you and make you want me as I want you...."

She drew a sharp breath and looked up at Thorn, wanting his kiss, the feel of his lips on hers, his mouth that awakened her to a glorious awareness of herself, of her ability to please him.

As he removed another pin and dropped it, he gazed into her eyes. "I want your hair down over your bare shoulders, to feel its silkiness...." Another pin fell, then another, until the long golden hair cascaded across her back.

Stepping away from her slightly, he said with a

rasp to his voice, "Put my hand where you want me to touch you, Sabrina."

She felt as if she couldn't breathe, absorbing the erotic power of his words. His hand slipped down her arm into her hand. "Where do you want my hand, love?" Thorn insisted softly.

Sabrina's heart thudded in her ears as her fingers closed over his. Without wavering, she gazed up at him as she placed his hand beneath her chin, his rough palm against her throat. As she continued to look into his eyes, she whispered, "See what you're doing to my pulse, just by looking at me that way...." And another whisper: "Here's where I want your hand, Thorn." She held his, felt the hard bony knuckles as she trailed his fingers slowly down over her heart. "This is yours...my heart, forever...."

She heard his deep intake of breath as he looked down at his hand before raising his eyes to meet hers again. "Is that where you want my hand—on that lace?" he asked.

A quiver shot through her. Still gazing into his eyes, she slipped her hand from under his. With both hands she reached up to grasp the neckline of the peasant blouse.

"This is what I want, Thorn." She tugged it down. His lips parted as his gaze lowered. The lace slid away easily beneath his palm.

"*Cara...*" he murmured. "I want you to feel what I feel—to need me as I need you." His hand molded her rounded breast, sending ripples of desire through her. The music from outside faded beneath the pounding of her heart.

"How many nights in that jungle I wanted to pull you down in my arms," Thorn muttered, caressing her amorously. He leaned forward to kiss her bare shoulder, his mouth drifting across her skin, following where his hand had been. "I wanted to do this—" he kissed a full soft curve "—and this.... I love you," he breathed hoarsely.

The words were a glory and a pain. In agony she whispered, "It's not forever."

Reaching up, his fingers touched her lips to silence her protest. "You gave me tonight, Sabrina...."

She twisted, caught his hand to press it again to her lips. "You're bound by honor to go into a marriage without love," she whispered. "What kind of life will you have? I wonder if I could bear it if you loved her, because at least I'd think you were happy. At home when I'll think of you...." She couldn't say any more. She held his wrist and kissed it lingeringly. "You've ruined me—and you've given me ecstasy."

"You'll forget," he breathed into her hair.

Tormented, she protested, "How can I forget to breathe, to live? You're that to me, Thorn—my life, my soul." Stepping back, she touched only her fingertips to his as she looked up at him.

"You've made your choice. You'll have your honor to keep you warm, while I spend night after night with memories of you, longing for you...." She could barely say the words; it was impossible to consider fully what lay ahead.

Again the unfairness of his honor-bound old-world way of life shook her. Taking a deep breath, she said, "During those nights in your marriage of duty and honor—think of this night, Thorn. Remember me sometimes. If a continent separates us, at least I'll know that there are moments when you think of me."

All her heart went into her words. "I don't want you to forget...." Slipping her hands beneath the elastic waistband of her lace skirt, she eased it slowly down her hips as she stood before him.

"I'm yours, Thorn. There's no holding back. Whenever you remember or think of me, you'll know at that moment that I love you and want you. There can't be another in my life." The skirt dropped softly around her slender ankles.

He groaned as he reached for her, crushing her in his arms, his fingers biting into her flesh as he kissed her passionately. She felt a tremor shake his powerful body, and she murmured against his throat, "Don't forget me, Thorn. Don't forget completely. Leave a small corner of your heart for me alone...."

"Sabrina, I can't go back on my word to Amanda. It would kill my father. I can't lose Bellefontaine." He raised his head, and she saw the anguish in his eyes. His voice was hoarse as he continued, "You're part of my heart, and no other woman on earth is or ever has been. I'm not complete without you."

For an instant she wished he'd throw aside all duty, his heritage and honor. Just as quickly, she knew that was impossible. She knew she couldn't ask him to give up everything that made his world—that made him the man he was—to give it up for marriage to her, because it would destroy him. Yet deep within, she was certain she'd never love another man as she did Thorn.

With a soft moan she tightened her arms around his neck for an instant, then, leaning back, unfastened the buttons on his shirt. "All those nights we were together, Thorn, you never wanted me one time more than I wanted you," she whispered.

He shrugged away his shirt, then placed his hands on her waist to move her back a step. Covered with a whisper of lace, her golden skin contrasted with his burnished tan.

Thorn lifted her effortlessly and carried her to the bed, then stood over her. His gray eyes were dark as they swept the length of her tremulous body. Her flaxen hair fanned over the pillow. With incredible tenderness he caught her foot, kissing her ankle. "You're beautiful, Sabrina." His lips trailed along her leg, causing her to twist and gasp with pleasure, while he continued to trace a fiery path across her skin.

"Belissima, cara," he murmured, then kissed her throat as he stretched out on the sheets and pulled her willing body against the length of his.

He shifted and lay on top of her, his long hard legs against hers, bracing his weight, yet still heavy and pressing her to the bed. She trembled with a longing that seared her veins until she reeled with the desire for his warm flesh, for him. She clung to him and gazed deeply into his eyes. His piercing look made her tighten her arms around his shoulders.

"How can I forget?" he murmured. "There won't ever be a time when I don't love you." His lips brushed her shoulder. "There never has been a time when I didn't. Our meeting at Congonhas was the most natural thing in the world. You belong in my arms." He turned his head to place his lips on hers again, his deep kiss confirming all that he'd said. The tingling she experienced at his touch deepened to a need only he could satisfy.

Thorn abruptly shifted to sit up, his breathing ragged and loud in the room. Dimly she noticed that the guitarist played on.

"Thorn, come here...."

He came down to crush her in his arms. His voice was torn with pain. "Sabrina, I promised, and I won't go back on it."

When she opened her mouth to protest, he placed his fingers against her lips. "Your innocence is safe, because I love you. But oh, love, you'll never know...." His voice faded as he groaned and buried his face in the full softness of her flesh.

Never would she have believed it possible to want anyone as she did Thorn. Her hands roamed over his angular body, while he caressed hers, arousing her, giving her pleasure that drove all thoughts but one from her mind—the infinite need for his love.

She responded to him with devastating intensity, giving completely, burning for ultimate consummation. But his eyes were bleak with bitter longing as he held her in his arms and whispered against her ear, "I want to know every response, to discover what pleases you. I want it branded on my soul, because the memory is all I'll have." Lowering his head, he traced a continuous circular pattern on her midriff with his tongue. "You're everything I thought, *cara*...this wild response...."

She writhed against him as he shifted beside her, still holding her. Her fingers locked in his dark hair; his head bent over her quivering body. "Thorn, it's you," she murmured. "It's you who evokes my response."

It was impossible to speak, she was so filled with need for him. She reached to pull him closer, to pull him down over her. Beneath him her body became fluid motion, a molten eagerness for him.

Suddenly he pulled away from her and sprang to his feet. Then he was gone through the connecting door to his room. The key turned in the lock. She heard a clatter and wondered if he'd flung the key across the room.

"Thorn!" The cry was wrenched from her. She rolled over to peer through the dim light at the flat impersonal barrier of the door.

"Oh, Thorn..." she sighed. Harsh unrelenting pain replaced the throbbing yearning of only seconds earlier.

Hot tears streamed down her cheeks. Then everything—the champagne, the long days in the jungle, the excitement of reaching civilization, the pain of his rejection—all worked together to cause a languor to overwhelm her. Her eyes fixed on the connecting door, Sabrina became aware of the iron will of the man behind it, and an exhaustion so complete that she couldn't combat it took over.

She burned from his touch, his kisses. The bed was warm from his body. A shudder shot through her. At the sound of the key she turned her head to see the door swing open and Thorn enter. Carrying two glasses of champagne, he was dressed again in the white shirt and dark slacks. When he reached the bed, he extended a glass to her.

Pulling up the sheet to cover herself, she sat up and accepted the glass. It took an immense effort to hold back all the words of longing she wanted to say. Thorn sat on the foot of the bed and placed his champagne on the floor while he lit a cigarette.

His voice was deep and husky as he remarked in a deliberately conversational tone, "I just came in for a moment to drink a glass of champagne with you and tell you good-night."

Without a word she waited, but she longed to toss aside the sheet and throw her arms around him. His hand dropped lightly to touch her foot, and he caressed her ankle while he quietly smoked. After a few minutes he asked, "Will you sleep?"

"Thorn...."

He stood up and caught her chin with his fingers, tilting her face up to his. "I think I've loved you since that first day we met. I'll never be the same." He sank down beside her, brushing the back of his hand gently against her cheek. "You have to forget...."

She felt his hand tremble, and she grasped his wrist to press her lips hard against his palm, stifling the sobs that racked her.

Agony flared in his eyes. Suddenly he swept her to him, taking her mouth passionately, conveying all his torment. "Lord, Sabrina, my control isn't as great as I thought. Good night, love...."

He left and locked the door.

With a pounding heart she gazed after him. "I love you," she whispered. She drank the champagne, staring numbly at the door, until finally she lay down and gazed miserably into space. The music had stopped outside.

SABRINA DOZED FITFULLY and awakened to sunlight pouring in through the windows and the open balcony doors. For a moment she stared blankly at the ceiling, feeling something was wrong. She glanced around. Like a great stone rolling over her heart, memory crowded in. They were returning to Bellefontaine today.

She got up and discovered another outfit spread on the chair. Glancing in surprise at Thorn's door, knowing that he'd furnished the new clothing, she picked up the sky-blue cotton blouse and skirt, a blue ribbon for her hair and brown sandals. By the time Thorn knocked on their connecting door, she'd finished dressing. She opened the door.

"Good morning, Sabrina," he greeted her, apparently relaxed, dressed in a clean khaki bush shirt and pants. Only for an instant did she catch the burning hunger in his gray eyes, to be replaced by a shuttered impassive mask.

Behind him she heard men's voices. When she entered his room, Thorn introduced her to two reporters, and she greeted Joao Fabrizio, Thorn's pilot. Within the hour the reporters were gone and Joao, Thorn and Sabrina had finished breakfast. Another half hour and they were airborne, flying above a thick green canopy dotted with purple jacaranda and the red leaves of the jatoba trees.

Joao had brought a stack of papers that it was urgent for Thorn to review, and with each passing second, as his dark head remained bent over the open briefcase, Sabrina knew she was losing him forever.

The insulation of their constant togetherness, their isolation from the world, their companionship—the effects of these were peeling away, leaving her vulnerable and heartbroken. She studied him as he worked. His strong brown fingers moved over the papers to make notations. He looked extremely fit and handsome, and glancing down at her simple clothing, the sandals, the plain blouse and skirt, Sabrina wished she appeared more glamorous for the ordeal ahead.

Thorn had instructed Joao to land at São Paulo in order to get their physicals and satisfy publicity seekers. When the pilot had informed Thorn that except for his father, the family would be at Congonhas Airport to greet them, Thorn's face had brightened with pleasure, but as the plane banked and touched the runway, his brows drew together in a frown.

When they taxied to a halt on the incredibly short runway, Sabrina realized with dismay that it had been almost three weeks since she'd landed at Congonhas the first time. *Three weeks and one lifetime,* she thought.

Thorn took her hand, his slate-gray eyes somber as he leaned forward and kissed her lightly on the forehead. Praying she could get through the minutes ahead, Sabrina stepped out beside him to applause and cheers as flashbulbs popped. Thorn took her arm, and she descended at his side.

The family rushed forward, but the tall breathtaking figure that emerged ahead of them was the only one Sabrina could see. Amanda reached Thorn and threw her arms dramatically around his neck.

"Thorn, my darling!" she cried. "You've come back to me!"

CHAPTER FOURTEEN

SABRINA COULDN'T TAKE her eyes away as Thorn embraced Amanda and leaned forward to kiss her mouth.

Amanda's eyes were closed, the flawless skin pale against the luxurious black page boy waves that swirled around her shoulders.

In red crepe de chine her marvelous figure was displayed to perfection. Silk clung to her voluptuous curves, and when she walked, the wraparound dress parted to expose her long shapely legs. Amanda wound her arms more tightly around Thorn's neck. Golden bracelets tumbled and clinked on her wrist.

Comparing herself to Amanda at that moment, Sabrina felt she looked like a peasant schoolgirl. She shifted her gaze to Thorn, and he straightened to look past his fiancée to Sabrina.

She felt as if her heart were grinding slowly to bits. The wind whipped against her, blowing her skirt around her legs while she stood immobile. In that moment, as she gazed at him, she knew it was goodbye. She'd lost part of herself; without him she'd never feel whole. She memorized his mouth, remembering it against hers, his strong shoulders, the brown hand on Amanda's waist. Last night it had caressed her bare skin.

Around them people talked and moved, but Sabrina was oblivious. She raised her eyes to peer into Thorn's.

If she'd felt an ache when he'd looked at her the first time, it was like a blow to her midriff now. His face paled as he thrust his jaw forward. A frown creased his brow.

She wondered if she actually swayed toward him or if she just felt as though she wanted to. Her throat ached, and she clenched her fists tightly at her sides. *Do you want me as much as I want you,* she wondered. *You look as if you hurt. Can it be as unbearable for you?*

Laurel hugged her and chattered, but mesmerized by Thorn's stony features Sabrina merely went through the motions of returning her greeting. Amanda regarded her sharply, glancing back and forth between them before taking Thorn's arm.

When he turned away, the world spun, brightening to a blinding light, and Sabrina felt giddy. An arm steadied her as Wade said, "Come on, we'll go to the car."

She went with him, climbing into the sleek Maserati and putting her hand over her eyes. She was numb with despair. She hadn't know it was possible to feel as miserable as she did at that moment. When Wade slid behind the wheel, she glanced at him and asked, "Don't we have to wait for any of them?"

"No," he stated, twisting in his seat to check for traffic. Straightening, he shifted the gears, and the car shot ahead onto the road. His dark eyes went over her in a quick appraisal. "You look gorgeous, Sabrina. You don't look as if you could have endured one minute's hardship."

She laughed shakily. "Wade, you're a delight! How good it is to be with you!" she exclaimed fervently. "But why are you here and not off somewhere married?"

He frowned against the sunlight, then glanced quickly at her. "I took your advice, Sabrina," he began, running his hand through his hair in a gesture that instantly reminded her of Thorn. "Instead of getting married that night, I brought Estralita back to Bellefontaine."

"I'm so glad!" she exclaimed, then noticed the stubborn thrust of his jaw. "What happened?"

"I told Thorn on the phone. Papa had a stroke that afternoon while I was still in Manaus. At least none of us did anything to precipitate it. He's improving, though, and Thorn's return will help."

Passing apartments, shops and houses, they wound through a labyrinth of streets in São Paulo. Wade stared silently ahead. His face was flushed, and his hands gripped the wheel tightly. Sabrina wondered what had occurred with Estralita, why he hadn't answered her, but she held her peace.

Suddenly he glanced at her, and the anger went out of him. "Here I am unloading my troubles on you the first moment you step off the plane. Tell me about your experience. What happened?"

For one minute she thought of the previous evening—of lying naked in Thorn's arms, bodies entwined. *Will it always be this way,* she wondered. In the center of a busy city in bright daylight while riding with a friend, suddenly in her heart, in her mind, she was back in a small room or a tiny hut, feasting her eyes on Thorn's strong body, hearing his husky voice.... Wade glanced at her sharply. He seemed to sense something of what she was feeling, and she looked down at her hands as she felt a blush rise in her cheeks.

"Wade, if Thorn hadn't been there, I never could have made it back. It was beautiful, it was terrifying, it was dreadful and it was marvelous."

"Will you go home right away?"

"No. Thorn promised to work with us on the research—all that Roddy and I came for." She heard his quick intake of breath and looked at him shrewdly. "You want me to leave, don't you?"

His head jerked around, and he reached over to squeeze her hand quickly. "I want what's best for you. You're far too sweet to get hurt any more. Every minute you're around Thorn may make it worse."

"It can't get much worse," she whispered, and twisted her fingers together.

"Oh, yes, it can," he stated grimly. "I was the one who broke the news to Amanda that you'd gone down together." He paused. "Sabrina, she'll make your life hell if you're underfoot. She'll throw herself all over Thorn in front of you, out of pure meanness. Her mother's back and staying with us, too. Her father stays at Fairoaks to supervise the work. Damn!" His fist hit the steering wheel, and he ran his hand distractedly through his hair again, making Sabrina suspect it was more than Amanda that was disturbing him.

"Hasn't your father accepted Estralita?"

Wade frowned. "Papa's confined to his bed. He doesn't even know she exists. Dr. Andrade said to wait until he's stronger to tell him, and our house is big enough that he'll never know until then."

Startled by his news, Sabrina became silent. Sao Paulo, sidewalks crowded with people, horns honking and the steady flow of traffic made Sabrina realize that the night before had been an illusion. Reality crowded in, and she knew Thorn would marry Amanda. He had never hinted he would do anything else.

But even though the hurt could only deepen, she had to remain to do the assignment she had come for.

They reached the hospital at last, where Sabrina was whisked away for a physical. She was given medication for her insect bites but was otherwise pronounced fit and in good condition. It was late afternoon before she was released to join Wade again for the drive to Bellefontaine. She hadn't seen Thorn during the entire time at the hospital.

Without asking, Sabrina guessed that Amanda had stayed with Thorn. Later, when Sabrina looked back on the day, she recalled it as one of the worst of her life.

Arriving at Bellefontaine, she learned that one wing on the ground floor had been turned over to Mr. Catlin, his doctor, nurses and servants. Sitting in the front hall waiting to greet her were Laurel and

Roddy. Laurel stood quietly beside him and watched while Sabrina hugged him, then drew away.

Roddy smiled warmly at her. "I can't wait to hear about everything." He glanced at Laurel and remarked dryly, "Only I'm interested in the scientific aspect—not wild animals."

Laurel's continual grin became noticeable, and suddenly Sabrina was aware that all three of them were waiting expectantly. Puzzled, she asked, "All right, what is it? There's something causing that smile, Laurel."

Laurel looked at Roddy, and to Sabrina's surprise he reached out and put his arm around Laurel's waist. "We're going to get married!" Roddy stated.

Sabrina said the first thing that came to mind. "You'll have to tell Thorn."

They glanced at each other, obviously worried. "Yes," Roddy agreed. "But for now, Sabrina, I wish you'd keep it quiet. I'm waiting for an opportune moment."

"I can understand that," she commented. Then it dawned on her that both of them were shyly waiting for her opinion. "I'm so happy for you both," she said sincerely, and hugged Laurel. "I'll have to get used to the idea, though. That's the last thing I expected to have happen while we were in the Amazon."

They both laughed and looked at each other, and in a flash Sabrina felt shut out—not from their happiness, but from her own with Thorn.

"I imagine Sabrina would like nothing better than

a little rest at the moment," Wade interjected smoothly.

Both Roddy and Laurel murmured apologies at the same time. Roddy gazed at her wonderingly. "You look beautiful, Sabrina—amazing under the circumstances."

"Thank you, Roddy." She laughed. "You had to get engaged to notice!"

They all laughed as Wade took her arm and accompanied her up the stairs. Glancing back over her shoulder, Sabrina watched Roddy and Laurel disappear into the library. She thought of Mr. Catlin. "I suppose I won't be allowed to see your father."

"Surprisingly enough," he answered, "you will. Not right now, because this is the time of day he sleeps, and you need some quiet, I'm sure. Papa has asked to see you. We finally had to tell him about the crash because he insisted on seeing Thorn. Go visit him in about an hour."

Wade reached around her to open the door to her room. "It's good to have you back," he said as he followed her into the room, "and thank God you're all right. I would have suffered a guilty conscience for the rest of my life if anything had happened to you and Thorn. You'll never know how I felt when I received word that you were missing—after all, I was the cause of the flight."

"I'll have to admit I was angry with you, but you can't blame yourself for the crash. You can't control natural disasters."

Jamming his hands into his pockets, he rocked on his heels and commented miserably, "At the moment

I don't think I can control anything—not even my own life!"

Sabrina looked up at him, waiting, but he said no more, and she didn't want to pry. "Thanks for rescuing me at the airport. I needed it desperately."

"Sabrina, my brother is cold and ruthless and arrogant. Make no mistake—he'll marry Amanda."

At the expression on her face he pulled her gently into his arms to comfort her. They stood quietly, and he murmured, "Thank God you're home," adding, "Thorn will break your heart if you don't do something to protect yourself. Pack your things and go. Let the government send another agronomist. Let Roddy do this job." He stepped back to look down at her. "You're in more danger now than you were when that plane went down."

"I know that," she answered solemnly, "but we don't always follow the wisest course."

He moved toward the door but halted abruptly and turned to her. "The men in this family seem to have a penchant for wanting to marry the wrong woman," he stated bitterly. "I'll see you at dinner, Sabrina. It'll be remarkable if you survive that!"

Touching familiar things around the room, she made her way to the windows and looked out. Bellefontaine seemed like home. Wade was right, of course. She should pack and get back to the States as quickly as possible—and she would as soon as this job was done.

A cloud of red dust appeared on the road as a car approached and stopped at the side of the house. Thorn emerged and crossed to hold the door open for

Amanda. Looking fresh and sparkling, she stepped out, linked her arm through Thorn's and then climbed the veranda stairs.

Sabrina gazed at him with unbearable longing. How would she ever live without him? Those magical moments spent in a remote town on the Tapajós tributary were gone forever. Sabrina turned resolutely away from the window.

Before going down to dinner, she stopped off briefly to greet Mr. Catlin. He grasped her hand wordlessly in his cool dry fingers, and Sabrina sat quietly at his side for a few moments, Otília hovering nearby.

Within a few minutes after she had joined the others downstairs, dinner was announced, and they entered the small dining room. Thorn looked preoccupied. His gray eyes were clouded, and Sabrina wondered if it was concern for his father that accounted for his silence during most of the meal.

What Thorn lacked in conversation was made up for by Amanda and her mother, a gaunt haughty woman with graying hair. Both continued to dwell on childhood memories that included Thorn but effectively shut out the others at the table.

Wearing a deep blue dress with a daring halter top, its clinging soft material dark against her pale skin, Amanda sat at Thorn's right. She gazed at him with rapt attention, occasionally touching his hand or arm.

But the biggest shock of all to Sabrina was the introduction of Estralita. Dark skinned, with flashing black eyes and a mass of midnight curls, she was beautiful in a full-blown, voluptuous way that was staggering. Her eyes were large, heavy-lidded and long-lashed. Her red mouth was full and sensuous. Her low-cut red jersey dress revealed every contour. Her ample breasts threatened to spill out of the bodice.

Estralita said little, eating with gusto and sending sultry looks in Wade's direction. Sabrina studied him obliquely, aware that something was terribly wrong.

Before dinner, Estralita had shown off her immense diamond engagement ring, first to Sabrina, then, on his arrival, to Thorn. Now Sabrina watched as Thorn turned his courteous charm on Estralita, realizing how well he could mask his true feelings.

Roddy and Laurel were filled with questions about their experiences in the jungle. At one point Laurel's enthusiasm bubbled over, and she asked, "How did you sleep, Thorn? On bare ground or in trees?"

For one fleeting instant he looked into Sabrina's eyes, and she thought of the nights she'd lain in his arms. She looked down at her plate quickly, feeling an embarrassing warmth rise in her cheeks.

Thorn laughed easily. "Laurel, we could hardly sleep in the trees—you should know better than that. The branches are too high to reach and filled with screeching howling monkeys, macaws and God knows what else. No, we stayed on the ground. The most dangerous encounters involved the insects and the rapids, of course." He continued talking in an unruffled casual tone, but Sabrina had lost her appetite.

Her gaze fluttered up briefly and caught Amanda's

eyes resting on her. She read pure murderous rage in their depths. Amanda turned away quickly, but there had been no mistaking that look.

In fact, there was a general undercurrent of tension in the room, and Sabrina sensed that she, Amanda and Thorn weren't the only source. Wade looked angry, his dark eyes smoldering, while Estralita serenely ate with relish. Even Laurel seemed nervous and keyed up. Finally Sabrina decided that their father's illness might be the cause. In the meantime Amanda interspersed every few words addressed to Thorn with, "Darling," until Sabrina felt she couldn't get away from them soon enough. The moment dinner was over she headed for the stairs.

As she reached them, Thorn called out to her, and she turned warily.

"Sabrina, I'd like to talk to you."

Amanda stood, one hip thrust out, her arm around his waist. Smiling down at her, he said, "Excuse us a minute, Amanda. I'll be out on the veranda shortly."

"Certainly, Thorn," she answered, and moved sinuously past him down the hall.

His gaze shifted to Sabrina. "I haven't had a chance before, Sabrina, but we need to talk." His gray eyes appeared cool and impassive as he went on. "I'm so behind on work now that Lizardo, one of our crop specialists, has agreed to work with you in my place. He knows his business. Will that be agreeable?"

Sabrina nodded quickly. "Of course, Thorn," she replied, and began to walk up the stairs.

"Wait a minute," he said. When she turned, he

added, "Come into the library, where we can have some privacy."

Sabrina studied him in silence for a moment. She didn't feel she could face another emotional scene with Thorn. She was certain he wanted to explain yet again why he was duty bound to marry Amanda, and Sabrina didn't want to listen to his excuses.

"Not now, Thorn. I'm exhausted."

"Thorn, darling—" Amanda's voice carried clearly, "—have you finished your discussion with Miss Devon?"

His black brows drew together. "Not quite," he answered evenly.

Quickly Sabrina mumbled, "We'll talk tomorrow, Thorn. Go join Amanda." She turned and almost ran to her room, closing the door sharply behind her.

Bitter disappointment swept through her. Yet the rational part of her mind told her it was probably best that she wouldn't be working closely with Thorn.

She moved restlessly around the room, opening the doors to the balcony for the breeze and pulling out the work sheets she had brought with her. She sat down at the desk and spread them in front of her, but had barely started to read when someone knocked on the door. Her heart hammered loudly as she called out, "Come in."

Her involuntary eagerness was instantly dashed when Amanda stepped inside and closed the door. "May I talk with you a moment, Miss Devon?"

Sabrina stared at her curiously. "Yes."

Moving across the room, Amanda glanced at the

papers spread on the desk. "Working?" she asked, then sat down in a chair close at hand. "Miss Devon, Thorn told me he's going to allow you to complete the project you came here for."

"That's right," Sabrina replied evenly.

"I hope that won't take a great deal of time, because we'll be getting ready for a wedding. Thorn has enough burdens on his shoulders at the moment without your adding another—but then your little job must be highly important to you. I imagine you're in a hurry to get it out of the way. Perhaps there's a boyfriend waiting at home?" Sabrina remained silent.

"If there's no boyfriend, I'm certain you'll find one," Amanda continued coolly, studying her long blood-red nails. "There'll be a great deal of publicity about your survival." She raised her eyes and fixed them on Sabrina. "Even if there's no truth to the rumors, I don't care to have my fiancé romantically linked with another woman."

Sabrina looked down at the papers under her hands to hide her reaction to Amanda's words. She knew she was foolish to feel hurt, but she couldn't help it. Thorn had never given her reason to expect anything.

Amanda continued relentlessly. "As a matter of fact, Miss Devon, men don't like sticky situations, either."

Sabrina looked up warily. "What do you mean?"

"I think you have the impression Thorn feels some affection for you. Don't be misled by his actions in the jungle."

Sabrina's hands grew cold. She thought of Thorn sitting on the foot of her bed, caressing her ankle, bending to kiss her...all those moments less than twenty-four hours earlier. Listening to the high-pitched voice, Sabrina gripped the edge of the desk tightly.

"I told him to stop in H. Stern Jeweler's and get you a pretty diamond necklace to ease your disappointment. I'm sure you can understand. When you were in the jungle, uncertain of survival, things may have been said or done that would be meaningless now. It's all quite different once you're back among your own, isn't it?"

Sabrina couldn't bear to hear any more. Amanda's words were cutting her heart into shreds. She turned her back to stand near the balcony door. "Amanda, tell Thorn not to bother with any gift. I wouldn't think of accepting a diamond necklace."

Amanda laughed softly. "Don't be foolish! It would take more than a year's income for you to buy a diamond necklace, and it means nothing to Thorn. Besides, it would assuage his somewhat guilty conscience." Her voice hardened. "I want to make myself clear. I don't want sensational news stories or any gossip to mar my wedding. Finish your business and go. You don't belong here, and it's an embarrassment to Thorn to have to get rid of you."

Amanda turned and left then. The instant the door banged shut behind her, the tears that had been swimming in Sabrina's eyes spilled over. She cried until there were no tears left, and that night she lay exhausted, staring into darkness for hours before she slept.

SHE GOT UP EARLY, dressed in a white shirt and blue jeans, then headed downstairs. Instead of Lizardo, she was startled to find Thorn waiting. His back was to her, and Sabrina quickly studied his dark head and tall angular frame. Breathing deeply, she clenched her fists, determined to hide how much she hurt. He turned and looked up at her, and it was like a blow.

I love you so much, she thought, hoping it didn't show. "Where's Lizardo?" she asked.

Thorn regarded her solemnly. "I want you to come with me. I want to show you something."

His somber countenance made her bite back her questions. He took her arm, and they started out of the house. Thorn was dressed in khaki shirt and trousers, as if he intended to work in the field, and she wondered where he was taking her.

They crossed the gravel drive, where he stopped for a moment. "Sabrina, are you afraid to fly with me again?"

Mystified, she shook her head. "No." *I'd never be afraid to do anything with you,* she wanted to add.

He turned to continue toward the hangar, where a helicopter waited. "It'll be noisy," Thorn warned her.

That'll be of little consequence, she thought, *because there's nothing left to say.* She couldn't trust herself to speak. Wade was right. She needed to return to Washington and let Roddy finish this job.

Thorn placed his hands on her waist to help her inside, then hesitated. "Sabrina, you've told me about your brother Andy. Send him down here for a while."

She shook her head, and he added quickly, "I mean it. I can keep a fifteen-year-old out of trouble, because there's enough work to occupy every minute of his time." He looked around. "It would be good for him."

"Thank you, Thorn," she answered, and tried to smile. How simple that would be—yet how dreadful to hear continually about Thorn and Amanda from Andy. She realized the offer would be a solution to many of her family's problems and give Andy an opportunity he wouldn't have otherwise. But she forgot about his offer as her attention centered on the two strong hands that lifted her quickly into the helicopter.

Fastening the seat belt, she waited while Thorn climbed in and started the motor. The long blades began to rotate noisily.

She turned. "Where are we going, Thorn?"

"I want to show you something."

That seemed to be all he wanted to say on the subject, so she, too, became silent, watching as they lifted off the ground, then swept above the hangar. They gained altitude and flew over the vastness of Bellefontaine.

The wind whipped through the open doors of the helicopter. In the distance dark clouds boiled on the horizon, as if threatening rain. Looking below, Sabrina caught sight of the magnificent house surrounded by well-tended flower beds and grounds.

Behind the house the swimming pool was a dazzling patch of blue.

Sabrina wondered if she would ever see anything like Bellefontaine after she left Brazil. She gazed back at the white roofs of barns and stables, the shiny tin roofs of the labs and the long experimental greenhouses. In the distance she glimpsed the red-tile roof of the sugar mill.

The rumble of the motor and the chop of the propellers were too loud to allow easy conversation. She glanced briefly at Thorn, and he turned momentarily to look at her. They passed over fields of sugarcane ready for April harvest, their green stalks topped by fluffy arrows that blew in the wind. The fields blended into a stretch of wild prohibited land. Then suddenly it was gone. In the center of a large clearing stood a long building surrounded by steel drums, lumber, heavy equipment and crates.

Dipping lower, they flew directly above the building. At her questioning glance he spoke above the noise. "It's the gold mine."

Suddenly Sabrina understood. If Mr. Catlin disapproved of developing the mine and Thorn was going against his father's wishes, she could see the reason for the signs, the fence and the jungle that Thorn had left untouched. Until he won his father over, the mine would remain hidden from view.

Fascinated, she continued to gaze at the land below. Like a surrealistic painting, the bare red earth—or *terra roxa*, as she had learned the *paulistas* called it—had been carved in an intricate design by nature, the convolutions gouged deep into the earth, layer upon layer. A road snaked over the barren ground, and traveling along it Sabrina spotted the largest truck she had ever seen.

"That's a sixty-five ton truck," Thorn commented. "It's taking a load of ore to the crusher, where it is reduced to sand. Then it goes through those tanks," he continued, pointing to four settling tanks dotting the red ground like bright blue jewels. "They're thickener tanks to settle out the waste," he shouted over the din. "Gold-bearing cyanide flows off the top."

Sabrina watched the work below, intrigued, and temporarily forgot her problems. Leaning close to her, Thorn said, "We may go through twenty tons of ore to get three troy ounces of gold. Are you bored by all this?" When she shook her head, he added, "I don't know how I could ever have misunderstood you about the gold. I suppose my showing you all this now is my way of saying I'm sorry." In spite of her misery, Sabrina couldn't help but be warmed by his words.

They regained altitude to rise above a cloud of billowing red dust where the power shovel bit into the earth. The shovel's boom dipped into the hillside, then dropped its load into another large truck.

One thing had registered with Sabrina as they flew over the mine site. Everything she had just witnessed meant wealth. It would take vast funds to buy that equipment, and obviously, gold would increase the Catlins' worth beyond her imaginings.

Looking down at the neat row upon row of trees below, she realized they were hovering over an orchard. Where was Thorn taking her and why?

She glanced at him and decided that whatever his purpose, it must be grim. His features were hard, the scar he had sustained in the crash adding to the harshness. Too clearly she recalled how that severity melted away in tenderness or laughter. His jaw was clamped shut, and he held his shoulders stiffly. His obvious tension made her spirits droop even more.

What kind of wife would Amanda make? Would she try to please him? Sabrina doubted it, but she realized that Thorn was utterly self-sufficient, that his first love was the vast plantation spread out below them.

Her throat felt tight, and she wished they would get to wherever they were going. The wind whipped noisily around them with greater force. Below, resembling a white zipper in a long dress of green, a fence appeared. They passed over it and continued.

It was impossible to talk, so Sabrina settled in the seat and tried to close her mind to all speculation about Thorn. She thought of her brothers. How they would love such a helicopter ride! The fields of fruit trees seemed to go on forever. Then, across the hills, she spotted a house under construction.

Although uncompleted, judging from its looks the house would be as palatial as Bellefontaine. Behind it a small lake glistened, diamond bright in the morning sun. To the west stood a compound similar to Bellefontaine's, with offices, greenhouses, barns and various workers' houses.

Without being told, Sabrina was positive she was staring at Fairoaks, Amanda's home. At the same moment Thorn confirmed her suspicion. "Fairoaks," he said.

She nodded and looked down, but she had seen all she wanted to of Amanda's home. As if he were obeying her command, Thorn swept the helicopter into a turn for the journey back to Bellefontaine.

Another certainty was growing within her: on this flight Thorn was confirming his reasons for marrying Amanda. The wealth of the gold mine, the orchards, these vast holdings—he risked losing it all if he went against his father's wishes. Even if that were not a consideration, Thorn was bound by traditions that made upholding one's honor and one's word as important as life itself.

Touching her arm, Thorn pointed below. Like a giant piece of nubby tweed flung over the ground, rows of green trees dotted the red earth. Occasionally the pattern was broken by workers' houses or neatly crisscrossed lines of roads.

Thorn raised his voice to say, "Those are our coffee trees."

He then indicated a stretch of rectangular plots and explained, "That's where the berries are spread to dry. For days, sometimes weeks, they are raked back and forth on drying floors. Each night the berries are covered with canvas so that the dampness won't hurt them."

The interest that the sight of the gold mine had aroused in her faded as Sabrina decided the reason for this flight. Yes, Thorn had a lot to lose—but she didn't want to see any more of it. She touched his arm lightly and asked, "Can we go back now?"

She immediately recognized his look of stubborn determination. "One more thing, Sabrina."

Shrugging with apparent indifference, she twisted in her seat to look down at the coffee trees as the helicopter rose higher in the sky. Ahead the land grew rugged. The dark clouds in the distance were a welcome sight, because she felt certain rain would end this little jaunt. She looked below to where a cliff jutted out over water.

To her surprise, Thorn began a descent at that moment, setting the helicopter down near the edge of the bluff. He cut the motor, and the blades began to slow as he jumped out and came around to lift her down.

Looking around, Sabrina couldn't imagine why Thorn had brought her to such a place, so high and barren. Near the edge of the cliff a pile of boulders stood, and beside them a tall mimosa that was still in bloom. Only when she was away from the sidewalks and buildings of São Paulo, as she was here, did Sabrina think about the reversal of South America's seasons. Because they had crossed the equator, it was spring in Washington and fall in São Paulo.

A warm gust of wind tinged with the freshness of rain whipped at her clothing. Thorn took her hand, and they strolled beneath the mimosa. The tree's feathery pink blossoms exuded a rain-drenched sweetness. Shade prevented much growth beneath the tree, and red dirt showed between the patches of weeds.

Why did he bring me here, Sabrina wondered again. When she looked up at him, she found him studying her with an intentness that took her breath away. "Why are we here, Thorn?" she finally asked bluntly.

He put his arm around her shoulders and turned her to look out over the view. His voice was as harsh as his expression. "I've come here since I was old enough to ride alone. I've flown up here before. This is the highest spot on Bellefontaine. Look at it, Sabrina."

She did as he instructed—and knew she had been right in her guess about his reason for flying over Bellefontaine and Fairoaks.

"Sabrina, this is my life. This is all I've ever known. It's all I've worked for since I was eight years old. I started working in the fields then."

She turned to look at him. "Thorn, our lives and our worlds are as different as can be. I know you can't give this up for me—"

He groaned and interrupted her. "I've little choice, unless I want to destroy my father. I've given my word that I'll marry Amanda. Years ago my father gave his promise that I would. I'm duty bound to that." His black brows flew together, his expression as bleak and dark as the thunderclouds gathering behind them.

"I know you are, Thorn," she answered, her voice nearly drowned out by thunder. A puff of wind blew red dust against them.

His eyes were filled with agony. "Sabrina, I can't give up Bellefontaine. I can't fight papa, either. Are you aware that he doesn't even know Estralita is at our house? Dr. Andrade told Wade it would be too hard on him. How much worse will it be if I tell him I don't want to marry Amanda?"

Sabrina felt as if a knife were cutting through her, as if her heart were being smashed and ground into pieces by his words. She fought against the tears that were rising to the surface. "You can't, Thorn. It's impossible, and I know that. Please, I want to get back to Bellefontaine. I'm going home as soon as possible."

She turned away and had taken only a few steps when his hand closed around her wrist and pulled her to him.

She looked up frantically. "Thorn, don't...."

He swore and tightened his arms around her waist. Then his mouth was on hers, demanding a response, filled with fire. Sabrina's heart pounded. All of her being quivered with longing and love for this tall strong man.

His hand slipped beneath her hair. Then the barrette was gone, and the wind blew her long flaxen hair across their faces. A sob racked her, and she pushed him away with all her strength. "Take me home, Thorn. You've made your decision."

His face became shuttered and remote. He turned for the helicopter. Without his help she scrambled into her seat. She wasn't certain how long she could remain strong; it had taken all her will to demand to be flown back to Bellefontaine. She wanted Thorn; she loved him beyond belief. The long ride home was agony. Trying with all her might to hold back a flood of tears, Sabrina sat stiffly and gazed straight ahead. The instant they landed, she jumped down and started for the house.

Ahead she saw Amanda start down the driveway in

the Ferrari. Before Sabrina had taken many steps, Thorn caught up with her.

"Sabrina."

She kept walking, until he grasped her shoulder and turned her to face him. One look at his face and there wasn't any question that his decision was as agonizing for him as it was for her. He spoke slowly and clearly. "One goodbye kiss, Sabrina. Then I'll leave you alone."

"No," she whispered again, and shook her head. But it was impossible to stop herself from raising her lips to his. He stepped forward, and she was in his arms, held so tightly she couldn't breathe, while he kissed her with a consuming hunger.

He had denied her his love, forsaken any claim to her, refused any future together, but there was no disregarding the passion that blazed between them, that made his hard rugged body quiver as much as hers. His kiss, probing, intense, fanned to life all their banked fires, destroying her because she knew it was the last time....

In desperation she pushed free and ran. Stumbling on the loose stones in the driveway, she dashed for the house and almost collided with the parked Ferrari. Sabrina looked up startled, to face Amanda.

Amanda's skin had paled drastically except for a bright spot of color in each cheek. She stood rigidly, fists clenched, eyes narrowed to slits. Sabrina turned away and ran. She didn't have to cope with Amanda; that was Thorn's problem.

Reaching her room, Sabrina closed the door and

rushed toward the bed. Suddenly she froze and threw her hand over her mouth to stifle a scream.

On the crisp white coverlet in the center of the bed lay a small doll, arms and legs pulled off, a long gleaming pin piercing its heart. Finding it under the present circumstances made it all the more frightful, obscene and cruel. Sabrina began to shake violently and struggled to gain control of her emotions. A hard rap sounded on the door, and she jumped.

"Sabrina!" Wade called through the closed door.

She didn't want him to see the doll. As he knocked again, she snatched it up to shoved it beneath a pillow. "Come in, Wade," she answered, and turned to face him.

He stepped in, looking cool in dark blue slacks and a blue shirt. "I saw you return and—" He stopped and swore, crossing quickly to her side and taking her in his arms.

His kindness dissolved her control, and she began to sob helplessly. He patted her shoulder and started to speak. "Sabrina, make a plane reserva—" Suddenly he released her and brushed past her. The determined set of his shoulders made her glance anxiously in the direction he was headed. Too late she discovered she had not completely covered the doll.

He flung aside the pillow, then whirled to glare at her. "When did you find this?"

She gazed up at him. "Wade, I'm not afraid of it. Promise me you won't worry Thorn with it."

"No," he stated firmly. "Thorn's in charge here, and he knows everything that goes on. He should know about this."

She didn't want to cause Thorn any more grief. "Wade, you owe me something for what you did that day you left me in the research lab."

"Dammit, Sabrina—" his eyes flashed "—that's not fair!" Then he sighed heavily. "I should make it up to you for what I did, but I don't like this at all. Still, I'll take this monstrosity out of your sight."

"Thank you, Wade," she said quietly.

The anger still showed in his face. He moved to the door and paused. "Just be damn careful where you go and what you do until you're on a plane headed home!"

She suspected there was more troubling Wade than the present situation. He hadn't been the same since she'd returned. She spoke softly. "Before you go, Wade, perhaps I'm the one who owes you something."

He cocked his head to one side. "Why?"

"I talked you into bringing Estralita here instead of running off and getting married that night—yet you seem far more unhappy now than you did then."

His lips clamped shut, and he stared at her angrily. "Does Thorn object to Estralita?" Sabrina asked.

He shook his head. "No, my brother surprised me. He's accepted her completely. He'll never cling to the old ways when papa is gone. I know now that Thorn loves the new Brazil too much and wants to be part of it. No, Thorn was gracious." His eyes clouded. "But now that Estralita's here, it isn't how I expected it to be."

"Why not?"

"She doesn't want to stay at Bellefontaine."

"That shouldn't seem so bad, Wade. You don't want to stay here, either," Sabrina pointed out.

Closing the door, he placed the doll on a table and jammed his hands into his pockets. "That's just it. I'm not certain anymore. While you and Thorn were gone, responsibility for Bellefontaine fell on my shoulders. I don't feel the same way about it as I did." He sighed. "I want my wife with me at home. I don't want her to have an acting career. I can't follow Estralita from film to film." As if he had forgotten Sabrina's presence, he began to pace up and down. "But she wants to act. I thought that would only be temporary, but it's not."

He whirled to face Sabrina. "She hates it here. She's bored. She isn't interested in the land—not one inch of it. She hates horses, and she doesn't like the quiet solitary life—at least to Estralita it's solitary."

Sabrina said nothing, and he continued, "What kind of life have we got ahead of us? I've been thinking about law. I'm not certain I want to give up my studies. There are things around here I'd be equipped to do if I had a legal background. There's no way Thorn can take time to study it, but if I did, we could work together. It's just not at all as I thought."

"Wade—" Sabrina spoke gently "—you're not in love with Estralita."

"Oh, no, it's not that. I feel—" He broke off and looked at her, then muttered, "Damn, Sabrina, I don't know what I feel. I love her, but we have all these problems."

"Wade, if you really loved her, you'd want her

more than a place to live, a house, studying law—anything on earth."

He stared at her assessingly, and his eyes narrowed. "Do you feel that way about Thorn? If he asked you to give up living in the United States, to give up your job—" he waved his hand "—or if he had to give up all this to marry you.... Be honest, Sabrina. If Thorn were penniless, would he be as appealing?"

She stiffened. "Of course, Wade!"

Suddenly his features softened, and he crossed the room to place his hands on her shoulders. "Dear Sabrina, calm down. You look as fierce as a mother cat defending her kittens."

"That's all right, Wade—" she patted his hand "—but it's the truth."

"I didn't mean to be insulting. I'm just trying to sort things out. Maybe I'm not ready for marriage," he sighed. "I seem to have managed to foul up my own life in much the same way as Thorn has." He gazed at her solemnly. "The only difference is, my brother approached his engagement coldly and ruthlessly. I thought I was in love with Estralita." Abruptly he changed the subject. "Well, we're having guests for dinner tonight—just a small party. I'd better leave."

"You'll work it out, Wade," she said encouragingly.

Turning away, he picked up the doll again. "I hope so." At the door he glanced back, a worried frown creasing his brow. "Be careful, Sabrina."

He left the door ajar, and in a moment Roddy

knocked. When Sabrina motioned to him, he rolled in in his wheelchair.

"How did your work go today?" He frowned at her expression. "What's wrong?"

She shook her head and moved to sit down in a chair facing him. "Nothing. Today hasn't gone too well, that's all. Thorn took me for a tour, but I haven't accomplished anything. Tomorrow should be better, Roddy."

He looked at her intently. "I haven't heard profuse congratulations—or even eager remarks—from you about my engagement."

She glanced down at her hands a moment. "No. I'm happy for you, Roddy—" she looked up at him "—but I keep thinking about her wanting to run away. I know how you feel about marriage, and I'd hate to see you get hurt. Laurel is very inexperienced."

"And you think this is another whim," he stated quietly.

She glanced at him with embarrassment, then said, "I just don't want to see either of you hurt. She's young—"

"But I'm not," he interrupted. "I'm thirty-four years old, Sabrina, and I'm in love. I know I want to marry Laurel." He grinned suddenly. "I'll have to admit, I probably owe this to my broken legs. I've never had idle time before. For once I had to notice more of the life—and people—around me. I've been afraid of deep commitment, but this slipped up on me unexpectedly." His smile disappeared. "I know what I want, Sabrina, and I'm no love-struck teenager.

"The biggest drawback is that I can't give Laurel this kind of life. I'm not part of this community, but then neither is Estralita, and Thorn seems to be accepting her. I'll just talk to Thorn about Laurel and promise him I'll do the best I can. She'll always have a comfortable life—that I can assure him. I love her, Sabrina, and it'll be forever."

She moved to kneel beside the wheelchair and hug him. "I'm so glad, Roddy. I didn't mean to pry."

He patted her shoulder. "Thank you, Sabrina."

When she moved away, he added earnestly, "Thorn may never consent, though. There are enough reasons not to, goodness knows, and this family places a light premium on love."

Feeling miserable, she nodded. "I want to get this job done quickly and get home. In fact, I may have to leave you to complete the work. But we'll talk about that later when I'm more up to it. There's time to work this afternoon, Roddy, if I can find Lizardo."

He gazed at her rather oddly, but started agreeably toward the door. "Go on. I'll see you tonight."

After watching him out of sight down the hall, she left to look for Lizardo. As soon as she found the tall dark-haired crop specialist, they went to one of the fields to begin her study.

Sabrina took notes on the conditions under which cane was grown—the ideal rainfall, the amount of irrigation, the type of fertilizers used. She measured the distance between the inner nodes, from leaf to leaf, as well as making notes on the varieties grown. For a time, moving along tall rows of plants, she forgot her troubles, immersing herself in acquiring knowledge of the sugarcane that she finally had access to.

Lizardo was as cooperative as she'd hoped, agreeing to pack samples in dry ice and have them shipped to Washington for her. Finishing for the day, she went to her room to bathe and dress in a simple white sheath. Her only jewelry was the thin gold chain around her neck.

Knowing she couldn't bear to watch Thorn with Amanda, she waited to go downstairs until the last few minutes before dinner. When she entered the large salon off the dining room, she paused in the doorway to look at the small crowd of guests. Thorn's height made him easily visible. He stood across the room with Amanda in a circle of people, his profile to her. His dark blue blazer and pale gray slacks, his white shirt, fitted to perfection.

Sabrina felt as if all the other females in the room paled in comparison to Amanda's stunning beauty. Dark and flashing, her eyes were heavily made up. Her daring black dress bared one ivory shoulder, while a full ruffle of taffeta swirled over the other and tucked into a crimson sash. Around her slender throat hung a necklace of blood-red rubies and sparkling diamonds. Sabrina tried to tear her eyes away, and just then Thorn turned his head to look at her.

Something inside her felt as if it flipped over. At that moment dinner was announced, and the doors to the dining room opened.

Sabrina sat between Roddy and Wade, down the

length of the table from Thorn. Candles flickered and burned in tall silver candelabra, adding warmth to a room filled with chattering guests. The sweet scent of waxen gardenias mingled with the exotic aroma of Brazilian cooking.

As Sabrina reached for her glass of chilled white wine, she remembered a certain hotel meal and looked at Thorn.

Lifting his glass to his lips, he paused, gazing over the rim at her. With the slightest motion he raised it in an unmistakable toast to her. Lowering the glass slowly to the table, he settled back in his chair.

His unwavering gaze was unsettling, disturbing, and Sabrina realized his face was flushed, the color in his cheeks unusually dark, and wondered at the change in him. For a moment she stared uncomfortably at her plate, but it was impossible to resist raising her head to look at him again.

He was still watching her intently, and she began to feel something churn inside her. With deliberation his gaze drifted slowly over her shoulders, her white dress. She remembered those moments in the restaurant when, in spite of his protests to the contrary, his eyes had blatantly made love to her.

He was doing it again. Silently, down the length of the table, separated as they were by people and dishes, he let his eyes devour her. She knew what was on his mind, what he was saying with his eyes, and it set her aflame. She put her fork down on her plate and glanced at Amanda, who was busily chatting with a handsome man on her left, both seemingly oblivious to Thorn.

Indeed, no one seemed to be looking in their direction, but along with the response Thorn evoked in her, her immediate reaction to him, she felt a stirring of anger that he'd do this to her in front of his fiancée.

Then her irritation was swamped by an even more powerful wave of desire. A flush rose in her cheeks. She knew she should look away from that riveting silvery gaze, but she couldn't. His eyes lowered, and as clearly as if he'd spoken, she remembered his husky voice saying, "I'm...letting my eyes touch you where my hands would like to...." Crossing her legs, she shifted in her chair and saw him smile.

"Well, I'll be damned!" Wade murmured softly beside her. He leaned closer to whisper, "You know, you may not have to pack and go home after all."

Glancing quickly at him, she became even more embarrassed. "You've noticed...."

He grinned. "By God, I think you're making headway! Quit looking at your plate, Sabrina. Give her some competition!"

But she was struggling to keep from looking past him at Thorn. "He shouldn't do this to me—not with Amanda here."

"She doesn't love him, Sabrina. If he lost Bellefontaine, she wouldn't marry him. With her for his wife, how happy do you think he'll be?"

Knowing the answer, still she insisted, "Wade, it's useless."

"Not if he's looking at you like that, Sabrina. Give Thorn the full benefit of those big blue eyes. I'd sure as hell rather have you for my sister-in-law!"

She laughed. "Wade, you're impossible!" Softly she added, "Both of you are." Without thinking, she glanced down the table and into Thorn's eyes. All laughter died at his piercing hungry look.

It was the same intense expression she'd seen on his face in the restaurant when he'd pushed back his chair to come around and kiss her. He moved his chair back a fraction now, and her heart slammed against her ribs. For a moment she thought he might do the same again, as improbable as it was. She glanced at Amanda to see if she'd noticed. Still chattering on, Amanda paid no attention to Thorn.

He continued to study Sabrina deliberately. As clearly as words, his eyes conveyed an unmistakable message of love. Her heart began a rolling drumbeat beneath his unwavering gray eyes. She felt as if she were a puppet with all the strings in Thorn's hands—that he could draw her to him. Why? Why was he doing it? Just hours ago he'd kissed her goodbye. Yet now he was letting down the barrier of remoteness, that cool facade he'd shown since they're returned from Amazonia.

She quirked an eyebrow at him questioningly. Why was he flirting with her? A faint smile touched his lips, and he winked at her. Amazed, she watched him turn his head as a guest spoke to him. Then Amanda shifted in her chair to talk to him.

Sabrina didn't dare speculate on his actions. She wouldn't allow herself to hope, because Amanda was still at his side, was still his fiancée.

Her curiosity deepened when they left the table and

Thorn suddenly appeared beside her. "I have to talk to you later."

There wasn't a chance to answer before he was gone, Amanda clinging to his arm, smiling up at him.

Gazing after him, Sabrina closed her mind to his strange behavior. She turned to spend a few minutes talking to Wade and Estralita. Then, excusing herself, she left.

When she reached her room, she sat on the balcony, feeling numb. Only a sliver of a moon and some fleeting clouds drifted in the sky. The air was relatively cool. What did Thorn want to talk to her about? The question kept surfacing, and each time she refused to dwell on it, determined to wait until she got the answer directly from Thorn.

Finally, when she got up and moved inside, something caught her eye—a folded piece of white paper that had been slipped under her door. Retrieving it, she unfolded it and read the large scrawl.

> Sabrina, meet me in the garden by the west fountain. Please come. It's urgent that we talk away from the house, and I have something to give you.
>
> Thorn

Why were the Catlins such a complicated family? None of them ever did anything in a simple way. Sabrina read the note again. Without thought, afraid to consider Thorn's reasons for wanting to see her because she might be disappointed again, she threw a shawl around her shoulders and descended the stairs to the front door.

Crossing the darkened empty veranda, she hurried through the garden to the west fountain. In the shadows near the fountain a figure moved. She rushed forward and called softly, "Thorn?"

"Senhorita Devon?" A small wiry man dressed in white pants and shirt stepped out of the night.

"Yes," she answered.

"You come, please. Senhor Catlin ask me to bring you to him. He say no one else but Senhorita Devon. We go quickly. You understand, yes?"

Sabrina looked around. "Where is he?"

"He send me to bring you. Not far."

Sabrina fell willingly into step behind him, but after a long walk on a path leading away from the house, doubts began to nag at her. She forced them back and followed the man. As if reading her thoughts, he turned. "Not much farther, *senhorita*."

"Not much farther" proved to be an inaccurate calculation. After another fifteen minutes' walk Sabrina began to grow both angry and alarmed.

She was alone, far from the house, headed for the forbidden part of Bellefontaine with a small man about whom she knew nothing. She couldn't decide whether to continue or return to the house. A bird screeched loudly, and she jumped nervously. Halting decisively, she said, "I'm going back."

The man stopped to look at her. "He not like, but I tell the *senhor*," he replied indifferently.

She studied him for a moment. He'd taken her announcement quite calmly. Maybe she was letting her imagination run away with her. "Very well, I'll come," she sighed. "How much farther away is Senhor Catlin?"

The man raised both hands expressively. "Not far." He turned and moved on, and she followed.

What did Thorn intend to give her? She remembered Amanda's statement about the diamond necklace. Sabrina hoped that wasn't the reason for the note. Surely it couldn't be the reason for his sensual looks down the length of the dinner table.

Within a short time her qualms returned. They reached a row of cane and proceeded to walk alongside it. Sabrina glanced back once more at the house, lights ablaze in only one wing and was amazed at the distance she had come. Why would Thorn need to meet her in such a remote place? Her uncertainty mounted, and a sense of helplessness swept through her.

She was in high heels, wearing a white dress and shawl that could be seen clearly in the darkness and carrying nothing for protection. She wished heartily that she were back in her room, sitting on the balcony.

And for the first time in weeks, Sabrina recalled the *mae-de-santo's* warning of danger. She clutched the shawl closer as her hands turned cold. Ahead stretched the fence that divided the sugarcane from the wild tangle of trees surrounding the mine.

Convinced now that something was wrong, that she had acted foolishly, Sabrina wanted nothing more than to escape from the small man marching ahead of her. As quietly as possible she edged into the cane and slipped through to the next row.

The stalks scraped against her; the man's footsteps began to fade. Soon she could detect only the sounds of insects and frogs. Every passing second confirmed her suspicions. The man was not thrashing through the cane field, nor was he calling out to her—which would be the natural reaction if he thought she'd got lost.

The seconds became minutes, and still there was no sound of him anywhere. Sabrina longed to move. Yet she was afraid to do so.

She heard a rustling nearby, and she jumped. She held her breath. Every nerve was stretched taut with apprehension. Where had the man gone? Why had she been so foolhardy as to wander from the house with a total stranger? Could the man possibly have moved on and not be aware that she wasn't behind him?

She recalled the many times Thorn had done unpredictable things. Then she remembered the doll on her bed. Was this another threat from Amanda to frighten her? Perhaps it was in retaliation for the kiss Amanda had witnessed. But Sabrina banished that idea.

Her legs began to ache. If she remained in the cane field until morning, would it be any safer to venture out then? If Thorn was actually waiting for her and she was reported missing in the morning and was found hiding in the field, she would feel ridiculous.

Some of the tension left her shoulders. Perhaps she was being foolish, frightened by *macumba* warnings, made nervous by the darkness and the strange request. Yet the thought of moving and making noise, even a small amount, filled her with reluctance.

Nagging doubts continued to plague her, to hold her immobile as the night passed. She wished with all her heart that she were back at the haven of Bellefontaine—that large fortress of a house with its ever present staff. Then she realized it was neither the house nor the staff that had given her a sense of security—it had been Thorn's presence.

Thorn. The very thought of his strength, his ability to cope so confidently with danger, sent such a pang of longing through her that she almost cried out his name.

She guessed it had been an hour since she'd first hidden herself among the rows of cane, and there was no indication that the man was still around. She was allowing her fears to overwhelm her. She belonged at Bellefontaine, and she had to return.

Pushing aside the sturdy stalks, she moved cautiously, then halted to listen. As quietly as she could, Sabrina edged forward. Yet it was impossible to make her way through without some noise.

Nearby something stirred, and she stopped instantly in her tracks. Goose bumps broke out on her skin. Chiding herself for being so easily frightened, Sabrina crept forward.

The cane stalks stirred behind her. Panic swept through her. She hurried ahead, but after a few steps terror caused her to break into a run. Her pulse raced, and she gasped for breath. There were footsteps behind her; she could hear someone coming!

Again she stopped to listen, and a terrifying quiet

descended. Perspiration beaded her brow. She thought of the safety of Thorn's strong arms and decided to stay still and wait until the sun was bright overhead and the workers were out.

Suddenly there was a noise directly behind her. Before she could turn around, something prodded into her back and the man hissed softly, "Ah, Senhorita Devon, I've had quite a search for you!"

CHAPTER FIFTEEN

SABRINA GASPED and spun around.

Instantly he commanded, "Be still! If you do not obey, you will have a bullet." He motioned away from the house. "Now we go."

Sabrina did as he ordered. When they reached the fenced boundary of the cane field, she asked, "Where are we going?"

"You will see," was the noncommittal reply.

They plunged through the bushes until they reached the clearing near the mine, and immediately Sabrina thought of alarms. The hope formed in her mind that they would encounter a guard or set off a warning system. Directly ahead were metal sheds, the steel drums and lumber and the wooden building that she had flown over earlier that day.

Sabrina gazed frantically around. Somewhere there should be some kind of alarm, or else how did the Catlins know when there were prowlers? Outside, the lamps on the building and the posts lighted the entire area.

Her shoulders prickled. She knew the man was behind her. Moving across the hard-packed clay toward the office, she jumped when he shouted, "Stop, *senhorita.*"

Studying her surroundings, she paused and turned. Heavy bulldozers and a dump truck were parked outside the ring of light. The steel gasoline drums close at hand were marked with danger warnings. On the seat of one of the bulldozers lay a machete. Several wires were strung from the building to the poles outside, and Sabrina guessed there was a phone inside, possibly connecting to the main house.

She was standing beside the row of steps leading up to the door of the building. The man held the gun steady while he removed a cigarette and placed it between his lips. Keeping his eyes on her all the time, he struck a match and lit the cigarette. A puff of smoke rose in the air and drifted away.

Sabrina peered into the darkness and thought of the times she had seen Thorn patrol the grounds. If only he would appear now! But nothing changed. The insects continued whining; the frogs croaked—nothing more.

She looked at her captor. "Why am I here?"

He eyed her through a haze of smoke. "You are trouble to somebody."

"How can I be!" she snapped. "I leave for the United States soon and I'll never be back!"

She detected surprise in his face and pressed her point. "Can't we just return and I'll forget about this?"

He stared at her for a second and shook his head. "I have to give back pay if I not do this," he replied in such a casual manner that Sabrina's blood chilled.

"You can't be that cold-blooded!" she cried.

He shrugged. "I do this before."

Even though her hands were cold and clammy, she felt perspiration trickling down her cheeks. How could he stand so calmly before her and admit to such evil? She licked her dry lips and asked, "What do you intend to do?"

He shrugged, exhaling a stream of smoke. "You have an accident."

She looked all around. "No one will believe that!" she snapped.

"I no care," he stated with supreme indifference. "They not find you."

Sabrina could have accepted his words if he had decided to dispose of her in the surrounding wild bush, but surely not here in this clearing. She stared at him curiously. "How could they not find me here?"

He glanced to her right. "Old pit is here. There is no bottom."

Sabrina stared at him in horror and consternation. "There has to be a bottom somewhere!" she exclaimed.

"Wherever it is, *senhorita*, you be there." He grinned wickedly, and his eyes went over her insolently. "Give me your necklace."

Sabrina reached up to unfasten it. "However much you've been paid, I'll double it if you'll let me go."

He cocked his head to one side and remained silent for a moment. While he mulled over her offer, Sabrina unfastened the necklace and held it in her hand. Her heartbeats quickened at the thought that he could be won over, but her spirits sank when he shook his head slowly.

"No." The answer was flat and final.

"Why not?"

Staring at her, he puffed on his cigarette, then dropped the tiny stub to the hard bare ground. "I have no way to make certain you pay. Besides, other *senhorita* has strong power. No."

He closed the distance between them, and with a lust impossible to miss, his dark eyes studied her. Terror filled Sabrina. He glanced at the office door, then motioned. "We go inside."

Tremors shook her body. She had no choice but to mount the steps ahead of him. She had to find something—an alarm, a phone, some way out. As she reached the locked door, he spoke. "Give me the necklace."

She dropped it in his hand, and he laughed greedily. "A beautiful lady...." The words shook her to the core. Raising the gun, he fired at the lock on the door.

His action brought home to her how remote a place they were in, how little chance of rescue she could expect. She watched the door swing open easily on the broken lock. "I thought there were alarms here," Sabrina said nervously.

"I cut the wire."

She stared at him in growing horror and in that instant realized the extent of the evil that threatened her. She felt like screaming and running—anything to get away from him. With a supreme effort she stood quietly, while her mind raced to discover some way of escape.

Turning on the lights, the man motioned toward a brown leather couch. Desperately she gazed around the office: four large desks, a water cooler, files, a stack of wooden crates that were padlocked and marked Explosives and the long leather sofa. Sitting on one of the desks was the knife Thorn had worn in the Amazon, and Sabrina almost sobbed aloud.

With deliberation the man placed the gun on the desk and moved toward her. All her chances for escape seemed to be dwindling to nothing.

"Senhorita," he whispered.

Throwing all her weight forward in a lunge, she shoved him backward and leaped for the gun.

He went down, swearing and kicking. His foot hit the gun. When it slid across the desk and dropped off the opposite side, out of her reach, Sabrina nearly fainted in alarm. She turned and fled, switching off lights as she went.

She ran wildly around the building. There was nothing to use for safety—nowhere to hide—except behind a stack of boards leaing against the building. She heard her sinister captor shouting at her and guessed he had come outside.

Dropping quickly, she scooted under the structure. He jumped off the steps and paused. His feet and legs appeared in her line of vision. He turned to run to the left. As quickly as possible she crawled to the front, then climbed out and started to race toward the brush.

Then she noticed a matchbox lying on the ground where the man had stopped to light his cigarette. She glanced back at the tall gasoline drums.

Snatching up the matches, Sabrina ran to the metal containers. From the other side of the building the man shouted, now irate. Then his voice faded a bit, as though he had run a short way into the brush. With shaking fingers she fumbled and snapped off a round lid, then pushed. The drum felt as if it weighed as much as the building itself. It wouldn't budge.

Panic tore through her. She put her shoulder against the drum and strained, scraping her skin on the rusty metal. It tipped and thudded to the ground. Brown gasoline spilled and ran across the earth underneath the office and around the machinery. She heard the man approaching, but she forced herself to stay there and fling the top off the next drum.

He rounded the corner just as she was putting her shoulder against the last metal container. She shoved, and the drum tipped. The gasoline reeked, splashing in a wider circle, spreading in all directions.

Sabrina jumped back to keep her feet out of the volatile liquid. She fumbled for matches, while the man swore at her, his face distorted by fury.

He swung for her. Sabrina ran, but he caught her and yanked her roughly off her feet. She hit the ground with a jolt that made her cry out, then scrambled out of his grasp, trying wildly to strike a match. A tiny orange flame leaped.

He lunged for her again. Sabrina tossed the match at the liquid.

The instantaneous flame made an arc through the air. The man ran. Sabrina jumped to her feet to do the same, breaking away from him, off to the right. The fire leaped from pool to pool. With a roar and a blinding flash, the area exploded into flame.

Sabrina was overcome by a wave of heat that

rolled out from the fire. She ran into the brush and heard the man coming after her, swearing. Her life wouldn't be worth anything if he caught her. Heedless of pain, scratches—of everything except her relentless angry pursuer—she ran.

Panting hoarsely, she glanced over her shoulder a few seconds later. The building had caught on fire, and for one brief second she thought of Thorn's work that would go up in flames. Then all thought of the office or anything except her own life disappeared as the distance narrowed. The man was determined to catch her, and Sabrina knew it was useless—that he would.

Her lungs were bursting. She was wringing wet with perspiration—cut, bleeding and in pain from the fall. She couldn't keep up this pace. She thought of the man's hard wiry body and realized he could probably run for hours without having to stop.

She gasped for breath. A cry was torn from her, carried on the wind. "Thorn! Thorn...."

A hand clamped on her shoulder. The man spun her around to slap her viciously with a blow that echoed like the crack of a rifle in the night.

Her head jerked, and the golden hair swung against her neck as tears poured down her face. Swearing angrily, he hit her again. His words poured out in bitter Portuguese as he yanked her back toward the fire. Her face stinging, Sabrina sobbed as he pulled her in the direction of the roaring inferno.

She looked up in horror. All he had to do now was push her in. There would be nothing left—no trace, no ashes.... The flames shot high in the air, sending a rolling boil of gray smoke into the sky. Bright sparks sailed upward, twinkling in the darkness overhead. The roar was deafening, the heat intense as flames gobbled up everything. Looking at the building, Sabrina remembered the wooden boxes of dynamite and realized that if she and her captor continued toward the fire, they'd be blown up.

At the edge of the clearing the heat became unbearable. A dull rumble emanated from the inferno, great clouds of smoke soaring upward. Then suddenly, from the brush opposite them, a horse and rider burst into sight.

CHAPTER SIXTEEN

"THORN!" SABRINA CRIED. He was off the horse and running toward them.

Flinging her to the ground, her captor raised his fists to swing at Thorn. Before he could land a blow, Thorn's fist shot out and hit him. As the man fell to the ground, Sabrina screamed, "Thorn, the dynamite!"

Thorn whirled to yank her up, but the man was on his feet in an instant, jerking Thorn around. His fist smashed into Thorn's face seconds before Thorn slugged him again. The man staggered backward, then turned to run.

Holding Sabrina's arm, Thorn sprinted in the opposite direction. After a quick glance over his shoulder, he shoved her to the ground and dropped on top of her.

A wave of heat churned over them as a blast shook the ground, sending a rippling vibration beneath her. Bits of debris hit her hands, and she cried out, struggling to move. Fearful that by protecting her, Thorn would be hurt, she fought to push him away. But his strength was superior to hers, and he held her down.

When the danger was past, he rose and pulled her into his arms. As if he were the only solid thing in the world, she wrapped her arms around his neck and clung tightly. Safety. Shivering with reaction, she twisted to look up at him.

"Belissima cara," he murmured, and kissed her temple, then swung her into his arms as he emitted a high piercing whistle.

Within seconds she heard a whinny in the distance, and Thorn headed in the direction of the sound.

He marched into the brush with her, and she fought a wave of dizziness. The smoke was acrid, burning her throat and her eyes as she clung to Thorn's strong shoulders. His face was lit by flames. An orange reflection danced over his cheekbones. The scar was dark along his temple where it wasn't hidden by his windblown black hair. His mouth was cut. A smudge of dirt covered his cheek. To Sabrina he was the most wonderful sight in the world.

He whistled again, changing direction toward the sounds of an answering whinny. It seemed too much effort to fight the faintness. Sabrina yielded to the blackness that closed in on her.

LATER, WHEN SHE STIRRED and opened her eyes, she saw Bellefontaine, every window ablaze with lights. She twisted in the saddle to gaze up at Thorn. "How did you know?" she whispered.

Looking as fiery as the conflagration they'd just left, his face darkened. "I wrung it out of Amanda."

Her mind felt fuzzy. It was too much of an effort to think, to sort things out. As they raced toward the house, she saw Wade come out, then Amanda.

"Sabrina...." Thorn tugged the reins to slow the

horse. At his change of tone she looked at him in wonder. His voice was husky as his arm tightened convulsively around her. "I love you. Will you marry me?"

She couldn't have heard correctly. "Thorn... Bellefontaine... your father...."

All faintness and pain diminished as she looked into his eyes and heard his deep baritone. "After all my reasons today, when I kissed you goodbye after that flight, I knew I couldn't let you go. I had to wait until papa was awake to talk to him—" he frowned "—or this might have been prevented." For a moment his frown vanished, and he grinned wickedly. "Didn't you get my message at dinner?"

She smiled with intense relief. "I got a message, all right! If only I'd known!"

Abruptly he sobered and said, "After I saw papa, I talked to Amanda. She became so angry I guessed something had happened. I got enough information from her to come after you."

A tightness closed her throat; she felt overwhelmed. It was difficult to ask, but she said, "Will you lose Bellefontaine?"

He kissed her temple tenderly. "If it meant having you, I wouldn't give a damn," he murmured against her ear. Pulling away slightly, he suddenly smiled. "My father may be arrogant, stubborn and difficult, but he's acquired excellent taste in women. You've been kind to him. He's enjoyed your company, and for some reason he thinks you'll make me happier than Amanda would."

"Oh, Thorn!" Joy burst through her.

He squeezed her in response. "I told you I will love you always. You're the only woman I've felt this for—I meant that, love." He looked past her for a moment at the house. "None of it is important if I don't have you." He leaned forward to kiss her, and for a moment she forgot everything else. Blazing with passion, his kiss assured her she needn't doubt his love. Raising his head a fraction, Thorn murmured, "We'll finish what we started in that jungle...."

Sabrina smiled up at him and touched his jaw. "You mean, finish what we started at Congonhas Airport!"

"Here they come," he remarked as they reached the house. He was off the horse in an instant, swinging her into his arms as Wade came running.

"Take over, Wade," Thorn commanded. "Try to get that fire under control where the mine equipment is."

His arms tightened around Sabrina. "I'm taking Sabrina into town to the hospital. I want to make certain she's all right. She has a nasty cut on her arm."

Amazed, Sabrina looked down and realized she hadn't felt or noticed anything before this. Shock upon shock had put her beyond feeling anything except joy from Thorn's proposal.

Wade grinned. "Take Estralita with you. She's afraid of fire. She's leaving." He looked at Sabrina and winked. "We've broken our engagement."

Thorn frowned. "You don't sound unhappy."

"I'm not. I'll explain later."

Thorn began to move away but said over his shoulder, "Someone else can take her, Wade. I want Sabrina to myself."

"Thorn!" The word was a scream. He turned to face Amanda.

Her face was contorted with fury. "You can't do this. Bellefontaine was to be mine!" Her mouth was an angry red slash against her white skin as she shook her clenched fist in the air.

Thorn spoke in a deadly tone. "You deserve to be charged with attempted murder—" his voice dropped "—and I intend to see that you are! Goodbye, Amanda" He passed her quickly, carrying Sabrina away from the house toward the hangar.

Thorn looked down at her yearningly. "As soon as we can get that family of yours down here, we're going to have a wedding," and added, "This trip, when you fly with me, Joao can pilot. I have something else to occupy my time!" He leaned forward and kissed her hungrily.

Sabrina's arms tightened around his neck, and she returned his kiss. Her heart pounded with joy as he enfolded her, safe, in a love as strong as his arms.

Harlequin Salutes... ANNE MATHER

The author whose romances have sold more than 90 million copies!

Harlequin is proud to salute Anne Mather with 6 of her bestselling Presents novels—

1. **Master of Falcon's Head** (#69)
2. **The Japanese Screen** (#77)
3. **Rachel Trevellyan** (#86)
4. **Mask of Scars** (#92)
5. **Dark Moonless Night** (#100)
6. **Witchstone** (#110)

Wherever paperback books are sold, or complete and mail the coupon below.

Harlequin Reader Service

In the U.S.
P.O. Box 22188
Tempe, AZ 85282

In Canada
649 Ontario Street
Stratford, Ontario N5A 6W2

Please send me the following editions of **Harlequin Salutes Anne Mather**. I am enclosing my check or money order for $1.75 for each copy ordered, plus 75¢ to cover postage and handling.

☐ 1   ☐ 2   ☐ 3   ☐ 4   ☐ 5   ☐ 6

Number of books checked _____ @ $1.75 each = $ _____

N.Y. state and Ariz. residents add appropriate sales tax $ _____

Postage and handling $ .75

TOTAL $ _____

I enclose _____
(Please send check or money order. We cannot be responsible for cash sent through the mail.) Price subject to change without notice.

NAME _____
(Please Print)
ADDRESS _____
CITY _____
STATE/PROV. _____ ZIP/POSTAL CODE _____

Offer expires July 31, 1983

30356000000

FREE!
THIS GREAT SUPERROMANCE

Yours FREE, with a home subscription to
SUPERROMANCE ™

Now you never have to miss reading the newest **SUPERROMANCES**... because they'll be delivered right to your door.

Start with your **FREE** LOVE BEYOND DESIRE. You'll be enthralled by this powerful love story... from the moment Robin meets the dark, handsome Carlos and finds herself involved in the jealousies, bitterness and secret passions of the Lopez family. Where her own forbidden love threatens to shatter her life.

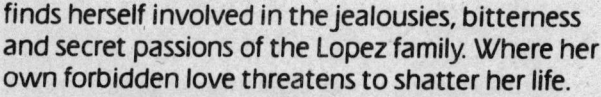

Your **FREE** LOVE BEYOND DESIRE is only the beginning. A subscription to **SUPERROMANCE** lets you look forward to a long love affair. Month after month, you'll receive four love stories of heroic dimension. Novels that will involve you in spellbinding intrigue, forbidden love and fiery passions.

You'll begin this series of sensuous, exciting contemporary novels... written by some of the top romance novelists of the day... with four every month.

And this big value... each novel, almost 400 pages of compelling reading... is yours for only $2.50 a book. Hours of entertainment every month for so little. Far less than a first-run movie or pay-TV. Newly published novels, with beautifully illustrated covers, filled with page after page of delicious escape into a world of romantic love... delivered right to your home.

Begin a long love affair with
SUPERROMANCE.
Accept LOVE BEYOND DESIRE, **FREE**.

Complete and mail the coupon below, today!

- -

FREE! Mail to: SUPERROMANCE

In the U.S.
1440 South Priest Drive
Tempe, AZ 85281

In Canada
649 Ontario St.
Stratford, Ontario N5A 6W2

YES, please send me FREE and without any obligation, my **SUPERROMANCE** novel, LOVE BEYOND DESIRE. If you do not hear from me after I have examined my FREE book, please send me the 4 new **SUPERROMANCE** books every month as soon as they come off the press. I understand that I will be billed only $2.50 for each book (total $10.00). There are no shipping and handling or any other hidden charges. There is no minimum number of books that I have to purchase. In fact, I may cancel this arrangement at any time. LOVE BEYOND DESIRE is mine to keep as a FREE gift, even if I do not buy any additional books.

NAME _____ (Please Print)

ADDRESS _____ APT. NO.

CITY _____

STATE/PROV. _____ ZIP/POSTAL CODE

SIGNATURE (If under 18, parent or guardian must sign.)

This offer is limited to one order per household and not valid to present subscribers. Prices subject to change without notice.

Offer expires July 31, 1983

PR303